SIDE JOBS

Jim Butcher

SIDE JOBS

STORIES FROM THE DRESDEN FILES

A ROC BOOK

ROC
Published by New American Library, a division of
Penguin Group (USA) Inc., 375 Hudson Street,
New York, New York 10014, USA
Penguin Group (Canada), 90 Eglinton Avenue East, Suite 700, Toronto,
Ontario M4P 2Y3, Canada (a division of Pearson Penguin Canada Inc.)
Penguin Books Ltd., 80 Strand, London WC2R 0RL, England
Penguin Ireland, 25 St. Stephen's Green, Dublin 2,
Ireland (a division of Penguin Books Ltd.)
Penguin Group (Australia), 250 Camberwell Road, Camberwell, Victoria 3124,
Australia (a division of Pearson Australia Group Pty. Ltd.)
Penguin Books India Pvt. Ltd., 11 Community Centre, Panchsheel Park,
New Delhi - 110 017, India
Penguin Group (NZ), 67 Apollo Drive, Rosedale, North Shore 0632,
New Zealand (a division of Pearson New Zealand Ltd.)
Penguin Books (South Africa) (Pty.) Ltd., 24 Sturdee Avenue,
Rosebank, Johannesburg 2196, South Africa

Penguin Books Ltd., Registered Offices:
80 Strand, London WC2R 0RL, England

First published by Roc, an imprint of New American Library,
a division of Penguin Group (USA) Inc.

First Printing, November 2010
10 9 8 7 6 5 4 3 2 1

Copyright © Jim Butcher, 2010
For additional copyright information, refer to p. 419
All rights reserved

RoC REGISTERED TRADEMARK—MARCA REGISTRADA

LIBRARY OF CONGRESS CATALOGING-IN-PUBLICATION DATA:
Butcher, Jim, 1971–
    Side jobs: stories from the Dresden files/Jim Butcher.
      p.   cm.
    ISBN 978-0-451-46365-4
    1. Dresden, Harry (Fictitious character)—Fiction.   2. Wizards—Fiction.
3. Chicago (Ill.)—Fiction.   I. Title.
    PS3602.U85S53   2010
    813'.6—dc22   2010028768

Set in Janson Text
Designed by Ginger Legato

Printed in the United States of America

TABLE OF CONTENTS

SIDE JOBS

A RESTORATION OF FAITH

Takes place before *Storm Front*

This is the first of the Dresden Files stories, chronologically, and it was the first time I tried to write short fiction for the professional market. I originally put it together as a class assignment at the University of Oklahoma's Professional Writing program, more than two years before *Storm Front* found a home at Roc.

This one won't win any awards, because it is, quite frankly, a novice effort. It was perhaps the third or fourth short story I'd ever written, if you include projects in grade school. I had barely learned to keep my feet under me as a writer, and to some degree that shows in this piece. Certainly, the editors to whom I submitted this story seemed to think it wasn't up to par for professional publication, and I think that was a perfectly fair assessment.

Read this story for what it is—an anxious beginner's first effort, meant to be simple, straightforward fun.

struggled to hold on to the yowling child while fumbling a quarter into the pay phone and jamming down the buttons to dial Nick's mobile.

"Ragged Angel Investigations," Nick answered. His voice was tense, I thought, anxious.

"It's Harry," I said. "You can relax, man. I found her."

"You did?" Nick asked. He let out a long exhalation. "Oh, Jesus, Harry."

The kid lifted up one of her oxford shoes and mule-kicked her leg back at my shin. She connected, hard enough to make me jump. She looked like a parent's dream at eight or nine years old, with her dimples and dark pigtails—even in her street-stained schoolgirl's uniform. And she had strong legs.

I got a better hold on the girl and lifted her up off the ground again while she twisted and wriggled. "Ow. Hold still."

"Let me go, beanpole," she responded, turning to glower back at me before starting to kick again.

"Listen to me, Harry," Nick said. "You've got to let the kid go right this minute and walk away."

"What?" I said. "Nick, the Astors are going to give us twenty-five grand to return her before nine p.m."

"I got some bad news, Harry. They aren't going to pay us the money."

I winced. "Ouch. Maybe I should just drop her off at the nearest precinct house, then."

"The news gets worse. The parents reported the girl kidnapped. The police band is sending two descriptions around town to Chicago PD, and they match guess who."

"Mickey and Donald?"

"Heh," Nick said. I heard him flick his Bic and take a drag. "We should be so lucky."

"I guess it's more embarrassing for Mr. and Mrs. High-and-Mighty to have their kid run away than it is to have her kidnapped."

"Hell. Kidnapped girl gives them something to talk about at their parties for months. Makes them look richer and more famous than their friends, too. Of course, we'll be in jail, but what the hell?"

"They came to us," I protested.

"That won't be the way they tell it."

"Dammit," I said.

"If you get caught with her, it could be trouble for both of us. The Astors got connections. Ditch the girl and get back home. You were there all night."

"No, Nick," I said. "I can't do that."

"Let the boys in blue bring her in. That'll clear you and me both."

"I'm up on North Avenue, and it's after dark. I'm not leaving a nine-year-old girl out here by herself."

"Ten," shouted the girl, furious. "I'm ten, you insensitive jerk!" She started kicking again, and I kept myself more or less out of the way of her feet.

"She sounds so cute. Just let her run, Harry, and let the criminal types beware."

"Nick."

"Aw, hell, Harry. You're getting moral on me again."

I smiled, but it felt tight on my mouth, and my stomach churned with anger. "Look, we'll think of something. Just get down here and pick us up."

"What happened to your car?"

"Broke down this afternoon."

"Again? What about the El?"

"I'm broke. Nick, I need a ride. I can't walk back to the office with her, and I don't want to stand here in a public booth fighting her, either. So get down here and get us."

"I don't want to spend time in jail because you can't salve your conscience, Harry."

"What about your conscience?" I shot back. Nick was all bluster. When it came down to the wire, he couldn't have left the girl alone in that part of town, either.

Nick growled out something that sounded vaguely obscene, then said, "Fine, whatever. But I can't get across the river very easy, so I'll be on the far side of the bridge. All you have to do is cross the bridge with her and stay out of sight. Police patrols in the area will be looking for you. Half an hour. If you're not there, I'm not waiting. Bad neighborhood."

"Have faith, man. I'll be there."

We hung up without saying good-bye.

"All right, kid," I said. "Stop kicking me and let's talk."

"To hell with you, mister," she shouted. "Let me go before I break your leg."

I winced at the shrill note her voice hit and stepped away from the phone, half dragging and half carrying her with me while I looked around nervously. The last thing I needed was a bunch of good citizens running to the kid's aid.

The streets were empty, the gathering dark rushing in quickly to fill the spaces left by the broken streetlights. There were lights in the windows, but no one came out in response to the girl's shouting. It was the sort of neighborhood where people looked the other way and let live.

Ah, Chicago. You just gotta love big, sprawling American cities. Ain't modern living grand? I could have been a real sicko, rather than just looking like one, and no one would have done anything.

It made me feel a little nauseated. "Look. I know you're angry right now, but believe me, I'm doing what's best for you."

She stopped kicking and glared up at me. "How should you know what's best for me?"

"I'm older than you. Wiser."

"Then why are you wearing that coat?"

I looked down at my big black duster, with its heavy mantle and long canvas folds flapping around my rather spare frame. "What's wrong with it?"

"It belongs on the set of *El Dorado*," she snapped. "Who are you supposed to be, Ichabod Crane or the Marlboro Man?"

I snorted. "I'm a wizard."

She gave me a look of skepticism you can really only get from children who have recently gone through the sobering trauma of discovering there is no Santa Claus. (Ironically, there is, but he can't operate on the sort of scale that used to make everyone believe in him.)

"You've got to be kidding me," she said.

"I found you, didn't I?"

She frowned at me. "How did you find me? I thought that spot was perfect."

I continued walking toward the bridge. "It would have been, for another ten minutes or so. Then that Dumpster would have been full of rats looking for something to eat."

The girl's expression turned faintly green. "Rats?"

I nodded. With luck, maybe I could win the kid over. "Good thing your mother had your brush in her purse. I was able to get a couple of hairs from it."

"So?"

I sighed. "So, I used a little thaumaturgy, and it led me straight to you. I had to walk most of the way, but straight to you."

"Thauma-what?"

Questions were better than kicks any day. I kept answering them. Heck, I like to answer questions about magic. Professional pride, maybe. "Thaumaturgy. It's ritual magic. You draw symbolic links between actual persons, places, or events, and representative models. Then you invest a little energy to make something happen on the small scale, and something happens on the large scale as well—"

The second I was distracted with answering her question, the kid bent her head and bit my hand.

I yelled something I probably shouldn't have around a kid and jerked my hand away. The kid dropped to the ground, agile as a monkey, and took off toward the bridge. I shook my hand, growled at myself, and took off after her. She was fast, her pigtails flying out behind her, her shoes and stained kneesocks flashing.

She got to the bridge first. It was an ancient, two-lane affair that arched over the Chicago River. She hurled herself out onto it.

"Wait!" I shouted after her. "Don't!" She didn't know this town like I did.

"Sucker," she called back, her voice merry. She kept on running.

That is, until a great rubbery, hairy arm slithered out from beneath a manhole cover at the apex of the bridge and wrapped its greasy fingers around one of her ankles. The kid screamed in sudden terror, pitching forward onto the asphalt and raking the skin from both knees. She turned and twisted, kicking at her attacker. Blood was a dark stain on her socks in the glow of the few functioning streetlights.

I cursed beneath my breath and raced toward her along the bridge, my lungs laboring. The hand tightened its grip and started dragging her toward the manhole. I could hear deep, growling laughter coming from the darkness in the hole that led down to the understructure of the bridge.

She screamed, "What is it? What is it? Make it let go!"

"Kid!" I shouted. I ran toward the manhole, jumped, and came down as hard as I could on the hairy arm, right at the wrist, the heels of both hiking boots thumping down onto the grimy flesh.

A bellow erupted from the manhole, and the fingers loosened. The girl twisted her leg, and though it cost her one of her expensive oxfords and one kneesock, she dragged herself free of its grasp, sobbing. I gathered her up and backpedaled away, turning so that I wasn't leaving my back to the manhole.

The troll shouldn't have been able to squeeze his way out of a hole that small, but he did. First came that grimy arm, followed by a lumpy shoulder, and then his malformed head and hideous face. He looked at me and growled, jerking his way out of the hole with rubbery ease, until he stood in the middle of the bridge between me and the far side of the river, like some professional wrestler who had fallen victim to a correspondence course for plastic surgeons. In one hand, he held a meat cleaver approximately two feet long, with a bone handle and suspicious-looking stains of dark brown on it.

"Harry Dresden," the troll rumbled. "Wizard deprive Gogoth of his lawful prey." He whipped the cleaver left and right. It made a little whistling sound.

I lifted my chin and set my jaw. It's never smart to let a troll see that you're afraid of him. "What are you talking about, Gogoth? You know as well as I do that mortals aren't all fair game anymore. The Unseelie Accords settled that."

The troll's face split into a truly disgusting leer. "Naughty children," he rumbled. "Naughty children still mine." He narrowed his eyes, and they started burning with malicious hunger. "Give! Now!" The troll rolled toward me a few paces, gathering momentum.

I lifted my right hand, forced out a little will, and the silver ring upon my third finger abruptly shone with a clear, cool light, brighter than the illumination around us.

"Law of the jungle, Gogoth," I said, keeping my voice calm. "Survival of the fittest. You take another step and you're going to land smack in the 'too stupid to live' category."

The troll growled, not slowing, and raised one meaty fist.

"Think about it, darkspawn," I snarled. The light pouring from my ring took on a hellish, almost nuclear tone. "One more step and you're vapor."

The troll came to a lumbering halt, and his rubber-slime lips drew back from fetid fangs. "No," he snarled. Drool slithered down his fangs and spattered on the asphalt as he stared at the girl. "She is mine. Wizard cannot interfere in this."

"Oh yeah?" I said. "Watch me." And with that, I lowered my hand (and with it the fierce silver light), gave the troll my best sneer, and turned in a flare of my dark duster to walk back to North Avenue with long, confident strides. The girl stared over my shoulder, her eyes wide.

"Is he coming after us?" I asked quietly.

She blinked back at the troll, and then at me. "Uh, no. He's just staring at you."

"Okay. If he starts this way, let me know."

"So you can vapor him?" she asked, her voice unsteady.

"Hell, no. So we can run."

"But what about . . . ?" She touched the ring on my hand.

"I lied, kid."

"What!?"

"I lied," I repeated. "I'm not a good liar, but trolls aren't too bright. It was just a light show, but he fell for it, and that's all that counts."

"I thought you said you were a wizard," she accused me.

"I am," I replied, annoyed. "A wizard who was at a séance-slash-exorcism before breakfast. Then I had to find two wedding rings and a set of car keys, and then I spent the rest of my day running after you. I'm pooped."

"You couldn't blow that . . . that thing up?"

"It's a troll. Sure I could," I said cheerfully. "If I weren't so worn-out, and if I were able to focus enough to keep from blowing myself up along with him. My aim's bad when I'm this tired."

We reached the edge of the bridge, and, I hoped, Gogoth's territory. I started to swing the girl down. She was too big to be carrying. Then I saw her one bare foot dangling and the blood forming into dark scabs on her knees. I sighed and started walking along North Avenue. If I could go down the long city block to the next bridge, cross it, and make my way back down the other block within half an hour, I could still meet Nick on the other side.

"How's your leg?" I asked.

She shrugged, though her face was pained. "Okay, I guess. Was that thing for real?"

"You bet," I said.

"But it was . . . It wasn't . . ."

"Human," I said. "No. But hell, kid. A lot of people I know aren't really human. Look around us. Bundy, Manson, those other animals. Right here in Chicago, you've got the Vargassis working out of Little Italy, the Jamaican posses, others. Animals. World's full of them."

The girl sniffed. I glanced at her face. She looked sad, and too wise for her years. My heart softened.

"I know," she said. "My parents are like that, a little. They don't think about anyone else, really. Just themselves. Not even each other—except what they can do for each other. And I'm just some toy that should get stuck in the closet and dragged out when people come over, so I can be prettier and more perfect than their toys. The rest of the time, I'm in their way."

"Hey, come on," I said. "It's not that bad, is it?"

She glanced at me, and then away. "I'm not going back to them," she said. "I don't care who you are or what you can do. You can't make me go back to them."

"There's where you're wrong," I said. "I'm not going to leave you down here."

"I heard you talking to your friend," she said. "My parents are trying to screw you over. Why are you still doing this?"

"I have another six months to work for a licensed investigator before I can get a license of my own. And I got this stupid thing about leaving kids in the middle of big, mean cities after dark."

"At least down here, no one tries to lie and tell me that they care, mister. I see all these Disney shows about how much parents love their kids. How there's some sort of magical bond of love. But it's a lie. Like you and that troll." She laid her head against my shoulder, and I could feel the exhaustion in her body as she sagged against me. "There's no magic."

I fell silent for several paces as I carried her. It was hard to hear that from a kid. A ten-year-old girl's world should be full of music and giggling and notes and dolls and dreams—not harsh, barren, jaded reality. If there was no light in the heart of a child, a little girl like this, then what hope did any of us have?

A few paces later, I realized something I hadn't been admitting to myself. A quiet, cool little voice had been trying to tell me something I hadn't been willing to listen to. I was in the business of wizardry to try to help people; to try to make things better. But no matter how many evil spirits I confronted, no matter how many would-be black magicians I tracked down, there was always something else—something worse waiting for me in the dark. No matter how many lost children I found, there would always be ten times as many who disappeared for good.

No matter how much I did, how much trash I cleaned up, it was only a drop in the ocean.

Pretty heavy thoughts for a tired and beaten guy like me, my arms burdened with the girl's weight.

Flashing lights made me look up. The mouth to one of the alleys between the buildings had been sealed off with police tape, and four cars, blue bulbs awhirl, were parked on the street around the alley. A couple of EMTs were toting a covered shape out of the alley on a stretcher. The flashing strobes of cameras lit the alleyway in bursts of white.

I came to a stop, hesitant.

"What?" the girl murmured.

"Police. Maybe I should hand you over."

I felt her weary shrug. "They're only going to take me home. I don't care." She sagged against me again.

I swallowed. The Astors were Chicago's elite crowd. They carried enough clout around the old town to get a bum would-be private investigator put away for a good long time. And they could afford the best of lawyers.

It's a lousy world, Dresden, the cool little voice told me. *And the good guys don't win unless they have an expensive attorney, too. You'd be in jail before you could blink.*

My mouth twisted into a bitter smile as one of the uniform cops, a woman, noticed me and cast a long frown in my direction. I turned around and started walking the other way.

"Hey," the cop said. I kept walking. "Hey!" she said again, and I heard brisk footsteps on the sidewalk.

I hurried along into the dark and stepped into the first alley. The shadows behind a pile of crates created an ideal refuge, and I carried the girl into it with me. I crouched there in the darkness and waited while the cop's footsteps came near and then passed on by.

I waited in the dark, feeling all the heaviness and darkness settle into my skin, into my flesh. The girl just shivered and lay against me, unmoving.

"Just leave me," she said, finally. "Go over the bridge. The troll will let you cross the bridge if I'm not with you."

"Yes," I said.

"So go on. I'll walk up to the police after you're gone. Or something."

She was lying. I'm not sure how I could tell, but I could.

She would go to the bridge.

I'm told that bravery is doing what you need to do, even when you're afraid. But sometimes I wonder if courage isn't a lot more complicated than that. Sometimes, I think, courage is pulling yourself up off the ground one more time. Doing one more set of paperwork, even when you don't want to. Maybe that's just plain stubbornness; I don't know.

It didn't matter. Not to me. I'm a wizard. I don't really belong here. Our world sucks. It might suit the trolls and the vampires and all those nasty, leering things that haunt our nightmares (while we clutch our physics books to our chests and reassure ourselves that they cannot exist), but I'm not a part of it. I won't be a part of it.

I took a breath, in the dark, and asked, "What's your name?"

She was silent for a moment and then said, in a very uncertain voice, "Faith."

"Faith," I said. I smiled, so that she could hear it. "My name's Harry Dresden."

"Hi," she said, her voice a whisper.

"Hi. Have you ever seen something like this?" I cupped my hand, summoned some of the last dregs of my power, and cast a warm, glowing light into the ring on my right hand. It lit Faith's face, and I could see on her smooth cheeks the streaks of the tears I had not heard.

She shook her head.

"Here," I said, and took the ring from my finger. I slipped it onto hers, over her right thumb, where it hung a bit loose. The light died away as I did it, leaving us in the dark again. "Let me show you something."

"Battery went out," she mumbled. "I don't have money for another one."

"Faith? Do you remember the very best day of your life?"

She was quiet for a minute. Then she said, her voice a bare whisper, "Yes. A Christmas. When Gremma was still alive. Gremma was nice to me."

"Tell me about it," I urged quietly, covering her hand with my own.

I felt her shrug. "Gremma came over Christmas Eve. We played games. She would play with me. And we stayed up, on the floor by the Christmas tree, waiting for Santa Claus. She let me open just one present, for Christmas Eve. It was one she'd gotten me."

Faith took a shuddering breath. "It was a dolly. A real baby dolly. Mother and Father had gotten me Barbie stuff, the whole line for that year. They said that if I left them all in the original boxes, they would be worth a lot of money later. But Gremma listened to what I really wanted." Then I heard it, the tiny smile in her voice. "Gremma cared about me."

I moved my hand, and a soft, pinkish light flowed up out of the ring around her thumb, a loving, gentle warmth. I heard Faith draw in a little gasp of surprise, and then a delighted smile spread over her mouth.

"But how?" she whispered.

I gave her a smile. "Magic," I said. "The best kind. A little light in the dark."

She looked up at me, studying my face, my eyes. I shied away from the perception of that gaze. "I need to go back, don't I?" she asked.

I brushed a stray bit of hair from her forehead. "There are people who love you, Faith. Or who one day will. Even if you can't see them beside you, right here, right now, they're out there. But if you let the dark get into your eyes, you might never find them. So it's best to keep a little light with you, along the way. Do you think you can remember that?"

She nodded up at me, her face lit by the light from the ring.

"Whenever it gets too dark, think of the good things you have, the good times you've had. It will help. I promise."

She leaned against me and gave me a simple, trusting hug. I felt my cheeks warm up as she did. Aw, shucks.

"We need to go," I told her. "We've got to get across the bridge and meet my friend Nick."

She chewed on her lip, her expression immediately worried. "But the troll."

I winked. "Leave him to me."

The girl didn't feel anywhere near so heavy as when I carried her back. I studied the bridge as we approached. Maybe, if I was lucky, I'd be able to sprint across without the troll being able to stop me.

Yeah. And maybe one day I'd go to an art museum and become well-rounded.

Bridges are a troll's specialty; either because of some magic or just because of aptitude, you never get across the bridge without facing the troll. That's life, I guess.

I set the girl down on the ground next to me and stepped out onto the bridge. "All right, Faith," I said. "Whatever happens, you run across that bridge. My friend Nick is going to pull up on the far side any minute now."

"What about you?"

I gave her a casual roll of my neck. "I'm a wizard," I said. "I can handle him."

Faith gave me another look of supreme skepticism and fumbled to hold my hand. Her fingers felt very small and very warm inside of mine, and a fierce surge of determination coursed through me. No matter what happened, I would let no harm come to this child.

We walked out onto the bridge. The few lights that had been burning brightly earlier were gone—Gogoth's work, doubtless. Night reigned over the bridge, and the Chicago River gurgled by, smooth and cold and black below us.

"I'm scared," Faith whispered.

"He's just a big bully," I told her. "Face him down and he'll back off." I hoped very much that was true. We kept walking and skirted wide around the manhole at the apex of the bridge; I kept my body between Faith and the entrance to the troll's lair.

Gogoth must have been counting on that.

I heard Faith scream again and whirled my head to see the troll's thick, hairy arm stretched up over the edge of the bridge, while the troll clung to the side of the bridge like some huge, overweight spider. I snarled and stomped his fingers once more, and the troll bellowed in rage. Faith slipped free, and I half hurled her toward the far side of the bridge. "Run, Faith!"

The troll's arm swept my legs out from beneath me and he came surging up over the railing at the side of the bridge, too supple and swift for his bulk. His burning eyes focused on the fleeing Faith, and more of his slimy drool spattered out of his mouth. He scythed his cleaver through the air and crouched to leap after the child.

I got my feet under me, screamed, and threw myself at the troll's leg, swinging my long legs around to tangle with the creature's. He roared in fury and went down in a tumble with me. I heard myself cackling and decided, without a doubt, that I had at least one screw loose.

The troll caught me by the corner of my jacket and threw me against the railing hard enough to make me see stars.

"Wizard," Gogoth snarled, spitting drool and foam. The cleaver swept the air again, and the troll stalked toward me. "Now you die, and Gogoth chew your bones."

I gathered myself to my feet, but it was too late. There was no way I could run or throw myself over the railing in time.

Faith screamed, "Harry!" and a brilliant flash of pink light flooded the bridge, making the troll whip his ugly head toward the far side of the river. I ducked to my left and ran, toward Faith and away from the troll. Looking up, I saw Nick's car roaring toward the bridge with enough speed to tell me my partner had seen that something was going on.

The troll followed me, and though I had gained a few paces on him, I had the sinking realization that the beast was lighter on his feet than I was. There was a whistling sound of the cleaver cutting the air, and I felt something skim past my scalp. I bobbed to my right, ducking, and the second swipe missed by an even narrower margin. I stumbled, and fell, and the troll was on top of me in a heartbeat. I rolled in time to see him lift his bloodstained cleaver high above him, and I felt his drool splatter onto my chest.

"Wizard!" the troll bellowed.

There was a yell, and then the cop, the one who had followed us before, hurled herself onto the troll's back and locked her nightstick across his throat. She gave the stick a practiced twist, and the troll's eyes bulged. The huge cleaver clanged as it tumbled from Gogoth's grip and hit the pavement.

The cop leaned back, making the troll's spine arch into a bow—but this wasn't a man she was dealing with. The thing twisted his head, squirmed, and popped out of her grip, then opened his jaws in a frenzied roar that literally blew the patrolwoman's cap off her head and sent her stumbling back with a wide-eyed stare. The troll, maddened, slammed one fist into the pavement, cracking it, and drew the other back to drive toward her skull.

"Hey, ugly," I shouted.

The troll turned in time to see me grunt and swing the massive cleaver at his side.

The rotten, grimy flesh just beneath his ribs split open with a howl of sound and a burst of motion. Gogoth leaned his head back and let out a high-pitched, wailing yowl. I backed off, knowing what came next.

The poor cop stared in white-faced horror as the troll's wound split and dozens, hundreds, thousands of tiny, wriggling figures, squalling and squealing, poured out of the split in his flesh. The massive thews of the beast deflated like old basketballs, slowly sinking in upon themselves as the bridge became littered with a myriad of tiny trolls, their ugly little heads no bigger than the head of a president on a coin. They poured out of Gogoth in a flood, spilling onto the bridge in a writhing, wriggling horde.

The troll's cheeks hollowed, and his eyes vanished. His mouth opened in a slack-jawed yawn, and, as the leathery, grimy sack of tiny trolls emptied, he sank to the ground until he lay there like a discarded, disgusting raincoat.

The cop stared, mouth wide, attempting to form words of a prayer or a curse. Nick's headlights whirled and spilled across the bridge, and with twice ten thousand screams of protest, the tiny trolls dispersed before the light in all directions.

A few seconds later, there were only myself, Faith, the cop, and Nick, who was approaching us across the bridge. Faith threw herself at me and gave me a quick hug around the waist. Her eyes were bright with excitement. "That was the most disgusting thing I have ever seen. I want to be a wizard when I grow up."

"That was . . . was . . ." the cop said, stunned. She was short, stocky, and the loss of her cap revealed tightly braided, pale hair.

I winked down at Faith and nodded to the cop. "A troll. I know." I walked over to the cap and dusted it off. A few trolls, squealing in protest, fell to the street and scampered away. The cop watched with stunned eyes. "Hey, thanks a lot for the help, Officer"—I squinted down at her badge—"Murphy." I smiled and offered her the hat.

She took it with numb fingers. "Oh, Jesus. I really have lost it." She blinked a few times and then scowled up at my face. "You. You're the perp on the Astor kidnapping."

I opened my mouth to defend myself, but I needn't have bothered.

"Are you kidding?" Faith Astor sneered. "This . . . buffoon? Kidnap me? He couldn't bum a cigarette off the Marlboro Man." She turned toward me and gave me a wink. Then she offered both her wrists to Murphy. "I admit it, Officer. I ran away. Take me to the pokey and throw away the key."

Murphy, to her credit, seemed to be handling things fairly well for someone who had just confronted the monster under the bed. She recovered her nightstick and went to Faith, examining her for injuries before directing a suspicious gaze at Nick and me.

"Hoo boy," Nick said, planting his stocky bulk squarely beside mine. "Here it comes. You get the top bunk, stilts, but I'm not going to pick up your soap in the shower."

The cop looked at me and Nick. Then she looked at the girl. Then, more thoughtfully, she looked at the leathery lump that had been Gogoth the troll. Her eyes flashed back to Nick and me, and she said, "Aren't you two the ones who run Ragged Angel, the agency that looks for lost kids?"

"I run it," Nick said, his voice resigned. "He works for me."

"Yeah, what he said," I threw in, just to let Nick know he wasn't going to the big house alone.

Murphy nodded and eyed the girl. "Are you all right, honey?"

Faith sniffed and smiled up at Murphy. "A little hungry, and I could use something to clean up these scrapes. But other than that, I'm quite well."

"And these two didn't kidnap you?"

Faith snorted. "Please."

Murphy nodded and then jabbed her nightstick at Nick and me. "I've got to call this in. You two vanish before my partner gets here." She glanced down at Faith and winked. Faith grinned up at her in return.

Murphy took the girl back toward the far side of the bridge and the other police units. Nick and I ambled back toward his car. Nick's broad, honest face was set in an expression of nervous glee. "I can't believe it," he said. "I can't believe that happened. Was that the troll, what's-his-name?"

"That was Gogoth," I said cheerfully. "Nothing bigger than a breadcrumb is going to be bothered by trolls on this bridge for a long, long time."

"I can't believe it," Nick said again. "I thought we were so dead. I can't believe it."

I glanced back over the bridge. On the far side, the girl was standing up on her tiptoes, waving. Soft pink light flowed from the ring on her right thumb. I could see the smile on her face. The cop was watching me, too, her expression thoughtful. It turned into a smile.

Modern living might suck. And the world we've made can be a dark place. But at least I don't have to be there alone.

I put an arm around Nick's shoulders and grinned at him. "It's like I keep telling you, man. You've got to have faith."

VIGNETTE

Takes place between *Death Masks* and *Blood Rites*

This was a very short piece I wrote at the request of my editor, Jennifer Heddle, who needed it for some kind of promotional thing—one of those free sampler booklets they sometimes hand out at conventions, I believe. I lost track of it in the clutter of life, then realized the deadline was the following morning.

It probably would have been helpful to have remembered at seven or eight, instead of at two a.m.

I'm not even sure I can claim to be the author of this piece, since it was almost entirely written by a coalition of caffeine molecules and exhausted twitches.

I sat on a stool in the cluttered laboratory beneath my basement apartment. It was chilly enough to make me wear a robe, but the dozen or so candles burning around the room made it look warm. The phone book lay on the table in front of me.

I stared at my ad in the Yellow Pages:

HARRY DRESDEN—WIZARD

**Lost Items Found. Paranormal Investigations.
Consulting. Advice. Reasonable Rates.
No Love Potions, Endless Purses, Parties, or
Other Entertainment**

I looked up at the skull on the shelf above my lab table and said, "I don't get it."

"Flat, Harry," said Bob the Skull. Flickering orange lights danced in the skull's eye sockets. "It's flat."

I flipped through several pages. "Yeah, well. Most of them are. I don't think they offer raised lettering."

Bob rolled his eyelights. "Not literally flat, dimwit. Flat in the aesthetic sense. It has no panache. No moxy. No chutzpah."

"No what?"

Bob's skull turned to one side and banged what would have been its forehead against a heavy bronze candleholder. After several thumps, it turned back toward me and said, "It's boring."

"Oh," I said. I rubbed at my jaw. "You think I should have gone four-color?"

Bob stared at me for a second and said, "I have nightmares about Hell, where all I do is add up numbers and try to have conversations with people like you."

I glowered up at the skull and nodded. "Okay, fine. You think it needs more drama."

"More anything. Drama would do. Or breasts."

I sighed and saw where that line of thought was going. "I am not going to hire a leggy secretary, Bob. Get over it."

"I didn't say anything about legs. But as long as we're on the subject . . ."

I set the Yellow Pages aside and picked up my pencil again. "I'm doing formulas here, Bob."

"It's formulae, O Maestro of Latin, and if you don't drum up some business, you aren't going to need those new spells for much of anything. Unless you're working on a spell to help you shoplift groceries."

I set the pencil down hard enough that the tip broke, and I stared at Bob in annoyance. "So what do you think it should say?"

Bob's eyelights brightened. "Talk about monsters. Monsters are good."

"Give me a break."

"I'm serious, Harry! Instead of that line about consulting and finding things, put, 'Fiends foiled, monsters mangled, vampires vanquished, demons demolished.'"

"Oh yeah," I said. "That kind of alliteration will bring in the business."

"It will!"

"It will bring in the nutso business," I said. "Bob, I don't know if anyone's told you this, but most people don't believe that monsters and fiends and whatnot even exist."

"Most people don't believe in love potions, either, but you've got that in there."

I held on to a flash of bad temper. "The point," I told Bob, "is to have an advertisement that looks solid, professional, and reliable."

"Yeah. Advertising is all about lying," Bob said.

"Hey!"

"You suck at lying, Harry. You really do. You should trust me on this one."

"No monsters," I insisted.

"Fine, fine," Bob said. "How about we do a positive-side spin, then? Something like, 'Maidens rescued, enchantments broken, villains unmasked, unicorns protected.'"

"Unicorns?"

"Chicks are into unicorns."

I rolled my eyes. "It's an ad for my investigative business, not a dating service. Besides, the only unicorn I ever saw tried to skewer me."

"You're sort of missing the entire 'Advertising is lying' concept, Harry."

"No unicorns," I said firmly. "It's fine the way it is."

"No style at all," Bob complained.

I put on a mentally challenged accent. "Style is as style does."

"Okay, fine. Suppose we throw intelligence to the winds and print only the truth. 'Vampire slayer, ghost remover, faerie fighter, werewolf exterminator, police consultant, foe of the foot soldiers of Hell.'"

I thought about it for a minute, then got a fresh piece of paper and wrote it down. I stared at the words.

"See?" Bob said. "That would look really hot, attract notice, and it would be the truth. What have you got to lose?"

"This week's gas money," I said, finally. "Too many letters. Besides, Lieutenant Murphy would kill me if I went around blowing trumpets about how I help the cops."

"You're hopeless," Bob said.

I shook my head. "No. I'm not in this for the money."

"Then what are you in it for, Harry? Hell, in the past few years you've been all but killed about a million times. Why do you do it?"

I squinted up at the skull. "Because someone has to."

"Hopeless," Bob repeated.

I smiled, picked up a fresh pencil, and went back to my formulas—formulae. "Pretty much."

Bob sighed and fell quiet. My pencil scratched over clean white paper while the candles burned warm and steady.

SOMETHING BORROWED

—from *My Big Fat Supernatural Wedding*,
edited by P. N. Elrod

Takes place between *Dead Beat*
and *Proven Guilty*

I wrote this for the very first anthology in which I'd ever been invited to participate. I'd met Pat Elrod at a convention and thought she was quite a cool person, and when she asked me to take part in her anthology, I was more than happy to do so.

When I wrote this story, I was thinking that the Alphas hadn't gotten nearly enough stage time in the series thus far, and it seemed like a good opportunity to give them some more attention, while at the same time showing the progression of their lives since their college days, which I felt was best demonstrated by Billy and Georgia's wedding.

Inane trivia: While I was in school writing the first three books of the Dresden Files, my wife, Shannon, watched *Ally McBeal* in the evenings, often while I was plunking away at a keyboard. I didn't pay too much attention to the show, and it took me years to realize I had unconsciously named Billy and Georgia after those characters in *Ally McBeal*.

Who knew? TV really *does* rot your brain!

Steel pierced my leg and my body went rigid with pain, but I could not allow myself to move. "Billy," I growled through my teeth, "kill him."

Billy the Werewolf squinted up at me from his seat and said, "That might be a little extreme."

"This is torture," I said.

"Oh, for crying out loud, Dresden," Billy said, his tone amused. "He's just fitting the tux."

Yanof the tailor, a squat, sturdy little guy who had recently immigrated to Chicago from Outer Sloboviakastan or somewhere, glared up at me, with another dozen pins clutched between his lips and resentment in his eyes. I'm better than six and a half feet tall. It can't be fun to be told you've got to fit a tux to someone my height only a few hours before the wedding.

"It ought to be Kirby standing here," I said.

"Yeah. But it would be harder to fit the tux around the body cast and all those traction cables."

"I keep telling you guys," I said. "Werewolves or not, you've got to be more careful."

Ordinarily, I would not have mentioned Billy's talent for shapeshifting into a wolf in front of a stranger, but Yanof didn't speak a word of English. Evidently, his skills with needle and thread were such that he had no pressing need to learn. As Chicago's resident wizard, I'd worked with Billy on several occasions, and we were friends.

His bachelor party the night before had gotten interesting on the walk back to Billy's place, when we happened across a ghoul terrorizing an old woman in a parking lot.

It hadn't been a pretty fight. Mostly because we'd all had too many stripper-induced Jell-O shots.

Billy's injuries had all been bruises and all to the body. They wouldn't spoil the wedding. Alex had a nasty set of gashes on his throat from the ghoul's clawlike nails, but he could probably pass them off as particularly enthusiastic hickeys. Mitchell had broken two teeth when he'd charged the ghoul but hit a wall instead. He was going to be a dedicated disciple of Anbesol until he got to the dentist.

All I had to remember the evening by was a splitting headache, and not from the fight. Jell-O shots are far more dangerous, if you ask me.

Billy's best man, Kirby, had gotten unlucky. The ghoul slammed him into a brick wall so hard that it broke both his legs and cracked a vertebra.

"We handled him, didn't we?" Billy asked.

"Let's ask Kirby," I said. "Look, there isn't always going to be a broken metal fence post sticking up out of the ground like that, Billy. We got lucky."

Billy's eyes went flat and he abruptly stood up. "All right," he said, his voice hard. "I've had just about enough of you telling me what I should and should not do, Harry. You aren't my father."

"No," I said, "but—"

"In fact," he continued, "if I remember correctly, the other Alphas and I have saved your life twice now."

"Yes," I said. "But—"

His face turned red with anger. Billy wasn't tall, but he was built like an armored truck. "But *what*? You don't want to share the spotlight with any of us mere one-trick wonders? Don't you *dare* belittle what Kirby did, what the others have done and sacrificed."

I am a trained investigator. Instincts honed by years of observation warned me that Billy might be angry. "Great hostility I sense in you," I said in a Muppety voice.

Billy's steady glower continued for a few more seconds, and then it broke. He shook his head and looked away. "I'm sorry. For my tone."

Yanof jabbed me again, but I ignored it. "You didn't sleep last night."

He shook his head again. "No excuse. But between the fight and Kirby and"—he waved a vague hand—"today. I mean, *today*."

"Ah," I said. "Cold feet?"

Billy took a deep breath. "Well, it's a big step, isn't it?" He shook his head. "And after next year, most of the Alphas are going to be done with school. Getting jobs." He paused. "Splitting up."

"And that's where you met Georgia," I said.

"Yeah." He shook his head again. "What if we don't have anything else in common? I mean, good grief. Have you seen her family's place? And I'm going to be in debt for seven or eight years just paying off the student loans. How do you know if you're ready to get married?"

Yanof stood up, gestured at my pants, and said something that sounded like, "Hahklha ah lafala krepata khem."

"I'm not seeing people right now," I told him as I took off the pants and passed them over. "Or else you'd have a shot, you charmer."

Yanof sniffed, muttered something else, and toddled back into the shop.

"Billy," I said, "you think Georgia would have fought that thing last night?"

"Yes," he said without a second's hesitation.

"She going to be upset that you did it?"

"No."

"Even though some folks got hurt?"

He blinked at me. "No."

"How do you know?" I asked.

"Because"—he shook his head—"because she won't. I know her. Upset by the injuries, yes, but not by the fight." He shifted to a tone he probably didn't realize was an imitation of Georgia's voice. "People get hurt in fights. That's why they're called fights."

"You know her well enough to answer serious questions for her when she isn't even in the room, man," I said quietly. "You're ready. Keep the big picture in mind. You and her."

He looked at me for a second and then said, "I thought you'd say something about love."

I sighed. "Billy. You knob. If you didn't love her, you wouldn't be stressed about losing what you have with her, would you."

"Good point," he said.

"Remember the important thing. You and her."

He took a deep breath and let it out. "Yeah," he said. "Georgia and me. The rest doesn't matter."

I was going to mumble something vaguely supportive, when the door to the fitting room opened and an absolutely ravishing raven-haired woman in an expensive lavender silk skirt-suit came in. She might have been my age, and she had a lot of gold and diamonds, a lot of perfect white teeth, and the kind of curves that come only from surgery. Her shoes and purse together probably cost more than my car.

"Well," she snapped, and put a fist on her hip, glaring first at Billy and then at me. "I see you are already doing your best to disrupt the ceremony."

"Eve," Billy said in a kind of stilted, formally polite voice. "Um. What are you talking about?"

"For one thing, this," she said, flicking a hand at me. Then she gave me a second, more evaluative look.

I tried to look casual and confident, there in my Spider-Man T-shirt and black briefs. I managed to keep myself from diving toward my jeans. I turned aside to put them on, maintaining my dignity.

"Your underwear has a hole," Eve said sweetly.

I jerked my jeans on, blushing. Stupid dignity.

"Bad enough that you insist on this . . . petty criminal taking part in a ceremony before polite society. Yanof is beside himself," Eve continued, speaking to Billy. "He threatened to quit."

"Wow," I said. "You speak Sloboviakstanese?"

She blinked at me. "What?"

"Because Yanof doesn't speak any English. So how did you know he threatened to quit?" I smiled sweetly at her.

Eve gave me a glare of haughty anger and defended herself by pretending I hadn't said anything. "And now we're going to have to leave out one of the bridesmaids. To say nothing of the fact that with *him* standing up there on one side of you and Georgia on the other, you're going to look like a midget. The photographer will have to be notified, and I have no idea how we'll manage to rearrange everything at the last moment."

I swore I could hear Billy's teeth grind. "Harry," he said in that same polite, strained voice, "this is Eve McAlister. My stepmother-in-law."

"I do not care for that term, as I have told you often. I am your mother-in-law," she said. "Or will be, whenever this ongoing disaster you've created from a respectable wedding breathes its last."

"I'm sure we can work something out," Billy assured her, his tone hopeless.

"Georgia is late and is letting the voice mail answer her phone—as though I needed something else to occupy my thoughts." She shook her head. "I assume the lowlifes you introduced her to kept her out too late last night. Just like this one did to you."

"Hey, come on," I said, careful to keep my tone as reasonable and friendly as I could. "Billy's had a rough night. I'm sure he can help you out if you just give him a chance to—"

She made a disgusted sound and interrupted me. "Did I say or do something to imply that I cared to hear your opinion, charlatan? Lowlifes. I warned her about folk like you."

"You don't even know me, lady," I said.

"Yes, I do," she informed me. "I know all about you. I saw you on *Larry Fowler.*"

I narrowed my eyes at Eve.

Billy's expression came close to panic, and he held up both hands, palms out, giving me a pleading look. But my hangover ached, and life is too short to waste it taking verbal abuse from petty tyrants who watch bad talk shows.

"Okay, Billy's stepmom," I began.

Her eyes flashed. "Do *not* call me that."

"You don't care to be called a stepmother?" I asked.

"Not at all."

"Though you obviously aren't Georgia's mother. Howsabout I call you trophy wife?" I suggested.

She blinked at me once, her eyes widening.

Billy put his face in his hands.

"Bed warmer?" I mused. "Mistress made good? Midlife crisis by-product?" I shook my head. "When in doubt, go with the classics." I leaned a little closer and gave her a crocodilian smile. "*Gold digger.*"

The blood drained out of Eve's face, leaving ugly pinkish blotches high on her cheeks. "Why, you . . . you . . ."

I waved my hand. "No, it's all right; I don't mind finding alternate terms. I understand that you're under pressure. Must be hard trying to look good in front of the old money when they all know that you were really just a receptionist or an actress or a model or something."

Her mouth dropped completely open.

"We're all having a tough day, dear." I flipped my hand at her. "Shoo."

She stared at me for a second, then let out a snarled curse you'd hardly expect from a lady of her station, spun on the heel of one Italian-leather pump, and stalked from the room. I heard a couple of beeps as she crossed to the shop's door, and then she started screeching into a cell phone. I could hear her for about ten seconds after she went outside.

Mission accomplished. Spleen vented. Dragon lady routed. I felt pleased with myself.

Billy heaved a sigh. "You had to talk to her like that?"

"Yeah." I glowered out after the departed Eve. "Once my mouth was open and my lips started moving, it was pretty much inevitable."

"Dammit, Harry." Billy sighed.

"Oh, come on, man. Sticks and stones may break her bones, but one wiseass will never hurt her. It's not a big deal."

"Not for you: You don't have to live with it. I do. So does Georgia."

I chewed on my lower lip for a second. I hadn't thought about it in those terms. I suddenly felt less than mature. "Ah," I said. "Oh. Um. Maybe I should apologize?"

He bent his head and pinched the bridge of his nose between his fingers. "Oh, God, no. Things are bad enough already."

I frowned at him. "Is it really that important to you? The ceremony?"

"It's important to Georgia."

I winced. "Oh," I said. "Ah."

"Look, we've got a few hours. I'll stay here and try to sort things out with Eve," Billy said. "Do me a favor?"

"Hey, what's a best man for? Other than tackling a panicked groom if he tries to run."

He gave me a quick grin. "See if you can contact Georgia first? Maybe she's had car trouble or overslept or something. Or maybe she just left her phone on all night and it went dead."

"Sure," I said, "I'll take care of it."

I CALLED BILLY and Georgia's apartment and got no answer. Knowing Georgia, I expected her to be at the hospital, visiting Kirby. Billy might have been the combat leader of the merry band of college kids who had learned shapeshifting from an actual wolf, but Georgia was the manager, surrogate mom, and brains when there wasn't any violence on.

Kirby was on painkillers and groggy, but he told me Georgia hadn't been there. I talked to the duty nurse and confirmed that though his family was flying in from Texas to see him, he'd had no visitors since Billy and I had left.

Odd.

I thought about mentioning it to Billy, but I didn't really know anything yet, and it wasn't as though he needed *more* pressure.

"Don't get paranoid, Harry," I told myself. "Maybe she's got a hangover, too. Maybe she ran off with a male stripper." I waited to see if I was buying it, then shook my head. "And maybe Elvis and JFK are shacked up in a retirement home somewhere."

I went to Billy and Georgia's apartment.

They live in a place near the University of Chicago's campus, in a neighborhood that missed being an ugly one by maybe a hundred yards. It still wasn't the kind of place you'd want to hang around outside after dark. I didn't have a key to get into the building, so I pressed buttons one at a time until someone buzzed me in, and I took the stairs up.

As I neared the apartment door, I knew something was wrong. It wasn't that I saw or heard anything, magical or otherwise, but when I stopped before the door, I had a nebulous but strong conviction that something bad had gone down.

I knocked. The door rattled and fell off the lower hinge. It swung open a few inches, drunkenly, upper hinges squealing. Splits and cracks, invisible until the door moved, appeared in the wood, and the dead bolt rattled dully against the inside of the door, loose in its setting.

I stopped there for a long second, waiting and listening. Other than the whirring of a window fan at the end of the hall and someone playing an easy-listening station on the floor above me, there was nothing. I closed my eyes for a moment and extended my wizard's senses, testing the air nearby for any touch of magic upon it.

I felt nothing but the subtle energy that surrounded any home, a form of naturally occurring protective magic called the threshold. Billy and Georgia's apartment was the nominal headquarters of the Werewolves, and members came and went at all hours. It was never intended to be a permanent home—but there had been a lot of living in the little apartment, and its threshold was stronger than most. I slowly pushed the door open with my right hand.

The apartment had been torn to pieces.

A futon lay on its side, its metal frame twisted like a pretzel. The entertainment center had been pulled down from the wall, shattering equipment, scattering CDs and DVDs and vintage *Star Wars* action figures everywhere. The wooden table had been broken in two precisely at its center. One of the half-dozen chairs survived. The others were kindling. The microwave protruded from the drywall of an interior wall. The door of the fridge had taken out the bookcase across the room. Everything in the kitchen had been pulled down and scattered.

I moved in as quietly as I could—which was pretty damn quiet. I had done a lot of sneaking around. The bathroom looked like someone had taken a chain saw to it and followed up with explosives. The bedroom used to house computers and electronic stuff looked like the site of an airplane crash.

Billy and Georgia's bedroom was the worst of all of them.

There was blood on the floor and one wall.

Whatever had happened, I had missed it. Dammit. I wanted to kill something, I wanted to scream in frustration, and I wanted to throw up in fear for Georgia.

But in my business, that kind of thing doesn't help much.

I went back into the living room. The phone near the door had survived. I dialed.

"Lieutenant Murphy, Special Investigations," answered a professional, bland voice.

"It's me, Murph," I told her.

Murphy knows me. Her tone changed at once. "My God, Harry, what's wrong?"

"I'm at Billy and Georgia's apartment," I said. "The place has been torn apart. There's blood."

"Are you all right?"

"I'm fine," I said. "Georgia's missing." I paused and said, "It's her wedding day, Murph."

"Five minutes," she said at once.

"I need you to pick something up for me on the way."

MURPHY CAME THROUGH the door eight minutes later. She was the head of Chicago PD's Special Investigations Department. They were the cops who got to handle all the crimes that didn't fall into anyone else's purview—stuff like vampire attacks and mystical assaults, as well as more mundane crimes like grave robbing, plus all the really messy cases the other cops didn't want to bother with. SI is supposed to make everything fit neatly into the official reports, explaining away anything weird with logical, rational investigation.

SI spends a lot of time struggling with that last one. Murphy writes more fiction than most novelists.

Murphy doesn't look like a cop, much less a monster cop. She's five nothing. She's got blond hair, blue eyes, and a cute nose. She's also got about a zillion gunnery awards and a shelfful of open-tournament martial arts trophies, and I once saw her kill a giant plant monster with a chain saw. She wore jeans, a white tee, sneakers, a baseball cap, and her hair was pulled back into a tail. She wore her gun in a shoulder rig, her badge around her neck, and she had a backpack slung over one shoulder.

She came through the door and stopped in her tracks. She surveyed the room for a minute and then said, "What did this?"

I nodded at the twisted futon frame. "Something strong."

"I wish I were a big-time private investigator like you. Then I could figure these things out for myself."

"You bring it?" I asked.

She tossed me the backpack. "The rest is in the car. What's it for?"

I opened the pack, took out a bleached-white human skull, and put it down on the kitchen counter. "Bob, wake up."

Orange lights appeared in the skull's shadowed eye sockets, and then slowly grew brighter. The skull's jaws twitched and then opened into a pantomime of a wide yawn. A voice issued out, the sound odd, like when you talk while on a racquetball court. "What's up, boss?"

"Jesus, Mary, and Joseph," Murphy swore. She took a step back and almost fell over the remains of the entertainment center.

Bob the Skull's eyelights brightened. "Hey, the cute blonde! Did you do her, Harry?" The skull spun in place on the counter and surveyed the damage. "Wow. You *did*! Way to go, stud!"

My face felt hot. "No, Bob," I growled.

"Oh," the skull said, crestfallen.

Murphy closed her mouth, blinking at the skull. "Uh. Harry?"

"This is Bob the Skull," I told her.

"It's a skull," she said. "That talks."

"Bob is actually the spirit inside. The skull is just the container it's in."

She looked blankly at me and then said, "It's a *skull*. That *talks*."

"Hey!" Bob protested. "I am not an it! I am definitely a he!"

"Bob is my lab assistant," I explained.

Murphy looked back at Bob and shook her head. "Just when I start thinking this magic stuff couldn't get weirder."

"Bob," I said, "take a look around. Tell me what did this."

The skull spun obediently and promptly said, "Something strong."

Murphy gave me an oblique look.

"Oh, bite me," I told her. "Bob, I need to know if you can sense any residual magic."

"Ungawa, bwana," Bob said. He did another turnaround, this one slower, and the orange eyelights narrowed.

"Residual magic?" Murphy asked.

"Anytime you use magic, it can leave a kind of mark on the area around you. Mostly it's so faint that sunrise wipes it away every morning. I can't always sense it."

"But *he* can?" Murphy asked.

"But he *can*!" Bob agreed. "Though not with all this chatter. I'm working over here."

I shook my head and picked up the phone again.

"Yes," said Billy. He sounded harried, and there was an enormous amount of background noise.

"I'm at your apartment," I said. "I came here looking for Georgia."

"What?" he said.

"Your apartment," I said louder.

"Oh, Harry," Billy said. "Sorry—this phone is giving me fits. Eve just talked to Georgia. She's here at the resort."

I frowned. "What? Is she all right?"

"Why wouldn't she be?" Billy said. Someone started shrieking in the background. "Crap, this battery's dying. Problem solved; come on up. I brought your tux."

"Billy, wait."

He hung up.

I called him back and got nothing but voice mail.

"Aha!" Bob said. "Someone used that wolf spell the naked chick taught to Billy and the Werewolves, back over there by the bedroom," he reported. "And there were faeries here."

I frowned. "Faeries. You sure?"

"One hundred percent, boss. They tried to cover their tracks, but the threshold must have taken the zing out of their illusion."

I nodded and exhaled. "Dammit." Then I strode into the bathroom and hunkered down, pawing through the rubble.

"What are you doing?" Murphy asked.

"Looking for Georgia," I said. I found a plastic brush full of long strands the color of Georgia's hair and took several of them in hand.

I've gotten a lot of mileage out of my tracking spell, refining it over the years. I stepped out into the hall and drew a circle on the floor around me with a piece of chalk. Then I took Georgia's hairs and pressed them against my forehead, summoning up my focus and will. I shaped the magic I wanted to create, focused on the hairs, and released my will as I murmured, "*Interessari, interressarium.*"

Magic surged out of me, into the hairs and back. I broke the circle with my foot, and the spell flowed into action, creating a faint sense of pressure against the back of my head. I turned, and the sensation flowed over my skull in response, over my ear, then over my cheekbone, and finally came to rest directly between my eyes.

"She's this way," I said. "Uh-oh."

"Uh-oh?"

"I'm facing south," I said.

"Which is a problem?"

"Billy says she's at the wedding. Twenty miles north of here."

Murphy's eyes widened in comprehension. "A faerie has taken her place."

"Yeah."

"Why? Are they trying to place a spy?"

"No," I said quietly. "This is malicious. Probably because Billy and company backed me up during the battle when the last Summer Knight was murdered."

"That was years ago."

"Faeries are patient," I said, "and they don't forget. Billy's in danger."

"I'd say Georgia was the one in danger," Murphy said.

"I mean that Billy's in danger, too," I said.

"How so?"

"This isn't happening on their wedding day by chance. The faeries want to use it against them."

Murphy frowned. "What?"

"A wedding isn't just a ceremony," I said. "There's power in it. A pledging of one to another, a blending of energies. There's magic all through it."

"If you say so," she said, her tone wry. "What happens to him if he marries a faerie?"

"Conservatives get real upset," I said absently. "But I'm not sure, magically speaking. Bob?"

"Oh," Bob said. "Um. Well, if we assume this is one of the Winter Sidhe, then he's going to be lucky to survive the honeymoon. If he does, well, she'll be able to influence him, long term. He'll be bound to her, the way the Winter Knights are bound to the Winter Queens. She'll be able to impose her will over his. Change the way he thinks and feels about things."

I ground my teeth. "And if she changes him enough, it will drive him insane."

"Usually, yup," Bob said. His voice brightened. "But don't worry, boss. Odds are he'll be dead before sunrise tomorrow. He might even die happy."

"That isn't going to happen," I said. I checked my watch. "The wedding is in three hours. Georgia might need help now." I looked back at Murphy. "You carrying?"

"Two on me. More in the car."

"Now, there's a girl who knows how to party!" Bob said.

I popped the skull back into my backpack harder than I strictly had to and zipped it shut. "Feel like saving the day?"

Her eyes sparkled, but she kept her tone bored. "On the weekend? Sounds too much like work."

We started from the apartment together. "I'll pay you in doughnuts."

"Dresden, you pig. That cop-doughnut thing is a vicious stereotype."

"Doughnuts with little pink sprinkles," I said.

"Professional profiling is just as bad as racial profiling."

I nodded. "Yeah. But I know you want the little pink sprinkles."

"That isn't the point," she said loftily, and we got into her car.

We buckled in, and I said more quietly, "You don't have to come with me, Karrin."

"Yes," she said. "I do."

I nodded and focused on the tracking spell, turning my head south. "Thataway."

THE WORST THING about being a wizard is all the presumption; people's expectations. Pretty much everyone expects me to be some kind of con artist, since it is a well-known fact that there is no such thing as magic. Of those who know better, most of them think I can just snap my fingers, poof, and have whatever I want. Dirty dishes? Snap my fingers and they wash themselves, like in *The Sorcerer's Apprentice*. Need to talk to a friend? Poof, teleport them in from wherever they are, because the magic knows where to find them, all by itself.

Magic ain't like that. Or I sure as hell wouldn't drive a beat-up old Volkswagen.

It's powerful, true, and useful, and enormously advantageous, but ultimately it is an art, a science, a craft, a tool. It doesn't go out and do things by itself. It doesn't create something from nothing. Using it takes talent and discipline and practice and a lot of work, and none of it comes free.

Which was why my spell led us to downtown Chicago and suddenly became less useful.

"We've circled this block three times," Murphy told me. "Can't you get a more precise fix on it?"

"Do I look like one of those GPS thingies?" I sighed.

"Define *thingie*," Murphy said.

"It's my spell," I said. "It's oriented to the points of the compass. I didn't really have the z-axis in mind when I designed it, and it only works for that when I'm right on top of the target. I keep meaning to go back and fix that, but there's never time."

"I had a marriage like that," Murphy said. She stopped at a light and stared up. The block held six buildings—three apartments, two office buildings, and an old church. "In there. Somewhere. It could take a lot of time to search that."

"So call in all the king's horses and all the king's men," I said.

She shook her head. "I might be able to get a couple, but since Rudolph moved to Internal Affairs, I've been flagged. If I start calling in people left and right without a damn good logical, rational, wholly normal reason . . ."

I grunted. "I get it. We need to get closer. The closer I get to Georgia, the more precise the tracking spell will be."

Murphy nodded once and pulled over in front of a fire hydrant, parking the car. "Let's be smart about this. Six buildings. Where would a faerie take her?"

"Not the church. Holy ground is uncomfortable for them." I shook my head. "Not the apartments. Too many people there. Too easy for someone to hear or see something."

"Office buildings on a weekend," Murphy said. "Empty as you can find in Chicago. Which one?"

"Let's take a look. Maybe the spell can give me an idea."

It took ten minutes to walk around the outsides of both buildings. The spell remained wonderfully nonspecific, though I knew Georgia was within a hundred yards or so. I sat down at the curb in disgust. "Dammit," I said, pushing at my hair. "There has to be something."

"Would a faerie be able to magick herself in and out of there?"

"Yes and no," I said. "She couldn't just wander in through the wall, or poof herself inside. But she could walk in under a veil, so that no one saw her—or else saw an illusion of what she wanted them to see."

"Can't you look for residual whatsit again?"

It was a good idea. I got Bob and tried it, while Murphy found a phone and tried to reach Billy or anyone who could reach Billy. After an hour's effort, we had accomplished enormous amounts of nothing.

"In case I haven't mentioned it before," I said, "dealing with faeries is a pain in the ass." Someone in a passing car flicked a still-smoldering cigarette butt onto the concrete near me. I kicked it through a sewer grate in disgust.

"She covered her tracks again?"

"Yeah."

"How?"

I shrugged. "Lot of ways. Scatter little glamours around to misdirect us. Only used her magic very lightly, to keep from leaving a big footprint. If she did her thing in a crowded area, enough people's life force passing by would cover it. Or she could have used running water to—"

I stopped talking, and my gaze snapped back to the sewer grate.

I could hear water running through it in a low, steady stream.

"Down there," I said. "She's taken Georgia to Undertown."

MURPHY STARED AT the stairs leading down to a tunnel with brick walls and shook her head. "I wouldn't have believed this was here."

We stood at the end of an uncompleted wing of Chicago's underground commuter tunnels, at a broken section of wall hidden behind a few old tarps that led down into the darkness of Undertown.

Murphy had thrown on an old Cubs jacket over her shirt. She switched guns, putting her favorite Sig away in exchange for the Glock she wore holstered on one hip. The gun had a little flashlight built onto the underside of its barrel, and she flicked it on. "I mean, I knew there were some old tunnels," Murphy said, "but not this."

I grunted and took off the silver pentacle amulet I wore around my neck. I held it in my right hand, my fingers clutching the chain against the solid, round length of oak in my right hand, about two feet long and covered with carved runes and sigils—my blasting rod. I sent an effort of will into the amulet, and the silver pentacle began to glow with a gentle, blue-white light. "Yeah. The Manhattan Project was run out of the tunnels here until they moved it to the Southwest. Plus the town kept sinking into the swamp for a hundred and fifty years. There are whole buildings sunk right into the ground. The Mob dug places during Prohibition. People built bomb shelters during the fifties and sixties. And other things have added more, plus gateways back and forth to the spirit world."

"Other things?" Murphy asked, gun steady on the darkness below. "Like what?"

"Things," I said, staring down at the patient, lightless murk of Undertown. "Anything that doesn't like sunlight or company. Vampires, ghouls, some of the nastier faeries, obviously. Once, I fought this wacko who kept summoning up fungus demons."

"Are you stalling?" Murphy asked.

"Maybe I am." I sighed. "I've been down there a few times. Never been good."

"How you wanna do this?"

"Like we did the vampire lair. Let me go first with the shield. Something jumps out at us, I'll drop and hold it off until you kill it."

Murphy nodded soberly. I swallowed a lump of fear out of my throat. It settled into my stomach like a nugget of ice. I prepared my shield, and the same color light as emanated from my pentacle surrounded it, drizzling heatless blue-white sparks in an irregular stream. I prepared myself to use my blasting rod if I had to, and started down the stairs, following the tracking spell toward Georgia.

The old brick stairs ended at a rough stone slope into the earth. Water ran down the walls and in rivulets down the sides of the tunnel. We went forward, through an old building that might have been a schoolhouse, judging by the rotted piles of wood and a single old slate chalkboard fallen from one wall. The floor was tilted to one side. The next section of tunnel was full of freezing, dirty, knee-deep water until it sloped up out of the water, went round a corner where the walls had been cut by rough tools, and then opened into a wider chamber.

It was a low-ceilinged cave—low for me, anyway. Most folks wouldn't have been troubled. Three feet from the doorway, the floor dropped away into silent, black water that stretched out beyond the reach of my blue wizard light. Murphy stepped up next to me, and the light on her gun sent a silver spear of white light out over the water.

There, on a slab of stone that rose up no more than an inch or two from the water's surface, lay Georgia.

Murphy's light played over her. Georgia was a tall woman—in high-enough heels, she could have looked me in the eye. She'd been stork-skinny and frizzy haired when I met her. The years in between had softened her lines and brought out a natural confidence and intelligence that made her an extraordinarily attractive, if not precisely beautiful, woman. She was naked, laid on her back with her arms crossed over her chest in repose, funeral-style. She took slow breaths. Her skin was discolored from the cold, her lips tinged blue.

"Georgia?" I called, feeling like a dummy. But I didn't know of any other way to see if she was awake. She didn't stir.

"What now?" Murphy asked. "You go get her while I cover you?"

I shook my head. "Can't be as easy as it looks."

"Why not?"

"Because it never is." I bowed my head for a moment, pressed my fingertips lightly to my forehead, between my eyebrows, and concentrated on bringing up my Sight.

One of the things common to all wizards is the Sight. Call it a sixth sense, a third eye, whatever you please; around the world everyone with enough magic has the Sight. It lets you actually see the forces of energy at work in the world around you—life, death, magic, what have you. It isn't always easy to understand what I see, and sometimes it isn't pretty—and anything a wizard views with his Sight is there, in Technicolor, never fading—forever.

That's why you have to be careful what you choose to Look at. I don't like doing it, ever. You never know what it is you'll See.

But when it came to finding out what kinds of magic might be between Georgia and me, I didn't have many options. I opened my Sight and Looked out over the water to Georgia.

The water was shot through with slithery tendrils of greenish light—a spell of some kind, just under its placid surface. If the water moved, the spell would react. I couldn't tell how. The stone Georgia lay upon held a dull, pulsing energy, a sullen violet radiance that wound in slow, hypnotic spirals through the rock. A binding was in effect, I was sure, something to keep her from moving. Another spell played over and through Georgia herself—a cloud of deep blue sparkles that lay against her skin, especially around her head. A sleeping spell? I couldn't make out any details from here.

"Well?" Murphy said.

I closed my eyes and released my Sight, always a mildly disorienting experience. The remnants of my hangover made it worse than usual. I reported my findings to Murphy.

"Well," she said, "I sure am glad we have a wizard on the case. Otherwise we might be standing here without any idea what to do next."

I grimaced and stepped to the water's edge. "This is water magic. It's tricky stuff. I'll try to take down the alarm spell on the surface of the pool, then swim out and get Geo—"

Without warning, the water erupted into a boiling froth at my feet, and a claw, a freaking pincer as big as a couple of basketballs, shot out of the water and clamped down on my ankle.

I let out a battle cry. Sure, a lot of people might have mistaken it for a sudden yelp of unmanly fear, but trust me: It was a battle cry.

The thing, whatever it was, pulled my leg out from under me, trying to drag me in. I could see slick, wet black shell. I whipped my blasting rod around to point at the thing and snarled, *"Fuego!"*

A lance of fire as thick as my thumb lashed from the tip of my blasting rod, which was pointed at the thing's main body. It hit the water and boiled into steam. It smashed into the shell of the creature with such force that it simply ripped the thing's body from its clawed limb. I brought my shield up, a pale, fragile-looking quarter dome of blue light that coalesced into place before the steam boiled back into my eyes.

I squirmed away from the water on my butt, shaking wildly at the severed limb that still clutched me.

The waters surged again, and another slick-shelled *thing* grabbed at me. And another. And another. Dozens of the creatures were rushing toward our side of the pool, and the pressure wave rushing before them rose a foot off the pool's surface.

"Shellycobbs!" I shouted, and flicked another burst of flame at the nearest, driving it back. "They're shellycobbs!"

"Whatever," Murphy said, stepped up beside me, and started shooting. The third shellycobb took three hits in the same center area of its shell and cracked like a restaurant lobster.

It bought me a second to act, and I raised the blasting rod and tried something new on the fly, a blending of a blast of fire with my shield magic. I pointed the rod at one side of the shore, gathered my will, and thundered, *"Ignus defendarius!"*

A bar of flame, bright enough to hurt my eyes, shot out to one side of the room. I drew a line across the stone with the tip of the blasting rod, and as the flame touched the stone, it adhered, spooling out from my blasting rod until it had formed a solid line between us and the water, and an opaque curtain of flame three feet high separated us from the shellycobbs. Angry rattles and splashes came from the far side of the curtain.

If the fire dropped, the faerie water monsters would swarm us.

The fire took a lot of energy to keep up, and if I tried to hold it too long, I'd probably black out. Worse, it was still fire—it needed oxygen to keep burning, and in those cramped tunnels there wasn't going to be much of it around for breathing if the fire stayed lit too long. All of this meant we had only seconds and had to do something—fast.

"Murph!" I snapped. "Could you carry her?"

She turned wide blue eyes to me, her gun still held ready and pointing at the shellycobbs. "What?"

"Can you carry her?"

She gritted her teeth and nodded once.

I met her eyes for a dangerous second and asked, "Do you trust me?"

Fire crackled. Water boiled. Steam hissed.

"Yes, Harry," she whispered.

I flashed her a grin. "Jump the fire. Run to her."

"Run to her?"

"And hurry," I said, lifting my left arm, focusing as my shield bracelet began to glow, blue-white energy swiftly becoming incandescent. "Now!"

Murphy broke into a run and hurtled over the wall of fire.

"*Forzare!*" I shouted, and extended my left arm and my will.

I reshaped the shield, this time forming it in a straight, flat plane about three feet wide. It shot through the wall of flame, over the water, to the stone upon which Georgia lay. Murphy landed on the bridge of pure force, kept her balance, and poured on the speed, sprinting over the water to the unconscious young woman.

Murphy slapped her gun back into its holster, grabbed Georgia, and, with a shout and a grunt of effort, managed to get the tall girl into a fireman's carry. She started back, much more slowly than she'd gone forward.

The shellycobbs thrashed even more furiously, and the strain of holding both spells started to become a physical sensation, a spidery, trembling weakness in my arms and legs. I clenched my teeth and my will, focusing on holding the wall and the bridge until Murphy could return. My vision distorted, shrinking down to a tunnel.

And then Murphy shouted again and plunged through the fire, this time more slowly. She let out a gasp of pain as she got singed, then stumbled past me.

I released the bridge with a gasp of relief. "Go!" I said. "Come on, let's go!"

Together, we were barely able to get Georgia lifted. I was only able to hold the wall of flame against the shellycobbs for about fifty feet when I had to release the spell or risk passing out. I guess the shelly-cobbs weren't sprinters, because Murphy and I outran them, dragging the naked girl out of her Undertown prison and back to Murphy's car.

In all that time, Georgia never stirred.

Murphy had a blanket in her trunk. I wrapped Georgia in it and got in the backseat with her. Murphy gunned the car and headed for the Lincolnshire Marriott Resort Hotel, twenty miles north of town and one of the most ostentatious places in the area to hold a wedding. Traffic wasn't good, and according to the clock in Murphy's car, we had less than ten minutes before the wedding was supposed to begin.

I struggled in the backseat, fumbling to keep Georgia from bouncing off the ceiling, to get my backpack open, and to ignore the cuts the shellycobb's pincer left on my leg.

"Is that blood on her face?" Murphy asked.

"Yeah," I said. "Dried. But I figure it wasn't hers. Bob said she wolfed out in the apartment. I think Georgia got her fangs into Jenny Green-teeth before she got grabbed."

"Jenny who?"

"Jenny Greenteeth," I said. "She's one of the sidhe. Faerie nobility, sidekick to the Winter Lady."

"Are her teeth green?"

"Like steamed spinach. I saw her leading a big old bunch of shellycobbs just like those guys, back at the faerie war. If Maeve wanted to lay out some payback for Billy and company, Jenny's the one she'd send."

"She's dangerous?"

"You know the stories about things that tempt you down to the water's edge and then drown you? Sirens that lure sailors to their deaths? Mermaids who carry men off to their homes under the sea?"

"Yeah?"

"That's Jenny. Only she's not so cuddly."

I dug Bob out of my backpack. The skull took one look at the sleeping, naked Georgia and leered. "First you get demolition-level sex with the cop chick, and now a threesome, all in the same day!" he cried. "Harry, you have to write *Penthouse* about this!"

"Not now, Bob. I need you to identify the spell that's been laid on Georgia."

The skull made a disgusted sound but focused on the girl. "Oh," he said after a second. "Wow. That's a good one. Definitely sidhe work."

"I figure it's Jenny Greenteeth. Give me details."

"Jenny got game. It's a sleep spell," he said. "A seriously good one, too. Malicious as hell."

"How do I lift it?"

"You can't," Bob said.

"Fine. How do I break it?"

"You don't understand. It's been tied into the victim. It's being fueled by the victim's life force. If you shatter the spell . . ."

I nodded, getting it. "I'll do the same to her. Is it impossible to get rid of it?"

"No, not at all. I'm saying that *you* couldn't lift it. Whoever threw it could do that, of course. But there's another key."

I grew wroth and scowled. "What key, Bob?"

"Uh," he said, somehow giving the impression that he'd shrugged. "A kiss ought to do it. You know. True love, Prince Charming, that kind of thing."

"That won't be hard," I said, relaxing a little. "We'll definitely get to the wedding before he goes off alone with Jenny and gets drowned."

"Oh, good," Bob said. "Of course, the girl still kicks off, but you can't save all the people, all the time."

"What?" I demanded. "Why does Georgia die?"

"Oh, if the Werewolf kid goes through the ceremony with Jenny and plights his troth and so on, it's going to contaminate him. I mean, if he's married to another, it can't really be pure love. Jenny's claim on him would prevent the kiss from lifting the spell."

"Which means Georgia won't wake up," I said, chewing on my lip. "At what point in the wedding does it happen, exactly?"

"You mean, when will it be too late?" Bob asked.

"Yeah, I mean, when they say, 'I do,' when they swap rings, or what?"

"Rings and vows," Bob said, mild scorn in his voice. "Way overrated."

Murphy glanced up at me in the rearview mirror and said, "It's the kiss, Harry. It's the kiss."

"Buffy's right!" Bob agreed cheerily.

I met Murphy's eyes in the mirror for just a second and then said, "Yeah. I guess I should have figured."

Murphy smiled a little.

"The kiss seals the deal," Bob prattled. "If Billy kisses Jenny Green-teeth, the girl with the long legs ain't waking up, and he ain't long for the world, either."

"Murph," I said, tense.

She rolled down the car's window, slapped a magnetic cop light on the roof, and started up the siren. Then she stomped on the gas and all but gave me whiplash.

UNDER NORMAL CIRCUMSTANCES, the trip to the resort would have taken half an hour. I'm not saying Murphy's driving was suicidal. Not quite. But after the third near collision, I closed my eyes and fought off the urge to chant, "There's no place like home."

Murphy got us there in twenty minutes.

Tires screeched as she swung into the resort's parking lot. "Drop me there," I said, pointing. "Park behind the reception tent so folks won't see Georgia. I'll go get Billy."

Clutching my blasting rod, I bailed out of the car, which never actually came to a full stop, and ran into the hotel. The concierge blinked at me from behind her desk.

"Wedding!" I barked at her. "Where?"

She blinked and pointed a finger down the hall. "Um. The ballroom."

"Right!" I said, and sprinted that way. I could see the open double doors and heard a man's voice over a loudspeaker saying, "Until death do you part?"

Eve McAlister stood at the doorway in her lavender silk outfit, and when she saw me, her eyes narrowed into sharp little chips of ice. "There, that's him. That's the man."

Two big, beefy guys in matching badly fitted maroon dress coats appeared—hotel security goons. They stepped directly into my path, and the larger one said, "Sir, I'm sorry, but this is a private function. I'll have to ask you to leave."

I ground my teeth. "You have got to be kidding me! Private? I'm the best-fucking-man!"

The loudspeaker voice in the ballroom said, "Then by the power vested in me . . ."

"I will not allow you to further disrupt this wedding, or tarnish my good name," Eve said in a triumphant tone. "Gentlemen, please escort him from the premises before he causes a scene."

"Yes, ma'am," the bigger goon said. He stepped toward me, glancing down at the blasting rod. "Sir, let's walk to the doors now."

Instead, I darted forward, toward the doors, taking the goons by surprise with the abrupt action. "Billy!" I shouted.

The goons recovered in an eyeblink and tackled me. They were professional goons. I went down under them, and it drove the breath out of me.

The loudspeaker voice said, "Man and wife. You may now kiss the bride."

I lay there on my back under maybe five hundred pounds of security goon, struggling to breathe and staring at nothing but ceiling.

A ceiling lined with a whole bunch of automated fire extinguishers.

I slammed my head into the Boss Goon's nose and bit Backup Goon on the arm until he screamed and jerked it away, freeing my right arm.

I pointed the blasting rod up, reached for my power, and wheezed, "*Fuego . . .*"

Flame billowed up to the ceiling.

A fire alarm howled. The sprinklers flicked on and turned the inside of the hotel into a miniature monsoon.

Chaos erupted. The ballroom was filled with screams. The floor shook a little as hundreds of guests leapt to their feet and started looking for an exit. The security goons, smart enough to realize they suddenly had an enormous problem on their hands, scrambled away from the doorway before they could be trampled.

I got to my feet in time to see a minister fleeing a raised platform, where a figure in Georgia's wedding dress had hunched over, while Billy, spiffy in his tux, stared at her in pure shock. That much running water grounded out whatever glamour the bride might have been using, and her features melted back into those I'd seen before—she lost an inch or two of height and her proportions changed. Georgia's rather sharp features flowed into a visage of haunting, unearthly beauty. Georgia's brown hair became the same green as emeralds and seaweed.

Jenny Greenteeth turned toward Billy, her trademark choppers bared in a viridian snarl, and her hand swept at his throat, inhuman nails gleaming.

Billy may have been shocked, but not so much that he didn't recognize the threat. His arm intercepted Jenny's and he drove into her, pushing both hands forward with the power of his arms, shoulders, and legs. Billy had a low center of gravity, and was no skinny weakling. The push sent Jenny back several steps and off the edge of the platform. She fell in a tangle of white fabric and lace.

"Billy!" I shouted again, almost managing to make it loud. My voice was lost in the sounds of panic and the wailing fire alarms, so I gritted my teeth, brought my shield bracelet up to its flashiest, sparkliest, shiniest charge, and thrust into the press of the crowd. To them, it must have looked like someone waving a road flare around, and there was a steady stream of interjections that averaged out to "Eek!" I forged ahead through them.

By the time I was past the crowd, Jenny Greenteeth had risen to her feet, tearing the bridal gown off as if it were made of tissue paper. She stretched one hand into a grasping claw and clenched at the air. Ripples of angry power fluttered between her fingers, and an ugly green sphere of light appeared in her hand.

She leapt nimbly back up to the platform, unencumbered by the dress, and flung the green sphere at Billy. He ducked. It flew over his head, leaving a hole with blackened, crumbling edges in the wall behind him.

Jenny howled and summoned another sphere, but by that time I was within reach. Standing on the floor by the platform gave me a perfect shot at her knees, and I swung my blasting rod with both hands. The blow elicited a shriek of pain from the sidhe woman, and she flung the second sphere at me. I caught it on my shield bracelet and it rebounded upon her, searing a black line across the outside of one thigh.

The sidhe screamed and threw herself back, her weight mostly on one leg, and snarled to me, "Thou wouldst have saved this one, Wizard. But I will yet exact my Lady's vengeance twofold."

And with a graceful leap, she flew over our heads, forty feet to the door, and vanished from sight as swiftly and nimbly as a deer.

"Harry!" Billy said, staring in shock at the soaking-wet room. "What the hell is happening here? What the hell was that thing?"

I grabbed his tux. "No time. Come with me."

He did but asked, "Why?"

"I need you to kiss Georgia."

"Uh," he said. "What?"

"I found Georgia. She's outside. The watery tart knows it. She's going to kill her. You gotta kiss her, *now*."

"Oh," he said.

We both ran, and suddenly the bottom fell out of my stomach. Vengeance twofold.

Oh, God.

Jenny Greenteeth would kill Murphy, too.

THE AREA OUTSIDE the hotel was a mess. People were wandering around in herds. Emergency sirens were already on the way. A couple of cars had smashed into each other in the parking lot, probably as they both gunned it for the road. Everyone out there seemed to be determined to get in our way, slowing our pursuit.

We ran to where Murphy had parked her car.

It was lying on its side. Windows were broken. One of the doors had been torn off. I didn't see anyone around. But Billy suddenly cocked his head to one side and then pointed at the reception tent. We ran for it as quietly as we could, and Billy threw himself inside. I heard him let out a short cry.

I followed.

Georgia lay on the ground, hardly covered by the blanket at all, limbs sprawled bonelessly. Billy rushed over to her.

Just past them I saw Murphy.

Jenny Greenteeth stood over her at the refreshments table, pushing her face down into a full punch bowl, hands locked in Murphy's hair. The wicked faerie's eyes were alight with rage and madness and an almost sexual arousal. Murphy's arms twitched a little, and Jenny gasped, lips parting, and pushed down harder.

Murphy's hand fluttered one more time and went still.

The next thing I knew, I was smashing my blasting rod down onto Jenny Greenteeth, screaming incoherently and pounding as hard as I possibly could. I drove the faerie back from Murphy, who slid limply to the ground. Then Jenny recovered her balance, struck out at me with one arm, and I found out a fact I hadn't known before.

Jenny Greenteeth was something strong.

I landed several feet away, not far from Billy and Georgia, watching birdies and little lights fly around. On another table, next to me, was another punch bowl.

Jenny Greenteeth flew at me, lust in her inhumanly lovely features, her feline eyes smoldering.

"Billy!" I slurred. "Dammit, kiss her! Now!"

Billy blinked at me.

Then he turned to Georgia, lifting the upper half of her body in his arms, and kissed her with a desperation and passion that no one could fake.

I didn't get to see what happened, because faster than you could say "oxygen deprivation," Jenny Greenteeth had seized my hair and smashed my face against the bottom of the punch bowl.

I fought her, but she was stronger than anything human, and she had all kinds of leverage. I could feel her pressed against me, body tensing and shifting, rubbing against me: She was getting off as she murdered me. The lights started to go out. This was what she did. She knew what she was doing.

Lucky for me, she wasn't the only one.

I suddenly fell, getting the whole huge punch bowl to turn over on me as I did, drenching me in bright red punch. I gasped and wiped stinging liquid from my eyes and looked up in time to see a pair of wolves, one tall and lean, one smaller and heavier, leap at Jenny Green-teeth and bring her to the ground. Screams and snarls blended, and none of them sounded human.

Jenny tried to run, but the lean wolf ripped across the back of her unwounded leg with its fangs, severing the hamstring. The faerie went down. The wolves were on her before she could scream again. The wheel turns, and Jenny Greenteeth never had a chance. The wolves knew what they were doing.

This was what *they* did.

I crawled over to Murphy. Her eyes were open and staring, her body and features slack. Some part of my brain remembered the steps for CPR. I started doing it. I adjusted her position, sealed my lips to Murphy's, and breathed for her. Then compressions. Breathe. Compressions.

"Come on, Murph," I whispered. "Come on."

I covered her mouth with mine and breathed again.

For one second, for one teeny, tiny instant, I felt her mouth move. I felt her head tilt, her lips soften, and my oh-so-professional CPR— just for a second, mind you—felt almost, *almost* like a kiss.

Then she started coughing and sputtering, and I sank back from her in relief. She turned on her side, breathing hard for a moment, and then looked up at me with dazed blue eyes. "Harry?"

I leaned down, causing runnels of punch to slide into one of my eyes, and asked quietly, "Yeah?"

"You have fruit-punch mouth," she whispered.

Her hand found mine, weak but warm. I held it. We sat together.

BILLY AND GEORGIA got married that night in Father Forthill's study, at St. Mary of the Angels, an enormous old church. No one was there but them, the padre, Murphy, and me. After all, as far as most anyone else knew, they'd been married at that disastrous travesty of a farce in Lincolnshire.

The ceremony was simple and heartfelt. I stood with Billy. Murphy stood with Georgia. They both looked radiantly happy. They held hands the whole time, except when exchanging rings.

Murphy and I stepped back when they got to the vows.

"Not exactly a fairy-tale wedding," she whispered.

"Sure it was," I said. "Had a kiss and an evil stepmother and everything."

Murphy smiled at me.

"Then by the power vested in me," the padre said, beaming at the pair from behind his spectacles, "I now pronounce you man and wife. You may kiss th—"

They beat him to it.

IT'S MY BIRTHDAY, TOO

—from *Many Bloody Returns*,
edited by Charlaine Harris

Takes place between *White Night*
and *Small Favor*

I've met people who are sweeter and nicer and more likeable than Charlaine Harris—but I really can't remember when. Every author I've ever talked with who knows Charlaine just couldn't be happier about the success of her books and the HBO series *True Blood*. She's that nice. I can't even bring myself to be jealous. She's *that* nice.

So when she invited me to contribute, I said, "Heck, yeah!"

Using a birthday theme (since the book, originally, was supposed to be published on Vlad Dracula's something-hundredth birthday) was sort of a challenge. Birthdays are about families. Whether they're a biological family or one that's come together by choice, it's your family who gathers to celebrate the anniversary of *you*.

It's kind of a profound thing, when you think about it.

But Dresden hadn't ever really associated his birthday with that kind of joy—only with the knowledge that he'd never really *had* a family. So I decided to do a story about Harry coping with the unfamiliar role of being the guy celebrating the life of his half brother. I found a very good mall in Chicago that I could demolish with the usual Dresdenesque shenanigans, set the story against the backdrop of a vampire-ish LARP, and knocked this one out over the course of about three weeks.

Hey, Miyagi-san," my apprentice said. Her jeans still dripped with purple-brown mucus. "You think the dry cleaner can get this out?"

I threw my car keys down on my kitchen counter, leaned my slimed, rune-carved wooden staff next to them, and said, "The last time I took something stained by a slime golem to a cleaner, the owner burned his place down the next day and tried to collect on the insurance."

Molly, my apprentice, was just barely out of her teens, and it was impossible not to notice what great legs she had when she stripped out of her trendily mangled jeans. She wrinkled her nose as she tossed them into the kitchen trash can. "Have I told you how much I love the wizard business, Harry?"

"Neither of us is in the hospital, kid. This was a good day at work." I took my mantled leather duster off. It was generously covered in splatters of the sticky, smelly mucus as well. I toted it over to the fireplace in my basement apartment, which I keep going during the winter. Given that I have to live without the benefits of electricity, it's necessary. I made sure the fire was burning strongly and tossed the coat in.

"Hey!" Molly said. "Not the coat!"

"Relax," I told her. "The spells on it should protect it. They'll bake the slime hard and I'll chisel it off tomorrow."

"Oh, good. I like the coat." The girl subsided as she tossed her secondhand combat boots and socks into my trash after her ruined jeans. She was tall for a woman and built like a schoolboy's fantasy of the Scandinavian exchange student. Her hair was shoulder length and the color of white gold, except for the tips, which had been dyed in a blend of blue, red, and purple. She'd lost a couple of the piercings she'd previously worn on her face, and was now down to only one eyebrow, one nostril, her tongue, and her lower lip. She went over to the throw rug in the middle of my living room floor, hauled it to one side, and opened the trapdoor leading down to my lab in the subbasement. She lit a candle in the fire, wrinkling her nose at the stink from the greasy smoke coming up from my coat, and padded down the stepladder stairs into the lab.

Mouse, my pet saber-toothed retriever, trotted out of my bedroom and spread his doggy jaws in a big yawn, wagging his shaggy grey tail. He took one step toward me, then froze as the smell of the mucus hit his nose. The big grey dog turned around at once and padded back into the bedroom.

"Coward!" I called after him. I glanced up at Mister, my tomcat, who drowsed upon the top of my heaviest bookshelf, catching the updraft from the fireplace. "At least you haven't deserted me."

Mister glanced at me, then gave his head a little shake as the pungent smoke from the fireplace rose to him. He flicked his ears at me, obviously annoyed, and descended from the bookshelf with gracefully offended dignity to follow Mouse into the relative aromatic safety of my bedroom.

"Wimp," I muttered. I eyed my staff. It was crusty with the ichor. I'd have to take it off with sandpaper and repair the carvings. I'd probably have to do the blasting rod, too. Stupid freaking amateurs, playing with things they didn't understand. Slime golems are just disgusting.

Molly thumped back up the stairs, now dressed in her backup clothes. Her experiences in training with me had taught her that lesson in about six months, and she had a second set of clothing stored in a gym bag underneath the little desk I let her keep in the lab. She came up in a black broomstick skirt—those skirts that are supposed to look wrinkled—and Birkenstocks, inappropriate for the winter weather but way less inappropriate than black athletic panties. "Harry, are you going to be able to drive me home?"

I frowned and checked the clock. It was after nine—too late for a young woman to trust herself to Chicago's public transportation. Given Molly's skills, she probably wouldn't be in any real danger, but it was best not to tempt fate. "Could you call your folks?"

She shook her head. "On Valentine's Day? Are you kidding? They'll have barricaded themselves upstairs and forced the older kids to wear the little ones out so they'll sleep through the noise." Molly shuddered. "I'm not interrupting them. Way too disturbing."

"Valentine's Day," I groaned. "Dammit."

"What?"

"Oh, I forgot, what with the excitement. It's, uh, someone's birthday. I got them a present and wanted to get it to them today."

"Oh?" Molly chirped. "Who?"

I hesitated for a minute, but Molly had earned a certain amount of candor—and trust. "Thomas," I said.

"The vampire?" Molly asked.

"Yeah," I said.

"Wow, Harry," she said, her blue eyes sparkling. "That's odd. I mean, why would you get *him* a birthday present?" She frowned prettily. "I mean, you didn't get my dad one, and you're friends with him, and he's a Knight of the Sword and one of the good guys, and he's saved your life about twenty times and all."

"More like four times," I said testily. "And I do Christmas for hi—"

Molly was looking at me, a smug smile on her face.

"You figured it out," I said.

"That Thomas was your brother?" Molly asked innocently. "Yep." I blinked at her. "How?"

"I've seen you two fight." She lifted both pale eyebrows. "What?

Have you *seen* how many brothers and sisters I have? I know my sibling conflicts."

"Hell's bells." I sighed. "Molly—"

She lifted a hand. "I know, boss. I know. Big secret; safe with me." Her expression turned serious, and she gave me a look that was very knowing for someone so young. "Family is important."

I'd grown up in a succession of orphanages and foster homes. "Yeah," I said, "it is."

She nodded. "So you haven't given family presents much. And your brother doesn't exactly have a ton of people bringing him presents on his birthday, does he?"

I just looked at her for a second. Molly was growing up into a person I thought I was going to like.

"No," I said quietly. "I haven't, and he doesn't."

"Well, then," she said, smiling. "Let's go give him one."

I FROWNED AT the intercom outside Thomas's apartment building and said, "I don't get it. He's always home this time of night."

"Maybe he's out to dinner," Molly said, shivering in the cold—after all, her backup clothing had been summer wear.

I shook my head. "He limits himself pretty drastically when it comes to exposing himself to the public."

"Why?"

"He's a White Court vampire, an incubus," I said. "Pretty much every woman who looks at him gets ideas."

Molly coughed delicately. "Oh. It's not just me, then."

"No. I followed him around town once. It was like watching one of those campy cologne commercials."

"But he *does* go out, right?"

"Sure."

She nodded and immediately started digging into her backpack. "Then maybe we could use a tracking spell and run him down. I think I've got some materials we can use."

"Me, too," I said, and produced two quarters from my pocket, holding them up between my fingers with slow, ominous flair, like David Blaine.

Then I took two steps to the pay phone next to the apartment building's entrance, plugged the coins in, and called Thomas's cell phone.

Molly gave me a level look and folded her arms.

"Hey," I told her as it rang. "We're wizards, kid. We have trouble using technology. Doesn't mean we can't be smart about it."

Molly rolled her eyes and muttered to herself, and I paid attention to the phone call.

"'Allo," Thomas answered, the word thick with the French accent he used in his public persona.

"Hello, France?" I responded. "I found a dead mouse in my can of French roast coffee, and I've called to complain. I'm an American, and I refuse to stand for that kind of thing from you people."

My half brother sighed. "A moment, please," he said in his accent. I could hear music playing and people talking behind him. A party? A door clicked shut and he said, without any accent, "Hey, Harry."

"I'm standing outside your apartment in the freaking snow with your birthday present."

"That won't do you much good," he said. "I'm not there."

"Being a professional detective, I had deduced that much," I said.

"A birthday present, huh?" he said.

"I get much colder and I'm going to burn it for warmth."

He laughed. "I'm at the Woodfield Mall in Schaumburg."

I glanced at my watch. "This late?"

"Uh-huh. I'm doing a favor for one of my employees. I'll be here until midnight or so. Look, just come back tomorrow evening."

"No," I said stubbornly. "Your birthday is today. I'll drive there."

"Uh," Thomas said. "Yeah. I guess, uh. Okay."

I frowned. "What are you doing out there?"

"Gotta go." He hung up on me.

I traded a look with Molly. "Huh."

She tilted her head. "What's going on?"

I turned and headed back for the car. "Let's find out."

WOODFIELD MALL IS the largest such establishment in the state, but its parking lots were all but entirely empty. The mall had been closed for more than an hour.

"How are we supposed to find him?" Molly asked.

I drove my car, the beat-up old Volkswagen Bug I had dubbed the *Blue Beetle*, around for a few minutes. "There," I said, nodding at a white sedan parked among a dozen other vehicles, the largest concentration of such transport left at the mall. "That's his car." I started to say something else but stopped myself before I wasted an opportunity to Yoda the trainee. "Molly, tell me what you see."

She scrunched up her nose, frowning, as I drove through the lot to park next to Thomas's car. The tires crunched over the thin dusting of snow that had frosted itself over scraped asphalt, streaks of salt and ice melt, and stubborn patches of ice. I killed the engine. It ticked for a few seconds, and then the car filled with the kind of soft, heavy silence you get only on a winter night with snow on the ground.

"The mall is closed," Molly said. "But there are cars at this entrance. There is a single section of lights on inside when the rest of them are out. I think one of the shops is lit inside. There's no curtain down over it, even though the rest of the shops have them."

"So what should we be asking?" I prompted.

"What is Thomas doing, in a group, in a closed mall, on Valentine's Day night?" Her tone rose at the end, questioning.

"Good; the date might have some significance," I said. "But the real question is this: Is it a coincidence that the exterior security camera facing that door is broken?"

Molly blinked at me, then frowned, looking around.

I pointed a finger up. "Remember to look in all three dimensions. Human instincts don't tend toward checking above us or directly at our feet, in general. You have to make yourself pick up the habit."

Molly frowned and then leaned over, peering up through the Beetle's window to the tall streetlamp pole above us.

Maybe ten feet up, there was the square, black metal housing of a security camera. Several bare wires dangled beneath it, their ends connected to nothing. I'd seen it as I pulled the car in.

My apprentice drew in a nervous breath. "You think something is happening?"

"I think we don't have enough information to make any assumptions," I said. "It's probably nothing. But let's keep our eyes open."

No sooner had the words left my mouth than two figures stepped out of the night, walking briskly down the sidewalk outside the mall toward the lighted entrance.

They both wore long black capes with hoods.

Not your standard wear for Chicago shoppers.

Molly opened her mouth to stammer something.

"Quiet," I hissed. "Do not move."

The two figures went by only thirty or forty feet away. I caught a glimpse of a very, very pale face within one of the figure's hoods, eyes sunken into the skull-like pits. They both turned to the door without so much as glancing at us, opened it as though they expected it to be unlocked, and proceeded inside.

"All right," I said quietly. "It might be something."

"Um," Molly said. "W-were those v-vampires?"

"Deep breaths, kid," I told her. "Fear isn't stupid, but don't let it control you. I have no idea what they were." I made sure my old fleece-lined heavy denim coat was buttoned up, and I got out of the car.

"Uh. Then where are you going?" she asked.

"Inside," I said, walking around to the Beetle's trunk. I unwrapped the wire that had held it closed ever since a dozen vehicular mishaps ago. "Whatever they are, Thomas doesn't know about them. He'd have said something."

I couldn't see her through the lifted hood, but Molly rolled down the window enough to talk to me. "B-but you don't have your staff or blasting rod or coat or anything. They're all back at your apartment."

I opened the case that held my .44 revolver and the box that held my ammunition, slipped shells into the weapon, and put it in my coat pocket. I dropped some extra rounds into the front pocket of my jeans and shut the hood. "They're only toys, Padawan." Familiar, capable, proven toys that I felt naked without, but a true wizard shouldn't absolutely rely on them—or teach his apprentice to do so. "Stay here, start up the car, and be ready to roll if we need to leave in a hurry."

"Right," she said, and wriggled over into the driver's seat. To give Molly credit, she might have been nervous, but she had learned the job of wheelman—sorry, political correctioners, wheel*person*—fairly well.

I kept my right hand in my coat pocket, on the handle of my gun, hunched my shoulders against a small breath of frozen wind, and hurried to the mall entrance, my shoes crunching and squeaking on the little coating of snow. I walked toward the doors as if I owned them, shoved them open like any shopper, and got a quick look around.

The mall was dark, except for the entrance and that single open shop—a little bistro with tinted windows that would have been dimly lit even when all the lights were on. I could see figures seated at tables inside and at a long dining counter and bar. They wore lots of black, and none of them looked much older than Molly, though the dim lights revealed few details.

I narrowed my eyes a bit, debating. Vampires gave off a certain amount of energy that someone like me could sense, but depending on which breed you were talking about, that energy could vary. Sometimes my sense of an approaching vampire was as overtly creepy as a child's giggle coming from an open grave. Other times there was barely anything at all, and it registered on my senses as something as subtle as simple, instinctive dislike for the creature in question. For White Court vamps like my half brother, there was nothing at all, unless they were doing something overtly vampiric. From outside the shop, I couldn't tell anything.

This was assuming they were vampires at all—which was a fairly large assumption. They didn't meet up in the open like this.

Vampires didn't apologize to the normal world for existing, but they didn't exactly run around auditioning for the latest reality TV shows, either.

There was one way to find out. I opened the door to the bistro, hand on my gun, took a step inside, holding the door open in case I needed to flee, and peered around warily at the occupants. The nearest was a pair of young men, speaking earnestly at a table over two cups of what looked like coffee and . . .

And they had acne—not like disfiguring acne or anything, just a few zits.

In case no one's told you, here's a monster-hunting tip for free: Vampires have little to no need for Clearasil.

Seen in that light, the two young men's costumes looked like exactly that—costumes. They had two big cloaks, dripping a little melt-water, hung over the backs of their chairs, and I caught the distinctive aroma of weed coming from their general direction. Two kids slipping out from the gathering to toke up and then come back inside. One of them produced a candy bar from a pocket and tore into it, to the reassurance of the people who make Clearasil, I'm sure.

I looked around the room. There were more people; mostly young, mostly with the thinness that goes with youth, as opposed to the leanly cadaverous kind that goes with being a bloodsucking fiend. They were mostly dressed in similar costume-style clothing, unless there had been a big sale at Goths-R-Us.

I felt my shoulders sag in relief, and I slipped my hand out of my pocket. Anytime one of my bouts of constructive paranoia didn't pan out was a good time.

"Sir," said a gruff voice from behind me. "The mall is closed. You want to tell me what you're doing here?"

I turned to face a squat, blocky man with watery blue eyes and no chin. He'd grown a thick brown-gold walrus mustache that emphasized rather than distracted from the lack. He had a high hairline, a brown uniform, and what looked like a cop's weapon belt until you saw that he had a walkie-talkie where the sidearm would be, next to a tiny can of Mace. His name tag read RAYMOND.

"Observing suspicious activity, Raymond," I said, and hooked my chin vaguely back at the bistro. "See that? People hanging around in the mall after hours. Weird."

He narrowed his eyes. "Wait. Don't I know you?"

I pursed my lips and thought. "Oh, right. Six, seven years ago, at Shoegasm."

He grunted in recognition. "The phony psychic."

"Consultant," I responded. "And from what I hear, their inventory stopped shrinking. Which hadn't happened before I showed up."

Raymond gave me a look that would have cowed lesser men. Much, much lesser men. Like maybe fourth graders. "If you aren't with the group, you're gone. You want to leave, or would you rather I took care of it for you?"

"Stop," I said. "You're scaring me."

Raymond's mustache quivered. He apparently wasn't used to people who didn't take him seriously. Plus, I was much, much bigger than he was.

"'Allo, 'Ah-ree," came my brother's voice from behind me.

I turned to find Thomas there, dressed in tight black pants and a blousy red silk shirt. His shoulder-length hair was tied back in a tail with a matching red ribbon. His face didn't look much like mine, except around the eyes and maybe the chin. Thomas was good-looking the way Mozart was talented. There were people on the covers of magazines and on television and on movie screens who despaired of ever looking as good as Thomas.

On his arm was a slim young girl, quite pretty and wholesome-looking, wearing leather pants that rode low on her hips and a red bikini top, her silky brown hair artfully mussed. I recognized her from Thomas's shop, a young woman named Sarah.

"Harry!" she said. "Oh, it's nice to see you again." She nudged Thomas with her hip. "Isn't it?"

"Always," Thomas, smiling, said in his French accent.

"Hello, Mr. Raymond!" Sarah said, brightly.

Raymond scowled at me and asked Sarah, "He with you?"

"But of course," Thomas said in that annoying French way, giving Raymond his most brilliant smile.

Raymond grunted and took his hand away from the radio. Lucky me. I had evidently been dismissed from Raymond's world. "I was going to tell you I'm going to be in the parking lot, replacing a camera we've got down, if you need me."

"*Merci*," Thomas said, still smiling.

Raymond grunted. He gave me a sour look, picked up a toolbox from where he'd set it aside, along with his coat and a stepladder, and headed out to the parking lot.

"'Ah-ree, you know Say-rah," Thomas said.

"Never had the pleasure of an introduction," I said, and offered Sarah my hand.

She took it, smiling. "I take it you aren't here to play Evernight?"

I looked from her to the costumed people. "Oh," I said. "*Oh*, it's a . . . game of some kind, I take it?"

"A LARP," she said.

I looked blank for a second. "Is that like a lark?"

She grinned. "LARP," she repeated. "Live action role-playing."

"Live action . . . vampire role-playing, I guess," I said. I looked at Thomas. "And this is why you are here?"

Thomas gave me a sunny smile and nodded. "She asked me to pretend to be a vampire, just for tonight," he said. "And straight."

No wonder he was having a good time.

Sarah beamed at me. "Thomas *never* talks about his, ah, personal life. So you're quite the man of mystery at the shop. We all speculate about you, all the time."

I'll just bet they did. There were times when my brother's cover as a flamingly gay hairdresser really grated. And it wasn't as though I could go around telling people we were related—not with the White Council of Wizards at war with the Vampire Courts.

"How nice," I told Sarah. I was never getting out of the role people had assumed for me around Thomas. "Thomas, can we talk for a moment?"

"*Mais oui*," he said. He smiled at Sarah, took her hand, and gave her a little bow over it. She beamed fondly at him, and then hurried back inside.

I watched her go, in her tight pants and skimpy top, and sighed. She had an awfully appealing curve of back and hip, and just enough bounce to make the motion pleasant, and there was no way I could ever even think about flirting with her.

"Roll your tongue back up into your mouth before someone notices," Thomas said, sotto voce. "I've got a cover to keep."

"Tell them I'm larping like I'm straight," I said, and we turned to walk down the entry hall, a little away from the bistro. "Pretending to be a vampire, huh?"

"It's fun," Thomas said. "I'm like a guest star on the season finale."

I eyed him. "Vampires aren't fun and games."

"I know that," Thomas said. "You know that. But *they* don't know that."

"You aren't doing them any favors," I said.

"Lighten up," Thomas said. The words were teasing, but there were serious undertones to his voice. "They're having fun, and I'm helping. I don't get a chance to do that very often."

"By making light of something that is a very real danger."

He stopped and faced me. "They're *innocent*, Harry. They don't know any better. They've never been hurt by a vampire or lost loved ones to a vampire." He lifted his eyebrows. "I thought that was what your people were fighting for in the first place."

I gave him a sour look. "If you weren't my brother, I'd probably tell you that you have some awfully nerdy hobbies."

We reached the front doors. Thomas studied himself in the glass and struck a pose. "True, but I look gorgeous doing them. Besides, Sarah worked eleven Fridays to Mondays in a row without a complaint. She earned a favor."

Outside, the snow was thickening. Raymond was atop his ladder, fiddling with the camera. Molly was watching him. I waved until I got her attention, then made a little outline figure of a box with my fingers, and beckoned her. She nodded and killed the engine.

"I came in here expecting trouble. We're lucky I didn't bounce a few of these kids off the ceiling before I realized they weren't something from the dark side."

"Bah," Thomas said. "Never happen. You're careful."

I snorted. "I hope you won't mind if I just give you your present and run."

"Wow," Thomas said. "Gracious much?"

"Up yours," I said as Molly grabbed the present and hurried in through the cold, shivering all the way. "And happy birthday."

He turned to me and gave me a small, genuinely pleased smile. "Thank you."

There was a *click* of high heels in the hall behind us, and a young woman appeared. She was pretty enough, I suspected, but in the tight black dress, black hose, and with her hair slicked back like that, she came off sort of threatening. She gave me a slow, cold look and said, "So. I see you're keeping low company after all, Ravenius."

Ever suave, I replied, "Uh. What?"

"'Ah-ree," Thomas said.

I glanced at him.

He put his hand flat on the top of his head and said, "Do this."

I peered at him.

He gave me a look.

I sighed and put my hand on the top of my head.

The girl in the black dress promptly did the same thing and gave me a smile. "Oh, right, sorry. I didn't realize."

"I will be back in one moment," Thomas said, his accent back. "Personal business."

"Right," she said, "sorry. I figured Ennui had stumbled onto a sub-plot." She smiled again, then took her hand off the top of her head, reassumed that cold, haughty expression, and stalked *clickety-clack* back to the bistro.

I watched her go, turned to my brother while we both stood there with our hands flat on top of our heads, elbows sticking out like chicken wings, and said, "What does this mean?"

"We're out of character," Thomas said.

"Oh," I said. "And not a subplot."

"If we had our hands crossed over our chests," Thomas said, "we'd be invisible."

"I missed dinner," I said. I put my other hand on my stomach. Then, just to prove that I could, I patted my head and rubbed my stomach. "Now I'm out of character—and hungry."

"You're always hungry. How is that out of character?"

"True," I said. I frowned, then looked back. "What's taking Molly—"

My apprentice stood facing away from me, her back pressed to the glass doors. She stood rigid, one hand pressed to her mouth. Thomas's birthday present, in its pink and red Valentine's Day wrapping paper, lay on its side among grains of snowmelt on the sidewalk. Molly trembled violently.

Thomas was a beat slow to catch on to what was happening. "Isn't that skirt a little light for the weather? Look, she's freezing."

Before he got to "skirt," I was out the door. I seized Molly and dragged her inside, eyes on the parking lot. I noticed two things.

First, that Raymond's ladder was tipped over and lay on its side in the parking lot. Flakes of snow were already gathering upon it. In fact, the snow was coming down more and more heavily, despite the weather forecast that had called for clearing skies.

Second, there were droplets of blood on my car and the cars immediately around it, the ones closest to Raymond's ladder. They were rapidly freezing and they glittered under the parking lot's lamps like tiny brilliant rubies.

"What?" Thomas asked as I brought Molly back in. "What is—" He stared out the windows for a second and answered the question for himself. "Crap."

"Yeah," I said. "Molly?"

She gave me a wild-eyed glance, shook her head once, then bowed it and closed her eyes, speaking in a low, repetitive whisper.

"What the hell?" Thomas said.

"She's in psychic shock," I said quietly.

"Never seen you in psychic shock," my brother said.

"Different talents. I blow things up. Molly's a sensitive, and getting more so," I told him. "She'll snap herself out of it, but she needs a minute."

"Uh-huh," Thomas said quietly. He stared intently at the shuddering young woman, his eyes shifting colors slightly, from deep grey to something paler.

"Hey," I said to him. "Focus."

He gave his head a little shake, his eyes gradually darkening again. "Right. Come on. Let's get her a chair and some coffee and stop standing around in front of big glass windows making targets of ourselves."

We did, dragging her into the bistro and to the table nearest the door, where Thomas could stand watching the darkness while I grabbed the girl some coffee from a dispenser, holding my hand on top of my silly head the whole while.

Molly got her act together within a couple of minutes after I sat down. It surprised me: Despite my casual words to Thomas, I hadn't seen her that badly shaken up before. She grabbed at the coffee, shaking, and slurped some.

"Okay, grasshopper," I said. "What happened?"

"I was on the way in," she replied, her voice distant and oddly flat. "The security man. S-something killed him." A hint of something desperate crept into her voice. "I f-felt him die. It was horrible."

"What?" I asked her. "Give me some details to work with."

Molly shook her head rapidly. "D-didn't see. It was too fast. I sensed something moving behind me—m-maybe a footstep. Then there was a quiet sound and h-he *died*. . . ." Her breaths started coming rapidly again.

"Easy," I told her, keeping my voice in the steady cadence I'd used when teaching her how to maintain self-control under stress. "Breathe. Focus. Remember who you are."

"Okay," she said, several breaths later. "Okay."

"This sound. What was it?"

She stared down at the steam coming up off her coffee. "I . . . A thump, maybe. Lighter."

"A snap?" I asked.

She grimaced but nodded. "And I turned around, fast as I could. But he was gone. I didn't *see* anything there, Harry."

Thomas, ten feet away, could hear our quiet conversation as clearly as if he'd been sitting with us. "Something grabbed Raymond," he said. "Something moving fast enough to cross her whole field of vision in a second or two. It didn't stop moving when it took him. She probably heard his neck breaking from the whiplash."

There wasn't much to say to that. The whole concept was disturbing as hell.

Thomas glanced back at me and said, "It's a great way to do a grab and snatch if you're fast enough. My father showed me how it was done once." His head whipped around toward the parking lot.

I felt myself tense. "What?"

"The streetlights just went out."

I sat back in my chair, thinking furiously. "Only one reason to do that."

"To blind us," Thomas said. "Prevent anyone from reaching the vehicles."

"Also keeps anyone outside from seeing what is happening here," I said. "How are you guys using this place after hours?"

"Sarah's uncle owns it," Thomas said.

"Get her," I said, rising to take up watching the door. "Hurry."

Thomas brought her over to me a moment later. By the time he did, the larpers had become aware that something was wrong, and their awkwardly sinister role-playing dwindled into an uncertain silence as Sarah hurried over. Before, I had watched her and her scarlet bikini top in appraisal. Now I couldn't help but think how slender and vulnerable it made her neck look.

"What is it?" Sarah asked me.

"Trouble," I said. "We may be in danger, and I need you to answer a few questions for me, right now."

She opened her mouth and started to ask me something.

"First," I said, interrupting her, "do you know how many security men are present at night?"

She blinked at me for a second. Then she said, "Uh, four before closing, two after. But the two who leave are usually here until midnight, doing maintenance and some of the cleaning."

"Where?"

She shook her head. "The security office, in administration."

"Right," I said. "This place have a phone?"

"Of course."

"Take me to it."

She did, back in the little place's tiny kitchen. I picked it up, got a dial tone, and slammed Murphy's phone number across the keypad. If the bad guys, whoever or whatever they were, were afraid of attracting attention from the outside world, I might be able to avoid the entire situation by calling in lots of police cars and flashy lights.

The phone rang once, twice.

And then it went dead, along with the lights, the music playing on the speakers, and the constant blowing sigh of the heating system.

Several short, breathy screams came from the front of the bistro, and I heard Thomas shout for silence and call, "Harry?"

"The security office," I said to Sarah. "Where is it?"

"Um. It's at the far end of the mall from here."

"Easy to find?"

"No," she said, shaking her head. "You have to go through the administrative hall and—"

I shook my head. "You can show me. Come on." I stalked out to the front room of the bistro. "Thomas? Anything?"

All the larpers had gathered in close, herd instinct kicking in under the tension. Thomas stepped closer to me so that he could answer me under his breath.

"Nothing yet," Thomas said. "But I saw something moving out there."

I grunted. "Here's the plan. Molly, Sarah, and I are going to go down to the security office and try to reach someone."

"Bad idea," Thomas said. "We need to get out of here."

"We're too vulnerable. They're between us and the cars," I said. "Whatever they are. We'll never make it out all the way across the parking lot without getting caught."

"Fine," he said. "You fort up here and I'll go."

"No. Once we're gone, you'll try to get through to the cops on a cell phone. There's not a prayer of getting one to work if Molly and I are anywhere nearby—not with both of us this nervous."

He didn't like that answer, but he couldn't refute it. "All right," he said, grimacing. "Watch your back."

I nodded to him and raised my voice. "All right, everyone. I'm not sure exactly what is going on here, but I'm going to go find security. I want everyone to stay here until I get back and we're sure it's safe."

There was a round of halfhearted protests at that, but Thomas quelled them with a look. It wasn't an angry or threatening look. It was simply a steady gaze.

Everyone shut up.

I headed out with Molly and Sarah in tow, and as we stepped out of the bistro, there was an enormous crashing sound, and a car came flying sideways through the glass wall of the entranceway about eight feet off the ground. It hit the ground, broken glass and steel foaming around it like crashing surf, bounced with a shockingly loud crunch, and tumbled ponderously toward us, heralded by a rush of freezing air.

Molly was already moving, but Sarah only stood there staring incredulously as the car came toward us. I grabbed her around the waist and all but hauled her off her feet, dragging her away. I ran straight away from the oncoming missile, which was not the smartest way to go—but since a little perfume kiosk was blocking my path, it was the *only* way.

I was fast, and we got a little bit lucky. I pulled Sarah past the kiosk just as the car hit it. The vehicle's momentum was almost gone by the time it hit, and the car crashed to a halt, a small wave of safety glass washing past our shoes. Sarah wobbled and nearly fell. I caught her and kept going. She started to scream or shout or ask a question—but I clapped my hand over her mouth and hissed, "Quiet!"

I didn't stop until we were around the corner and the crashing racket was coming to a halt. Then I stopped with my back against the wall and got Sarah's attention.

I didn't speak. I raised one finger to my lips with as much physical emphasis as I could manage. Sarah, trembling violently, nodded at me. I turned to give the same signal to Molly, who looked pale but in control of herself. She nodded as well, and we turned and slipped away from that arm of the mall.

I listened as hard as I could, which was actually quite hard. It's a talent I seem to have developed, maybe because I'm a wizard, and maybe just because some people can hear really well. It was difficult to make out anything at all, much less any kind of detail, but I was sure I heard one thing—footsteps, coming in the crushed door of the mall, crunching on broken glass and debris.

Something fast enough to snap a man's neck with the whiplash of its passage and strong enough to throw that car through a wall of glass had just walked into the mall behind us. I figured it was a very, very good idea not to let it know we were there and sneaking away.

We got away with it, walking slowly and silently out through the mall, which yawned all around us, three levels of darkened stores, deserted shops, and closed metal grates and doors. I stopped a dozen shops later, after we'd gone past the central plaza of the mall and were far enough away for the space to swallow up quiet conversation.

"Oh my God," Sarah whimpered, her voice a strangled little whisper. "Oh my God. What is happening? Is it terrorists?"

I probably would have had a more suave answer if she hadn't been pressed up against my side, mostly naked from the hips up, warm and lithe and trembling. The adrenaline rush that had hit me when the car nearly smashed us caught up to me, and I suddenly found it difficult to keep from shivering, myself. I had a sudden, insanely intense need to rip off the strings on that red bikini top and kiss her, purely for the sake of how good it would feel. All things considered, though, it would have been less than appropriate. "Uh," I mumbled, forcing myself to look back the way we'd come. "They're . . . bad guys of some kind, yeah. Are you hurt?"

"No," Sarah said.

"Molly?" I asked.

"I'm fine," my apprentice answered.

"The security office," I said.

Sarah stared at me for a second, her eyes intense. "But . . . but I don't understand why—"

I put my hand firmly over her mouth. "Sarah," I said, meeting her eyes for as long as I dared, "I've been in trouble before, and I know what I'm doing. I need you to trust me. All right?"

Her eyes widened for a second. She reached up to lightly touch my wrist, and I let her push my hand gently away from her mouth. She swallowed and nodded once.

"There's no time. We have to find the security office now."

"A-all right," she said. "This way."

She led us off and we followed her, creeping through the cavernous dimness of the unlit mall. Molly leaned in close to me to whisper. "Even if we get the security guards, what are they going to do against something that can do *that*?"

"They'll have radios," I whispered back. "Cell phones. They'll know all the ways out. If we can't call in help, they'll give us the best shot of getting these people out of here in one—"

Lights began flickering on and off—not blinking, not starting up and shutting down in rhythm, but irregularly. First they came on over a section of the third floor for a few seconds. Then they went out. A few seconds later, it was a far section of the second floor. Then they went out. Then light shone from one of the distant wings for a moment and vanished again. It was like watching a child experiment with the switches.

Then the PA system let out a crackle and a little squeal of feedback. It shut off again and came back on. "Testing," said a dry, rasping voice over the speakers. "Testing one, two, three."

Sarah froze in place, and then backed up warily, looking at me. I stepped up next to her, and she pressed in close to me, shivering.

"There," said the voice. It was a horrible thing to listen to—like Linda Blair's impression of a demon-possessed victim, only less melodious. "I'm sure you all can hear me now."

And I'd heard such a voice before. "Oh, hell," I breathed.

"This is Constance," continued the voice. "Constance Bushnell. I'm sure you all remember me."

I glanced at Molly, who shook her head. Sarah looked frightened and confused, but when she caught my look, she shook her head, too.

"You might also remember me," she continued, "as Drulinda." And then the voice started singing "Happy Birthday." The tune wasn't even vaguely close to the actual song, but the "Happy birthday to me" lyrics were unmistakable.

Sarah's eyes had widened. "Drulinda?"

"Who the hell is Drulinda?" I asked.

Sarah shook her head. "One of our characters. But her player ran away from home or something."

"And you didn't recognize her actual name?"

Sarah gave me a slightly guilty glance. "Well, I never played with her much. She wasn't really very, you know—popular."

"Uh-huh," I said. "Tell me whatever you can about her."

She shook her head. "Um. About five four, sort of . . . plain. You know, not ugly or anything, but not really pretty. Maybe a little heavy."

"Not that." I sighed. "Tell me something *important* about her. People make fun of her?"

"Some did," she said. "I never liked it, but . . ."

"Crap." I looked at Molly and said, "Code Carrie. We're in trouble."

The horrible, dusty song came to an end. "It's been a year since I left you," Drulinda's voice said. "A year since I found what all you whining losers were looking for. And I decided to give myself a present." There was a horrible pause, and then the voice said, "You. All of you."

"Code what?" Molly asked me.

I shook my head. "Sarah, do you know where the announcement system is?"

"Yes," Sarah said. "Administration. Right by—"

"The security office." I sighed.

Drulinda's voice continued. "The entrances are closed and watched. But you should feel free to run for them. You all taste *so* much better when you've had time to be properly terrified. I've *so* been looking forward to seeing your reaction to the new me."

With that, the PA system shut off, but a second later, it started playing music—"Only You," by the Platters.

"Molly," I hissed, suddenly realizing the danger. "Veil us, *now.*"

She blinked at me, then nodded, bowing her head with a frown of concentration and folding her arms across her chest. I felt her gather up her will and release it with a word and a surge of energy that made the air sparkle like diamond dust for a half second.

Inside the veil, the air suddenly turned a few degrees cooler, and the area outside it seemed to become even dimmer than it had been a second before. I could sense the delicate tracery of the veil's magic in the air around us, though I knew that, from the other side, none of that would be detectable—assuming Molly had done it correctly, of course. Veils were one of her strongest areas, and I was gambling our lives that she had gotten it right.

Not more than a breath or two later, there was a swift pattering sound and a dim blur in the shadows, which ceased moving abruptly maybe twenty feet away and revealed the presence of a vampire of the Black Court.

Drulinda, or so I presumed her to be, was dressed in dark jeans, a red knit sweater, and a long black leather coat. If she'd been heavy in life, death had taken care of that problem for her. She was sunken and shriveled, as bony and dried up as the year-old corpse she now was. Unlike the older vamps of her breed, she still had most of her hair, though it had clearly not been washed or styled. Most of the Black Court I'd run into had never been terribly body conscious. I suppose once you'd seen it rot, there just wasn't much more that could happen to sway your opinion of it, either way.

Unlike the older vampires I'd faced, she stank. I don't mean that she carried a little whiff of the grave along with her. I mean she smelled like a year-old corpse that still had a few juicy corners left and wasn't entirely done returning to the earth. It was noxious enough to make me gag—and I'd spent my day tracking down and dismantling a freaking slime golem.

She stood there for a moment, while the Platters went through the first verse, looking all around her. She'd sensed something, but she wasn't sure what. The vampire turned a slow circle, her shriveled lips moving in time with the music coming over the PA system, and as she did, two more of the creatures, slower than Drulinda, appeared out of the darkness.

They were freshly made vampires—so much so that for a second, I thought them human. Both men wore brown uniforms identical to Raymond's. Both were stained with blood, and both had narrow scoops of flesh missing from the sides of their throats—at the jugular and carotid, specifically. They moved stiffly, making many little twitching motions of their arms and legs, as if struggling against the onset of rigor mortis.

"What is it?" slurred one of them. His voice was ragged but not the horrible parody Drulinda's was.

Her hand blurred, its movement too fast to see. The newborn vampire reacted with inhuman speed, but not nearly enough of it, and the blow threw him from his feet to land on the floor, shattered teeth scattering out from him like coins from a dropped purse. "You can talk," Drulinda rasped, "when I say you can talk. Speak again, and I will rip you apart and throw you into Lake Michigan. You can spend eternity down there with no arms, no legs, no light, and no blood."

The vampire, his nose smashed into shapelessness, rose as if he'd just slipped and fallen on his ass. He nodded, his body language twitchy and cringing.

Drulinda's leathery lips peeled back from yellow teeth stained with drying brownish blood. Then she turned and darted ahead, her footsteps making that light, swift patter on the tiles of the floor. She was gone and around the corner, heading for the bistro, in maybe two or three seconds. The two newbie vampires went after her, if far more slowly.

"Crap," I whispered as they vanished. "Dammit, dammit, dammit."

"What was that, Harry?" Molly whispered.

"Black Court vampires," I replied, trying not to inhale too deeply. The stench was fading, but it wasn't gone. "Some of the fastest, strongest, meanest things out there."

"Vampires?" Sarah hissed, incredulous. She didn't look so good. Her face was turning green. "No, this is, no, no, no—" She broke off and was violently sick. I avoided joining in by the narrowest of margins. Molly had an easier time of it than I, focused as she was on maintaining the veil over us, but I saw her swallow very carefully.

"Okay, Molly," I said quietly, "listen to me."

She nodded, turning abstracted eyes to me.

"Black Court vampires," I told her. "The ones Stoker's book outed. All their weaknesses—sunlight, garlic, holy water, symbols of faith. Remember?"

She nodded. "Yes."

"Most of the strengths, too. Strong, fast. Don't look them in the eyes." I swallowed. "Don't let them take you alive."

My apprentice's eyes flickered with both apprehension and a sudden, fierce fire. "I understand. What do you want me to do?"

"Keep the veil up. Take Sarah here. Find a shady spot and lie low. This should be over in half an hour, maybe less. By then, there's going to be a ruckus getting people's attention, one way or another."

"But I can—"

"Get me killed trying to cover you," I said firmly. "You aren't in this league, grasshopper. Not yet. I have to move fast. And I have friends here. I won't be alone."

Molly stared at me for a moment, her eyes shining with brief, frustrated tears. Then she nodded once and said, "Isn't there anything I can do?"

I peered at her, then down at her Birkenstocks. "Yeah. Give me your shoes."

Molly hadn't been my apprentice in the bizarre for a year and a half for nothing. She didn't even blink, much less ask questions. She just took off her shoes and handed them to me.

I put a gentle hand on her shoulder, then touched Sarah's face until she lifted her eyes to me. "I don't understand what's happening," she whispered.

"Stay with Molly," I told Sarah. "She's going to take care of you. Do whatever she says. All right?" I frowned down at her expensive black heels. "Gucci?"

"Prada," she said in a numb voice.

Being all manly, I know dick about shoes, but hopefully it wouldn't blow my cover as Thomas's mystery man. "Give them to me."

"All right," she said, and did, too shocked to argue.

Thomas had been right about the larpers. The corpse of Sarah's innocence lay on the floor along with her last meal, and she was taking it pretty hard.

I fought down a surge of anger and rose without another word, padding out from the protection of Molly's veil, shoes gripped in one hand, my gun in the other. The .44 might as well have been Linus's security blanket. It wouldn't do a thing to help me against a vampire of the Black Court—it just made me feel better.

I went as fast as I could without making an enormous racket and stalked up the nearest stairs—a deactivated escalator. Once I'd reached the second level, I took a right and hurried toward Shoegasm.

It was a fairly spacious shop that had originally occupied only a tiny spot, but after ironing out some early troubles, the prosperous little store had expanded into the space beside it. Now, behind a steel mesh security curtain, the store was arranged in an oh-so-trendy fashion and sported several huge signs that went on with a thematically appropriate orgasmic enthusiasm about the store's quality money-back guarantee.

"I am totally underappreciated," I muttered. Then I raised my voice a little, forcing a very slight effort of will, of magic, into the words as I spoke. "Keef! Hey, Keef! It's Harry Dresden!"

I waited for a long moment, peering through the grating, but I couldn't see anything in the dim shadows of the store. I took a chance, slipping the silver pentacle amulet from its chain around my neck, and with a murmur willed a whisper of magic through the piece of jewelry. A soft blue radiance began to emanate from the silver, though I tried to keep the light it let out to a minimum. If Drulinda or her vampire buddies were looking even vaguely in my direction, I was going to stand out like a freaking moron holding the only light in an entire darkened shopping mall.

"Keef!" I called again.

The cobb appeared from an expensive handbag hung over the arm of a dressing dummy wearing a pair of six-hundred-dollar Italian boots. He was a tiny thing, maybe ten inches tall, with a big puff of fine white hair like Albert Einstein. He was dressed in something vaguely approximating nineteenth-century urban-European wear—dark trousers, boots, a white shirt, and suspenders. He also wore a leather work belt thick with tiny tools, and he had a pair of odd-looking goggles pushed up over his forehead.

Keef hopped down from the dressing dummy and hurried across the floor to the security grate. He put on a pair of gloves and pulled out a couple of straps from his work belt. Then, nearly as nimble as a squirrel and very careful not to touch the metal with his bare skin, he climbed up the metal grate using a pair of carabiners. Keef was a faerie, one of the Little Folk who dwelled within the shadows and hidden places of our own world, and the touch of steel was painful to him.

"Wizard Dresden," he greeted me in a Germanic accent as he came level with my head. The cobb's voice was pitched low, even for someone as tiny as he. "The market this night danger roams. Here you should not be."

"Don't I know it," I replied. "But there are people in danger."

"Ah," Keef said. "The mortals you insist to defend. Unwise that battle is."

"I need your help," I said.

Keef eyed me and gave me a firm shake of his head. "The walking dead very dangerous are. My people's blood it could cost. That I will risk not."

"You owe me, Keef," I growled.

"Our living. Not our lives."

"Have it your way," I said. Then I lifted up one of Sarah's shoes and, without looking away from the little cobb, snapped the heel off.

"Ach!" Keef cried in horror, his little feet slipping off the metal grate. "*Nein!*"

There was a chorus of similar gasps and cries from inside Shoegasm.

I held up the other shoe and did it again.

Keef wailed in protest. All of a sudden, thirty of the little cobbs, male and female, pressed up to the security grate. All of them had the same frizzy white hair, all of them dressed like something from Oktoberfest, and all of them were horrified.

"*Nein!*" Keef wailed again. "Those are Italian leather! Handmade! What are you doing?"

I took a step to my left and held the broken shoes over a trash can.

The cobbler elves gasped, all together, and froze in place.

"Do not do this," Keef begged me. "Lost all is not. Repaired they can be. Good as new we can fix them. Good as new! Do not throw them away."

I didn't waver. "I know things have been hard for your people since cobblers have gone out of business," I said. "I got you permission for your clan to work here, fixing shoes, in exchange for taking what you need from the vending machine. True?"

"True," Keef said, his eyes on the broken shoes in my hand. "Wizard, over the trash you need not hold them. If dropped they are, trash they become, and touch them we may not. Lost to all will they be. Anything we both will regret let us not do."

Anxious murmurs of agreement rose from the other cobbs.

Enough of the stick—it was time to show them the carrot. I held up Molly's battered old Birkenstocks. The sight made several of the more matronly cobbs cluck their tongues in disapproval.

"I helped set you up with a good deal here at Shoegasm," I said. "But I can see you're getting a little crowded. I can get you another good setup—a family, seven kids, mom and dad, all of them active."

The cobbs murmured in sudden excitement.

Keef coughed delicately and said, staring anxiously at the broken heels in my hand, "And the shoes?"

"I'll turn them over to you," I said, "if you help me."

Keef narrowed his eyes. "Slaves to you we are," he snapped. "Threatened and bribed."

"You know the cause I fight for," I said. "I protect mortals. I've never tried to hide that, and I've never lied to you. I need your help, Keef. I'll do what it takes to get it—but you know my reputation by now. I deal fairly with the Little Folk, and I always show gratitude for their help."

The leader of the cobbs regarded me steadily for a moment. Nobody likes being strong-armed, not even the Little Folk, who are used to getting walked on, but I didn't have time for diplomacy.

Keef's gaze kept getting distracted by the shoes, dangling over the trash can, and he made no answer. The other cobbs all waited, clearly taking their cue from Keef.

"Show of good faith, Keef," I said quietly. I took the broken shoes and set them gently on the ground in front of the shop. "I'll trust you and your people to repair them and return them. And I'll pay in pizza."

The cobbs gasped, staring at me as if I'd just offered them a map to El Dorado. I heard one of the younger cobbs exclaim, "*True*, it is!"

"Fleeting, pizza is," Keef said sternly. "Eternal are shoes and leather goods."

"Shoes and leather goods," the rest of the cobbs intoned, their tiny voices solemn.

"Few mortals to the Little Folk show respect, these days," Keef said quietly. "Or trust. True it is that beneath this roof we are crowded. And unto the wizard, debt is owed." He gave the shoes a professional glance and nodded once. "Under your terms, and within our means, our aid is given. Your need unto us speak."

"Scouts," I said at once. "I know there are Black Court vampires in the mall. I need to know exactly how many and exactly where they are."

"Done it will be," Keef barked. "Cobbs!"

There was a little gust of wind, and I was suddenly alone. Oh, and both Sarah's expensive heels and Molly's clunky sandals were gone, the latter right out of my hands and so smoothly that I hadn't even noticed them being taken. I checked, just to be careful, but my own shoes remained safely on my feet, which was a relief. You can't ever be certain with cobbs. The little faeries, at times, could get awfully fixated upon whatever their particular area of concern might be, and messing around with it was more dangerous than most realized. Despite the metal screen between the cobbs and me, I'd been playing with fire when I held those Pradas over the trash can.

Another thing that most people don't realize is just how much the Little Folk can learn, and how fast they can do it—especially when things are happening on their own turf. It took Keef and his people about thirty seconds to go and return.

"Four, there are," Keef reported. "Three lesser, who of late this place did guard. One greater, who gave them not-life."

"Four," I breathed. "Where?"

"One outside near the group of cars waits and watches," Keef said. "One outside the bistro where the mortals hide stands watch. One beside his mistress stands within."

I got a sick little feeling in my stomach. "Has anyone been hurt?"

Keef shook his head. "Taunt them, she does. Frighten them." He shrugged. "It is not as their kind often is."

"No. She's there for vengeance, not food." I frowned. "I need you to get me something. Can you?"

I told him what I needed, and Keef gave me a mildly offended look. "Of course."

"Good. Now, the one outside," I said. "Can you show me a way I could get close to him without being seen?"

Keef's eyes glittered with a sudden ferocity that was wholly at odds with his size and appearance. "This way, Wizard."

I went at what was practically a run, but the tiny cobb had no trouble staying ahead of me. He led me through a service access door that required a key to open—until it suddenly swung open from the other side, a dozen young male cobbs dangling from the security bar and cheering. My amulet cast the only light as Keef led me down a flight of stairs and through a long, low tunnel.

"Access to the drains and watering system, this passage is," Keef called to me. We stopped at a ladder leading up. A small paper sack sat on the floor by the ladder. "Your weapons," he said, nodding at the bag. He pointed at the ladder. "Behind the vampire, this opens."

I opened the bag and found two plastic cylinders. I didn't want the crinkling paper, so I put one of them in my jacket pocket, kept the other in hand, and crept up the ladder. At the top was a hatch made of some kind of heavy synthetic, rather than wood or steel, and it opened without a sound. I poked my head up and looked cautiously around the parking lot.

The lights were out, but there was enough snow on the ground to bounce around plenty of light, giving the outdoors an oddly close, quiet quality, almost as if someone had put a roof overhead, just barely out of sight. Over by the last group of cars in the mall parking lot, next to the *Blue Beetle* in fact, stood the vampire.

He was little more than a black form, and though human in shape, he was inhumanly still, every bit as motionless as the other inanimate objects in the parking lot. Snow had begun to gather on his head and shoulders, just as it had on the roofs and hoods of the parked cars. He stood facing the darkened mall, where snow blew into the hole left by the thrown car. He was watching, I supposed, for anyone who might come running out, screaming.

A newborn vampire might not be anywhere near as dangerous as an older one, but that was like saying a Mack truck was nowhere near as dangerous as a main battle tank. If you happened to be the guy standing in the road in front of one, it wouldn't much matter to you which of them crushed you to pulp. If I'd had my staff and rod with me, I might have chanced a stand-up fight. But I didn't have my gear, and even if I had, my usual magic would have made plenty of noise and warned the vampire's companions.

Vampires are tough. They take a lot of killing. I had to take this one out suddenly and with tremendous violence without making any noise. If I had to face it openly, I'd have no chance.

Which is why I had used the cobbs' intelligence to get sneaky.

I drew in my will, the magic I had been born with and that I had spent a lifetime exercising, practicing, and focusing. As the power came into me, it made the skin of my arms ripple with goose bumps, and I could feel a strange pressure at the back of my head and pressing against the *inside* of my forehead. Once I had the power ready, I started shaping it with my thoughts, focusing my will and intent on the desired outcome.

The spell I worked up wasn't one of my better evocations. It took me more than twenty seconds to get it together. For fast and dirty combat magic, that's the next-best thing to forever.

For treacherous, backstabbing, sucker-punch magic, though, it's just fine.

At the very last second, the vampire seemed to sense something. It turned its head toward me.

I clenched my fist as I released my will and snarled, *"Gravitus!"*

The magic lashed out into the ground beneath the vampire's feet, and the steady, slow, immovable power of the earth suddenly stirred, concentrating, reaching up for the vampire standing upon it. In technical terms, I didn't actually *increase* the gravity of the earth beneath it. I only concentrated it a little. In a circle fifty yards across, for just a fraction of a second, gravity vanished. The cars all surged up against their shock absorbers and settled again. The thin coat of snow leapt several inches off the parking lot and fell back.

In that same fraction of a second, all of that gravity from all of that area concentrated itself into a circle, maybe eighteen inches across, directly at the vampire's feet.

There was no explosion, no flash of light—and no scream. The vampire just went down, slammed to the earth as suddenly and violently as if I'd dropped an anvil on it. There was a rippling, crackling sound as hundreds of bones shattered all together, and a splatter of sludgy liquid that splashed all over the cars around the vampire—mostly upon the Beetle, really.

The effort of gathering and releasing so much energy left me gasping. I was out of shape when it came to earth magic. It had never been my strongest suit—too slow, most of the time, to seem like it would have been worth the bother. As I hauled myself out of the ground, though, I had to admit that when there was enough time to actually use it, it sure as hell was impressive.

I padded to the car, watching the mall entrance, but there was no outcry and no sudden appearance of Drulinda or the other vampires of her scourge.

The vampire was still alive.

Un-alive. Whatever. The thing was still trying to move.

It was mostly just a mass of pulped, squishy meat. In the cold, at least, it hadn't begun to rot, so that cut down on the smell. One eye rolled around in its mashed skull. Muscles twitched, but without a solid framework of bone to work with, they didn't accomplish much beyond an odd, pulsing motion. It could probably put itself back together, given blood and time, but I didn't feel like letting it have either. I held the plastic cylinder over it.

"Nothing personal," I told the vampire. Then I dumped powdered garlic from the pizzeria in the mall's food court all over it.

I can't say the vampire screamed, really. It died the way a salted slug does, in silent, pulsing agony. I had to fight to keep my stomach from emptying itself, but only for a second. Absolutely disgusting demises are par for the course when fighting vampires. A few wisps of smoke rose up, and after a few seconds, the mass of undead flesh became simple dead flesh again.

One down.

Three to go.

I stalked toward the mall, moving with all the silence I could manage. After years working as a private investigator, and more years fighting a magical war against the vampires in the shadows, I knew how to be quiet. I slipped up to within thirty feet of the entrance and spotted the second vampire before he noticed me, right where Keef's people said he was.

He stood facing the door of the bistro, apparently intent on what was happening within. I could hear voices inside, though I could make out no details over the continued, repeated playing of "Only You," beyond that one of the voices was Drulinda's leathery rasp. There were no sounds of fighting, which wasn't good. Thomas certainly wouldn't have allowed them to hurt anyone without putting up a struggle, and given the mutual capabilities of everyone involved, it would have been noticeable.

A second's thought told me that it might also be a good sign. If they'd killed him, they would have made a big mess doing it. Assuming he hadn't gone down without getting to put up much of a fight— and I refused to assume anything else. I knew my brother too well—something else had to be happening.

My brother could go toe-to-toe with a vampire of the Black Court, if he had to, but the last time he'd done it, the effort had nearly killed both him and the woman he'd had to feed from in order to recover. There were two of them inside, and though Thomas was as combat capable as any of the White Court's best, he wasn't going to start a slugfest if he thought he could get a better fight by biding his time, doing what the White Court did—looking human and using guile. My instincts told me that Thomas was stalling, choosing his moment. Hell, he was probably waiting for me to show up and help.

I looked down and found his birthday present, untouched by the flying debris, lying in its bright red and pink paper where Molly had dropped it on the sidewalk outside the doors.

I found myself smiling.

Twenty seconds or so later, I tossed the present underhand. It tumbled through the air and landed on the floor directly outside the bistro's entrance. The head of the vampire on guard jerked around, focusing on the present. It tilted its head to one side. Then it whipped around toward me, baring its teeth in a snarl.

"*Gravitus!*" I thundered, releasing a second earthcrafting.

Once again, everything jumped up—but this time, it wasn't quiet. The circle of nullified gravity embraced every shop nearby in the mall, sending merchandise and shelves and dishes and furniture and cash registers and dressing dummies and God knew what other sundry objects flying up, to come crashing back down to the floor again. A great uproar of hundreds of impacts came down from the floors above us as well.

Once again, the circle of supergravity crushed a brown-shirted vampire flat to the floor—only I'd forgotten about the levels above. There was a shriek of tortured metal, and a great crashing rain of debris came down in a nearly solid column as floors and ceilings gave way under the sudden, enormous stress. It all thundered down on the pulped vampire.

There was a second of shocked silence, while objects continued falling from their shelves and bins and who knew what else. Evidently, the damage to the ceiling had torn through some plumbing; a steady stream of water began to patter down from overhead onto the mound of rubble, along with occasional bits of still-falling material.

Then two things happened, almost at the same time.

First, my brother chose his moment.

The front wall of the bistro exploded outward. I saw the flying form of another vampire security guard hurtle across the hallway into the opposite wall with no detectable loss of altitude, and it smashed against a metal security grate with terrifying force.

Second, Drulinda let out an eerie howl of fury. It was a horrible sound, nasty and rasping and somehow spidery, for all that it was of inhuman volume. There was a crash from inside the bistro. Young men and women started screaming.

There wasn't any time to waste. I ran for the vampire my brother had thrown from the bistro. It had bounced off and fallen on the ground and was still gathering itself up. I had hoped it would take it a moment to recover from the blow, to give me time to get close enough to act.

It didn't work out that way.

The vampire was on its feet again before I could get halfway there, one of its shoulders twisted and deformed by the impact, one arm hanging loosely. It spun toward me with no sense of discomfort evident in its expression or posture, and it let out a very human-sounding scream of fury and flung itself at me.

I reacted with instant instinct, raising my right hand, with my will, and calling, "*Fuego!*"

Fire kindled from my open palm and rushed out in a furious torrent, spewing raggedly across the tile floor in a great, slewing cone. It splashed against the floor, up onto the metal grate, and all over the vampire in question, a sudden, if clumsy, immolation.

But without my blasting rod to help me focus the attack, it was diffused; the heat was spread out over a broad area instead of focused into a single, searing beam. Though I'm sure it hurt like hell, and though it set the security guard vampire's uniform on fire, it didn't cripple him. It might have sent up an older, more withered vampire like a torch, but the newbie was still too . . . juicy. It didn't burn him up so much as broil him a bit.

Pretty much, it just pissed him off.

The vampire came at me with another, higher-pitched scream, and swung a flaming arm at me. Maybe the fire had disoriented him a little, because I was able to get out of the way of the blow—sort of. It missed my head and neck and instead slammed into my left shoulder like a train wreck.

Pain flooded through me, and the canister of garlic went flying. The force of the blow spun me around, and I fell to the floor. The vampire came down on top of me, teeth bared, still on freaking *fire* as he leaned in with his non-pointy, still-white teeth, which were plenty strong enough to rip my throat open.

"Harry!" Thomas screamed. There was a rushing sound, and a tremendous force pulled the vampire off me. I sat up in time to see my brother drive his shoulder into the vampire's chest, slamming the un-dead thing back against the concrete wall between two stalls. Then Thomas whipped out what looked like a broken chair leg and drove the shattered end of the wood directly into the vampire's chest, a cou-ple of inches below the gold, metallic security badge on his left breast, slightly off center.

The vampire's mouth opened, too-dark blood exploding from it in a gasp. The creature reached for the chair leg with its remaining arm.

Thomas solved that problem in the most brutal way imaginable. His face set in fury, my brother ignored the flames of the vampire's burning clothing, seized the remaining arm with both of his hands, and with a twist of his hips and shoulders, ripped it out of the socket.

More blood splashed out, if only for a second—without a heartbeat to keep pumping it, blood loss is mostly about leakage—and then the mortally crippled vampire fell, twitching and dying as the stake of wood through its heart put an end to its unlife.

I felt Drulinda coming, more than I saw it happen, the cold presence of a Black Court vampire in a fury, rubbing abrasively against my wizard's senses. "Thomas!"

My brother turned in time to duck a blow so swift I didn't even *see* it. He returned it with one of his own, but Drulinda, though new to the trade, was a master vampire, a creature with its own terrible will and power. Thomas had fought other Black Court vamps before—but not a master.

He was on the defensive from the outset. Though my brother was unthinkably strong and swift when drawing upon his vampiric nature, he wasn't strong or swift enough. I lay sprawled on the ground, still half paralyzed by the pain in the left side of my body, and tried to think of what to do next.

"Get out!" I screamed at the bistro. "Get out of here, people! Get the hell out now!"

While I screamed, Drulinda slammed my brother's back into a metal security grate so hard that it left a broad smear of his pale red blood on its bars.

People started hurrying out of the bistro, running for the parking lot.

Drulinda looked over her shoulder and let out another hissing squall of rage. At this opening, Thomas managed to get a grip on her arm, set his feet, and swing her into the wall, sending cracks streaking through the concrete. On the rebound, he swung her up and around and then down, smashing her down onto the floor, then up from that and into a security mesh again, crushing tile and bending metal with every impact.

I heard a scream and looked up to see Ennui fall from her impossibly high black heels in her tiny, tight black dress, as she tried to flee the bistro.

A horribly disfigured hand had reached out from the rubble over the crushed vampire, and now it held her.

I ran for the girl as my brother laid into Drulinda. My left arm wasn't talking to me, and I fumbled the second canister out of my left jacket pocket with my right arm, then dumped garlic over the outstretched vampire's hand.

It began smoking and spasming. Ennui screamed as the crushing grip broke her ankle. I stood up in frustration and started stomping down on the vampire's arm. Supernaturally strong it might be, but its bones were made of bone, and it couldn't maintain its grip on the girl without them.

It took a lot of stomping, but I was finally able to pull the girl free. I tried to get Ennui to her feet, but her weight came down on her broken ankle, and from there it came down on my wounded shoulder. I went down to one knee, and it was all I could do not to fall.

I almost didn't notice when my brother flew through the air just over my head, smashed out what had to be the last remaining pane of glass at the mall entrance, and landed limply in the parking lot.

I felt Drulinda's presence coming up behind me.

The vampire let out a dusty laugh. "I thought it was just some poor pretty boy to play with. Silly me."

I fumbled with the canister for a second, and then whirled, flinging its contents at Drulinda in a slewing arc.

The vampire blurred to one side, dodging the garlic with ease. She looked battered and was covered with dust. Her undead flesh was approximately the consistency of wood, and so it wasn't cut and damaged so much as chipped and crushed. Her clothes were torn and ruined—and none of that mattered. She was just as functional and just as deadly as she had been before the fight.

I dropped the canister and drew forth my pentacle amulet, lifting it as a talisman against her.

The old bit with the crucifix works on the Black Court—but it isn't purely about Christianity. They are repelled not by the holy symbol itself, but by the faith of the one holding it up against them. I'd seen vampires repulsed by crosses, crucifixes, strips of paper written with holy symbols by a Shinto priest—once even a Star of David.

Me, I used the pentacle, because that was what I believed in. The five-pointed star, to me, represented the five elements of earth, air, water, fire, and spirit, bound within the solid circle of mortal will. I believed that magic was a force intended to be used to create, to protect, and to preserve. I believed that magic was a gift that had to be used responsibly and wisely—and that it especially had to be used against creatures like Drulinda, against literal, personified *evil*, to protect those who couldn't protect themselves. That was what I thought, and I'd spent my life acting in accordance with it.

I *believed*.

Pale blue light began to spill from the symbol—and Drulinda stopped with a hiss of sudden rage.

"You," she said after a few seconds. "I have heard of you. The wizard. Dresden."

I nodded slowly. Behind her, the fire from my earlier spell was spreading. The power was out, and I had no doubt that Drulinda and her former security-guard lackeys had disabled the alarms. It wouldn't take long for a fire to go insane in this place, once it got its teeth sunk in. We needed to get out.

"Go," I mumbled at Ennui.

She sobbed and started crawling for the exit, while I held Drulinda off with the amulet.

The vampire stared steadily at me for a second, her eyes all milky white, corpse cataracts glinting in the reflected light of the fire. Then she smiled and moved.

She was just too damn fast. I tried to turn to keep up with her, but by the time I did, Ennui screamed, and Drulinda had seized her hair and dragged her back, out of the immediate circle of light cast by the amulet.

She lifted the struggling girl with ease, so that I could see her mascara-streaked face. "Wizard," Drulinda said. Ennui had been cut by flying glass or the fall at some point, and some blood had streaked out of her slicked-back hair, over her ear, and down one side of her throat. The vampire leaned in, extending a tongue like a strip of beef jerky, and licked blood from the girl's skin. "You can hide behind your light. But you can't save her."

I ground my teeth and said nothing.

"But your death will profit me, grant me standing with others of my kind. The feared and vaunted Wizard Dresden." She bared yellowed teeth in a smile. "So I offer you this bargain. Throw away the amulet. I will let the girl go. You have my word." She leaned her teeth in close and brushed them over the girl's neck. "Otherwise . . . Well, all of my new friends are gone. I'll have to make more."

That made me shudder. Dying was one thing. Dying and being made into *one of those* . . .

I lowered the amulet. I hesitated for a second, and then dropped it.

Drulinda let out a low, eager sound and tossed Ennui aside like an empty candy wrapper. Then she was on me, letting out rasping *giggles*, for God's sake, pressing me down. "I can smell your fear, Wizard," she rasped. "I think I'm going to enjoy this."

She leaned closer, slowly, as she bared her teeth, her face only inches from mine.

Which was where I wanted her to be.

I reared up my head and spat out a gooey mouthful of powdered garlic directly into those cataract eyes.

Drulinda let out a scream, bounding away in a violent rush, clawing at her eyes with her fingers—and getting them burned, too. She thrashed in wild agony, swinging randomly at anything she touched or bumped into, tearing great, gaping gashes in metal fences, smashing holes in concrete walls.

"Couple words of advice," I growled, my mouth burning with the remains of the garlic I'd stuffed it with as she'd come sneaking up on me. "First, anytime I'm not shooting my mouth off to a clichéd, two-bit creature of the night like you, it's because I'm up to something."

Drulinda howled more and rushed toward me—tripping on some rubble and sprawling on the ground, only to rush about on all fours like some kind of ungainly, horrible insect.

I checked behind me. Ennui was already out, and Thomas was beginning to stir, maybe roused by the snow now falling on him. I turned back to the blinded, pain-maddened vampire. We were the only ones left in that wing of the mall.

"Second," I spat, "never touch my brother on his fucking birthday."

I reached for my will, lifted my hand, and snarled, *"Fuego!"*

Fire roared out to eagerly engulf the vampire.

What the hell. The building was burning down, anyway.

"FREAKING AMATEUR VILLAINS," I muttered, glowering down at the splatters on my car.

Thomas leaned against it with one hand pressed to his head, a grimace of pain on his face. "You okay?"

I waved my left arm a little. "Feeling's coming back. I'll have Butters check me out later. Thanks for loaning Molly your car."

"Least I could do. Let her drive Sarah and Ennui to the hospital." He squinted at the rising smoke from the mall. "Think the whole thing will go?"

"Nah," I said. "This wing, maybe. They'll get here before too much more goes up. Keef and his folk should be all right."

My brother grunted. "How are they going to explain this one?"

"Who knows," I said. "Meteor, maybe. Smashed holes in the roof, crushed some poor security guard, set the place on fire."

"My vote is for terrorists," Thomas said. "Terrorists are real popular these days." He shook his head. "But I meant the larpers, not the cops."

"Oh," I said. "Probably, they won't talk to anyone about what they saw. Afraid people would think they were crazy."

"And they would," Thomas said.

"And they would," I agreed. "Come tomorrow, it will seem very unreal. A few months from now, they'll wonder if they didn't imagine some of it or if there wasn't some kind of gas leak or something that made them hallucinate. Give it a few more years, and they'll remember that Drulinda and some rough-looking types showed up to give them a hard time. They drove a car through the front of the mall. Maybe they were crazy people dressed in costumes who had been to a few too many larps themselves." I shook my head. "It's human nature to try to understand and explain everything. The world is less scary that way. But I don't think they'll be in any danger, really. No more so than anyone else."

"That's good," Thomas said quietly. "I guess."

"It's the way it is." In the distance, sirens were starting up and coming closer. I grunted and said, "We'd better go."

"Yeah."

We got into the Beetle. I started it up, and we headed out. I left the lights off—no sense attracting attention.

"You going to be all right?" I asked him.

He nodded. "Take me a few days to get enough back into me to feel normal, but"—he shrugged—"I'll make it."

"Thanks for the backup," I said.

"Kicked their freaky asses," he said, and held out his fist.

I rapped my knuckles lightly against it.

"Nice signal. The birthday present."

"I figured you'd get it," I said. Then I frowned. "Crap," I said. "Your present."

"You didn't remember to bring it?"

"I was a little busy," I said.

He was quiet for a minute. Then he asked, "What was it?"

"Rock'em Sock'em Robots," I said.

He blinked at me. "What?"

I repeated myself. "The little plastic robots you make fight."

"I know what they are, Harry," he responded. "I'm trying to figure out why you'd give me them."

I pursed my lips for a minute. Then I said, "Right after my dad died, they put me in an orphanage. It was Christmastime. On television, they had commercials for Rock'em Sock'em Robots. Two kids playing with them, you know? Two brothers." I shrugged. "That was a year when I really, really wanted to give those stupid plastic robots to my brother."

"Because it would mean you weren't alone," Thomas said quietly.

"Yeah," I said. "Sorry I forgot them. And happy birthday."

He glanced back at the burning mall. "Well," my brother said, "I suppose it's the thought that counts."

HEOROT

—from *My Big Fat Supernatural Honeymoon*,
edited by P. N. Elrod

Takes place between *White Night*
and *Small Favor*

Once more, Pat invited me to come play at her literary club-house, and once more, I cheerfully agreed.

What can I say? I fear change.

The last anthology's theme had been weddings, and this one was the logical sequel—honeymoons. Research into the etymology of "honeymoon" led me back to its roots in Scandinavia and in the British Isles, where a newly wed bride and groom would depart their village and remain in solitude for a lunar month, while being well provided with mead (which is made from honey).

I think the idea was to establish beyond a reasonable doubt that any child conceived in that time was the legitimate heir of the groom. Or maybe it was just to get a pretty young bride liquored up and wild for a month—Viking Girls Gone Wild, as it were.

I have no idea if the information I found, mostly on the Internet, was academically accurate. For my purposes, that wasn't nearly as important as finding a solid inspiration. So, from newlyweds, mead, and Norse-Scandinavian backgrounds, I developed a story using everything from the Dresden Files' story line that had the flimsiest of connections to those base ideas.

I put them all together, plopped Harry down in the middle of it, and gleefully watched as it caught fire.

was sitting in my office, sorting through my bills, when Mac called and said, "I need your help."

It was the first time I'd heard him use four whole words all together like that.

"Okay," I said. "Where?" I'd out-tersed him—another first.

"Loon Island Pub," Mac said. "Wrigleyville."

"On the way." I hung up, stood up, put on my black leather duster, and said to my dog, "We're on the job."

My dog, Mouse, who outweighs most European cars, bounced up eagerly from where he had been dozing near my office's single heating vent. He shook out his thick grey fur, especially the shaggy, almost leonine ruff growing heavy on his neck and shoulders, and we set out to help a friend.

October had brought in more rain and more cold than usual, and that day we had both, plus wind. I found parking for my battered old Volkswagen Bug, hunched my shoulders under my leather duster, and walked north along Clark, into the wind, Mouse keeping pace at my side.

Loon Island Pub was in sight of Wrigley Field, and a popular hangout before and after games. Bigger than most such businesses, it could host several hundred people throughout its various rooms and levels. Outside, large posters had been plastered to the brick siding of the building. Though the posters were soaked with rain, you could still read CHICAGO BEER ASSOCIATION and NIGHT OF THE LIVING BREWS, followed by an announcement of a home-brewed beer festival and competition, with today's date on it. There was a lot of foot traffic in and out.

"Aha," I told Mouse. "Explains why Mac is here, instead of at his own place. He's finally unleashed the new dark on the unsuspecting public."

Mouse glanced up at me rather reproachfully from under his shaggy brows; then he lowered his head, sighed, and continued plodding against the rain until we gained the pub. Mac was waiting for us at the front door. He was a sinewy, bald man dressed in dark slacks and a white shirt, somewhere between the age of thirty and fifty. He had a very average, unremarkable face, one that usually wore a steady expression of patience and contemplation.

Today, though, that expression was what I could only describe as grim.

I came in out of the rain, and passed off my six-foot oak staff to Mac to hold for me as I shrugged out of my duster. I shook the garment thoroughly, sending raindrops sheeting from it, and promptly put it back on.

Mac runs the pub where the supernatural community of Chicago does most of its hanging out. His place has seen more than its share of paranormal nasties, and if Mac looked that worried, I wanted the spell-reinforced leather of the duster between my tender skin and the source of his concern. I took the staff back from Mac, who nodded to me and then crouched down to Mouse, who had gravely offered a paw to shake. Mac shook, ruffled Mouse's ears, and said, "Missing girl."

I nodded, scarcely noticing the odd looks I was getting from several of the people inside. That was par for the course. "What do we know?"

"Husband," Mac said. He jerked his head at me, and I followed him deeper into the pub. Mouse stayed pressed against my side, his tail wagging in a friendly fashion. I suspected the gesture was an affectation. Mouse is an awful lot of dog, and people get nervous if he doesn't act overtly friendly.

Mac led me through a couple of rooms where each table and booth had been claimed by a different brewer. Homemade signs bearing a gratuitous number of exclamation points touted the various concoctions, except for the one Mac stopped at. There, a cardstock table tent was neatly lettered, simply reading MCANALLY'S DARK.

At the booth next to Mac's, a young man, good-looking in a reedy, librarianesque kind of way, was talking to a police officer while wringing his hands.

"But you don't get it," the young man said. "She wouldn't just leave. Not today. We start our honeymoon tonight."

The cop, a stocky, balding fellow whose nose was perhaps more red than warranted by the weather outside, shook his head. "Sir, I'm sorry, but she's been gone for what? An hour or two? We don't even start to look until twenty-four hours have passed."

"She wouldn't just *leave*," the young man half shouted.

"Look, kid," the cop said. "It wouldn't be the first time some guy's new wife panicked and ran off. You want my advice? Start calling up her old boyfriends."

"But—"

The cop thumped a finger into the young man's chest. "Get over it, buddy. Come back in twenty-four hours." He turned to walk away from the young man and almost bumped into me. He took a step back and scowled up at me. "You want something?"

"Just basking in the glow of your compassion, Officer," I replied.

His face darkened into a scowl, but before he could take a deep breath and start throwing his weight around, Mac pushed a mug of his dark ale into the cop's hand. The cop slugged it back immediately. He swished the last gulp around in his mouth, purely for form, and then tossed the mug back at McAnally, belched, and went on his way.

"Mr. McAnally," the young man said, turning to Mac. "Thank goodness. I still haven't seen her." He looked at me. "Is this him?"

Mac nodded.

I stuck out my hand. "Harry Dresden."

"Roger Braddock," the anxious young man said. "Someone has abducted my wife."

He gripped too hard, and his fingers were cold and a little clammy. I wasn't sure what was going on here, but Braddock was genuinely afraid. "Abducted her? Did you see it happen?"

"Well," he said, "no. Not really. No one did. But she *wouldn't* just walk out. Not today. We got married this morning, and we're leaving on our honeymoon tonight, soon as the festival is over."

I arched an eyebrow. "You put your honeymoon on hold to go to a beer festival?"

"I'm opening my own place," Braddock said. "Mr. McAnally has been giving me advice. Sort of mentoring me. This was . . . I mean, I've been here every year, and it's only once a year, and the prestige from a win is . . . The networking and . . ." His voice trailed off as he looked around.

Yeah. The looming specter of sudden loss has a way of making you reevaluate things. Sometimes it's tough to know what's really important until you realize it might be gone.

"You two were at this booth?" I prompted.

"Yes," he said. He licked his lips. "She went to pick up some napkins from the bar, right over there. She wasn't twenty feet away and somehow she just vanished."

Personally, I was more inclined to go with the cop's line of reasoning than the kid's. People in general tend to be selfish, greedy, and unreliable. There are individual exceptions, of course, but no one ever wants to believe that the petty portions of human nature might have come between themselves and someone they care about.

The kid seemed awfully sincere, but endearing, awfully sincere people, their decisions driven mostly by their emotions, are capable of being mistaken on an epic scale. The worse the situation looks, the harder they'll search for reasons not to believe it. It seemed more likely that his girl left him than that someone took her away.

On the other hand, likely isn't the same as true—and Mac isn't the kind to cry wolf.

"How long you two been together?" I asked Braddock.

"Since we were fifteen," he replied. An anemic smile fluttered around his mouth. "Almost ten years."

"Making it official, eh?"

"We both knew when it was right," he replied. He lost the smile. "Just like I know she didn't walk away. Not unless someone made her do it."

I stepped around Braddock and studied the high-backed booth for a moment. A keg sat on the table, next to a little cardstock sign that had a cartoon bee decked out with a Viking-style helmet, a baldric, and a greatsword. Words beneath the bee proclaimed BRADDOCK'S MID-NIGHT SUN CINNAMON.

I grunted and reached down, pulling a simple black leather ladies' purse from beneath the bench seating. Not an expensive purse, either. "Not much chance she'd walk without taking her bag," I said. "That's for damn sure."

Braddock bit his lip, closed his eyes, and said, "Elizabeth."

I sighed.

Well, dammit.

Now she had a name.

Elizabeth Braddock, newlywed—maybe she'd just run off, but maybe she hadn't. I didn't think I would like myself very much if I walked and it turned out that she really was in danger and really did get hurt.

What the hell? No harm in looking around.

"I guess the game's afoot," I said. I gestured vaguely with the purse. "May I?"

"Sure," Braddock said. "Sure, sure."

I dumped Elizabeth's purse out on the booth's table, behind the beer keg, and began rummaging through it. The usual—a wallet, some makeup, a cell phone, Kleenex, some feminine sanitary sundries, one of those plastic birth control pill holders with a folded piece of paper taped to it.

And there was a hairbrush, an antique-looking thing with a long, pointy silver handle.

I plucked several strands of dark wavy hair from the brush. "Is this your wife's hair?"

Braddock blinked at me for a second, then nodded. "Yes. Of course."

"Mind if I borrow this?"

He didn't. I pocketed the brush for the moment and glanced at the birth control pill case. I opened it. Only the first several slots were empty. I untaped the folded paper and opened it, finding instructions for the medicine's use.

Who keeps the instruction sheet, for crying out loud?

While I pondered it, a shadow fell across Braddock, and a beefy, heavily tattooed arm shoved him back against the spine of the partition between booths.

I looked up the arm to the beefy, heavily tattooed bruiser attached to it. He was only a couple of inches shorter than me, and layered with muscle gone to seed. He was bald and sported a bristling beard. Scar tissue around his eyes told me he'd been a fighter, and a lumpy, often-broken nose suggested that he might not have been much good at it. He wore black leather and rings heavy enough to serve as passable brass knuckles on every finger of his right hand. His voice was like the rest of him—thick and dull. He flung a little triangle of folded card-stock at Braddock. "Where's my keg, Braddock?"

"Caine," Braddock stammered, "what are you talking about?"

"My keg, bitch," the big man snarled. A couple of guys who wished they were more like Caine lurked behind him, propping up his ego. "It's gone. You figure you couldn't take the competition this year?"

I glanced at the fallen table tent. It also had a little Wagnerian cartoon bee on it, and the lettering, CAINE'S KICKASS.

"I don't have time for this," Braddock said.

Caine shoved him back against the booth again, harder. "We ain't done. Stay put, bitch, unless you want me to feed you your ass."

I glanced at Mac, who stared at Caine, frowning, but not doing anything. Mac doesn't like to get involved.

He's smarter than I am.

I stepped forward, seized Caine's hand in mine, and pumped it enthusiastically. "Hi, there. Harry Dresden, PI. How you doing?" I nodded at him, smiling, and smiled at his friends, too. "Hey, are you allergic to dogs?"

Caine was so startled that he almost forgot to try crushing my hand in his. When he got around to it, it hurt enough that I had to work not to wince. I'm not heavily built, but I'm more than six and a half feet tall, and it takes more strength than most have to make me feel it.

"What?" he said wittily. "Dog, what?"

"Allergic to dogs," I clarified, and nodded down at Mouse. "Occasionally someone has a bad reaction to my dog, and I'd hate that to happen here."

The biker scowled at me and then looked down.

Two hundred pounds of Mouse, not acting at *all* friendly now, stared steadily at Caine. Mouse didn't show any teeth or growl. He didn't need to. He just stared.

Caine lifted his lips up from his teeth in an ugly little smile. But he released my hand with a jerk, and then sneered at Braddock. "Say, where's that pretty little piece of yours? She run off to find a real man?"

Braddock might have been a sliver over half of Caine's size, but he went after the biker with complete sincerity and without a second thought.

This time Mac moved, interposing himself between Braddock and Caine, getting his shoulder against Braddock's chest. The older man braced himself and shoved Braddock back from the brink of a beating, though the younger man cursed and struggled against him.

Caine let out an ugly laugh and stepped forward, his big hands closing into fists. I leaned my staff so that he stepped into it, the blunt tip of the wood thrusting solidly against the hollow of his throat. He made a noise that sounded like *glurk*, and stepped back, scowling ferociously at me.

I tugged my staff back against my chest so that I could hold up both hands, palms out, just as the dumpy cop, attracted by Braddock's thumping and cursing, came into the room with one hand on his nightstick. "Easy there, big guy," I said, loud enough to make sure the cop heard. "The kid's just upset on account of his wife. He doesn't mean anything by it."

The bruiser lifted one closed fist as if he meant to drive it at my noggin, but one of his two buddies said urgently, "Cop."

Caine froze and glanced back over his shoulder. The officer might have been overweight, but he looked like he knew how to throw it around, and he had a club and a gun besides. Never mind all the other uniforms theoretically behind him.

Caine opened his fist, showing an empty hand, and lowered it again. "Sure," he said. "Sure. Misunderstanding. Happen to anybody."

"You want to walk away," the cop told Caine, "do it now. Otherwise you get a ride."

Caine and company departed in sullen silence, glaring daggers at me—well, glaring letter openers, anyway; Caine didn't seem real sharp.

The cop stalked over to me more lightly than he should have been able to—no question about it, the man knew how to play rough. He looked at me, then at my staff, and kept his nightstick in his hand. "You Dresden?"

"Uh-huh," I said.

"Heard of you. Work for Special Investigations sometimes. Call yourself a wizard."

"That's right."

"You know Rawlins?"

"Good man," I said.

The cop grunted. He jerked his head toward the departing Caine as he put the stick away. "Guy's a con. A hard case, too. Likes hurting people. You keep your eyes open, Mr. Wizard, or he'll make some of your teeth disappear."

"Yeah," I said. "Golly, he's scary."

The cop eyed me, then snorted and said, "Your dentures." He nod-ded, and walked out again, probably tailing Caine to make sure he left.

The cop and Caine weren't all that different, in some ways. The cop would have loved to take his stick to Caine's head as much as Caine had wanted to swat mine. They were both damn near equally sensitive about Braddock's missing wife, too. But at least the cop had channeled his inner thug into something that helped out the people around him—as long as he didn't have to run up too many stairs, I guessed.

I turned back to Mac and found him still standing between the kid and the door. Mac nodded his thanks to me. Braddock looked like he might be about to start crying, or maybe start screaming.

"No love lost there, eh?" I said to Braddock.

The kid snarled at the empty space where Caine had been. "Eliza-beth embarrassed him once. He doesn't take rejection well, and he never forgets. Do you think he did it?"

"Not really. Mac," I said, "something tipped you off that this was from the spooky side. Lights flicker?"

Mac grunted. "Twice."

Braddock stared at Mac and then at me. "What does that have to do with anything?"

"Active magic tends to interfere with electrical systems," I said. "It'll disrupt cell phones, screw up computers. Simpler things, like the lights, usually just flicker a bit."

Braddock had a look somewhere between uncertainty and nausea on his face. "Magic? You're kidding, right?"

"I'm tired of having this conversation," I said. I reached into my pocket for Elizabeth Braddock's fallen hairs. "This joint got a back door?"

Mac pointed silently.

"Thanks," I said. "Come on, Mouse."

THE BACK DOOR opened into a long, narrow, dirty alley running paral-lel to Clark. The wind had picked up, which meant that the cold rain was mostly striking the upper portion of one wall of the alley. Good for me. It's tough to get a solid spell put together under even a moderate rain. When it's really coming down, it's all but impossible, even for a relatively simple working—such as a tracking spell.

I'd done this hundreds of times, and by now it was pretty routine. I found a clear spot of concrete in the lee of the sheltering wall and sketched a quick circle around me with a piece of chalk, investing the motion with a deliberate effort of will.

As I completed the circle, I felt the immediate result—a screen of energy that rose up from the circle, enfolding me and warding out any random energy that might skew the spell. I took off my necklace, a silver chain with a battered old silver pentacle hanging from it, murmuring quietly, and tied several of Elizabeth's hairs through the center of the pentacle. After that, I gathered up my will, feeling the energy focused by the circle into something almost tangible, whispered in faux Latin, and released the gathered magic into the pentacle.

The silver five-pointed star flickered once, a dozen tiny sparks of static electricity fluttering over the metal surface and the hairs bound inside it. I grimaced. I'd been sloppy, to let some of the energy convert itself into static. And I'd been harping on my apprentice about the need for precision for a week.

I broke the circle by smudging the chalk with one foot, and glanced at Mouse, who sat patiently, mouth open in a doggy grin. Mouse had been there for some of those lessons, and he was smarter than the average dog. How much smarter remained to be seen, but I got the distinct impression he was laughing at me.

"It was the rain," I told him.

Mouse sneezed, tail wagging.

I glowered at him. I'm not sure I could take it if my dog was smarter than me.

The falling rain would wash away the spell on the amulet if I left it out in the open, so I shielded it as carefully as I could with the building and my hand. A hat would have come in handy for that purpose, actually. Maybe I should get one.

I held up the amulet, focusing on the spell. It quivered on the end of its chain, then swung toward the far end of the alley, in a sharp, sudden motion.

I drew my hand and the amulet back up into the sleeve of my duster, whistling. "She came right down this alley. And judging by the strength of the reaction, she was scared bad. Left a really big trail."

At that, Mouse made a chuffing sound and started down the alley, snuffling. The end of his short lead, mostly there for appearance's sake, dragged the ground. I kept pace, and by the time Mouse was twenty yards down the alley, he had begun growling low in his throat.

That was an occasion worth a raised eyebrow. Mouse didn't make noise unless there was Something Bad around. He increased his pace, and I lengthened my stride to keep up.

I found myself growling along with him. I'd gotten sick of Bad Things visiting themselves upon people in my town a long time ago.

When we hit the open street, Mouse slowed. Magic wasn't the only thing that a steady rain could screw up. He growled again and looked over his shoulder at me, tail drooping.

"I got your back," I told him. I lifted a section of my long leather duster with my staff, so that I could hold the amulet in the shelter it offered. I looked only moderately ridiculous while doing so.

I'm going to get a hat one of these days. I swear.

The tracking spell held, and the amulet led me down the street, toward Wrigley. The silent stadium loomed in the cold grey rain. Mouse, still snuffling dutifully, abruptly turned down another alley, his steps hurrying to a lope. I propped up my coat and consulted the amulet again.

I was so busy feeling damp and cold and self-conscious that I forgot to feel paranoid, and Caine came out of nowhere and swung something hard at my skull.

I turned my head and twitched sideways at the last second, taking the blow just to one side of the center of my forehead. There was a flash of light, and my legs went wobbly. I had time to watch Caine wind up again and saw that he was swinging a long, white, dirty athletic sock at me. He'd weighted one end with something, creating an improvised flail.

My hips bounced off a municipal trash can, and I got one arm between the flail and my face. The protective spells on my coat are good, but they're intended to protect me against gunfire and sharp, pointy things. The flail smashed into my right forearm. It went numb.

"So what, you steal my keg for Braddock, so his homo-bee cinnamon crap would win the division? I'm gonna take it out of your ass."

And with that pleasant mental image, Caine wound up again with that flail.

He'd made a mistake, though, pausing to get in a little dialogue like that. If he'd hit me again, immediately, he probably could have beaten me unconscious in short order. He hadn't hesitated long—but it had been long enough for me to pull my thoughts together. As he came in swinging, I snapped the lower end of my heavy staff into a rising quarter spin, right into his testicles. The thug's eyes snapped wide-open, and his mouth locked into a silent scream.

It's the little things in life you treasure.

Caine staggered and fell to one side, but one of the Cainettes came in hard behind him and pasted me in the mouth. By itself, I might have shrugged it off, but Caine had already rung my bells once. I went down to one knee and tried to figure out what was going on. Someone with big motorcycle boots kicked me in the guts. I fell to my back and drove a heel into his kneecap. There was a *crackle* and a *pop*, and he fell, howling.

The third guy had a tire iron. No time for magic—my damn eyes wouldn't focus, much less my thoughts. By some minor miracle, I caught the first two-handed swing on my staff.

And then two hundred pounds of wet dog slammed into Cainette Number Two's chest. Mouse didn't bite, presumably because there are some things even dogs won't put in their mouths. He just overbore the thug and smashed him to the ground, pinning him there. The two of them thrashed around.

I got up just as Caine came back in, swinging his flail.

I don't think Caine knew much about quarterstaff fighting. Murphy had been teaching it to me, however, for almost four years. I got the staff up as Caine swung and intercepted the sock. The weighted end wrapped around my staff, and I jerked the weapon out of his hands with a sweeping twist. With the same motion, I brought the other end of the staff around and popped him in the noggin.

Caine flopped to the ground.

I stood there panting and leaning on my staff. Hey, I'd won a brawl. That generally didn't happen when I wasn't using magic. Mouse seemed fine, if occupied holding his thug down.

"Jerk," I muttered to the unconscious Caine, and kicked him lightly in the ribs. "I have no idea what happened to your freaking keg."

"Oh my," said a woman's voice from behind me. She spoke perfectly clear English, marked with an accent that sounded vaguely Germanic or maybe Scandinavian. "I have to admit, I didn't expect you'd do that well against them."

I turned slightly, so that I could keep the thugs in my peripheral vision, and shifted my grip on the staff as I faced the speaker.

She was a tall blonde, six feet or so, even in flat, practical shoes. Her tailored grey suit didn't quite hide an athlete's body, nor did it make her look any less feminine. She had ice blue eyes, a stark, attractive face, and she carried a duffel bag in her right hand. I recognized her. She was the supernatural security consultant to John Marcone, the kingpin of Chicago crime.

"Miss Gard, isn't it?" I asked her, panting.

She nodded. "Mr. Dresden."

My arm throbbed and my ears were still ringing. I'd have a lovely goose egg right in the middle of my forehead in an hour. "Glad I could entertain you," I said. "Now if you'll excuse me, I'm working."

"I need to speak to you," she said.

"Call during office hours." Caine lay senseless, groaning. The guy I'd kicked in the knee whimpered and rocked mindlessly back and forth. I glared at the thug Mouse had pinned down.

He flinched. There wasn't any fight left in him. Thank God. There wasn't much left in me, either.

"Mouse," I said, and started down the alley.

Mouse rose up off the man, who said, "Oof!" as the dog planted both paws in the man's belly as he pushed up. Mouse followed me.

"I'm serious, Mr. Dresden," Gard said to my back, following us.

"Marcone is only a king in his own mind," I said without stopping. "He wants to send me a message, he can wait. I've got important things to do."

"I know," Gard said. "The girl. She's a brunette, maybe five foot five, brown eyes, green golf shirt, blue jeans, and scared half out of her mind."

I stopped and turned to bare my teeth at Gard. "Marcone is behind this? That son of a bitch is going to be sorry he ever *looked* at that—"

"No," Gard said sharply. "Look, Dresden, forget Marcone. This has nothing to do with Marcone. Today's my day off."

I stared at her for a moment, and only partly because the rain had begun to make the white shirt she wore beneath the suit jacket become transparent. She sounded sincere—which meant nothing. I've learned better than to trust my judgment when there's a blonde involved. Or a brunette. Or a redhead.

"What do you want?" I asked her.

"Almost the same thing you do," she replied. "You want the girl. I want the thing that took her."

"Why?"

"The girl doesn't have enough time for you to play twenty questions, Dresden. We can help each other and save her, or she can die."

I took a deep breath and then nodded once. "I'm listening."

"I lost the trail at the far end of this alley," she said. "Clearly, you haven't."

"Yeah," I said. "Skip to the part where you tell me how you can help me."

Wordlessly, she opened up the duffel bag and drew out—I kid you not—a double-bitted battle-ax that must have weighed fifteen pounds. She rested it on one shoulder. "If you can take me to the grendelkin, I'll deal with it while you get the girl out."

Grendelkin? What the hell was a grendelkin?

Don't get me wrong—I'm a wizard. I know about the supernatural. I could fill up a couple of loose-leaf notebooks with the names of various entities and creatures I recognized. That's the thing about knowledge, though. The more you learn, the more you realize how much there *is* to learn. The supernatural realms are bigger, far bigger, than the material world, and humanity is grossly outnumbered. I could learn about new beasties until I dropped dead of old age a few centuries from now and still not know a quarter of them.

This one was new on me.

"Dresden, seconds could matter, here," Gard said. Beneath the calm mask of her lovely face, I could sense a shadow of anxiety, of urgency.

As I absorbed that, there was a sharp clicking sound as a piece of broken brick or a small stone from roofing material fell to the ground farther down the alley.

Gard whirled, dropping instantly into a fighting crouch. Both hands were on her ax, which she held in a defensive position across the front of her body.

Yikes.

I'd seen Gard square off against a world-class necromancer and her pet ghoul without batting a golden eyelash. What the hell had her so spooked?

She came back out of her stance warily, then shook her head and muttered something under her breath before turning to me again. "What's going to happen to that girl . . . ? You have no idea. It shouldn't happen to anyone. So I'm begging you. Please help me."

I sighed.

Well, dammit.

She said please.

THE RAIN WAS weakening the tracking spell on my amulet and washing away both the scent of the grendelkin and the psychic trail left by the terrified Elizabeth, but between Mouse and me, we managed to find where the bad guy had, literally, gone to earth. The trail ended at an old storm cellar–style door in back of the buildings on the east side of Wrigley Field, under the tracks of the El, near Addison Station. The doors were ancient and looked as if they were rusted shut—though they couldn't have been, if the trail went through them. They were surrounded by a gateless metal fence. A sign on the fence declared the area dangerous and to keep out—you know, the usual sound advice that thrill-seeking blockheads and softhearted wizards with nagging headaches always ignore.

"You sure?" I asked Mouse. "It went in there?"

Mouse circled the fence, snuffling at the dry ground protected from the rain by the El track overhead. Then he focused intently on the doors and growled.

The amulet bobbed weakly, less definitely than it had a few minutes before. I grimaced and said, "It went down here, but it traveled north after that."

Gard grunted. "Crap."

"Crap," I concurred.

The grendelkin had fled into Undertown.

Chicago is an old city—at least by American standards. It's been flooded, burned down several times, been constructed and reconstructed ad nauseam. Large sections of the city have been built up as high as ten and twelve feet above the original ground level, while other buildings have settled into the swampy muck around Lake Michigan. Dozens and dozens of tunnel systems wind beneath its surface. No one knows exactly how many different tunnels and chambers people have created intentionally or by happenstance, and since most people regard the supernatural as one big scam, no one has noticed all the additional work done by not-people in the meantime.

Undertown begins somewhere just out of the usual traffic in the commuter and utility tunnels, where sections of wall and roof regularly collapse, and where people with good sense just aren't willing to go. From there, it gets dark, cold, treacherous, and jealously inhabited, increasingly so the farther you go.

Things live down there—all kinds of things.

A visit to Undertown bears more resemblance to suicide than exploration, and those who do it are begging to be Darwined out of the gene pool. Smart people don't go down there.

Gard slashed a long opening in the fence with her ax, and we descended crumbling old concrete steps into the darkness.

I murmured a word and made a small effort of will, and my amulet began to glow with a gentle blue-white light, illuminating the tunnel only dimly—enough, I hoped, to see by while still not giving away our approach. Gard produced a small red-filtered flashlight from her duffel bag, a backup light source. It made me feel better. When you're underground, making sure you have light is almost as important as making sure you have air. It meant that she knew what she was doing.

The utility tunnel we entered gave way to a ramshackle series of chambers, the spaces between what were now basements and the raised wall of the road that had been built up off the original ground level. Mouse went first, with me and my staff and my amulet right behind him. Gard brought up the rear, walking lightly and warily.

We went on for maybe ten minutes, through difficult-to-spot doorways and at one point through a tunnel flooded with a foot and a half of icy stagnant water. Twice, we descended deeper into the earth, and I began getting antsy about finding my way back. Spelunking is dangerous enough without adding in anything that could be described with the word *ravening*.

"This grendelkin," I said. "Tell me about it."

"You don't need to know."

"Like hell I don't," I said. "You want me to help you, you gotta help me. Tell me how we beat this thing."

"We don't," she said. "I do. That's all you need to know."

That sort of offended me, being so casually kept ignorant. Granted,

I'd done it to people myself about a million times, mostly to protect them, but that didn't make it any less frustrating—just ironic.

"And if it offs you instead?" I said. "I'd rather not be totally clueless when it's charging after me and the girl and I have to turn and fight."

"It shouldn't be a problem."

I stopped in my tracks and turned to regard her.

She stared back at me, eyebrows lifted. Water dripped somewhere nearby. There was a faint rumbling above us, maybe the El going by somewhere overhead.

She pressed her lips together and nodded, a gesture of concession. "It's a scion of Grendel."

I started walking again. "Whoa. Like, *the* Grendel?"

"Obviously." Gard sighed. "Before Beowulf faced him in Heorot—"

"*The* Grendel?" I asked. "*The* Beowulf?"

"Yes."

"And it actually happened like in the story?" I demanded.

"It isn't far wrong," Gard replied, an impatient note in her voice. "Before Beowulf faced him, Grendel had already taken a number of women on his previous visits. He got spawn upon them."

"Ick," I said. "But I think they make a cream for that now."

Gard gave me a flat look. "You have no idea what you're talking about."

"No kidding," I said. "That's the point of asking."

"You know all you need."

I ignored the statement, and the sentiment behind it to boot. A good private investigator is essentially a professional asker of questions. If I kept them coming, eventually I'd get some kind of answer. "Back at the pub, there was an electrical disruption. Does this thing use magic?"

"Not the way you do," Gard said.

See there? An answer. A vague answer, but an answer. I pressed ahead. "Then how?"

"Grendelkin are strong," Gard said. "Fast. And they can bend minds in an area around them."

"Bend how?"

"They can make people not notice them, or to notice only dimly. Disguise themselves, sometimes. It's how they get close. Sometimes they can cause malfunctions in technology."

"Veiling magic," I said. "Illusion. Been there, done that." I mused. "Mac said there were two disruptions. Is there any reason it would want to steal a keg from the beer festival?"

Gard shot me a sharp look. "Keg?"

"That's what those yahoos in the alley were upset about," I said. "Someone swiped their keg."

Gard spat out a word that would probably have gotten bleeped out had she said it on some kind of Scandinavian talk show. "What brew?"

"Eh?" I said.

"What kind of liquor was in the keg?" she demanded.

"How the hell should I know?" I asked. "I never even saw it."

"Dammit."

"But . . ." I scrunched up my nose, thinking. "The sign from his table had a drawing of a little Viking bee on it, and it was called Caine's Kickass."

"A bee," she said, her eyes glittering. "You're sure?"

"Yeah."

She swore again. "Mead."

I blinked at her. "This thing ripped off a keg of mead and a girl? Is she supposed to be its . . . bowl of bar nuts or something?"

"It isn't going to eat her," Gard said. "It wants the mead for the same reason it wants the girl."

I waited a beat for her to elaborate. She didn't. "I'm rapidly running out of willingness to keep playing along," I told her, "but I'll ask the question—why does it want the girl?"

"Procreation," she said.

"Thank you. Now I get it," I said. "The thing figures she'll need a good set of beer goggles before the deed."

"No," Gard said.

"Oh, right, because the grendelkin isn't human. The *thing* is going to need the beer goggles."

"No," Gard said, harder.

"I understand. Just setting the mood, then," I said. "Maybe it picked up some lounge music CDs, too."

"Dresden," Gard growled.

"Everybody needs somebody sometime," I sang—badly.

Gard stopped in her tracks and faced me, her pale blue eyes frozen with glacial rage. Her voice turned harsh. "But not everybody impregnates women with spawn that will rip its own way out of its mother's womb, killing her in the process."

See, another answer. It was harsher than I would have preferred.

I stopped singing and felt sort of insensitive.

"They're solitary," Gard continued in a voice made more terrible for its uninflected calm. "Most of the time, they abduct a victim, rape her, rip her to shreds, and eat her. This one has more in mind. There's something in mead that makes the grendelkin fertile. It's going to impregnate her. Create another of its kind."

A thought occurred to me. "That's what kind of person still has her instructions taped to her birth control medication. Someone who's never taken it until very recently."

"She's a virgin," Gard confirmed. "Grendelkin need virgins to reproduce."

"Kind of a scarce commodity these days," I said.

Gard snapped out a bitter bark of laughter. "Take it from me, Dresden. Teenagers have always been teenagers. Hormone-ridden, curious, and generally ignorant of the consequences of their actions. There's never been a glut on the virgin market. Not in Victorian times, not during the Renaissance, not at Hastings, and not now. But even if they were ten times as rare in the modern age, there would still be more virgins to choose from than at any other point in history." She shook her head. "There are so *many* people, now."

We walked along for several paces.

"Interesting inflection, there," I said. "Speaking about those times as if you'd seen them firsthand. You expect me to believe you're better than a thousand years old?"

"Would it be so incredible?" she asked.

She had me there. Lots of supernatural critters were immortal, or the next-best thing to it. Even mortal wizards could hang around for three or four centuries. On the other hand, I'd rarely run into an immortal who felt so human to my wizard's senses.

I stared at her for a second and then said, "You wear it pretty well, if it's true. I would have guessed you were about thirty."

Her teeth flashed in the dim light. "I believe it's currently considered more polite to guess twenty-nine."

"Me and polite have never been on close terms."

Gard nodded. "I like that about you. You say what you think. You act. It's rare in this age."

I kept on the trail, quiet for a time, until Mouse stopped in his tracks and made an almost inaudible sound in his chest. I held up a hand, halting. Gard went silent and still.

I knelt down by the dog and whispered, "What is it, boy?"

Mouse stared intently ahead, his nose quivering. Then he paced forward, uncertainly, and pawed at the floor near the wall.

I followed him, light in hand. On the wet stone floor were a few tufts of greyish hair. I chewed my lip and lifted the light to examine the wall. There were long scratches in the stone—not much wider than a thumbnail, but they were deep. You couldn't easily see the bottom of the scratch marks.

Gard came up and peered over my shoulder. Amid the scents of lime and mildew, her perfume, something floral I didn't recognize, was a pleasant distraction. "Something sharp made those," she murmured.

"Yeah," I said, collecting the hairs. "Hold up your ax."

She did. I touched the hairs to the edge of the blade. They curled away from it as they touched it, blackening and shriveling, and adding the scent of burned hair to the mix.

"Wonderful." I sighed.

Gard lifted her eyebrows and glanced at me. "Faeries?"

I nodded. "Malks, almost certainly."

"Malks?"

"Winterfae," I said. "Felines. About the size of a bobcat."

"Nothing steel can't handle, then," she said, rising briskly.

"Yeah," I said. "You could probably handle half a dozen."

She nodded once, brandished the ax, and turned to continue down the tunnel.

"Which is why they tend to run in packs of twenty," I added, a couple of steps later.

Gard stopped and gave me a glare.

"That's called sharing information," I said. I gestured at the wall. "These are territorial markings for the local pack. Malks are stronger than natural animals, quick, almost invisible when they want to be, and their claws are sharper and harder than surgical steel. I once saw a malk shred an aluminum baseball bat to slivers. And if that wasn't enough, they're sentient. Smarter than some people I know."

"Od's bodkin," Gard swore quietly. "Can you handle them?"

"They don't like fire," I said. "But in an enclosed space like this, I don't like it much, either."

Gard nodded once. "Can we treat with them?" she asked. "Buy passage?"

"They'll keep their word, like any fae," I said. "If you can get them to give it in the first place. But think of how cats enjoy hunting, even when they aren't hungry. Think about how they toy with their prey sometimes. Then distill that joyful little killer instinct out of every cat in Chicago and pour it all into one malk. They're to cats what Hannibal Lecter is to people."

"Negotiation isn't an option, then."

I shook my head. "I don't think we have anything to offer them that they'll want more than our screams and meat, no."

Gard nodded, frowning. "Best if they never notice us at all, then."

"Nice thought," I said. "But these things have a cat's senses. I could probably hide us from their sight or hearing, but not both. And they could still smell us."

Gard frowned. She reached into her coat pocket and drew out a slim box of aged, pale ivory. She opened it and began gingerly sorting through a number of small ivory squares.

"Scrabble tiles?" I asked. "I don't want to play with malks. They're really bad about using plurals and proper names."

"They're runes," Gard said quietly. She found the one she was after, took a steadying breath, and then removed a single square from the ivory box with the same cautious reverence I'd seen soldiers use with military explosives. She closed the box and put it back in her pocket, holding the single ivory chit carefully in front of her on her palm.

I was familiar with Norse runes. The rune on the ivory square in her hand was totally unknown to me. "Um. What's that?" I asked.

"A rune of Routine," she said quietly. "You said you were skilled with illusion magic. If you can make us look like them, even for a few moments, it should allow us to pass through them unnoticed, as if we were a normal part of their day."

Technically, I had told Gard I was *familiar* with illusion magic, not skilled. Truth be told, it was probably my weakest skill set. Nobody's good at everything, right? I'm good with the kaboom magic. My actual use of illusion hadn't passed much beyond the craft's equivalent of painting a few portraits of fruit bowls.

But I'd just have to hope that what Gard didn't know wouldn't get us both killed. Elizabeth didn't have much time, and I didn't have many options. Besides, what did we have to lose? If the bid to sneak by failed, we could always fall back on negotiating or slugging it out.

Mouse gave me a sober look.

"Groovy," I said. "Let's do it."

A GOOD ILLUSION is all about imagination. You create a picture in your mind, imagining every detail; imagining so hard that the image in your head becomes nearly tangible, almost real. You have to be able to see it, hear it, touch it, taste it, smell it, to engage all your senses in its (theoretical) reality. If you can do that, if you can really believe in your fake version of reality, then you can pour energy into it and create it in the minds and senses of everyone looking at it.

For the record, it's also how all the best liars do business—by making their imagined version of things so coherent that they almost believe it themselves.

I'm not a terribly good liar, but I knew the basics of how to make an illusion work, and I had two secret weapons. The first was the tuft of hair from an actual malk, which I could use to aid in the accuracy of my illusion. The second was a buddy of mine, a big grey tomcat named Mister who deigned to share his apartment with Mouse and me. Mister didn't come with me on cases, being above such trivial matters, but he found me pleasant company when I was at home and not moving around too much, except when he didn't, in which case he went rambling.

I closed my eyes once I'd drawn my chalk circle, gripped the malk hair in my hand, and started my image on a model of Mister. I'd seen malks a couple of times, and most of them bore the same kinds of battle scars Mister proudly wore. They didn't look exactly like cats, though. Their heads were shaped differently, and their fur was rougher, stiffer. The paws had one too many digits on them, too, and were wider than a cat's—but the motion as they moved was precisely the same.

"*Noctus ex illuminus,*" I murmured once the image was firmly fixed in my thoughts, that of three ugly, lean, battle-marked malks walking through on their own calm business. I sent out the energy that would power the glamour and broke the circle with a slow, careful motion.

"Is it working?" Gard asked quietly.

"Yeah," I said, focused on the illusion, my eyes still closed. I fumbled about until I found Mouse's broad back, then rested one hand on his fur. "Stop distracting me. Walk."

"Very well." She drew in a short breath, said something, and then there was a snapping sound and a flash of light. "The rune is active," she said. She put her hand on my shoulder. The malks weren't using any light sources, and if a group of apparent malks tried to walk through with one, it would kind of spoil the effect we were trying to achieve. So we'd have to make the walk in the dark. "We have perhaps five minutes."

I grunted, touched my dog, and we all started walking, trusting Mouse to guide our steps. Even though it was dark, I didn't dare open my eyes. Any distraction from the image in my head would cause it to disintegrate like toilet paper in a hurricane. So I walked, concentrating, and hoped like hell it worked.

I couldn't spare any brain-time for counting, but we walked for what felt like half an hour, and I was getting set to ask Gard if we were through yet, when an inhuman voice not a foot from my left ear said in plain English, "More of these new claws arrive every day. We are hungry. We should shred the ape and have done."

I nearly fell on my ass, it startled me so much, but I held on to the image in my head. I'd heard malks speak before, with their odd inflections and unsettling intonations, and the sound only reinforced the image in my head.

A round of both supporting and disparaging comments rose from all around me, all in lazy, malk-inflected English. There were more than twenty of them. There was a small horde.

"Patience," said another malk. The tone of voice somehow suggested this was a conversation that had repeated itself a million times. "Let the ape think it has cowed us into acting as its door wardens. It hunts in the wizard's territory. The wizard will come to face it. The Erlking will give us great favor when we bring the wizard's head."

Gosh. I felt famous.

"I'm weary of waiting," said another malk. "Let us kill the ape and its prey and then hunt the wizard down."

"Patience, hunters. The wizard will come to us," the first one said. "The ape's turn will come, after we have brought down the wizard." There was an unmistakable note of pleasure in its voice. "And his little dog, too."

Mouse made another subvocal rumble in his chest. I could, just barely, feel it in his back. He kept walking, though, and we passed through the stretch of tunnel occupied by the malks. It was another endless stretch of minutes and several turns before Gard let out her breath between her teeth and said, "There were more than twenty."

"Yeah, I kind of noticed that."

"I think we are past them."

I sighed and released the image I'd been holding in my head, calling forth dim light from my amulet. Or tried to release the image, at any rate. I opened my eyes and blinked several times, but my head was like one of those TVs at the department store, when one image has been burned into it for too long. I looked at Mouse and Gard, and had trouble shaking the picture of the savage, squash-headed malks I'd been imagining around them with such intensity.

"Do you have another of those rune things?" I asked her.

"No," Gard said.

"We'll have to get creative on the way out," I said.

"There's no need to worry about that yet," she said, and started walking forward again.

"Sure there is. Once we get the girl, we have to get *back* with her. Christ, haven't you read any Joseph Campbell at all?"

She shrugged one shoulder. "Grendelkin are difficult opponents. Either we'll die, or it will. So there's only a fifty-fifty chance that we'll need to worry about the malks on the way out. Why waste the effort until we know if it will be necessary?"

"Call me crazy, but I find that if I plan for the big things, like how to get back to the surface, it makes it a little simpler to manage the little things. Like how to keep on breathing."

She held up a hand and said, "Wait."

I stopped in my tracks, listening. Mouse came to a halt, snuffling at the air, his ears twitching around like little radar dishes, but he gave no sign that he'd detected lurking danger.

"We're close to its lair," she murmured.

I arched an eyebrow. The tunnel looked exactly the same as it had for several moments now. "How do you know?"

"I can feel it," she said.

"You can *do* that?"

She started forward. "Yes. It's how I knew it was moving in the city to begin with."

I ground my teeth. "It might be nice if you considered *sharing* that kind of information."

"It isn't far," she said. "We might be in time. Come on."

I felt my eyebrows go up. Mouse had us both beat when it came to purely physical sensory input, and he'd given no indication of a hostile presence ahead. My own senses were attuned to all kinds of supernatural energies, and I'd kept them focused ever since we'd entered Undertown. I hadn't sensed any stirring of any kind that would indicate some kind of malevolent presence.

If knowledge is power, then it follows that ignorance is weakness. In my line of work, ignorance can get you killed. Gard hadn't said anything about any kind of mystic connection between herself and this beastie, but it was the most likely explanation for how she could sense its presence when I couldn't.

The problem with that was that those kinds of connections generally didn't flow one-way. If she could sense the grendelkin, odds were the grendelkin could sense her right back.

"Whoa, wait," I said. "If this thing might know we're coming, we don't want to go rushing in blind."

"There's no time. It's almost ready to breed." There was a hint of a snarl in her words as the ax came down off her shoulder. Gard pulled what looked like a road flare out of her duffel bag and tossed the bag aside.

Then she threw back her head and let out a scream of pure, unholy defiance. The sound was so loud, so raw, so primal, it hardly seemed human. It wasn't a word, but that didn't stop her howl from eloquently declaring Gard's rage, her utter contempt for danger, for life—and for death. That battle cry scared the living snot out of me, and it wasn't even aimed in my direction.

Gard struck the flare to life with a flick of a wrist and shot me a glance over her shoulder. Eerie green light played up over her face, casting bizarre shadows, and her icy eyes were very wide and white-rimmed above a smile stretched so tightly that the blood had drained from her lips. Her voice quavered disconcertingly. "Enough talk."

Holy Schwarzenegger.

Gard had lost it.

This wasn't the reaction of the cool, reasoning professional I'd seen working for Marcone. I'd never actually *seen* anyone go truly, old-school *berserkergang*, but that scream . . . It was like hearing an echo rolling down through the centuries from an ancient world, a more savage world, now lost to the mists of time.

And suddenly I had no trouble at all believing her age.

She charged forward, whipping her ax lightly around with her right hand, holding the blazing star of the flare in her left. Gard let out another banshee shriek as she went, a wordless cry of challenge to the grendelkin that declared her intent as clearly as any horde of phonemes: *I am coming to kill you.*

And ahead of us in the tunnels, something much, much bigger than Gard answered her, a deep-chested, basso bellow that shook the walls of the tunnel in answer: *Bring it on.*

My knees turned shaky. Hell, even Mouse stood with his ears pressed against his skull, tail held low, body set in a slight crouch. I doubt I looked any more courageous than he did, but I kicked my brain into gear, spat out a nervous curse, and hurried after her.

Charging in headlong might be a really stupid idea, but it would be an even *worse* idea to stand around doing nothing, throwing away the only help I was likely to get. Besides, for better or worse, I'd agreed to work with Gard, and I wasn't going to let her go in without covering her back.

So I charged headlong down the tunnel toward the source of the terrifying bellow. Mouse, perhaps wiser than I, hesitated a few seconds longer, then made up for it on the way down the tunnel, until he was running a pace in front of me, matching my stride. We'd gone maybe twenty yards before his breath began to rumble out in a growl of pure hostility, and he let out his own roar of challenge.

Hey, when in Cimmeria, do as the Cimmerians do. I screamed, too. It got lost in all the echoes bouncing around the tunnels.

Gard, running hard ten paces ahead of me, burst into a chamber. She gathered herself in a sudden leap, flipping neatly in the air, and plummeted from sight. The falling green light of the flare showed me that the tunnel opened into the top of a chamber the size of a small hotel atrium, and if Mouse hadn't stopped first and leaned back against me, I might have slid over the edge before I could stop. As it was, I got a really good look at a drop of at least thirty feet to a wet stone floor.

Gard landed on her feet, turned the momentum into a forward roll, and a shaggy blur the size of an industrial freezer whipped past her, slamming into the wall with a coughing roar and a shudder of impact.

The blond woman bounced up, kicked off a stone wall, flipped over again, and came down on her feet, ax held high. She'd discarded the flare, leaving it in the center of the floor, and I got my first good look at the place, and at the things in it.

First of all, the chamber, cavern, whatever it was, was huge. Thirty feet from ceiling to floor, at least thirty feet wide, and it stretched out into the darkness beyond the sharp light cast by the flare. Most of it was natural stone. Some of the surfaces showed signs of being crudely cut with hand-wielded tools. A ledge about two feet wide ran along the edge of the chamber in a C-shape, up near the top. I'd nearly tumbled off the ledge into the cavern. There were stairs cut into the wall below me—if you could call the twelve-inch projections crudely hacked out of the stone every couple of feet a stairway.

My glance swept over the cavern below. A huge pile of newspapers, old blankets, bloodstained clothes, and unidentifiable bits of fabric must have served as a nest or bed for the creature. It was three feet high in the middle, and a good ten or twelve feet across. A mound of bones, nearby, was very nearly as large. The old ivory gleamed in the eerie light of the flare, cleared entirely of meat, though the mound was infested with rats and vermin, all tiny moving forms and glittering red eyes.

A huge stone had been placed in the center of the floor. A metal beer keg sat on top of it, between the tied-down, spread-eagled legs of a rather attractive and very naked young woman. She'd been tied down with rough ropes, directly over a thick layer of old bloodstains congealed into an almost-rubbery coating on the rock. Her eyes were wide, her face flushed with tears, and she was screaming.

Gard whipped her ax through a series of scything arcs in front of her, driving them at the big furry blur. I had no idea how she was covering the ground fast enough to keep up with the thing. They were both moving at Kung Fu Theater speed. One of Gard's swipes must have tagged it, because there was a sudden bellow of rage and it bounded into the shadows outside the light of the flare.

She let out a howl of frustration. The head of her ax was smeared with black fluid, and as it ran across the steel, flickers of silver fire appeared in the shape of more strange runes. "Wizard!" she bellowed. "Give me light!"

I was already on it, holding my amulet high and behind my head, ramming more will through the device. The dim wizard light flared into incandescence, throwing strong light at least a hundred feet down the long gallery—and drawing a shriek of pain and surprise from the grendelkin.

I saw it for maybe two seconds, while it crouched with one arm thrown up to shield its eyes. The grendelkin was flabby over a quarter ton of muscle, and the nails on its fingers and toes were black, long, and dangerous-looking. It was big, nine or ten feet, and covered in hair. It wasn't fur, like a bear or a dog, but *hair*, human hair, with pale skin easily seen beneath, so that the impression it gave was one of an exceptionally hirsute man, rather than that of a beast.

And the beast was definitely male; terrifyingly so—I'd seen smaller fire extinguishers. And from the looks of things, Gard and I must have interrupted him in the middle of foreplay.

No wonder he was pissed.

Gard saw the grendelkin and charged forward. I saw my chance to pitch in. I lifted my staff and pointed it at the creature, gathered another surge of will, and snarled, *"Fuego!"*

My staff was an important tool, allowing me to focus and direct energy much more precisely and with more concentration than I could manage without it. It didn't work as well as my more specialized blasting rod for directing fire, but for this purpose it would do just fine. A column of golden flame as wide as a whiskey barrel leapt across the cavern to the grendelkin, smashing into his head and upper body. It was too dispersed to kill the grendelkin outright, but hopefully it would blind and distract the beast enough to let Gard get in the killing blow.

The grendelkin lowered his arm, and I saw a quick flash of yellow eyes, a hideous face, and a mouthful of fangs. Those teeth spread into a smile, and I realized I might as well have hit him with the stream of water from a garden hose, for all the effect the fire had on him. He moved, an abrupt whipping of his massive shoulders, and flung a stone at me.

Take it from me, the grendelkin's talents were wasted on the abduct-rape-devour industry.

He should have been playing professional ball.

By the time I realized the rock was on the way, it had already hit me. There was a popping sound from my left shoulder, and a wave of agony. Something flung me to the ground, driving the breath out of my lungs. My amulet fell from my suddenly unresponsive fingers, and the brilliant light died at once.

Dammit, I had assumed big and hostile meant dumb, and the grendelkin wasn't. The beast had deliberately waited for Gard to charge forward out of the light of the dropped flare before he threw.

"Wizard!" Gard bellowed.

I couldn't see anything. The brief moment of brilliant illumination had blinded my eyes to the dimmer light of the flare, and Gard couldn't be in much better shape. I got to my feet, trying not to scream at the pain in my shoulder, and staggered back to look down at the room.

The grendelkin bellowed again, and Gard screamed—this time in pain. There was the sound of a heavy blow, and Gard, her hands empty, flew across the circle of green flare-light, a dim shadow. She struck the wall beneath me with an ugly, heavy sound.

It was all happening so *fast*. Hell's bells, but I was playing out of my league, here.

I turned to Mouse and snarled an instruction. My dog stared at me for a second, ears flattened to his skull, and didn't move.

"Go!" I screamed at him. "Go, go, go!"

Mouse spun and shot off back down the way we'd come.

Gard groaned on the floor beneath me, stirring weakly at the edge of the dim circle of light cast by the flare. I couldn't tell how badly she was hurt—but I knew that if I didn't move before the grendelkin finished her, she wasn't going to get any better. I could hear Elizabeth sobbing in despair.

"Get up, Harry," I growled at myself. "Get a move on."

I could barely move my left arm, so I gripped my staff in my right and began negotiating the precarious stone stairway.

A voice laughed out in the darkness. It was a deep voice, masculine, mellow, and smooth. When it spoke, it did so with precise, cultured pronunciation. "Geat bitch," the grendelkin murmured. "That's the most fun I've had in a century. Surt, but I wish there were a few more Choosers running about the world. You're a dying breed."

I could barely see the damned stairs in the flare's light. My foot slipped, and I nearly fell.

"Who's the *seidrmadr*?" the grendelkin asked.

"Gesundheit," I said.

The beast appeared at the far side of the circle of light, and I stopped in my tracks. The grendelkin's yellow eyes gleamed with malice and hunger. He flexed his claw-tipped hands very slowly, baring his teeth in another smile. My mouth felt utterly dry and my legs were shaking. I'd seen him move. If he rushed me, things could get ugly.

Strike that. *When* he rushed me, things *were* going to get ugly.

"Is that a fire extinguisher in your pocket?" I asked, studying the grendelkin intently. "Or are you just happy to see me?"

The grendelkin's smile spread wider. "Most definitely the latter. I'm going to have two mouths to feed, shortly. What did she promise you to fool you into coming with her?"

"You got it backward. I permitted her to tag along with me," I said.

The grendelkin let out a low, lazily wicked laugh. It was eerie as hell, hearing such a refined voice come from a package like that. "Do you think you're a threat to me, little man?"

"You think I'm not?"

Idly, the grendelkin dragged the clawed fingers of one hand around on the stone floor beside him. Little sparks jumped up here and there. "I've been countering *seld* since before I left the Old World. Without that, you're nothing more than a monkey with a stick." He paused and added, "A rather weak and clumsy monkey at that."

"Big guy like you shouldn't have any trouble with little old me, then," I said. His eyes were strange. I'd never seen any quite like that. His face, though pretty ugly, was similar to others I'd seen. "I guess you have some history with Miss Gard, there."

"Family feuds are always the worst," the grendelkin said.

"Have to take your word for it," I said. "Just like I'm going to have to take these women. I'd rather do it peaceably than the hard way. Your call. Walk away, big guy. We'll both be happier."

The grendelkin looked at me, and then threw his head back in a rich, deeply amused laugh. "It's not enough that I already have a brood-mare and a wounded little wildcat to play with; I also have a clown. It's practically a festival."

And with that, the grendelkin rushed me. A crushing fist the size of a volleyball flicked at my face. I was fast enough, barely, to slip the blow. I flung myself to the cavern floor, gasping as the shock of landing reached my shoulder. That sledgehammer of flesh and bone slammed into the wall with a brittle crunching sound. Chips of flying stone stung my cheek.

It scared the crap out of me, which was just as well. Terror makes a great fuel for some kinds of magic, and the get-the-hell-away-from-me blast of raw force I unleashed on the grendelkin would have flung a parked car to the other side of the street and into the building beyond.

The grendelkin hadn't been kidding about knowing counter-magic, though. All that naked force hit him and just sort of slid off him, like water pouring around a stone. It only drove him back about two steps—which was room enough to let me drop to one knee and swing my staff again. It wasn't a bone-crushing blow, powered as it was by only one hand and from a fairly unbalanced position.

But I got him in the fire extinguisher.

The grendelkin let out a howl about two octaves higher than his original bellows had been, and I scooted around him, running for the altar stone where Elizabeth Braddock lay helpless—away from Gard. I wanted the grendelkin to focus all his attention on me.

He did.

"Behind you!" Elizabeth screamed, her eyes wide with terror.

I whirled and a sweep of the grendelkin's arm ripped the staff out of my hand. Something like a steel vise clamped around my neck, and my feet came up off the ground.

The grendelkin lifted my face to his level. His breath smelled of blood and rotten meat. His eyes were bright with their fury. I kicked at him, but he held me out of reach of anything vital, and my kicks plunked uselessly into his belly and ribs.

"I was going to make it quick for you," he snarled. "For amusing me. But I'm going to start with your arms."

If I didn't have him right where I wanted him, I'd have been less than sanguine about my chances of survival. I'd accomplished that much, at least. He had his back to the tunnel.

"Rip them off one at a time, little *seidrmadr*." He paused. "Which, when viewed from a literary perspective, has a certain amount of irony." He showed me more teeth. "I'll let you watch me eat your hands. Let you see what I do to these bitches before I'm done with you."

Boy, was he going to get it.

One of his hands grabbed my left arm, and the pain of my dislocated shoulder made my world go white. I fought through the agony, ripped Elizabeth Braddock's pointy-handled hairbrush from my duster's pocket, and drove it like an ice pick into the grendelkin's forearm.

He roared and flung me into the nearest wall.

Which hurt. Lots.

I fell to the stone floor of the cavern in a heap. After that, my vision shrank to a tunnel and began to darken.

This was just as well—fewer distractions, that way. Now all I had to do was time it right.

A sound groaned down from the tunnel entrance above, an odd, ululating murmur, echoed into unintelligibility.

The furious grendelkin ripped the brush out of his arm and flung it away—but when he heard the sound, he turned his ugly kisser back toward the source.

I focused harder on the spell I had coming than upon anything I'd ever done. I had no circle to help me, lots of distractions, and absolutely no room to screw it up.

The strange sound resolved itself into a yowling chorus, like half a hundred band saws on helium, and Mouse burst out of the tunnel with a living thunderstorm of malks in hot pursuit.

My dog flung himself into the empty air, and malks bounded after him, determined not to let him escape. Mouse fell thirty feet, onto the huge pile of nesting material, landing with a yelp. The malks spilled after him, yowling in fury, dozens and dozens of malevolent eyes glittering in the light of the flare. Some jumped, some flowed seamlessly down the rough stairs, and others bounded forward, sank their claws into the stone of the far wall, and slid down it like a fireman down a pole.

I unleashed the spell.

"Useless vermin!" bellowed the grendelkin, his voice still pitched higher than before. He pointed at me, a battered-looking man in a long leather coat, and roared, "Kill the wizard or I'll eat every last one of you!"

The malks, now driven as much by fear as anger, immediately swarmed all over me. I gave them a pretty good time of it, but there were probably better than three dozen of them, and the leather coat couldn't cover everything.

Claws and fangs flashed.

Blood spattered.

The malks went insane with bloodlust.

I screamed, swinging wildly with both hands, killing a malk here or there, but unable to protect myself from all those claws and teeth. The grendelkin turned toward the helpless Elizabeth.

It was a real bitch, trying to undo the grendelkin's knotted ropes while still holding the illusion in place in my mind. Beneath the glamour that made him look like me, he fought furiously, clawing and swinging at the malks attacking him. It didn't help that Elizabeth was screaming again, thanks to the illusion of the grendelkin I was holding over myself, but hey. No plan is perfect.

"Mouse!" I cried.

A malk flew over my head, screaming, and splattered against a wall.

My dog bounded up just as I got the girl loose. I shoved her at him and said, "Get her out of here! Run! Go, go, go!"

Elizabeth didn't know what the hell was going on, but she understood that last part well enough. She fled, back toward the crude staircase. Mouse ran beside her, and when a malk flung itself at Elizabeth's naked back, my dog intercepted the little monster in the air, catching it as neatly as a Frisbee at the park. Mouse snarled and shook his jaws once. The malk's neck broke with an audible snap. My dog dropped it and fled on.

I grabbed my staff and ran to Gard. The malks hadn't noticed her yet. They were still busy mobbing the grendelkin—

Crap. My concentration had wavered. It looked like itself again, as did I.

I whirled and focused my will upon the giant pile of clean-picked bones. I extended my staff and snarled, "Counterspell this. *Forzare!*"

Hundreds of pounds of sharp white bone flung themselves at the grendelkin and the malks alike. I threw the bones hard, harder than the grendelkin had thrown his rock, and the bone shards ripped into them like the blast of an enormous shotgun.

Without waiting to see the results, I snatched up the still-burning flare and flung it into the pile of nesting fabric, bloody clothes, and old newspapers. The whole mound flared instantly into angry light and smothering smoke.

"Get up!" I screamed at Gard. One side of her face was bruised and swollen, and she had a visibly broken arm, one of the bones in her forearm protruding from the skin. With my help, she staggered up, dazed and choking on the smoke, which also blotted out the light. I got her onto the stairs, and even in our battered state, we set some kind of speed record going up them.

The deafening chorus of bellowing grendelkin and howling malks faded a little as the smoke started choking them, too. Air was moving in the tunnel, as the fire drew on it just as it might a chimney. I lit up my amulet again to show us the way out.

"Wait!" Gard gasped, fifty feet up the tunnel. "Wait!"

She fumbled at her jacket pocket, where she kept the little ivory box, but she couldn't reach it with her sound arm. I dug it out for her.

"Triangle, three lines over it," she said, leaning against a wall for support. "Get it out."

I poked through the little ivory Scrabble tiles until I found one that matched her description. "This one?" I demanded.

"Careful," she growled. "It's a Sunder rune." She grabbed it from me, took a couple of steps back toward the grendelkin's cavern, murmured under her breath, and snapped the little tile. There was a flicker of deep red light, and the tunnel itself quivered and groaned.

"Run!"

We did.

Behind us, the tunnel collapsed in on itself with a roar, sealing the malks and the grendelkin away beneath us, trapping them in the smothering smoke.

We both stopped for a moment after that, as dust billowed up the tunnel and the sound of furious supernatural beings cut off as if someone had flipped a switch. The silence was deafening.

We both stood there, panting and wounded. Gard sank to the floor to rest.

"You were right," I said. "I guess we didn't need to worry about the malks on the way out."

Gard gave me a weary smile. "That was my favorite ax."

"Go back for it," I suggested. "I'll wait for you here."

She snorted.

Mouse came shambling up out of the tunnel above us. Elizabeth Braddock clung to his collar, and looked acutely embarrassed about her lack of clothing. "Wh-what?" she whispered. "What happened here? I d-don't understand."

"It's all right, Mrs. Braddock," I said. "You're safe. We're going to take you back to your husband."

She closed her eyes, shuddered, and started to cry. She sank down to put her arms around Mouse's furry ruff, and buried her face in his fur. She was shivering with the cold. I shucked out of my coat and draped it around her.

Gard eyed her, then her own broken arm, and let out a sigh. "I need a drink."

I spat some grit out of my mouth. "Ditto. Come on."

I offered her a hand up. She took it.

SEVERAL HOURS AND doctors later, Gard and I wound up back at the pub, where the beer festival was winding to a conclusion. We sat at a table with Mac. The Braddocks had stammered a gratuitous number of thanks and rushed off together. Mac's keg had a blue ribbon taped to it. He'd drawn all of us a mug.

"Night of the Living Brews," I said. I had painkillers for my shoulder, but I was waiting until I was home and in bed to take one. As a result, I ached pretty much everywhere. "More like night of the living bruise."

Mac rose, drained his mug, and held it up in a salute to Gard and me. "Thanks."

"No problem," I said.

Gard smiled slightly and bowed her head to him. Mac departed.

Gard finished her own mug and examined the cast on her arm. "Close one."

"Little bit," I said. "Can I ask you something?"

She nodded.

"The grendelkin called you a Geat," I said.

"Yes, he did."

"I'm familiar with only one person referred to in that way," I said.

"There are a few more around," Gard said. "But everyone's heard of that one."

"You called the grendelkin a scion of Grendel," I said. "Am I to take it that you're a scion of the Geat?"

Gard smiled slightly. "My family and the grendelkin's have a long history."

"He called you a Chooser," I said.

She shrugged again, and kept her enigmatic smile.

"Gard isn't your real name," I said. "Is it?"

"Of course not," she replied.

I sipped some more of Mac's award-winning dark. "You're a Valkyrie. A real one."

Her expression was unreadable.

"I thought Valkyries mostly did pickups and deliveries," I said. "Choosing the best warriors from among the slain. Taking them off to Valhalla. Oh, and serving drinks there. Odin's virgin daughters, pouring mead for the warriors, partying until Ragnarok."

Gard threw back her head and laughed. "Virgin daughters." She rose, shaking her head, and glanced at her broken arm again. Then she leaned down and kissed me on the mouth. Her lips were a sweet, hungry little fire of sensation, and I felt the kiss all the way to my toes—some places more than others, ahem.

She drew away slowly, her pale blue eyes shining. Then she winked at me and said, "Don't believe everything you read, Dresden." She turned to go, then paused to glance over her shoulder. "Though, to be honest, sometimes he *does* like us to call him Daddy. I'm Sigrun."

I watched Sigrun go. Then I finished the last of the beer.

Mouse rose expectantly, his tail wagging, and we set off for home.

DAY OFF

—from *Blood Lite*,
edited by Kevin J. Anderson

Takes place between *Small Favor*
and *Turn Coat*

Kevin Anderson talked to me at NYCC and asked me if I'd be interested in participating in a new kind of anthology (for me, anyway) in which authors known for their work in supernatural and horror fiction tried their hands at comedy. I loved the idea.

Poor Dresden. I mean, I keep putting the weight of the world on the poor guy's shoulders—and I feel really bad about it. No, really. I'm serious. I feel awful, honestly.

Okay, well. Less "awful" and more "gleeful," but you get the point. It's easy to torture Harry when there are master vampires and superghouls and ghosts and demons and ogres traipsing all over the scenery. But I found myself intrigued with the idea of making him suffer just as much frustration and embarrassment in a situation where his opponents and problems were relatively trivial.

I don't really know how other people reacted to poor Harry struggling to get to enjoy a day off work—but I thought it was pretty darned funny.

The thief was examining another trapped doorway when I heard something—the tromp of approaching feet. The holy woman was in the middle of another sermon, about attentiveness or something, but I held up my hand for silence and she obliged. I could hear twenty sets of feet, maybe more.

I let out a low growl and reached for my sword. "Company."

"Easy, my son," the holy woman said. "We don't even know who it is yet."

The ruined mausoleum was far enough off the beaten path to make it unlikely that anyone had just wandered in on us. The holy woman was dreaming if she thought the company might be friendly. A moment later they appeared—the local magistrate and two dozen of his thugs.

"Always with the corrupt government officials," muttered the wizard from behind me. I glanced back at him and then looked for the thief. The nimble little minx was nowhere to be seen.

"You are trespassing!" boomed the magistrate. He had a big boomy voice. "Leave this place immediately on pain of punishment by the Crown's law!"

"Sir!" replied the holy woman. "Our mission here is of paramount importance. The writ we bear from your own liege requires you to render aid and assistance in this matter."

"But not to violate the graves of my subjects!" he boomed some more. "Begone! Before I unleash the nine fires of Atarak upon—"

"Enough talk!" I growled, and threw my heavy dagger at his chest.

Propelled by my massive thews, the dagger hit him two inches below his left nipple—a perfect heart shot. It struck with enough force to hurl him from his feet. His men howled with surprised fury.

I drew the huge sword from my back, let out a leonine roar, and charged the two dozen thugs.

"Enough talk!" I bellowed, and whipped the twenty-pound greatsword at the nearest target as if it were a wooden yardstick. He went down in a heap.

"Enough talk!" I howled, and kept swinging. I smashed through the next several thugs as if they were made of soft wax. Off to my left, the thief came out of nowhere and neatly sliced the Achilles tendons of another thug. The holy woman took a ready stance with her quarterstaff and chanted out a prayer to her deities at the top of her lungs.

The wizard shrieked, and a fireball whipped over my head, exploding twenty-one feet in front of me, then spread out in a perfect circle, like the shock wave of a nuke, burning and roasting thugs as it went and stopping a bare twelve inches shy of my nose.

"Oh, come on!" I said. "It doesn't work like that!"

"What?" demanded the wizard.

"It doesn't *work* like that!" I insisted. "Even if you call up fire with magic, it's still *fire*. It acts like *fire*. It expands in a sphere. And under a ceiling, that means it goes rushing much farther down hallways and tunnels. It *doesn't* just go twenty feet and then *stop*."

"Fireballs used to work like that." The wizard sighed. "But do you know what a chore it is to calculate exactly how far those things will spread? I mean, it slows everything down."

"It's simple math," I said. "And it's way better than the fire just spreading twenty feet regardless of what's around it. What, do fireballs carry tape measures or something?"

Billy the Werewolf sighed and put down his character sheet and his dice. "Harry," he protested gently, "repeat after me: It's only a game."

I folded my arms and frowned at him across his dining room table. It was littered with snacks, empty cans of pop, pieces of paper, and tiny model monsters and adventurers (including a massively thewed barbarian model for my character). Georgia, Billy's willowy brunette wife, sat at the table with us, as did the redheaded bombshell Andi, while lanky Kirby lurked behind several folding screens covered with fantasy art at the head of the table.

"I'm just saying," I said, "there's no reason the magic can't be portrayed at least a little more accurately, is there?"

"Again with *this* discussion." Andi sighed. "I mean, I know he's the actual wizard and all, but Christ."

Kirby nodded glumly. "It's like taking a physicist to a *Star Trek* movie."

"Harry," Georgia said firmly, "you're doing it again."

"Oh, no, I'm not!" I protested. "All I'm saying is that—"

Georgia arched an eyebrow and gave me a steady look down her aquiline nose. "You know the law, Dresden."

"He who kills the cheer springs for beer," chanted the rest of the table.

"Oh, bite me!" I muttered at them, but a grin was diluting my scowl as I dug out my wallet and tossed a twenty on the table.

"Okay," Kirby said. "Roll your fireball damage, Will."

Billy slung out a double handful of square dice and said, "Hah! One-point-two over median. Suck on that, henchmen!"

"They're all dead," Kirby confirmed. "We might as well break there until next week."

"Crap," I said. "I barely got to hit anybody."

"I only got to hit *one*!" Andi said.

Georgia shook her head. "I didn't even get to finish casting my spell."

"Oh, yes," Billy gloated. "Seven modules of identifying magic items and repairing things the stupid barbarian broke, but I've finally come into my own. Was it like that for you, Harry?"

"Let you know when I come into my own," I said, rising. "But my hopes are high. Why, this very morrow, I, Harry Dresden, have a day off."

"The devil you say!" Billy exclaimed, grinning at me as the group began cleaning up from the evening's gaming session.

I shrugged into my black leather duster. "No apprentice, no work, no errands for the Council, no Warden stuff, no trips out of town for Paranet business. My very own free time."

Georgia gave me a wide smile. "Tell me you aren't going to spend it puttering around that musty hole in the ground you call a lab."

"Um," I said.

"Look," Andi said. "He's blushing!"

"I am not blushing," I said. I swept up the empty bottles and pizza boxes, and headed into Billy and Georgia's little kitchen to dump them into the trash.

Georgia followed me in, reaching around me to send several pieces of paper into the trash, too. "Hot date with Stacy?" she asked, her voice pitched to keep the conversation private.

"I think if I ever called her 'Stacy,' Anastasia might beat the snot out of me for being too lazy to speak her entire name," I replied.

"You seem a little tense about it."

I shrugged a shoulder. "This is going to be the first time we spend a whole day together without something trying to rip us to pieces along the way. I . . . I want it to go right, you know?" I pushed my fingers back through my hair. "I mean, both of us could use a day off."

"Sure, sure," Georgia said, watching me with calm, knowing eyes. "Do you think it's going to go anywhere with her?"

I shrugged. "Don't know. She and I have very different ideas about . . . well, about basically everything except what to do with things that go around hurting people."

The tall, willowy Georgia glanced back toward the dining room, where her short, heavily muscled husband was putting away models. "Opposites attract. There's a song about it and everything."

"One thing at a time," I said. "Neither one of us is trying to inspire the poets for the ages. We like each other. We make each other laugh. God, that's nice, these days. . . ." I sighed and glanced up at Georgia, a little sheepishly. "I just want to show her a nice time tomorrow."

Georgia had a gentle smile on her narrow, intelligent face. "I think that's a very healthy attitude."

I WAS JUST getting into my car, a battered old Volkswagen Bug I've dubbed the *Blue Beetle*, when Andi came hurrying over to me.

There'd been a dozen Alphas when I'd first met them, college kids who had banded together and learned just enough magic to turn themselves into wolves. They'd spent their time as werewolves protecting and defending the town, which needed all the help it could get. The conclusion of their college educations had seen most of them move on in life, but Andi was one of the few who had stuck around.

Most of the Alphas adopted clothing that was easily discarded— the better to swiftly change into a large wolf without getting tangled up in jeans and underwear. On this particular summer evening, Andi was wearing a flirty little purple sundress and nothing else. Between her hair, her build, and her long, strong legs, Andi's picture belonged on the nose of a World War II bomber, and her hurried pace was intriguingly kinetic.

She noticed me noticing and gave me a wicked little smile and an extra jiggle the last few steps. She was the sort to appreciate being appreciated. "Harry," she said, "I know you hate to mix business with pleasure, but there's something I was hoping to talk to you about tomorrow."

"Sorry, sweetheart," I said in my best Bogey dialect. "Not tomorrow. Day off. Important things to do."

"I know," Andi said. "But I was hoping—"

"If it waited until after the Arcanos game, it can wait until after my d-day off," I said firmly.

Andi almost flinched at the tone, and nodded. "Okay."

I felt myself arch an eyebrow. I hadn't put *that* much harsh into it—and Andi wasn't exactly the sort to be fazed by verbal salvos, regardless of their nature or volume. Socially speaking, the woman was armored like a battleship.

"Okay," I replied. "I'll call." Kirby approached her as I got into the car, put an arm around her from behind, and tugged her backside against his front side, leaning down to sniff at her hair. She closed her eyes and pressed herself into him.

Yeah. I let myself feel a little smug as I pulled out of the lot and drove home. That one had just been a matter of time, despite everything Georgia had said. I totally called it.

I PULLED INTO the gravel parking lot beside the boardinghouse where I live and knew right away I had a problem. Perhaps it was my keenly developed intuition, honed by years of investigative work as the infamous Harry Dresden, Chicago's only professional wizard, shamus of the supernatural, gumshoe of the ghostly, wise guy of the weird, warning me with preternatural awareness of the shadow of Death passing nearby.

Or maybe it was the giant black van painted with flaming skulls, goat's head pentacles, and inverted crosses that was parked in front of my apartment door—six-six-six of one, half a dozen of another.

The van's doors opened as I pulled in and people in black spilled out with neither the precision of a professional team of hitters nor the calm swagger of competent thugs. They looked like I'd caught them in the middle of eating sack lunches. One of them had what looked like taco sauce spilled down the front of his frothy white lace shirt. The other four . . . Well, they looked like something.

They were all wearing mostly black, and mostly Gothware, which meant a lot of velvet with a little leather, rubber, and PVC to spice things up. Three women, two men, all of them fairly young. All of them carried wands and staves and crystals dangling from chains, and all of them had deadly serious expressions on their faces.

I parked the car, never looking directly at them, and then got out of it, stuck my hands in my duster pockets, and stood there waiting.

"You're Harry Dresden," said the tallest one there, a young man with long black hair and a matching goatee.

I squinted at nothing, like Clint Eastwood would do, and said nothing, like Chow Yun-Fat would do.

"You're the one who came to New Orleans last week." He said it, "Nawlins," even though the rest of his accent was Midwest standard. "You're the one who desecrated my works."

I blinked at him. "Whoa, wait a minute. There actually *was* a curse on that nice lady?"

He sneered at me. "She had earned my wrath."

"How about that," I said. "I figured it for some random bad feng shui."

His sneer vanished. "What?"

"To tell you the truth, it was so minor that I only did the ritual cleansing to make her feel better and show the Paranetters how to do it for themselves in the future." I shrugged. "Sorry about your wrath, there, Darth Wannabe."

He recovered his composure in seconds. "Apologies will do you no good, Wizard. Now!"

He and his posse all raised their various accoutrements, sneering malevolently. "Defend yourself!"

"Okay," I said, and pulled my .44 out of my pocket.

Darth Wannabe and his posse lost their sneers.

"Wh-what?" said one of the girls, who had a nose ring that I was pretty sure was a clip-on. "What are you doing?"

"I'm a-fixin' to defend myself," I drawled, Texas-style. I held the gun negligently, pointing down and to one side and not right at them. I didn't want to hurt anybody. "Look, kids. You really need to work on your image."

Darth opened his mouth. It just hung that way for a minute.

"I mean, the van's a bit overdone. But hell, I can't throw stones. My VW Bug has a big '53' inside a circle spray-painted on the hood. You're sort of slipping elsewhere, though." I nodded at one of the girls, a brunette holding a wand with a crystal on the tip. "Honey, I liked the *Harry Potter* movies, too, but that doesn't mean I ran out and got a Dark Mark tattooed onto my left forearm like you did." I eyed the other male. "And you're wearing a freakin' Slytherin scarf. I mean, Christ. How's anyone supposed to take *that* seriously?"

"You would dare—" Darth Wannabe began, obviously outraged.

"One more tip, kids. If you had any real talent, the air would practically have been on fire when you got ready to throw down. But you losers don't have enough magic between you to turn cereal into breakfast."

"You would dare—"

"I can tell, because I actually *am* a wizard. I went to school for this stuff."

"You would—"

"I mean, I know you guys have probably thrown your talents at other people in your weight class, had your little duels, and maybe someone got a nosebleed and someone went home with a migraine and it gave your inner megalomaniac a boner. But this is different." I nodded at one of the other girls, who had shaved her head clean. "Excuse me, miss. What time is it?"

She blinked at me. "Um. It's after one . . . ?"

"Thanks."

The Dim Lord tried for his dramatic dialogue again. "You would dare threaten us with mortal weapons?"

"It's after midnight," I told the idiot. "I'm off the clock."

That killed his momentum again. "What?"

"It's my day off, and I've got plans, so let's just skip ahead."

Darth floundered wordlessly. He was really out of his element—and he wasn't giving me anything to work with at all. If I waited around for him, this was going to take all night.

"All right, kid. You want some magic?" I pointed my gun at the van. "Howsabout I make your windows disappear."

Darth swallowed. Then he lowered his staff, a cheaply carved thing you could pick up at tourist traps in Acapulco, and said, "This is not over. We are your doom, Dresden."

"As long as you don't drag it out too much. Good night, children."

Darth sneered at me again, pulled the shreds of his dignity about him, and strode to the van. The rest of them followed him like good little darthlings. The van started up and tore away, throwing gravel spitefully into the *Blue Beetle*.

Could it sneer at them, the Beetle would have done so. Its dents had dents worse than what that van inflicted.

I spun the .44 once around my finger and put it back into my pocket. Clint Yun-Fat.

As if I didn't have enough to do without worrying about Darth Wannabe and his groupies. I went inside, greeted my pets in order of seniority—Mister, my oversized cat first, then Mouse, my undersized ankylosaurus—washed up, and went to bed.

THE MICKEY MOUSE alarm clock told me it was five in the morning when my apartment's front door opened. The door gets stuck, because a ham-handed amateur installed it, and it makes a racket when it's finally forced open. I came out of the bedroom in my underwear, with my blasting rod in one hand and my .44 in the other, ready to do battle with whatever had come a-calling.

"Hi, boss!" Molly chirped, giving my blasting rod and gun a passing glance but ignoring my almost-nudity.

I felt old.

My apprentice came in and set two Starbucks cups down on the coffee table, along with a bag that would be full of something expensive that Starbucks thought people should eat with coffee. Molly, who was young and tall and blond and built like a brick supermodel, offered me one of the cups. "You want to wake up now or would you rather I kept it warm for you?"

"Molly," I said, trying to be polite, "I can't stand the sight of you. Go away."

She held up a hand. "I know, I know, Captain Grumpypants. Your day off and your big date with Luccio."

"Yes," I said. I put as much hostility into it as I could.

Molly had been overexposed to my menace. It bounced right off her. "I just thought it would be a good time for me to work out some of the kinks on my invisibility potion. You've said I'm ready to use the lab alone."

"I said *unsupervised*. That isn't quite the same thing as alone." My glower deepened. "Much like having an apprentice puttering around the basement is not quite the same thing as being alone with Anastasia."

"You're going horseback riding," Molly said in a reasonable tone of voice. "You won't be here, and I'll be gone by the time you get back. And besides, I can make sure Mouse gets a walk or two while you're gone, so you won't have to come rushing back early. Isn't that thoughtful of me?"

Mouse's huge grey doggy head came up off the floor, and his tail twitched as she said, "Walk." He looked at me hopefully.

"Oh, for crying out—" I shook my head wearily. "Lock up behind you before you go downstairs."

She turned back to the front door and started pushing. "You got it, boss."

I staggered back to my bed to get whatever rest I could before my apprentice died in a fit of sleep-deprivation-induced psychotic mania.

FOR THE FIRST time ever, Mickey Mouse let me down.

Granted, being a wizard means that technology and I don't get along very well. Things tend to break down a lot faster in the presence of mortal magic than they would otherwise—but that's mostly electronics. My windup Mickey Mouse clock was pure springs and gears, and it had given me years and years of loyal service. It never went off, and when I woke up, Mickey was cheerfully indicating that I had less than half an hour before Anastasia was supposed to arrive.

I got up and threw myself into the shower, bringing my razor with me. I was only partway through shaving when the explosion rattled the apartment, hard enough to make a film of water droplets leap up off the shower floor.

I stumbled out, wrapped a towel around my waist, seized my blasting rod—just in case what was needed was *more* explosions—and went running into the living room. The trapdoor leading down to the lab in my subbasement was open, and pink and blue smoke was roiling up out of it in a thick, noxious plume.

"Hell's bells," I choked out, coughing. "Molly!?"

"Here," she called back through her own thick coughing. "I'm fine, I'm fine."

I opened a couple of the sunken windows, on opposite sides of the room, and the breeze began to thin out the smoke. "What about my lab?"

"I had it contained when it blew," she responded more clearly now. "Um. Just . . . just let me clean up a bit."

I eyed the trapdoor. "Molly," I said warningly.

"Don't come down!" she said, her voice near panic. "I'll have it cleaned up in a second. Okay?"

I thought about storming down there with a good hard lecture about the importance of not busting up your mentor's irreplaceable collection of gear, but I took a deep breath instead. If anything had been destroyed, the lecture wouldn't fix it. And I had only fifteen minutes to make myself look like a human being and find some way to get rid of the smell of Molly's alchemical misadventure. So I decided to go finish shaving.

Am I easygoing or what?

No sooner had I gotten bits of paper stuck to the spots on my face where I'd been in a hurry than someone began hammering on the front door.

"For crying out *loud*," I muttered. "It's my day *off.*" I stomped out to the living room and found the smoke mostly gone, if not the smell. Mouse paced along beside me on the way to the door. I unlocked it and wrenched it open, careful to open it only an inch or three, then peered outside.

Andi and Kirby crouched on the other side of my door. Both of them were dirty, haggard, and entirely covered with scratches. I could tell, because both were also entirely naked.

Kirby lowered his arm and stared warily at me. Then he let out a low growling sound, which I realized a second later had been meant to be my name. "Harry."

"You have got to be kidding me," I said. *"Today?"*

"Harry," Andi said, her eyes brimming. "Please. I don't know who else we can turn to."

"Dammit!" I snarled. "Dammit, dammit, dammit!" I wrenched the door the rest of the way open and muttered my wards down. "Come in. Hurry up, before someone sees you."

Kirby's nostrils flared as he entered, and his face twisted up in revulsion.

"Oh," Andi said as I shut the door. "That smells terrible."

"Tell me about it," I said. "You two look . . ." Well, I would have used different adjectives for Kirby than for Andi. "A little thrashed. What's up? You two get in a fight with a barbed wire golem or something?"

"N-no," Andi said. "Nothing like that. We've had . . . Kirby and I have . . . fleas."

I blinked.

Kirby nodded somber agreement and growled something unintelligible.

I checked the fireplace, which Molly had lit and which was crackling quietly. My coffeepot hung on a swinging arm near the fire, close enough to stay warm without boiling. I went to the pot and checked. She'd put my cup of expensive Starbucks elixir in there to stay warm. If I'd been preparing to murder her, that single act of compassion would have been reason enough to spare her life.

I poured the coffee into the mug Molly had left on the mantel and slugged some of it back. "Okay, okay," I said. "Start from the top. Fleas?"

"I don't know what else to call them," Andi said. "When we shift, they're there, in our fur. Biting and itching. It was just annoying at first, but now . . . it's just awful." She shuddered and began running her fingertips over her shoulders and ribs. "I can feel them right now. Chewing at me. Biting and digging into me." She shook her head and, with an almost visible effort, forced her hands to be still. "It's getting hard to th-think straight. To talk. Every time we ch-change, it gets worse."

I gulped down a bit of coffee, frowning. That *did* sound serious. I glanced down at the towel around my waist, and noted, idly, that I was the most heavily clothed person in the room. "All right, let me get dressed," I said. "I guess at least one of us should have clothes on."

Andi looked at me blankly. "What?"

"Clothes. You're naked, Andi."

She looked down at herself, and then back up at me. "Oh." A smile spread over her lips, and the angle of her hips shifted slightly and very noticeably. "Maybe you should do something about that."

Kirby looked up from where he'd settled down by the fireplace, pure murder in his eyes.

"Uh," I said, looking back and forth between them. No question about it—the kids were definitely operating under the influence of something. "I'll be right back."

I threw on some clothes, including my shield bracelet, in case the murderous look on Kirby's face got upgraded to a murderous lunge, and went back out into the living room. Kirby and Andi were both in front of the fireplace. They were . . . Well, *nuzzling* is both polite and generally accurate, even if it doesn't quite convey the blush factor the two were inspiring, I mean, they'd have been asked to leave any halfway reputable club for that kind of thing.

I lifted my hand to my eyes for a moment, concentrated, and opened up my Third Eye, my wizard's Sight. That was always a dicey move. The Sight showed you what truly was, all the patterns of magic and life that existed in the universe, as they truly were—but you got them in permanent ink. You didn't ever get to forget what you saw, no matter how bad it was. Still, if something was chewing up my friends, I needed to know about it. They were worth the risk.

I opened my eyes and immediately saw the thick bands of power that I'd laid into the very walls of my apartment when I'd built up its magical defenses. Further layers of power surrounded my lab in a second shell of insulating magic, beneath my feet. From his perch atop one of my bookshelves, Mister, the cat, appeared exactly as he always did, evidently beyond the reach of such petty concerns as the mere forces that created the universe, though my dog, Mouse, was surrounded by a calm, steady aurora of silver and blue light.

More to the point, Kirby and Andi were both engulfed in a number of different shimmering energies—the flame-colored tinges of lust and passion foremost among them, for obvious reason, but those weren't the only energies at play. Greenish energy that struck me as something primal and wild, that essence of the instinct of the wolf they'd been taught by the genuine article, maybe, remained strong all around them, as did an undercurrent of pink-purple fear. Whatever was happening to them, it was scaring the hell out of both of them, even if they weren't able to do anything about it, at the moment.

The golden lightning of a practitioner at work also flickered through their auras—which shouldn't have been happening. Oh, the Alphas all had a lot more talent than Darth Wannabe and his playmates. That went without saying. But they had become extremely focused upon a single use of their magic—shapeshifting into a wolf, which is a *lot* more complicated and difficult and useful than it looks or sounds. But that kind of activity should only have been working if they were actually in the process of changing shape—and they weren't.

I stepped closer, peering intently, and saw something I rather wouldn't have.

Creatures clung to both of them—tiny, tiny things, dozens of them. To my Sight, they looked something like tiny crabs, hard-shelled little things with oversized pincers that ripped and tore into their spiritual flesh—tearing out tiny pieces that each contained a single glowing mote of both green and gold energy.

"Ah!" I said. "Aha! You've got psychophagic mites!"

Andi and Kirby both jumped in shock. I guess they hadn't noticed me coming closer, being fully occupied with . . . Oh, wow. They'd sort of segued into NC-17 activities.

"Wh-what?" Andi managed to say.

"Psychophagic . . ." I shook my head, dismissing my Sight with an effort of will. "Psychic parasites. They've latched onto you from the Nevernever. They're exerting an influence on you both, pushing you to indulge your, um, more basic and primitive behavior patterns, and feeding on the energy of them."

Andi dragged lust-glazed eyes from Kirby to me. "Primitive . . . ?"

"Yeah," I said. I nodded to them. "Hence the two of you, um. And I imagine they make you want to change form."

Andi's eyelids fluttered. "Yes. Yes, that sounds lovely." She shook her head slightly and came to her feet, her eyes suddenly glimmering with tears. "Is it . . . Can you make them go away?"

I put a reassuring hand on her shoulder. "I can't figure out how they would have gotten there in the first place. I mean, these things are only attracted to very specific kinds of energy. And you'd only be vulnerable to them when you were actually drawing upon the matter of the Nevernever—when you were shifted. And"—I blinked and then rubbed at my forehead—"Andi. Please don't tell me that you and Kirby have been getting down while you were fuzzy."

The bombshell blushed, from the roots of her hair to the tips of her . . . toes.

"God, that's just . . . so wrong." I shook my head. "But to answer your question, yes, I think that—"

"Harry?" Molly called from the lab. "Um. Do you have a fire extinguisher?"

"*What!?*"

"I mean, if I needed one!" she amended, her voice quavering. "Hypothetically speaking!"

"Hypothetically speaking?" I half shouted. "Molly! Did you set my lab on fire?!"

Andi, a distracted expression on her face, idly lifted my hand from her shoulder and slid my index finger between her lips, suckling gently. A pleasant flicker of lightning shot up my arm, and I felt it all the way to the bottoms of my feet.

"Oh, hey, ho-ho-ho! Hold on there," I said, pulling my finger away.

It came out of her mouth with another intriguing sensation and a soft popping sound. "Andi. Ahem. We really need to focus, here."

Kirby let out a raw snarl and hit me with a right cross that sent me tumbling back across the room and into one of my bookshelves. I rebounded off it, fell on my ass, and sat there stunned for a second as copies of the Black Company novels fell from the shelf and bounced off my head.

I looked up to see Kirby seize Andi by the wrist and jerk her back behind him, placing his body between her and me in a gesture of raw possession. Then he balled up his hands into fists, snarled, and took a step toward me.

Mouse loomed up beside me then, two hundred pounds of shaggy grey muscle. He didn't growl at Kirby, or so much as bare his teeth. He did, however, stand directly in Kirby's path and face him without backing down.

Without blinking, Kirby's body seemed to shimmer and flow, and suddenly a black wolf nearly Mouse's size, but leaner and swifter looking, crouched across the apartment, white teeth bared, amber eyes glowing with rage.

Holy crap. Kirby was about half a second from losing it, and he had the skill and experience to cause some real mayhem. I mean, taking on an animal is one thing. Taking on an animal directed by a human intelligence with years of experience in battling the supernatural is a challenge at least an order of magnitude greater. If it came down to a fight, a real fight, between me and Kirby, I was sure I could beat him, but to do it I'd have to hit him fast and hard, without pulling any punches.

I was not at all confident that I could beat him without killing him.

"Kirby," I said, trying to keep my voice as low and steady as I could. "Kirby, man, think about this for a minute. It's Harry. Listen, man, this is Harry, and you've just blown your willpower check, like, completely. You need to take a deep breath and get some perspective here. You're my friend, you're under the influence, and I'm trying to help you."

"Harry?" Molly called out, her voice higher-pitched than ever. "Acid doesn't eat through concrete, right?"

I blinked at the trapdoor and screamed in frustration, "Hell's bells, what are you *doing* down there?!"

Kirby took another pace forward, wolf eyes bright, jaws slavering, head held low and ready for a fight. Behind him, Andi was watching the whole thing with a wide-eyed look that mixed terror, lust, excitement, and rage in equal parts, her impressive chest heaving. Her hands and lower arms had already begun to slowly change, sprouting curling russet fur, her nails lengthening into dark claws. Her eyes traveled to me and her mouth dropped open, revealing fangs that were already beginning to grow.

Super. In a fight against Kirby, I was worried about him not surviving. Against Kirby *and* Andi, in these quarters, it would be *me* who was running against long odds.

But I try to be an optimist: At least things weren't going to get any worse.

Above and behind me, a window broke.

A length of lead pipe, maybe a foot long, capped at both ends with plastic, landed on a rug five feet away from me. Cheap, Mardi Gras–style beads were wrapped around it.

A lit fuse sparked and fizzed at one end of the pipe.

It was maybe half an inch away from vanishing into the cap.

"But this is my day *off*!" I howled.

I know things looked bad. But I honestly think I could have handled it if Mister hadn't picked that exact moment to leap down from his perch and go streaking across the room, acting upon some feline imperative unknown and unknowable to mere mortals.

Kirby, already on the edge of a feral frenzy, did what any canine would do—he let out a snarl and gave immediate chase.

Mouse let out a sudden bellow of rage—for crying out loud, he hadn't gotten that worked up over *me* being in danger—and launched himself after Kirby. Andi, upon seeing Mouse in pursuit of her fellow werewolf, shifted entirely to her own wolf shape and flung herself after Mouse.

Mister rocketed around my tiny apartment, with several hundred pounds of furious canine in pursuit. Kirby bounded over and around furniture almost as nimbly as Mister. Mouse didn't bother with nimble. He simply plowed through whatever was in the way, smashing my coffee table and one easy chair, knocking over another bookcase, and churning the throw rugs on the floor into hummocks of fabric and fiber.

I leapt for the pipe bomb and picked it up, only to have my legs scythed out from beneath me by Kirby as he went by. Mouse accidently slammed a paw bearing his full weight down onto me as he rumbled past in pursuit, and got me right where the damn dog always gets a man. There was none of that delayed-reaction component to the pain, either. My testicles began reporting the damage instantly, loudly, and in nauseating intensity.

I had no time for pain. I lunged for the pipe bomb and nearly wet my pants as another explosion shook the floor—only this one was followed an instant later by an absolute flood of bright green smoke that billowed up from the lab.

I grabbed the pipe bomb and tried to pluck out the fuse, but it vanished into the cap and beyond the reach of my fingers. In a panic, I scrabbled across the floor to the door and ripped it open with terrified strength. I hauled back to throw the thing out and—

There was a sharp burst of sound.

My hand exploded into pins and needles.

I fell limply to the floor, my head falling in such a way as to bring my gaze over to where my hand had been clutching the pipe bomb a few seconds before and—

And I was still holding it now, unharmed. Heavy jets of scarlet and purple smoke were billowing wildly from both ends of the pipe, scented heavily with a familiar odor.

Smoke bombs.

The freaking thing had been loaded with something remarkably similar to Fourth of July smoke bombs, the kind kids play with. Bemused, I tugged one plastic cap off, and several little expended canisters fell out along with a note: *The next time you interfere with me, more than smoke will interfere with you.*

More than smoke will interfere with you?

Who *talks* like that?

Mouse roared, snapping my focus back to the here and now, as he pounced onto Kirby's back, smashing the werewolf to the floor by dint of sheer mass. Mister, sensing his opening, shot out the front door with a yowl of disapproval and vanished into the outdoors, seeking a safer environment, like maybe traffic.

Andi leapt onto Mouse's back, fangs ripping, but my dog held fast to Kirby—buying me a couple of precious seconds. I seized a bit of chalk from the basket by the door and, choking on smoke, ran in a circle around the embattled trio, drawing a line of chalk on the concrete floor. Then I willed the circle closed, and the magical construct snapped into existence, a silent and invisible field of energy that, among other things, completely severed the connection between the psychic parasites in the Nevernever and the werewolves whaling on my dog.

The fight stopped abruptly. Kirby and Andi both blinked their eyes several times and hurriedly removed their fangs from Mouse's hide. A few seconds later, they shimmered and resumed their human forms.

"Don't move!" I snapped at them, infuriated to no end. "Any of you! Don't break the circle or you'll go nuts again! Sit! Stay!"

That last was for Mouse.

Mostly.

I couldn't see what Molly had done to my lab, but the fumes down there were cloying and obviously dangerous. I hauled myself over to the trapdoor.

Molly hadn't made it up the folding staircase and just lay sprawled semiconscious against it. I had to grab her and haul her up the stairs. She was undressed from the waist up. I spotted her shirt and bra on the floor near the worktable, both of them riddled with acid-burned holes.

I got her laid out on her back, elevated her feet on a stray cushion from the smashed easy chair, and checked her breathing. It didn't take long, because she wasn't, though she did still have a faint pulse. I started rescue breathing for her—which is a *lot* more demanding than people think. Especially when the air is still thick with the smell of God only knows what chemical combinations.

I finally got her to cough, and my racing heartbeat subsided a little as she began breathing again, raggedly, and opened her eyes.

I sat up slowly, breathing hard, and found Anastasia Luccio standing in the open doorway to my apartment, her arms folded over her chest, one eyebrow arched.

Anastasia was a pretty girl—not glamorously lovely, but believably, genuinely pleasant to look at, with a fantastic smile and killer dimples. She looked like someone in her twenties, for reasons too complex to go into right now, but she was an older woman. A much older woman.

And there I was, apparently sitting up from kissing a topless girl, with a naked couple a few feet away, and the air thick with a pall of smoke and the smell of noxious fumes. For crying out loud, my apartment looked like the set of some kind of bizarre porno.

"Um," I said, and swallowed. "This isn't what it might appear to be."

Anastasia just stared at me. I knew it had been a long time since she'd opened up to anyone. It might not take much to make her close herself off again.

She shook her head, very slowly, and the smile lines at the corners of her eyes deepened along with her dimples. Then she burst out into a hearty belly laugh. "*Madre di Dio*, Harry. I cannot for the life of me imagine what it *does* appear to be."

I lifted my eyebrows in surprise. "You aren't upset?"

"By the time you get to be my age," she replied, "you've either worked out your insecurities, or they're there to stay. Besides, I simply *must* know how *this* happened."

I shook my head and then smiled at her. "I . . . My friends needed help."

She looked back and forth between the Alphas and Molly. "And still do," she said, nodding sharply. She came in and, as the only one actually wearing shoes, began picking up pieces of fallen glass from the broken window, literally rolling up her sleeves as she went. "Shall we?"

IT TOOK MOST of the day to get Molly to the hospital, gather the materials needed to fumigate Kirby's and Andi's auras, and actually perform the work to get the job done. By the time they left, all better and psychophage-free, it was after seven.

"So much for our day off," I said.

She turned to consider me. "Would you do it differently if you had it to do again?"

"No. Of course not."

She shrugged. "Then it was a day well spent. There will be others."

"You never can be sure of that, though, can you?"

Her cheeks dimpled again. "Today is not yet over. You mourn its death somewhat prematurely."

"I just wanted to show you a nice time for a day. Not get bogged down in more business."

Anastasia turned to me and put her fingers over my mouth. Then she replaced her fingers with her lips.

"Enough talk," she murmured.

I agreed.

BACKUP

—novelette from Subterranean Press

Takes place between *Small Favor*
and *Turn Coat*

This story was really fun to write. I'd been wanting to show a little more of Thomas and his world for several years, but it just hadn't ever been a feasible thing for Harry to encounter. The vampires of the Dresden Files, the White Court especially, see themselves as a nation of outcasts, banded together by similar concerns and dangerous enemies. The kind of culture that emerges from that sort of foundation simply doesn't make itself available to outsiders. If Harry had ever gotten to the "inside" to see that culture, it would have betrayed the us-against-them integrity of the White Court, and invalidated the whole setup.

So when Subterranean came to me with a proposal to produce a novelette illustrated by no less than Mike Mignola, I jumped at the chance. The challenge, here, was to present Thomas from his own viewpoint, one distinct from Harry's. And, even better, I wanted to pit brother against brother in such a way that their relationship of trust and mutual regard was maintained, but they still got to slug it out with each other.

I also got to bring some of the other background material of the Dresden Files story world into play. The Oblivion War was something I really loved, conceptually, but like the White Court, its very nature prevented Dresden from getting involved without causing the entire thing to implode. This was an ideal place for that piece of universe background, and it made me feel all warm and fuzzy to finally get it out where the readers could see it, too.

1

Let's get something clear right up front.

I'm not Harry Dresden.

Harry's a wizard. A genuine, honest-to-goodness wizard. He's Gandalf on crack and an IV of Red Bull, with a big leather coat and a .44 revolver in his pocket. He'll spit in the cye of gods and demons alike if he thinks it needs to be done, and to hell with the consequences—and yet somehow my little brother manages to remain a decent human being.

I'll be damned if I know how.

But then, I'll be damned regardless.

My name is Thomas Raith, and I'm a monster.

The computer in my little office clamored for my attention. I've got it set up to play Nazi Germany's national anthem whenever I receive e-mail from someone in my family. Not Harry, my half brother, naturally. Harry and e-mail go together like Robert Downey, Jr., and sobriety. I mean the other side of my family.

The monsters.

I finished cleaning off the workstation and checked the clock—five minutes until my next appointment. I took a quick look around my boutique, smiled at one of my regular customers, playfully scolded the young stylist working on her, and went back down the hall, around the corner, down the narrow stairwell, and then through ten feet of claustrophobic hallway to get to my office. I sat down at the desk and nudged my laptop to life. The virus scanner pored over the e-mail before it chimed again, a soft sound that a human wouldn't have heard from the end of the hall, much less from upstairs, and pronounced it safe.

The e-mail from admin@whitecourt.com was empty, but the subject line read, *Re: Ob.ll.vl.On*.

Oh.

Super.

Just what I needed.

I never really enjoyed hearing from that side of the family, even when the subject was something boring—like business pertaining to the war between the Vampire Courts and the wizards' White Council, for example. Whenever Lara wanted to get in touch with me, for any reason, it was bad news.

But when it was about an Oblivion matter, it was worse.

I had Lara's number on the speed dial on my cell phone. I gave her a ring.

"Brother-mine," purred my eldest sister, her voice pure honey. It was the kind of voice that would give men ideas—really bad ideas, though they'd never realize that part. "You hardly ever call me anymore."

"I've hardly ever called you, Lara. Period." I ignored the lure she was sliding into her voice. She'd fed very recently—or was doing so at the moment. "What do you want?"

"You received my e-mail?"

"Yes."

"There's a project I think you'll be interested in."

"Why?"

"Take a look at it," she said. "You'll understand."

The line was supposedly secure, but we both knew how much that was worth. Neither of us would mention any details over the phone—

and we certainly would not use the word *oblivion*. Too many Venatori had discovered, too late, that the enemy had very sharp ears, and that they would swiftly carry the war into the homes of those careless enough not to guard their tongues.

It had been nearly eight years since I had been involved in the Oblivion War. I suppose I had known I couldn't avoid being drawn back into the fight forever. Lara, the only other Venator in the White Court, was largely occupied with her current responsibilities—namely, spending her days manipulating our father like a puppet on her psychic strings and ruling the White Court from the shadows behind his throne. Naturally, if something came up, she would pass it along to me to deal with.

"I'm busy," I told her.

"Grooming pets?" she said. "Trimming their fur? Checking for fleas? Priorities, brother-mine."

Lara is most annoying when she has a point. "Where do you want to meet?"

She laughed, a warm little sound. "Tommy, Tommy, I'm flattered you want to be with me, but no. I've no time to spend playing games with you. I've sent a courier with everything you need and . . . Mmmmmm." Her voice turned into a sensual little purr of pleasure. "You know the stakes. Don't ask too many questions, brother-mine," she murmured. "Don't start using that pretty little head for anything taxing. Go back to your apartment. Talk to the courier. Take the job. Or you and I are going to have a very . . . ahhhhh . . ." Her breathing sped up. "A very serious falling-out."

I could hear other soft sounds in the background, and another voice. A woman. Maybe two. Most of my family isn't what you'd call particular, when it comes to feeding on mortals.

"I'd tell you that you were a much nicer person before you got into the power-behind-the-throne game, Lara," I said. "But you were a bitch then, too."

I hung up on her before she had a chance to reply and went back upstairs, thinking. It was always good to get as much thinking done as you could, before the actual mind-boggling crisis came down. That way, when it got there and you only had half a second to decide what to do before something from beyond the borders of sanity started ripping at your soul, you could skip the preliminaries and go straight to the mistake.

When you deal with someone like my sister, you never take anything at face value. She was up to something. Whatever it was, it included putting pressure on me to hurry. Lara wanted me to rush into the situation blindly. If that was what she wanted me to do, it was probably a good idea not to do it.

Besides, I didn't want Lara to start getting used to the idea that I would run to do her bidding every time she snapped her fingers. More important, I didn't want to get into the habit of obeying her. It was an important first step toward becoming ensnared by more inflexible means, the way she had done to our father.

Anyway, I had a business to run.

And I was hungry.

Michelle Marion, eldest daughter of the Honorable Senator Marion of the Great State of Illinois, had arrived a minute or two early for her haircut. My clients almost always did—especially the young ones. Michelle was a brunette, though you couldn't tell that by looking. Only her hairdresser knew for sure.

"Thomas!" she exclaimed, smiling at me, pronouncing it with the Latin emphasis. "What have you done with your hair?"

I had cut it a bit shorter after getting a rather large section of it burned off by a flaming arrow fired by a faerie assassin—but that isn't the sort of thing you share with your customers when you're supposed to be a flaming French master stylist. "Darling," I said, taking her hands and kissing her on either cheek.

The Hunger inside me stirred as my skin touched hers. The demon gleefully danced through her for a heartbeat or two, and as it did, she shivered, her heart rate rose, and her pupils dilated. The Hunger told me what it always did about Michelle. Though she looked sweet, gentle, and kind, her repressed desires, far darker, would make her easy prey. Fingers tightening in the back of her hair, feeling a man's body press hers against a wall—that was the stuff of her fantasies. She would follow me to the hall downstairs without hesitation. I could take her there. I could fulfill her desires, feed the Hunger, draw away her life, and take my fill. I could leave my mark ripped into her mind and soul so that forever after she would come to me willingly, eagerly, yearning to be taken again and again and agai—

Until she died.

I pushed the Hunger back down into the corruption that passes for my soul, and I smiled at Michelle, slipping on the accent as easily as an Italian leather glove. "I grew bored, so tediously bored, darling. I had half decided to shave it all, just to shock everyone."

The girl laughed, her cheeks still flushed with excitement, in the wake of my demon's touch. "Don't you dare!"

"Have no fear," I assured her, tucking her arm through mine and walking her to my station. "The men who prefer such things aren't really my type in any case."

She laughed again, and I kept up the inane chatter until I could lean her chair back to the sink and begin washing her hair.

The Hunger lunged forward, eager as always—and I let it begin to feed upon the girl.

Michelle's eyes glazed over slightly as I went through the wash—very slowly, very thoroughly, working a full-scalp massage into the process. I felt her mind slip into idle fantasy as the thin warmth of her aura pooled around my fingertips and slid up into me.

The Hunger screamed for me to do more, to take more, that it wasn't *enough*. But I didn't. Feeding would have been . . . delicious. But it might have hurt her, too. It might even have killed her. So I kept on with the steady, gentle circular motions, barely tasting of her life force. She sighed in bliss as her fantasies dissolved into a gentle euphoria, and I shuddered with the need to give in to my Hunger and take more.

Some days, it was more difficult than others to hold back. But it's what I do. It's what I have left.

Michelle left about an hour later, hair trimmed, color retouched, blissfully relaxed, flushed, happy, and humming to herself under her breath. I watched her go, and my Hunger snarled and paced about restlessly in the cage I'd built for it in my thoughts, furious that the prey had escaped. For just a second, I found myself turning toward her, my weight shifting as if to take a step forward, to follow her to someplace quiet and—

I turned away and went back to my station, beginning the routine of cleaning. Not today. One day, doubtless, the Hunger would gain the upper hand again, and feed and feed until it was the only thing inside and there was nothing left of me.

But not today.

2

I left the store in the good hands of my employees and went out to my car, a white Hummer, huge, expensive, and ostentatious as hell. It was also one of the more robust vehicles a civilian could buy. Entire sections of houses could fall on it without causing it more than minor inconvenience, as could giant demon insects, and before you ask, I know it from experience. Just as I know that having a really tough vehicle on hand is not at all a bad move when you've made the kinds of enemies I have—which is to say, all of my own and pretty much all of my little brother's to boot.

Before I got in, I checked the engine, the undercarriage, and the interior for explosives. One reason Lara might have wanted me to hurry out might have been to make me rush out to the car, turn the ignition key, and blow tiny pieces of me all over Chicago.

I pulled up a mix list on the truck's MP3 player—Cole Porter and Mozart, mostly, with a dash of Violent Femmes—and headed back home to my apartment, hoping that whatever Lara had in mind for me, it wouldn't send me running to all corners of the earth . . . again. Even though our breed of vampire doesn't share the others' weaknesses for sunlight and running water and so on, the kinds of places Oblivion missions had taken me hadn't exactly been tourist attractions.

I live in a trendy, expensive apartment building in Chicago's Gold Coast. It's not exactly to my taste, but it's the sort of place where Toemoss the French stylist would live. One thing you learn young when you're a vampire is how to camouflage yourself, and to do that you have to sell every aspect of the disguise. It's a high-security building, but Lara's courier would be waiting for me in my apartment despite that. My sister had the resources to get it done.

Before I got out of the truck, I reached under the seat and slipped the sheathed kukri knife there into my coat, then tucked the barrel of my Desert Eagle into the waist of my leather pants, in back, hiding the grip under my coat. It had occurred to me, ten minutes into Michelle's appointment, that telling me to expect a courier in my apartment would be an excellent way to get me to lower my guard against an assassin who lurked inside, waiting for my return.

I went up to my apartment, took the knife in my teeth, and drew the gun, holding it low, the barrel parallel to my leg. Then I stood as far to the left of the door as I could, unlocked it, and pushed it open. No one opened fire. I waited a moment more, just being quiet and listening, and picked out two things—the low throb of an excited heartbeat, and the scent of her shampoo.

Her shampoo.

I came through the door in a rush, discarding the weapons, and Justine met me on the other side. She threw her arms around me, and I had to fight to remember that if I didn't restrain my strength, I might hurt her as I hugged her back. She just pressed against me, everywhere, as if she wanted to just push herself inside me. She let out a soft little sob of laughter and pressed her face into my shirt.

She felt so good; soft and warm and alive.

We just stood there, holding each other for a long time.

My body surged with need, and an instant later, my Hunger howled in frenzied lust.

Justine. Our doe, our bottle of wine, ours, ours, ours. So many nights with her screaming under us, so many soft sighs, so many touches—so much rich, warm, madness-laced life rushing into us.

I ignored the demon—but while blocking it away, I moved my hand without really thinking about it, and I stroked it over her hair.

Pain, pain so unreal, so unimaginably intense that I could not adequately describe it, surged up my arm, as if the softness of those hairs had been the touch of high-power electrical cables. I hissed, my arm jerking away by pure reflex.

Sunlight, holy water, garlic, and crosses don't bother an incubus of the White Court much. But the touch of someone who truly loves and is loved in return is a different story.

I glanced at my hand. It was already blistering.

Justine drew away from me, her lovely face distressed. "I'm sorry," she said. "I'm sorry. I didn't think."

I shook my head. "It's all right," I said quietly, and stepped back from her, while the demon screamed its frustration behind my eyes.

She bit her lip and looked up at me uncertainly.

It had been a long time since I had seen Justine face-to-face. I had forgotten how beautiful she was. The lines of her face had changed, subtly. She looked leaner now, more confident, more assured. Maybe I was too used to dealing with things that were immortal, or practically so. It's easy to forget how much difference a couple of years can make.

Her dark hair, of course, was gone now. It was growing in just as rich, long, and curling as before, but now it was silver-white. I'd done that to her—fed on her, drained her to the very edge of death, almost torn the life from her body in my eagerness to sate the Hunger.

I closed my eyes for a moment at the memory of that pleasure, and shivered. I'd nearly killed the woman I loved, and remembering it was nearly as arousing as her touch had been. When I opened my eyes again, Justine's gaze was steady and calm—and knowing.

"It doesn't make you a monster to want," she said, her voice very gentle. "It's what you do with the want that matters."

Instead of answering her, I turned and shut the door, then picked up my hardware. It isn't gentlemanly to leave weapons lying around on the floor. They clashed with the apartment's décor, too. I studied Justine from the corner of my eye as I did, taking in her clothing—elegant business-wear, suitable for Lara's executive assistant.

Or for a corporate courier.

"Empty night," I swore, viciously, suddenly furious.

Justine blinked at me. "What is it?"

"Lara," I spat. "What did she tell you?"

Justine shook her head slowly, frowning at me, as though trying to read my thoughts from my expression. "She said to bring you a briefing on a situation you needed to know about. Nothing could be written down. I had to memorize it all and bring it to you, along with some photos, here." She put a slender hand on a valise that sat on my coffee table.

I stared at her intently. Then I sat slowly down on one of the chairs in my apartment's living room. It wasn't a comfortable chair, but it was very, very expensive. "I need you to tell me everything she told you," I said. "Absolutely every word."

Justine stared back for a long moment, her frown deepening. "Why?"

Because *knowing* certain things, simply being *aware* of them, was dangerous. Because Justine had been providing me with information from within Lara's operation, and which I had, in turn, been providing to Harry, and through him to the White Council. If Lara had found out about that, she might have brought Justine into the Oblivion War. If she had, I was going to kill my sister.

"I need you to trust me, love," I said quietly. "But I can't tell you."

"But *why* can't you tell me?"

The real bitch about the Oblivion War was that question.

"Justine," I said, spreading my hands. "Please. Trust me."

Justine narrowed her eyes in wary thought, which took me somewhat aback. It was not an expression I was used to seeing on her face.

No. I was used to seeing a look of dazed satiation after I'd fed, or of molten desire as I stalked her, or of shattering ecstasy as I took her—

I closed my eyes, took a deep breath, and shoved my demon down again.

"My poor Thomas," she said quietly, when I opened them again. She sat down across the table from me, her dark eyes compassionate. "When we were together, I never realized how hard it was for you. Your demon is much stronger than theirs. Stronger than any but hers, isn't it."

"It only matters if I give in to it," I replied, more harshly than I meant to. "Which means it doesn't matter. Tell me, Justine. Please."

She folded her arms across her body, biting on her bottom lip. "It really isn't much. She said to tell you that word had come to her through the usual channels that the Ladies of the Dark River were in town." She opened the valise. "And that you would know which one you were dealing with." She took out a full-page photo, and slid it across the table to me. It was grainy, but big enough to clearly show an image of a stark-featured, young-looking woman getting into a cab at O'Hare. The time stamp on the photo said it was from that morning.

"Yes," I said quietly. "I know her. I thought she was dead."

"Lara said that this person had taken a child," Justine continued. "Though she didn't say how she knew that. And that her aim was to draw out one who could do her cause great good."

I got a sick feeling in my stomach as Justine slid out the second photograph and pushed it across the table.

The photograph was simple, this time—a hallway, a picture of a door, its top half of frosted glass, bearing simple black lettering:

HARRY DRESDEN, WIZARD.

The door was closed, but I could see the outline of a tall, feminine form, facing an even taller, storkish, masculine outline.

The time stamp said it was barely two hours before.

So.

Lara had been trying to do me a favor, after all. She had protected Justine behind a layer of generalities. And I had dithered around cutting hair and indulging my Hunger and my suspicions, while the Stygian Sisterhood had suckered my brother into a ploy to bring back one of their monstrous matrons.

Justine had never been stupid. Even when she'd been deep in my influence, before, she'd walked into it with her eyes open. "He's in trouble, isn't he?"

"And he doesn't even know it yet," I said quietly.

She pursed her lips in thought. "And you can't tell him why, can you? Any more than you could tell me."

I looked up at her helplessly.

"What are you going to do?" she asked.

I rose and reclaimed my knife and gun. "He's my brother," I said. "I'm going to cover his back."

"How are you going to explain it to him?" she asked.

I tugged on a pair of leather gloves and went to her, so I could take her hands in mine, squeezing gently, before I turned to go.

"If he thinks he's helping her, and you interfere, he's not going to understand," she said. "How are you going to explain it to him, Thomas?"

It sucks to be a Venator.

"I'm not," I said quietly.

Then I and my demon went out to continue an ages-old silent war and help my brother.

I just hoped the two activities wouldn't be mutually exclusive.

3

Justine had a driver circling the block, waiting for her to call. She did. I walked her to the elevator, holding her hand in my gloved fingers, the whole way. We didn't speak again. She smiled at me, though, when the elevator arrived, and kissed my fingers through the glove.

Then she was gone.

Technically, there was always a huge empty place inside me—that was what the Hunger was, after all.

So I told myself that this wasn't any different, and I went back to my apartment to get to work.

Purely for form, I tried Harry's home and office phones before I left my apartment, but I got no answer at his apartment, and only his answering service at his office. I left a message that I needed to talk to him, but I doubted he would get it in time for it to be of any help. I grimaced as I took my cell phone out of my pocket and left it on my kitchen counter. There wasn't any point in carrying it with me. Technology doesn't get along well with magic. Twenty or thirty minutes in Harry's company could kill a cell phone if he was in a bad mood—less if he was actively throwing spells around.

My own remedial skills weren't any particular threat to the phone, but once I brought up the tracking spell I'd need to find my brother, my reception would go straight to hell, anyway.

Harry waxes poetic about magic. He'll go on and on about how it comes from your feelings, and how it's a deep statement about the nature of your soul, and then he'll whip out some kind of half-divine, half-insane philosophy he's cobbled together from the words of saints and comic books about the importance of handling power responsibly. Get him rolling, and he'll go on and on and on.

For someone on Harry's level, maybe it's relevant. For the rest of us, here's what you need to know about magic: It's a skill. Anyone can learn it to one degree or another. Not very many people can be *good* at it. It takes a lot of practice and patience, it makes you tired, leaves you with headaches and muscle cramps, and everyone and their dog has an opinion about the "correct" way to do it.

Harry's a master of the skill—as in simultaneous doctorates from MIT, Harvard, and Yale, and a master's from Oxford. By comparison, I went to a six-month vo-tech—which means I skipped a bunch of the flowery crap and focused on learning some useful things that work.

It took me a couple of minutes longer than it would have taken him, but I used the silver pentacle amulet my mother had given me for my fifth birthday to create a link to Harry's amulet, a battered twin to mine.

Early springtime in Chicago can come at you with a psychotic array of weather. This spring had been pleasantly mild, and by the time I'd used the tracking spell to catch up to my little brother, the day had faded into a pleasantly brisk evening.

I held the silver amulet in my right hand, its chain wrapped around my knuckles, four or five inches above the pendant left dangling. The pendant swung steadily, back and forth in one direction, no matter which way I turned, as if it had been guided by a tiny gyroscope. I'd paid a small fortune to park the Hummer—money well spent. Now I followed the swing of the pendant, and the spell guiding it, across the grounds of Millennium Park.

Millennium Park is something fairly rare—a genuinely beautiful park in the middle of a large city. Granted, the buildings spaced around the grounds look like something inspired by an Escher painting and a period of liberal chemical experimentation in an architect's underclassman years, but even they have their own kind of madman's charm. Even though night was coming on, the park was fairly busy. The skating rink stayed open until ten every night, and it would only stay open for a few more days before it would shut down until the seasons turned again. Kids and parents skated around the rink. Couples strolled together. Uniformed police officers patrolled in plain sight nearby, making sure the good people of Chicago were kept safe from predators.

I spotted Harry stalking along the side of the skating rink, walking away from me. He was head and shoulders taller than most of the people around him, professional-basketball-player tall, and rather forebidding in his big black duster. His head was down, his attention on something he was holding in his hands—probably a tracking spell of his own. I hurried across the distance to the skating rink to begin shadowing him.

I realized I was being followed about twenty seconds later.

Whoever they were, the Stygian hadn't told them they were dealing with a vampire. They hadn't stayed downwind, and a stray breeze had brought in the aromas of a couple of dozen humans who were nearby, the reek of a couple of trash cans, the scents of several nearby food vendors selling various temptations from their carts—and the distinct, rotten-meat and stale-sweat stench (badly hidden under generous splashes of Axe) of two ghouls.

That wasn't good. Like me, ghouls can pass for human. They're the cheap muscle-for-hire of the supernatural world. Doubtless, the Stygian had hired them on against the possibility of interference from the Venatori.

One ghoul I could handle, no problem. Though they were tough to kill, strong, fast, and vicious as the day is long, that's nothing I haven't slaughtered before. Two of them, though, changed the picture. It meant that if they had any brains going for them at all, they could make it very difficult, if not impossible, for me to take them out without being incapacitated myself.

True, hired thugs generally weren't known for their brains, but it wasn't a good time to start making assumptions about the opposition. I quickened my pace, attempting to catch up with Harry, and pretended I hadn't noticed the ghouls.

Harry turned aside and hurried across the park grounds toward the Pavilion. It was an enormous structure, which I always thought looked something like a medieval Mongol's war helmet. Giant Attila chapeau, turned into a building, where concerts were held on a regular basis for the good people of Chicago. Tonight, though, the Pavilion was dark and empty. It should have been locked up—and probably was. Locks, though, never seemed to pose much of an obstacle to my brother. He went to a door on the side of the stage building of the Pavilion and opened it, vanishing inside.

I hurried after him and called out his name. I was still a good fifty yards away, though, and he didn't hear me.

The ghouls did, though. I heard one of them snarl something to the other, and their footsteps quickened to a run.

I ran faster. I beat them to the door, and my demon and I shut it behind me, hard—hard enough to warp the metal door in its metal frame.

"Harry!" I shouted. "Harry, we need to talk!"

The ghouls hit the door and tried to open it. They didn't have much luck on the first try, but they settled in to wrench it open. The door was only metal. It wouldn't hold them out for long.

The interior of the building was empty and completely unlit, except for the faintest greenish radiance, which came through dimly, as though reflecting from many other interior surfaces, several rooms away. My demon had no trouble seeing through it, and I went through the halls in silent haste, following the faint light source toward its origin.

One of the ghouls ripped the door off its hinges, the metal shrieking behind me. One of the ghouls bounded through, snarling, the pitch and tenor of its voice changing as it came. It was changing form, growing less human and more dangerous as it ran down its prey.

I rounded a corner and ran toward a tall figure in a dark coat at the end of a hall, lit by a green luminescence—and realized within a few steps that the figure my tracking spell had taken me after was not my brother.

I drew the Desert Eagle from under my coat and opened fire. The form crouched, lifting an arm, and bullets bounced off something and began skittering around the concrete of the hallway. A magical defense—the Stygian. A hand lifted, and a sphere of light flashed toward me. I dove under it, but the incoming spell matched my movement and fell to meet me.

There was a flash of brighter light, and an instant of heat that I expected to become agony. Instead, there was just a whirl of confusing dizziness, and then I was back on my feet—just as the first ghoul, its arms now half again as long as they were, and ending in grotesque claws, its face distended into a gaping, fanged muzzle, rounded the corner and leapt at me.

I'd brought the kukri. It's a weapon that's served the Gurkhas well for a couple of centuries, and with good reason. The bent-bladed knife, the size of a small sword, carries a tremendous amount of striking power along its inner edge when wielded properly, enough to strike limbs and heads from bodies, even when used by relatively small and less powerful mortals.

In the hands of a vampire, it's the kind of thing that Jabberwocks get twitchy about.

The first ghoul led with a claw that was fast, but not fast enough. I left it on the floor of the hallway, hamstrung it on the back-stroke, and emptied the Desert Eagle into its back as it tried to flee, shattering its spine. It's one of a couple of ways to put a ghoul down fast and for keeps.

The second ghoul came at me a breath later, and hesitated for maybe a quarter of a second upon seeing what was left of the first ghoul. That isn't a long time in human terms. When you play in my league, the ghoul might as well have put a bullet through its own head. It would have amounted to the same thing.

I threw the kukri, hard, my demon lending me strength and precision, and the knife split the ghoul's skull open like rotten fruit—the other way to put ghouls down fast.

I slapped a new clip into the Desert Eagle and had it trained on the far end of the hall when the dark figure reappeared, lit by a faintly glowing green crystal she carried in her left hand. Her dark hair was tied back from her perfectly expressionless, motionless face, and her eyes were unreadably reptilian.

The Stygian.

"Balera, isn't it?" I asked her. The second ghoul's momentum had carried it to the ground beside me, and it lay there on his back, the handle of my knife sticking out of the center of its face, the interior of his skull open to view. One of his legs was still quivering. "Or are you Janera?"

"It matters little to us," she replied. Her voice was hollow, empty of something vital. It sounded about as much like a human voice as the old sixties electric pianos did like actual pianos. "You cannot win, Venator. The *Lexicon Malos* will be renewed. Depart now. Live to fight another day."

I leaned down and jerked my gore-soaked knife out of the dead ghoul. Then I started a steady, deliberate walk toward her. "That's what the other two members of the Stygian Sisterhood I've met have said. So far, it hasn't worked out that way." I started planning my shot. Every schmuck who can conjure up a shield that bounces bullets thinks he's hot stuff. But it takes concentration to do it, and the shields aren't omnidirectional. A ricochet shot can bounce right around a conjured shield—and besides, if I could get her focused on the gun, she might not realize I was using the knife on her until it was too late.

There was a nice, smooth, polished metal surface behind her, the cover to what must have been a heating unit or a lighting control panel or something. The steel looked heavy enough to suit my purpose. If I could put part of a shot into her back, even just a few fragments from a shattered bullet, it should be distraction enough to let me put her down. "Let's make this simple," I told her. "Hold still, smile pretty, and your sisters can have an open-casket service."

Her lower lip twitched down away from her teeth in a gesture that looked like something that had never been human attempting a smile. "But yours," she said, her voice suddenly a purr, "will never know you."

I stepped forward, ready to shoot, and caught a flicker of my own reflection in the metal behind the Stygian.

It wasn't me.

The man facing me *wasn't me.*

He looked older, rough faced, with shaggy greying hair and a scruff of a beard. His jaws were slightly distended, as were his lips, and I pegged him at once as a ghoul who had not quite managed to completely hide its true nature under a human outer appearance.

I lifted my left hand, and the knife in it, and the ghoul in the reflection did the same thing.

The Stygian gave me another not-smile and vanished around the corner.

It took me a second to recover and go running after her—but I needn't have bothered. A heavy door clanged shut as I rounded the corner, and flickering motes of greenish light danced over its surface before leaving me in total darkness. I'm not a member of the elite when it comes to the use of magic, but I knew better than to try to force that door against whatever energies the Stygian had laid across it in her wake.

I cursed savagely.

The entire affair had been an ambush, and I had walked right into it.

This was the difference between Harry's use of magic and mine. The link between our amulets was strong enough that his more sophisticated spells would never have been deceived. The Stygian must have used some kind of masking enchantment to trick my own grade-school version of a tracking spell, and then employed an illusion to give herself the appearance of my brother once she had lured me into position to . . . do whatever it was she had done to me.

Why change my face? The members of the Stygian Sisterhood were no amateurs when it came to dangerous, even lethal magic. Why had she done *that* instead of, for example, setting my intestines on fire? Even if my demon had been fully fed and at peak strength, I doubted I could have survived something like that.

Now that the actual fighting was over, I began to feel the fear. Had the Stygian wished it, I would be dead right now, and the knowledge was sobering, frightening. Harry had occasionally accused me of being reckless and overconfident—which is, believe me, hypocrisy of a staggering magnitude. But in this instance, he was probably right.

And after expending so much energy on running, fighting, and bending steel with my bare hands, I was *hungry*. The park outside this building was just brimming over with happy, oblivious kine. It would be so easy to cut one out of the herd, some tender little doe, and—

I had to focus and concentrate. I wasn't working with a safety net. Another stupid mistake could kill me.

"Get your game face on, Thomas," I snarled to myself. "Get your head together."

The darkness of the building was almost complete, but my demon let me see clearly enough. The ghouls were already rotting away. They'd be nothing but a stinking mess of sludge in a few hours. We were far enough into the building that I doubted the sound of the shots had carried out of it—but the cops on patrol in the park would notice the door the ghouls had torn off the building, probably sooner rather than later. I couldn't stay there.

I found another way out of the building and hurried back toward my truck. I couldn't trust my tracking spell, obviously, which meant that I had to find Harry another way. Karrin Murphy of Chicago PD might be able to find out if anyone had seen his car, but I had no way of knowing Harry would be in it, or even nearby. And even if I *did* find him, it was going to be hell convincing him of anything when a stranger walked up, told Harry that he was his brother, and asked him to abandon a case.

First things first, I decided. I had to find him, or none of the rest of it would matter.

I knew someone who could help.

4

Harry is one of the top wizards on the planet, and he lives in a basement.

His boardinghouse is a little run-down, but roomy. I guess the rent is cheap. His basement apartment is tiny, but the neighbors are elderly and quiet. He seems to like it. I've known him for years, and I still can't quite believe that he really keeps on living there.

Personally, I think that's why he hasn't had more trouble at home—I don't think his enemies can bring themselves to believe it, either. Maybe they figure it's a decoy he's constructed solely to give them somewhere obvious to attack, where he can lure them to their deaths. Certainly, the ones who show up don't like the welcome they receive. The defensive spells around his home could charbroil a herd of charging buffalo.

I used the crystal he'd given me to disarm his wards, and the key he'd given me to unlock his door and let myself in. His apartment was spotlessly clean, as usual—he'd turned into a neat freak a few years ago, for some reason, though he'd never talked about why.

An enormous, shaggy grey dog, two hundred pounds of muscle and fur and white, sharp fangs, appeared from the little kitchen-equipped alcove and growled at me.

"Whoa," I said, holding up my hands. "Mouse, it's me. Thomas."

Mouse's growl cut off suddenly. His ears twitched back and forth, and he tilted his head one way and then the other, peering at me, his nose twitching as he sniffed.

"Someone laid an illusion over me," I said. Harry had told me his dog was special and could understand human speech. I still wasn't sure whether he'd been pulling my leg when he said it. Harry's got a weird sense of humor, sometimes. But speaking quietly to animals when they appear nervous is always a good idea, and I did *not* want Mouse deciding that I was a threat. He was a Foo dog, and I'd seen him take on things no mortal animal could survive, much less overcome. "Look, boy, I think Harry might be in trouble. I need to talk to the skull."

Mouse came over to me and sniffed at me carefully. Then he made a chuffing sound, padded over to one of the throw rugs on the apartment's floor, and dragged it to one side, revealing the lift-up trapdoor that led down to the subbasement.

I paced over to it and ruffled the dog's ears. "Thanks, boy."

Mouse wagged his tail at me.

A folding stepladder led down into my brother's laboratory, which I always pronounced with five syllables, just to give him a hard time. I unfolded it and went down, stopping as soon as I could see the whole place.

You don't just wander around a wizard's lab. It's a bad idea.

The place was piled high with god only knows what kind of horribly disturbing, rare, expensive, and inane junk. There was a lead box on one shelf in which he kept dust made from depleted uranium, for crying out loud. There was also an eight-foot-long scale model of the heart of the Chicago skyline on a table in the center of the room. It's obsessively detailed, down to models of trees that actually *look* like the trees they represent, and one of the downtown buildings that was recently demolished.

It's a little bit creepy, actually. My brother's got a voodoo doll of the entire *town*.

He also has a human skull that sits on its own wooden shelf, between a pair of candles that have been burned down and replaced so many times that little volcano lumps of colored wax have formed at either end. There are romance paperbacks stacked up on either side of the skull, along with an old issue of *Playboy* from the seventies, with Bo Derek on the cover, and a long strip of scarlet ribbon.

"Hey," I said. "Skull. Bob, isn't it?"

The skull didn't move.

I was going to feel really stupid if it turned out that Harry had been pulling my leg about the skull the whole time. My brother, the ventriloquist. "Hey," I said. "Skull. Look, it's me, Thomas. I know I don't look like Thomas, but it's me. Harry's in trouble, and I need your help to go get him out of it."

There was a tiny flicker of orange lights in one of the eye sockets of the skull. Then the flicker grew brighter, and was joined by a second in the other socket. The skull twitched on the shelf, turning a little toward me, and said, "Holy Clay Face, Batman. What happened to you?"

I chewed on my bottom lip for a second, debating on what to tell the skull. I knew that Bob was Harry's lab assistant and technical adviser in matters magical, that he was some sort of spirit who resided inside the skull, and not a mortal being in his own right. All the same, he was beholden to Harry, and whatever Bob knew, Harry could potentially learn.

"There isn't much I can tell you," I said. "Harry's new client isn't what she appears to be. I was trying to warn him. She tricked me into following her and did this to my face. I think she did it to make it harder for me to warn Harry about her."

"Uh-huh," Bob said. "What do you want from me?"

"Help me get this thing off my face. Then help me find Harry so I can get him off this case before he gets hurt."

Bob snorted. "Yeah, right."

I frowned. "What? You think I'm lying to you?"

"Look, Thomas," the skull said, its tone patently patronizing. "I acknowledge you're cool beyond cool. You're good-looking, you get all the girls, and you send naked chicks to Harry's apartment dressed only in bits of red ribbon, all of which I admire in a person—but, uh. You're still kind of a vampire. From a house of vampires famous for being mind benders, no less."

I ground my teeth. "You think someone's controlled me into doing this?"

"I think that generally speaking, you don't have secrets from your brother, man," Bob said, yawning. "And besides, once Harry gets onto a case for a client, he doesn't come off it. He's like a tick, only his head doesn't come off quite as easy, and there's less chance of his giving you an infection."

"This is important, Bob," I told him.

"So is finding lost children," Bob said. "Or at least it is to Harry. I thought it might be because then their mother would be all appreciative and jump into bed with him, but apparently it's one of those morality things. Finding kids hits some kind of good-versus-evil hot button in his head."

That was what Lara had meant when she said the Stygian had taken a child. Crap. Now I could see the Stygian Sisterhood's plan.

And if I didn't stop them—stop Harry—the Oblivion War could be lost in a night.

"Dammit," I growled. "Bob, I need the help. I need you to do this."

"Sorry, chief," Bob said. "Don't work for you. Harry tells me different, that's a different story."

"But he's in *trouble*," I said.

"So you say. But you aren't offering me any details, which makes it sound fishy."

"Because if I gave you any details, they might get back to Harry, and he might be in even more trouble than he is right now."

Bob stared at me for a second. Then he said, "I hereby promote you from mackerel to tuna fish."

"Okay," I said, thinking. Bob was a spirit. Such beings were bound by their words and promises, by the contracts they made with mortals. "Okay, look. You serve Harry, right?"

"Yep."

"If I give you this information," I said, "and if in your judgment his possession of this information could prove detrimental to his well-being, I want you to swear to me that you will keep it from him or anyone else who asks you about it."

"Okay," Bob said, drawing out the word with tremendous skepticism.

"If you do that," I said, "I'll tell you. If you can't, I won't. And bad things are going to happen."

The skull's eyelights brightened with what looked surprisingly like curiosity. "Okay, okay. I'll bite. You have a bargain. I do so swear it to you, Vampire."

I took a deep breath and glanced around. If another Venator knew what I was doing, they'd put a bullet in my head without thinking twice.

"Have you ever heard of the Oblivion War?"

"No," the skull said promptly.

"For a reason," I said. "Because it's a war being waged for the memory of mankind."

"Uh," Bob said. "What?"

I sighed and brushed my gloved hand back over my hair. "Look. You know that for the most part, the old gods have grown less powerful over the years, or have changed as they were incorporated into other beliefs."

"Sure," Bob said. "There hasn't been a First Church of Marduk for a while now. But Tiamat got an illustration in the *Monster Manual* and had that role in that cartoon, so she's probably better off."

"Uh, okay," I said. "I'm not sure exactly what you're talking about, but generally speaking, you're right. Beings like Tiamat needed a certain amount of mortal belief to connect them to the mortal world."

The eyelights brightened. "Ah!" the skull said. "I get it! If no one *remembers* some has-been god, there's no connection left! It can't remain in the mortal world!"

"Right," I said quietly. "And we're not just talking about pagan gods. We're talking about things that people of today have no words for, no concept to adequately define. Demons of such appetites and fury that the only way mortals in some parts of the world survived them at *all* was with the help of some of those early gods. Demons who had to be stopped, permanently."

"You can't destroy a primal spiritual entity," Bob mused. "Even if you disperse it, it will just re-form in time."

"But you can forget them," I said. "Shut them away. Leave them forever lost, outside the mortal world and unable to do harm. You can consign them to Oblivion."

Bob made a whistling sound.

What the hell? *How?* He doesn't have any *lips*.

"Ballsy," Bob admitted. "I mean, fighting a war like that . . . The more people you brought in to fight on your side, the more the information would spread, and the stronger a hold these demons would have. So you'd have to control who had the information. You'd have to lock that down *hard*."

"Very," I said. "I know there are fewer than two hundred Venatori in the world. But we're organized in cells. I only know one other Venator."

"Venatori?" Bob said. "There's like five *thousand* of those dried-up old prunes. They've been helping the Council fight the war, remember?"

I waved a hand. "Those are the Venatori Umbrorum."

"Yeah," Bob said. "The Hunters of the Shadows."

"One way to translate their name," I said, "and it's the one they believe is correct. But it's more accurate to call them the Shadows of the Hunters. They don't know it, but we founded them. Gave them their store of knowledge. Use them to gather information, to help us keep an eye on things. And they're camouflage, too, to make our enemies have to work a little harder to find us."

"Enemies, right," Bob said. "A war has to have two sides."

I nodded. "Or more. There are a lot of . . . people . . . interested in the old demons. They're weak compared to what they once were, but they're still a route to power. Cults, priests, societies, individual lunatics. They're trying to keep the demons nailed to this world. We're trying to stop them." I shook my head. "The Oblivion War has been going on for more than five thousand years. Sometimes decades will pass without a single battle being fought. Sometimes it all goes insane."

"How many demons have you guys cut off?" Bob asked brightly. Then he chirped, "Oh, heh, I guess you wouldn't *know*, would you. If you kacked 'em, you don't even remember 'em."

"Yeah," I said.

"Kind of a thankless way to fight a war."

"Tell me about it," I said. "This is secret stuff, Bob. Just knowing it creates a kind of resonance in the mind. If someone knows to look for it, they can see it. If Harry finds out about the war, and anyone from either side realizes that he's aware . . ."

"The bad guys will assume he's a Venator or a rival and kill him," Bob said, his manner suddenly sober. "And the Venatori will assume he's a threat like the rest of the nut balls. They'll either consider him a security risk and kill him or impress him into joining their army. And he's already fighting one war."

"Yeah," I said.

"Um," Bob said. "One wonders why they won't do the same thing to me."

"You aren't mortal," I said. "Your knowledge won't bind anything to this world."

The skull somehow looked reassured. "That's true. Tell me about this client that's with my boss."

"You know about the Prosthanos Society?" I asked.

"Buncha lunatics in the Baltic region," Bob replied immediately. "They lop off their bits and pieces and replace them with grafts from inhuman sources. Demons and ghouls and such. Patchwork immortality."

I nodded. "The Stygian Sisterhood does the same thing—only with their psyches instead of with their physical bodies. They slice out the parts of their human personalities they don't want, and replace them with pieces torn from inhuman minds."

"Cheery," Bob leered. "Sorority, huh? They hot?"

"It's generally advantageous," I said. "So for the most part, yes. They're dedicated to the service of a number of old demon-goddesses whom they're trying to keep in the world through the publication of a book of rituals called the *Lexicon Malos*."

"So," the skull said, "hot girl comes into Harry's office. He drools on her shoes, acts like an idiot, and doesn't take her up on her offer to do morally questionable things to him right then and there."

"Uh," I said. "I'm not sure if—"

"Being a stupid hero, he tells her not to worry, that he'll find her obvious sob-story decoy—I mean, lost child. Only when he does find the kid, he finds this book of rituals, too."

"And being a stalwart Warden of the White Council now . . ." I said.

Bob snorted. "He'll take them this book of dangerous rituals anyone could use. And the Council will do with it what they did with the *Necronomicon* in order to defuse it."

I nodded. "They publish it, because they think that by making the rituals available to every nut who wants to try them, the power that comes out of them will be so diffused that it will never amount to any harm."

"Only the real danger isn't the rituals," Bob said. "But the knowledge of the beings behind them."

"And we might never be rid of them—just as we'll never be rid of the faeries."

Bob looked suddenly wistful. "You were trying to ditch the faeries?"

"The Venatori tried, yes," I said. "But the G-men stopped us cold."

"G-men? What, like the government?" Bob asked. "Like the Men in Black?"

"Like Gutenberg and the Grimms," I replied.

Bob narrowed his eyelights for a moment, apparently in thought. "This Stygian hottie. She laid a trap for you. She knew who you were, and what you'd do."

"I've crossed swords with the Sisterhood before. They know me." I shook my head. "I've got no idea why she messed up my face instead of killing me, though."

"Because Dresden would have sensed it," Bob said promptly.

"Eh?"

"Murdering someone with magic? It leaves an odor, and there isn't a body spray on earth that can hide it completely so soon after a kill. If Harry got close enough to sense a whiff of black magic on her, there wouldn't be any way she could pretend to be a damsel in distress."

"He'd still be able to tell she was a practitioner."

"Only if he actually touched her," Bob said. "And even then, if she's significantly different from a normal human, mentally, it'll alter the sense of her aura. Besides, sensing a little tingle of magical potential in a client is a whole lot different from realizing that she's spattered in supernatural gore."

"I get it. So instead she changed my face."

"Technically, she didn't *change* it," the skull said. "It's an illusion. You're still you under there. The question is why would she do *that*, particularly."

I frowned. "To slow me down," I said, thinking it through. It didn't take me long to figure out what the Stygian had in mind, and I clenched my teeth in frustration. "Oh, empty night. She's told Harry that there's a villain in the piece. She's shown him the picture of the bad man who took the poor kid." I gestured at my face. "And she's made *me* look like him."

"Damn," Bob said, admiration in his tone. "That's sneaky. Harry's awfully quick on the draw these days. If you mosey up, he might not give you a chance to explain anything."

I sighed. "The kind of day I'm having, he probably wouldn't. Are you going to help me or not?"

"Answer me one more question," the skull said, quieter now.

"Okay."

"Why?" he asked. "Why would vampires be a part of this? Why would something that eats people be interested in saving humanity from devouring demon gods?"

I snorted. "You want me to tell you that it's because in our secret hearts, we long to be heroes? Or that deep down, there's something in us that cries out for humanity, for redemption?" I shook my head and smiled at him, showing teeth. "At the end of the day? Because we don't like competition."

"Finally," Bob said, with a roll of his eyelights. "A motive I can *understand*. Okay."

"Okay?"

The skull turned on its shelf, to face the table. "I can show you how to find Harry. But the first thing we do is fix your face. Come on in, let me get a better look."

Mnemonic lightning flashed and boomed between my ears, and I felt myself smile. "No," I said.

The skull tilted slightly to one side, watching me. "No?"

"No. I've got a better idea."

5

The skull tried to explain why the tracking spell he showed me was going to work when my own had failed, but about five seconds into the technical talk I started substituting "blah blah blah" for everything he was saying.

I'm not a wizard, okay? I'm a cheap hack. I don't care *why* it works, as long as it works.

The Stygian had staged her little charade in a warehouse down in Hammond. When I caught up to my brother, he and the Stygian were lurking in an alley across the street from the warehouse, watching the place. The Stygian was playing her part, that of the frightened, nervous female, anxious with the need to bring her offspring safely home again. She was a reasonably good actress, too, for someone with so little humanity. She was probably a couple of centuries old. She'd had time to get in some practice.

I went up the side of the building adjacent to the warehouse, so that I could get a look at the place, too. There were a couple more ghouls guarding the building, wearing the brown uniforms of private security personnel. They kept up a regular walking routine around the warehouse's exterior and interior, and they weren't bothering to so much as glance up at the rooftop I was on. It was five floors up with no fire escape and nothing but bricks to hold on to. Why should they?

I paced down to the back side of the warehouse, where Harry and the Stygian couldn't spot me, waited until the pacing ghouls were both out of sight, and then leapt the forty feet or so from my rooftop to the roof of the warehouse. I landed in a roll, in near-complete silence, and froze for a long moment, waiting to see if anyone raised an outcry.

No one did. I hadn't been spotted.

I settled down to wait.

Harry made his move sometime between three and four in the morning, when the guards were most likely to be bored, tired, and convinced that nothing was going to happen tonight—and when there would be the fewest possible witnesses or innocent bystanders. From the front of the warehouse came his resonant baritone, crying out one of those pretend-Latin spell incantations he uses. There was a flash of light, a boom like thunder, and a crash of something slamming into sheet metal with the force of a cannonball.

Scratch one ghoul. My brother hates the creatures with a passion so pure that it's almost holy. If his first attack hadn't killed the thing, he'd finish it off before long. I heard the other ghoul shriek as it began to transform.

Once everyone's attention was on the attack at the front door, I went in through a skylight.

The warehouse was stacked high with years of accumulated junk, consisting mostly of the remains of shipping crates, stacks of loading pallets, and broken boxes. An area in the center of the floor had been cleared, and the concrete had been heavily marked up with oc-cult symbols painted in blood, around a table that was obviously in-tended to be an altar. A kid, a little boy maybe nine years old, was bound hand and foot on the table, his face blotchy from crying. He was screaming and struggling against the ropes, but was firmly se-cured to the table.

Harry cried out again. The glass in both windows at the front side of the warehouse exploded inward in a flash of scarlet light. Something that looked disturbingly like a severed arm went tumbling by the open doorway.

I kept looking until I spotted it—the *Lexicon Malos*, a leather-bound book, like a big old handwritten journal, just the kind of impressive grimoire occult nut-jobs like the Stygians are so giddy about. It rested on a little pedestal beside the table. It didn't actually have a flashing neon sign over it reading NOTICE ME, but it was pretty close.

I went hand over hand along the steel-beam rafters until I got to one of the girders that ran down the wall. Then I slid down it to the floor and hurried over to the altar and the pedestal. I opened the nylon backpack in my hands, stuffed the *Lexicon Malos* into it, zipped it closed, and then slid my arms through the shoulder straps.

I could have bailed then. I suppose it would have been the smartest thing. Once the book was removed from the equation, the Stygian's entire operation was blown. Granted, she and the other members of the Sisterhood would try it again somewhere else, but they would have been stopped for the time being.

But the bitch had messed with my brother.

"For the time being" wasn't good enough.

Harry came through the front door of the warehouse, with the Stygian treading fearfully behind him, pretending to tremble. Tall, skinny, sharp-featured, and somewhat rough-looking, Harry wore his usual wizarding gear—the black leather duster. He carried a carved staff in his left hand, a shorter, more heavily carved rod in his right, and the tip of the rod glowed with a sullen red-orange flame.

I was waiting for them.

I had wrapped the dark red blanket around my shoulders and upper body like some sort of dramatic ceremonial garb. I stood over the child, a wicked-looking knife I'd found lying on the altar in hand, with my head thrown back and a sneer on my illusion-covered face.

"So!" I boomed in my most overblown voice. "You have defeated my minions!"

"You have got to be kidding me," my brother said, staring at me with an expression somewhere between bemusement and naked contempt. "I mean . . . Jesus, look at this place. I've seen high school plays with a higher production value than this."

"Silence!" I thundered, pointing the knife at him. I had eyes only for the Stygian, in any case. She was staring at me with a look of blank surprise. Heh. Serves you right, sweetheart. You shouldn't make up stories about imaginary villains until you're certain they won't come true. "Who dares interrupt my—"

"Yeah, you know what?" Harry asked. *"Forzare!"*

His staff snapped forward and an invisible truck hit me at thirty miles an hour.

I flew backward, thirty feet or so, and hit a stack of loading pallets.

I went through them.

That hurt.

I hit the wall behind them.

I did not go through it.

That hurt even more.

I landed, dazed, and wobbled to my feet with the help of my demon. No problem, I told myself. I'd planned to fall back to this position in any case—just not quite that vigorously.

The circuit box for the building was on the wall two feet to my left. I reached out and killed the lights.

"Crouch down!" Harry shouted to the woman he thought he was protecting. "Stay still!"

My demon and I adjusted to the darkness almost instantly. The Stygian had done the same. She had produced a wavy-bladed dagger from nowhere and was running toward me on silent feet, her eyes narrowed and intent.

I threw the prop knife I'd been holding when she was ten feet away. She slipped to one side, and it went spinning through the air, striking sparks off the far wall. Her knife struck at me, but I slammed the edge of one hand against her forearm, knocking it away before it could do more than scratch me. I followed that with a pair of sharp blows to the body, driving her back a step, and then drew my kukri from beneath the red blanket-robes, slashing at her head. I missed her, and the follow-up rake at her eyes that I made with my other hand failed to connect as well.

In the background, Harry had his priorities straight. He'd brought forth a little light from his amulet, and was cutting the child free from the makeshift altar. I felt my mouth stretch into a fierce grin.

"So smug," hissed the Stygian, her reptile eyes flat. "But not for long." She raised her voice into a terrified scream. "Let me go! Don't touch me!"

Harry, holding the child over one shoulder in a fireman's carry, spun toward the sound, raising his blasting rod, and began hurrying toward me.

"Run, Venator," hissed the Stygian. "But the Blood of the Ancient Mothers is in your veins now. Enjoy your last hours."

The nick on my arm, the tiny cut from the dagger, suddenly felt very cold.

The book was out of Harry's hands. The child was safe.

I fled the building.

6

The wound was poisoned.

Without my demon, I don't think I would have lasted more than an hour. Even with its support, I was having trouble staying steady.

The pain was horrible, and my whole body poured sweat even as I shivered with cold. The Hunger can usually overcome any kind of foreign substance—but while my demon might have been a powerful one, it was not well fed, and I'd been using it hard all night. It had little strength left with which to fight the poison.

It was difficult, but I persevered for three hours.

That was how long it took for me to track the Stygian and catch her alone.

The sweep of my kukri had missed her head—but not the hairs growing out of it. And while my grasping fingers had not found her eyes an instant later, they had snatched those hairs out of the air before they could fall. The tracking spell the skull had taught me had been good enough to let me find the Stygian, despite any countermeasures she might have taken.

When she entered her hotel room, I was half an inch behind her. She never knew I was there until my lips touched the back of her neck, and I unleashed my demon upon her.

She let out a sudden gasp, as my Hunger, starved for so long, rushed into her flesh. Though she might have had the mind and thoughts of a dozen alien beings, she had a mortal life force and a mortal body—a woman's body, and, as I had told the skull, a rather lovely one at that.

She tried to struggle for five or six seconds, until her nervous system succumbed to my Hunger, until the first orgasm ripped a moan of equal parts ecstasy, need, and despair from her throat.

"Shhhh," I told her, my teeth gently finding her earlobe and my hands roaming. "It won't hurt. I promise."

She cried out in despair again, as her body began moving in helpless acquiescence to desire, and my own reservations flickered and died before the raw, aching need of my Hunger.

I spend most of my life fighting my darker nature.

Most of it.

Not all of it.

I bore the Stygian to the floor and fed her to my demon.

Lara would help me get rid of the body.

7

A long, long shower and the cleansing force of the rising sun had been enough to wash away the illusion that had obscured my true features.

I visited my brother at his office the next day.

"How's business?" I asked him.

He shook his head, scowling. "You know what? I've been doing so much gopher work for the Council and the Wardens, I think I must be forgetting how to be a private eye."

"Why's that?"

"Oh, I went up against this complete joke of a bad guy yesterday," he said. "Kidnapper. I mean, you should have seen this loser. He was a *joke*."

"Uh-huh," I said.

"And somehow he manages to get away from me." Harry shook his head. "I mean, I got the kid back, no problem, but the little skeeve skated out on me."

"Maybe you're getting old."

He glowered at me. "The worst part is that the chick who hired me, it turns out, isn't even his mother. She was playing me all along. The kid's been missing for three days, and his *real* parents are trying to get the cops to freaking *arrest* me. After I pull him off a freaking sacrificial altar—okay, a cheesy, stupid sacrificial altar, but a sacrificial altar all the same."

"Where's the chick?" I asked.

"Who knows?" Harry said, exasperated. "She's gone. Stiffed me, too. And good luck trying to get the kid's parents to pay me for the investigation and rescue. There's a better chance of electing a Libertarian president."

"The perils of the independent entrepreneur," I said. "You hungry?"

"You buying?"

"I'm buying."

He stood up. "I'm hungry." He put on his coat and walked with me toward the door, shaking his head. "I tell you, Thomas. Sometimes I feel completely unappreciated."

I found myself smiling.

"Wow," I said. "What's it like?"

THE WARRIOR

—novelette from *Mean Streets*

Takes place between *Small Favor*
and *Turn Coat* and before "Last Call"

Once upon a time, when moving into a new neighborhood, I spent a few days meeting the new neighbors. Nothing big, just visits to say hello, introduce myself to the other family with children my son's age, another family with a high-school-aged daughter who often babysat for the other families on the street, the usual sort of thing. I had a bunch of innocuous interactions with them that didn't look like anything special—at the time.

Fast-forward five years. Over the next few years, I came to learn that some of the most inane, unimportant little things I had done or said in that time had impacted several of my neighbors in enormous ways. Not necessarily good or bad, but significantly, and generally in a positive fashion, or so it seemed to me.

If I'd chosen different words to speak, or timed my actions only slightly differently, it might well have altered their lives—and if I hadn't been paying close attention, I might not have realized it had happened at all. It was my first real-life lesson in the law of unintended consequences—and the basis of my belief that big, important things are built from small and commonplace things, and that even our little acts of petty, everyday good or evil have a cumulative effect on our world. A lot of religions make a distinction between light and darkness, and paint portraits of dramatic battles between their champions.

But maybe the "fight on the ground" is a lot more common than we ever really think. It happens every day, and a lot of the time we might not even be aware that it's going on—until five years later, I guess. Our smallest actions and choices matter. They tell us about who we are.

That was the idea I tried to carry into "The Warrior."

That, and the idea that what seems like a good thing or a bad thing might not be either, seen from another point of view. Many readers were upset with Michael's fate at the end of *Small Favor*—how horrible that a character who was basically so decent got handed such a horrible fate, being shot and crippled for life by the champions of Hell itself. What a tragedy that he couldn't continue the fight.

Judge for yourself how tragic it was for him.

sat down next to Michael and said, "I think you're in danger."

Michael Carpenter was a large, brawny man, though he was leaner now than in all the time I'd known him. Months in bed and more months in therapy had left him a shadow of himself, and he had never added all the muscle back on. Even so, he looked larger and more fit than most, his salt-and-pepper hair and short beard going heavier on the salt these days.

He smiled at me. That hadn't changed. If anything, the smile had gotten deeper and more steady.

"Danger?" he said. "Heavens."

I leaned back on the old wooden bleachers at the park and scowled at him. "I'm serious."

Michael paused to shout a word of encouragement at the second baseman (or was that baseperson?) on his daughter Alicia's softball team. He settled back onto the bleachers. They were covered in old, peeling green paint, and it clashed with his powder blue and white shirt, which matched the uniform T-shirts of the girls below. It said COACH in big blue letters.

"I brought your sword. It's in the car."

"Harry," he said, unruffled, "I'm retired. You know that."

"Sure," I said, reaching into my coat. "I know that. But the bad guys apparently don't." I drew out an envelope and passed it to him.

Michael opened it and studied its contents. Then he replaced them, put the envelope back on the bench beside me, and rose. He started down onto the field, leaning heavily on the wooden cane that went everywhere with him now. Nerve damage had left one of his legs pretty near perfectly rigid, and his hip had been damaged as well. It gave him a rolling gait. I knew he couldn't see out of one of his clear, honest eyes very well anymore, either.

He took charge of the practice in the quiet, confident way he did everything, drawing smiles and laughter from his daughter and her teammates. They were obviously having fun.

It looked good on him.

I looked down at the envelope and wished I couldn't imagine the photos contained inside it quite so clearly. They were all professional, clear—Michael walking up the handicap access ramp to his church; Michael opening a door for his wife, Charity; Michael loading a big bucket of softballs into the back of the Carpenter family van; Michael at work, wearing a yellow hard hat, pointing up at a half-finished building as he spoke to a man beside him.

The pictures had come in the mail to my office, with no note, and no explanation. But their implications were ugly and clear.

My friend, the former Knight of the Cross, was in danger.

It took half an hour for the softball practice to end, and then Michael rolled back over to me. He stood staring up at me for a moment before he said, "The sword has passed out of my hands. I can't take it up again—especially not for the wrong reason. I won't live in fear, Harry."

"Could you maybe settle for living in caution?" I asked. "At least until I know more about what's going on?"

"I don't think His plan is for me to die now," he replied calmly. It was never hard to tell when Michael was talking about the Almighty. He could insert capital letters into spoken words. I'm not sure how.

"What happened to 'No man knows the day or the hour'?" I asked.

He gave me a wry smile. "You're taking that out of context."

I shrugged. "Michael. I'd like to believe in a loving, just God who looks out for everyone. But I see a lot of people get hurt who don't seem to deserve it. I don't want you to become one of them."

"I'm not afraid, Harry."

I grimaced. I'd figured he might react like this, and I'd come prepared to play dirty. "What about your kids, man? What about Charity? If someone comes for you, they aren't going to be particular about what happens to the people around you."

I'd seen him display less expression while being shot. His face turned pale, and he looked away from me.

"What do you have in mind?" he asked after a moment.

"I'm going to lurk and hover," I told him. "Maybe catch our photographer before things go any further."

"Whether or not I want you to do it," he said.

"Well. Yes."

He shook his head at me and gave me a tight smile. "Thank you, Harry. But no thank you. I'll manage."

MICHAEL'S HOME WAS an anomaly so close to the city proper—a fairly large old colonial house, complete with a white picket fence and a yard with trees in it. It had a quiet, solid sort of beauty. It was surrounded by other homes, but they never seemed quite as pleasant, homey, or clean as Michael's house. I knew he did a lot of work to keep it looking nice. Maybe it was that simple. Maybe it was a side effect of being visited by archangels and the like.

Or maybe it was all in the eye of the beholder.

I'm pretty sure there won't ever be a place like that for me.

Michael had given a couple of the girls—young women, I suppose— a ride home in his white pickup, so it had taken us a while to get there, and twilight was heavy on the city. I wasn't making any particular secret about tailing them, but I wasn't riding his back bumper, either, and I don't think either of them had noticed my beat-up old VW.

Michael and Alicia got out of the car and went into the house, while I drove a slow lap around their block, keeping my eyes peeled.

When I didn't spot any imminent maniacs or anticipatory fiends about to pounce, I parked a bit down the street and walked toward Michael's place.

It happened pretty fast. A soccer ball went bouncing by me, a small person came pelting after it, and just as it happened, I heard the crunchy hiss of tires on the street somewhere behind me and very near. I have long arms, and it was a good thing. I grabbed the kid, who must have been seven or eight, about half a second before the oncoming car hit the soccer ball and sent it sailing. Her feet went flying out ahead of her as I swung her up off the ground, and her toes missed hitting the car's fender by maybe six inches.

The car, one of those fancy new hybrids that run on batteries part of the time, went by in silence, without the sound of the motor to give any warning. The driver, a young man in a suit, was jabbering into a cell phone that he held to his ear with one hand. He never noticed. As he reached the end of the block, he turned on his headlights.

I turned to find the child, a girl with inky black hair and pink skin, staring at me with wide, dark eyes, her mouth open and uncertain. She had a bruise on her cheek a couple of days old.

"Hi," I said, trying to be as unthreatening as I could. I had limited success. Tall, severe-looking men in long black coats who need a shave are challenged that way. "Are you all right?"

She nodded her head slowly. "Am I in trouble?"

I put her down. "Not from me. But I heard that moms can get kind of worked up about—"

"Courtney!" gasped a woman's voice, and a woman I presumed to be the child's mother came hurrying from the nearest house. Like the child, she had black hair and very fair skin. She had the same wary eyes, too. She extended her hand to the little girl, and then pulled her until Courtney stood behind her mother. She peeked around at me.

"What do you think you're doing?" she demanded—or tried to. It came out as a nervous question. "Who are you?"

"Just trying to keep your little girl from becoming a victim of the Green movement," I said.

She didn't get it. Her expression changed, as she probably wondered something along the lines of *Is this person a lunatic?*

I get that a lot.

"There was a car, ma'am," I clarified. "She didn't see it coming."

"Oh," the woman said. "Oh. Th-thank you."

"Sure." I frowned at the girl. "You okay, sweetheart? I didn't give you that bruise, did I?"

"No," she said. "I fell off my bike."

"Without hurting your hands," I noted.

She stared at me for a second before her eyes widened, and she hid behind her mother a little more.

Mom blinked at me, and then at the child. Then she nodded to me, took the daughter by the shoulders, and frog-marched her toward the house without another word. I watched them go, and then started back toward Michael's place. I kicked Courtney's soccer ball back into her yard on the way.

Charity answered the door when I knocked. She was of an age with Michael, though her golden hair hid fairly well any strands of silver that might have shown. She was tall and broad-shouldered, for a woman, and I'd seen her crush more than one inhuman skull when one of her children was in danger. She looked tired—a year of seeing your husband undergoing intensely difficult physical therapy can do that, I guess. But she also looked happy. Our personal cold war had entered a state of détente, of late, and she smiled to see me.

"Hello, Harry. Surprise lesson? I think Molly went to bed early."

"Not exactly," I said, smiling. "Thought I'd just stop by to visit."

Charity's smile didn't exactly vanish, but it got cautious. "Really."

"Harry!" screamed a little voice, and Michael's youngest son, of the same name, flung himself into the air, trusting me to catch him. Little Harry was around Courtney's age, and generally regarded me as something interesting to climb on. I caught him and gave him a noisy kiss on the head, which elicited a giggle and a protesting "Yuck!"

Charity shook her head wryly. "Well, come in. Let me get you something to drink. Harry, he's not a jungle gym. Get down."

Little Harry developed spontaneous deafness and scrambled up onto my shoulders as we walked into the living room. Michael and Alicia, his dark-haired, quietly serious daughter, were just coming in from the garage, after putting away softball gear.

"Papa!" little Harry shouted, and promptly plunged forward, off my shoulders, arms outstretched to Michael.

He leaned forward and caught him, though I saw him wince and exhale tightly as he did it. My stomach rolled uncomfortably in sympathy.

"Alicia," Charity said.

Her daughter nodded, hung her ball cap on a wooden peg by the door, and took little Harry from Michael, tossing him up into the air and catching him, much to the child's protesting laughter. "Come on, squirt. Time for a bath."

"Leech!" Harry shouted, and immediately started climbing on his sister's shoulders, babbling about something to do with robots.

Michael smiled as he watched them exit. "I asked Harry to dinner tonight," he told Charity, kissing her on the cheek.

"Did you?" she said, in the exact same tone she'd used on me at the door.

Michael looked at her and sighed. Then he said, "My office."

We went into the study Michael used as his office—more cluttered than it had been before, now that he was actually using it all the time—and closed the door behind us. Without a word, I took out the photos I'd received and showed them to Charity.

Michael's wife was no dummy. She looked at them one at a time, in rapid succession, her eyes blazing brighter with every new image. When she spoke, her voice was cold. "Who took these?"

"I don't know yet," I told her. "Though Nicodemus's name does sort of leap to mind."

"No," Michael said quietly. "He can't harm me or my family anymore. We're protected."

"By what?" I asked.

"Faith," he said simply.

That would be a maddening answer under most circumstances—but I'd seen the power of faith in action around my friend, and it was every bit as real as the forces I could manage. Former presidents get a detail of Secret Service to protect them. Maybe former Knights of the Cross had a similar retirement package, only with more seraphim. "Oh."

"You're going to get to the bottom of this?" Charity asked.

"That's the idea," I said. "It might mean I intrude on you all a little."

"Harry," Michael said, "there's no need for that."

"Don't be ridiculous," Charity replied, turning to Michael. She took his hand, very gently, though her tone stayed firm. "And don't be proud."

He smiled at her. "It isn't a question of pride."

"I'm not so sure," she said quietly. "Father Forthill said we were only protected against supernatural dangers. If there's something else afoot . . . You've made so many enemies. We have to know what's happening."

"I often don't know what's happening," Michael said. "If I spent all my time trying to find out, there wouldn't be enough left to live in. This is more than likely being done for the sole purpose of making us worried and miserable."

"Michael," I said quietly, "one of the best ways I know to counter fear is with knowledge."

He tilted his head, frowning gently at me.

"You say you won't live in fear. Fine. Let me poke around and shine a light on things, so we know what's going on. If it turns out to be nothing, no harm done."

"And if it isn't?" Charity asked.

I kept a surge of quiet anger out of my voice and expression as I looked at her levelly. "No harm gets done to you and yours."

Her eyes flashed, and she nodded her chin once.

"Honey." Michael sighed.

Charity stared at him.

Michael might have slain a dragon, but he knew his limits. He lifted a hand in acceptance and said, "Why don't you make up the guest bedroom."

BY A LITTLE after nine, the Carpenter household was almost entirely silent. I had been shown into the little guest room kept at the end of an upstairs hallway. It was really Charity's sewing room, and was all but filled with colorful stacks of folded fabric, some of them in clear plastic containers, some of them loose. There was room around a little table with a sewing machine on it, and just barely enough space to get to the bed. I'd recuperated from injuries there before.

One thing was new—there was a very fine layer of dust on the sewing machine.

Huh.

I sat down on the bed and looked around. It was a quiet, warm, cheerful little room—almost manically so, now that I thought about it. Everything was soft and pleasant and ordered, and it took me maybe six or seven whole seconds to realize that this room had been Charity's haven. How many days and nights must she have been worried about Michael, off doing literally God only knew what, against foes so terrible that no one but he could have been trusted to deal with them? How many times had she wondered if it would be a solemn Father Forthill who came to the door, instead of the man she loved? How many hours had she spent in this well-lit room, working on making warm, soft things for her family, while her husband carried *Amoracchius*'s cold, bright steel into the darkness?

And now there was dust on the sewing machine.

Michael had nearly been killed, out there on that island. He had been crippled, forced by his injuries to lay aside the holy sword, along with the nearly invisible, deadly war that went with it. And he was happier than I'd ever seen him.

Maybe the Almighty worked in mysterious ways, after all.

Another thought occurred to me, as I sat there pondering: Whoever had sent those pictures hadn't sent them to Michael—he'd sent them to me. What if I'd put Michael and his family into real danger by showing up? What if I'd somehow reacted in exactly the way I'd been meant to react?

I grimaced around the cheerful room. So much for sleep.

I got up and padded back downstairs in my sock feet to raid the fridge, and while I was in the kitchen munching on an impromptu cold cuts sandwich, I saw a shadow move past the back window.

I had several options, but none of them was real appetizing. I settled for the one that might accomplish the most. I turned and padded as quickly and quietly as I could to the front door, slipped out, and snuck around the side of the house in the direction that would, I hoped, bring me up behind the intruder. A quick spat of rain had made the grass wet, and the night had grown cool enough to make my instantly soaked socks uncomfortable. I ignored them and went padding through the grass, keeping to the side of the house and watching all around me.

The backyard was empty.

I got an itchy feeling on the back of my neck and continued my circle. Had I given myself away somehow? Was the intruder even now circling just the way I was, hoping to sneak up on *me*? I took longer steps and stayed as quiet as I knew how—which was pretty darn quiet. I had developed my skulking to professional levels, over the years.

And as I rounded the corner, I spotted the intruder, a dark form hurrying down the sidewalk past Courtney's house. I couldn't follow him without being spotted pretty quickly, unless I cheated, which I promptly did. My ability to throw up a veil wasn't anything to write home about, but it ought to be good enough to hide me from view on a dark night, on a heavily shadowed street. I focused on my surroundings, on drawing the light and shadow around me in a cloak, and watched my own vision dim and blur somewhat as I did.

I half wished I'd woken up Molly. The kid is a natural at subtle stuff like veils. She can make you as invisible as Paris Hilton's ethical standards, and you can still see out with no more impediment than a pair of mildly tinted sunglasses. But, since it was me doing the job, I was probably just sort of indistinct and blurry, and my view of the street was like something seen through dark, thin fabric. I kept track of the pale concrete of the sidewalk and the movement of the intruder against the background of shadowy shapes and blurry bits of light, and walked softly.

The intruder crept down the street and then quickly crouched down beside my old Volkswagen, the *Blue Beetle*. It took him maybe five seconds to open the lock, reach into the car, and draw out the long, slender shape of a sheathed sword.

He must have come to the house first, and circled it to determine where I was. He could have spotted my staff, which I'd left resting against the wall by the front door, when he looked into the kitchen window. And I was pretty sure it was a he I was dealing with, too. The movement of his arms and legs was brusque, choppy, masculine.

I took a few steps to one side and picked up Courtney's soccer ball. Then I approached to within a few yards and tossed it up in a high arc. It came down with a rattling thump on the *Blue Beetle*'s hood.

Lurky-boy twitched, twisting his upper body toward the sound and freezing, and I hit him in a diving tackle with my body as rigid as a spear, all of my weight behind one shoulder, trying to drive it right through his spine and out his chest. He was completely unprepared for it and went down hard, driven to the sidewalk with a *whuff* of expelled air.

I grabbed him by the hair so that I could introduce his forehead to the sidewalk, but his hair was cut nearly military-short, and I didn't have a good grip. He twisted and got me in the floating rib with an elbow, and I wasn't in a good enough position to keep him from getting out from under me and scrambling away, the sheathed weapon still in hand.

I focused my will, flicked a hand at him, and spat, *"Forzare!"* Unseen force lashed out at the backs of his knees—

And hit the mystic equivalent of a brick wall. There was a burst of twinkling, shifting lights, and he let out a croaking sound as he kept running. Something that glowed like a dying ember fell to the sidewalk.

I pushed myself up to pursue him, slipped on the wet grass next to the sidewalk, and rolled my ankle painfully. By the time I'd gotten to my feet again, he was too far away for me to catch, even if my ankle had been steady. A second later, he hopped a fence and was out of sight.

I was left there, standing beside my car on one foot, while neighborhood dogs sent up a racket. I gimped forward and looked down at the glowing embers of the thing he'd dropped. It was an amulet, its leather cord snapped in the middle. It looked as though it had been a carving of wood and ivory, but it was scorched almost completely black, so I couldn't be certain. I picked it up, wrinkling my nose at the smell. Then I turned back to the car and closed the open door. After that, I untwisted the piece of wire that held the trunk closed, picked up a blanket-wrapped bundle, and went back to Michael's place.

MORNING ON A school day in the Carpenter household is like Southampton, just before June 6, 1944. There's a lot of yelling, running around, and organizing transport, and no one seems to be exactly sure what's going on. Or maybe that was just me, because by a little before eight, all the kids were trooping out to their bus stop, led by Alicia, the senior schoolchild.

"So he grabbed the sword and ran?" Molly asked, sipping coffee. She apparently had a cold, and her nose was stuffy and bright pink. My apprentice was her mother's daughter, tall and blond and too attractive for me ever to be entirely comfortable—even wrapped up in a pink fluffy robe and flannel pj's, with her hair a mess.

"Give me some credit," I said, unwrapping the blanket-wrapped bundle and producing *Amoracchius*. "He *thought* he took the sword."

Michael frowned at me as he put margarine on his toast. "I thought you told me the sword was best hidden in plain sight."

"I've been getting paranoid in my old age," I replied, munching on a bit of sausage. I blinked at the odd taste and looked at him.

"Turkey," Michael said mildly. "It's better for me."

"It's better for everyone," Charity said firmly. "Including you, Harry."

"Gee," I said. "Thanks."

She gave me an arch look. "Can't you just use the amulet to track him down?"

"Nope," I said, putting some salt on the turkey "sausage." "Tell her why not, grasshopper."

Molly spoke through a yawn. "It caught on fire. Fire's a purifying force. Wiped out whatever energy was on the amulet that might link back to the owner." She blinked watery eyes. "Besides, we don't need it."

Michael frowned at her.

"He took the decoy," I said, smiling. "And I know how to find that."

"Unless he's gotten rid of it, or taken steps to make it untraceable," Michael said in a patient, reasonable tone. "After all, he was evidently prepared with some sort of defensive measure against your abilities."

"Different situation entirely," I said. "Tracking someone by using one of their personal possessions depends upon following a frequency of energy inherently unstable and transient. I actually have a piece of the decoy sword, and the link between those two objects is much more concrete. It'd take one he—uh, heck of a serious countermeasure to stop me from finding it."

"But you didn't trail him last night?" Charity asked.

I shook my head. "I didn't know where I'd have been going, I wasn't prepared, and since apparently someone is interested in the swords, I didn't want to go off and leave . . ."

You.

"The sword . . ."

Unprotected.

"Here," I finished.

"What about the other one?" Michael asked quietly.

Fidelacchius, brother-sword to Michael's former blade, currently rested in a cluttered basket in my basement—next to the heavy locked gun safe that was warded with a dozen dangerous defensive spells.

Hopefully, anyone looking to take it would open the safe first and get a face full of boom. My lab was behind a screen of defensive magic, which was in turn behind an outer shell of defensive magic that protected my apartment. Plus there was my dog, Mouse, two hundred pounds of fur and muscle, who didn't take kindly to hostile visitors.

"It's safe," I told him. "After breakfast, I'll track buzz-cut guy down, have a little chat with him, and we'll put this whole thing to bed."

"Sounds simple," Michael said.

"It could happen."

Michael smiled, his eyes twinkling.

BUZZ, AS IT turned out, wasn't a dummy. He'd ditched the decoy sword in a Dumpster behind a fast-food joint less than four blocks from Michael's place. Michael sat behind the wheel of his truck, watching as I stood hip-deep in trash and dug for the sword.

"You sure you don't want to do this part?" I asked him sourly.

"I would, Harry," he replied, smiling, "but my leg. You know."

The bitch of it was, he was being sincere. Michael had never been afraid of work. "Why dump it here, do you think?"

I gestured at a nearby streetlight. "Dark last night, no moon. This is probably the first place he got a good look at it. Parked his car here, too, maybe." I found the handle of the cheap replica broadsword I'd picked up at what had amounted to a martial arts trinkets shop. "Aha," I said, and pulled it out.

There was another manila envelope duct-taped to the blade. I took the sword and the envelope back to the truck. Michael wrinkled up his nose at the smell coming up from my garbage-spattered jeans, but that expression faded when he looked at the envelope taped to the sword. He exhaled slowly.

"Well," he said, "no use just staring at it."

I nodded and peeled the envelope from around the blade. I opened it and looked in.

There were two more photos.

The first was of Michael, in the uniform shirt he wore when he coached his daughter's softball team. He was leaning back on the bleachers, as he had been when I'd first walked up to speak to him.

The second picture was of a weapon—a long-barreled rifle with a massive steel snout on the end of it, and what looked like a telescope for a sight. It lay on what looked like a bed with cheap motel sheets.

"Hell's bells," I muttered. "What is that?"

Michael glanced at the picture. "It's a Barrett," he said quietly. "Fifty-caliber semiautomatic rifle. Snipers in the Middle East who use them are claiming kills at two kilometers, sometimes more. It's one of the deadliest long-range weapons in the world." He looked up and around him at all the buildings. "Overkill for Chicago, really," he said with mild disapproval.

"You know what I'm thinking?" I said. "I'm thinking we shouldn't be sitting here in your truck right next to a spot Buzz expected us to go while he and his super-rifle are out there somewhere."

Michael looked unperturbed. "If he wanted to simply kill me here, he's had plenty of time to make the shot."

"Humor me," I said.

He smiled and then nodded. "I can take you to your place. You can get some clean clothes, perhaps."

"That hurts, man," I said, brushing uselessly at my jeans as the truck moved out. "You know what bugs me about this situation?"

Michael glanced aside at me for a second. "I think I do. But it might be different from what you were thinking."

I ignored him. "Why? I mean sure, we need to know who this guy is, but *why* is he doing this?"

"It's a good question."

"He sends the pictures to me, not you," I said. I held up the new photo of the sniper rifle. "I mean, this is obviously an escalation. But if what he wanted was to kill you, why . . . ? Why document it for me?"

"It looks to me," Michael said, "as if he wants you to be afraid."

"So he threatens *you*?" I demanded. "That's stupid."

He smiled. "Do people threaten you very often?"

"Sure. All the time."

"What happens when they do?" he asked.

I shrugged. "I say something mouthy," I said. "Then I clean their clocks for them at the first opportunity."

"Which is probably why our photographer here—"

"Call him Buzz," I said. "It will make things simpler."

"Why Buzz hasn't bothered threatening you."

I frowned. "So you're saying Buzz knows me."

"It stands to reason. It seems clear he's trying to push you into some sort of reaction. Something he thinks you'll do if you're frightened."

"Like what?" I asked.

"What do you think?" he replied.

I put my hand on the hilt of *Amoracchius*. The sword's tip rested on the floorboards of the truck, between my feet.

"That would be my guess, too," he said.

I frowned down at the blade and nodded. "Maybe Buzz figured I'd bring you the sword if you were in danger. So that . . ." I didn't finish.

"So that I'd have some way of defending myself," Michael said gently. "You can say it, Harry. You won't hurt my feelings."

I nodded at the true sword. "Sure you don't want it?"

Michael shook his head. "I told you, Harry. That part of my life is over."

"And what if Buzz makes good?" I asked quietly. "What if he kills you?"

Michael actually laughed. "I don't think that's going to happen," he said. "But if it does . . ." He shrugged. "Death isn't exactly a terrifying proposition for me, Harry. If it was, I could hardly have borne the sword for as long as I did. I know what awaits me, and I know that my family will be taken care of."

I rolled my eyes. "Yeah, I'm sure everything will be fine if your younger kids have to grow up without a father in their lives."

He winced, and then he pursed his lips thoughtfully for a few moments before he replied. "Other children have," he said finally.

"And that's it?" I asked, incredulous. "You just surrender to whatever is going to happen?"

"It isn't what I'd want—but a lot of things happen that I don't want. I'm just a man."

"The last thing I would expect from you," I said, "is fatalism."

"Not fatalism," he said, his voice suddenly and unexpectedly firm. "Faith, Harry. Faith. This is happening for a reason."

I didn't answer him. From where I was standing, it looked like it was happening because someone ruthless and fairly intelligent wanted to get his hands on one of the swords. And worse, it looked like he was probably a mortal, too. If what Charity had said was accurate, that meant Michael didn't have a heavenly insurance policy against the threat.

It also meant I would have to pull my punches—the First Law of Magic prohibited using it to kill a human being. There was some grey area involved with it, but not much, and it was the sort of thing that one didn't play around with. The White Council enforced the laws, and anyone who broke them faced the very real possibility of a death sentence.

"And that's all I need," I muttered.

"What?"

"Nothing."

Michael pulled the truck into the gravel parking lot of my apartment, in the basement of a big old boardinghouse. "I need to drop by a site before we go back to get your car. Is that all right?"

I took the sword with me as I got out of the truck. "Well," I said, "as long as it's all happening for a reason."

MICHAEL'S SMALL COMPANY built houses. Years of vanishing at irregular intervals to battle the forces of evil had probably held him back from moving up to building the really expensive, really profitable places. So he built homes for the upper couple of layers of the middle class instead. He probably would have made more money if he cut corners, but it was Michael. I was betting that never happened.

This house was a new property, down toward Wolf Lake, and it had the depressing look of all construction sites—naked earth, trees bulldozed and piled to one side, and the standard detritus of any such endeavor: mud, wood, garbage discarded by the workers, and big old boot tracks all over the ground. Half a dozen men were at work, putting up the house's skeleton.

"Shouldn't take me long," Michael said.

"Sure," I said. "Go to it."

Michael hopped down from the truck and gimped his way over to the house, moving with an energy and purpose I'd seldom seen from him. I frowned after him, and then pulled the first envelope out of my pocket and started looking at the photos inside.

The photo of Michael at a building site had been taken at this one. Buzz had been here, watching Michael.

He might still be here now.

I got out of the car and slung the sword's belt over my shoulder, so that it hung with its hilt sticking up next to my head. Photo in hand, I started circling the site, trying to determine where Buzz had been standing when he'd taken his picture. I got some looks from the men on the job—but as I said before, I'm used to that kind of thing.

It took me only a couple of minutes to find the spot Buzz had used—a shadowed area of weeds and scrub brush behind the pile of felled trees. It was obscured enough to offer a good hiding spot, if no one was looking particularly hard, but far enough away that he had to have used a zoom lens of some kind to get those pictures. I had heard that digital cameras could zoom in to truly ridiculous levels these days.

I found footprints.

Don't read too much into that. I'm not Ranger Rick or anything, but I had a teacher who made sure I spent my share of time hiking and camping in the rugged country of the Ozarks, and he taught me the basics—where to look, and what to look for. The showers last night had wiped away any subtle signs, but I wouldn't have trusted my own interpretation of them in any case. I did find one clear footprint, of a man's left boot, fairly deep, and half a dozen partials and a few broken branches in a line leading away. He'd come here, hung around for a while, then left.

Which just about anyone could have deduced from the photo, even if he hadn't seen any tracks.

I had this guy practically captured already.

There weren't any bubble-gum wrappers, discarded cigarettes, or fortuitously misplaced business cards that would reveal Buzz's identity. I hadn't really thought there would be, but you always look.

I slogged across the muddy ground back toward the truck, when the door of one of the contractors' vans opened, and a prematurely balding thin guy with a tool belt and a two-foot reel of electrician's wire staggered out. He had a shirt with a name tag that read CHUCK. Chuck wobbled to one side, dragging the handles of some tools along the side panel of Michael's truck, leaving some marks.

I glanced into the van. There was an empty bottle of Jim Beam inside, with a little still dribbling out the mouth.

"Hey, Chuck," I said. "Give you a hand with that?"

He gave me a bleary glance that didn't seem to pick up on anything out of the ordinary about me or the big old sword hanging over my shoulder. "Nah. I got it."

"It's cool," I said. "I'm going that way anyhow. And those things are heavy." I went over to him and seized one end of the reel, taking some of the weight.

The electrician's breath was practically explosive. He nodded a couple of times and shifted his grip on the reel. "Okay, buddy. Thanks."

We carried the heavy reel of wire over to the house. I had to adjust my steps several times, to keep up with the occasional drunken lurch from Chuck. We took the wire to the poured-concrete slab that was going to be the garage at some point, it looked like, and dropped it off.

"Thanks, man," Chuck said, his sibilants all mushy.

"Sure," I said. "Look, uh. Do you really think you should be work-ing with electricity right now, Chuck?"

He gave me an indignant, drunken glare. "What's that supposed to mean?"

"Oh, you just, uh, look a little sick, that's all."

"I'm just fine," Chuck slurred, scowling. "I got a job to do."

"Yeah," I said. "Kind of a dangerous job. In a big pile of kindling."

He peered at me. "What?" It came out more like "*Wha?*"

"I've been in some burning buildings, man, and take it from me, *this* place . . ." I looked around at the wooden framework. "Fwoosh. I'm just saying. Fwoosh."

He worked on that one for a moment, and then his face darkened into a scowl again. He turned and picked up a wrench from a nearby toolbox. "Buzz off, freak. Before I get upset."

I wasn't going to do anyone any favors by getting into half of a drunken brawl with one of Michael's subcontractors. I looked around to see if anyone had noticed, but they were all at other parts of the house, I guessed. So I just held up one hand in front of me and said, mildly, "Okay. I'm going."

Chuck watched me as I walked out of the garage. I looked around until I spotted the power lines running into the house, and then I fol-lowed the trench they were buried in back to the street until I got to the transformer. I looked up at it, glanced around a little guiltily, and sighed. Then I waved my hand at the thing, exerted my will, and mut-tered, "*Hexus.*"

Wizards and technology don't get along. At all. Prolonged expo-sure to an active wizard has really detrimental effects on just about anything manufactured after World War II or so, especially anything involving electricity. My car breaks down every couple of weeks, and that's when I'm not even trying. When I'm making an effort?

The transformer exploded in a humming shower of blue-white sparks, and the sound of an electric saw, somewhere on the site, died down to nothing.

I went back to the truck and sat quietly until Michael returned. He gave me a steady look.

"It was in the name of good," I said. "Your electrician was snockered. By the time the city gets by to repair it, he'll have sobered up."

"Ah," Michael said. "Chuck. He's having trouble at home."

"How do you know?"

"He's got a wife, a daughter," Michael said. "And I know the look."

"Maybe if he spent less time with Jim Beam," I said, "it'd go better."

"The booze is new," Michael said, looking worriedly at the house. "He's a good man. He's in a bad time." He glanced back at me a moment later. "Thank you. Though perhaps next time . . . you could just come tell me about it?"

Duh, Harry. That probably would have worked, too. I shook my head calmly. "That's not how I roll."

"How you roll?" Michael asked, smiling.

"I heard Molly say it once. So it must be cool."

"How you roll." Michael shook his head and started the truck. "Well. You were trying to help. That's the important thing."

Harry Dresden. Saving the world, one act of random destruction at a time.

"Okay," I said to Molly as I prepared to get into my car. "Just keep your wits about you."

"I know," she said calmly.

"If there's any trouble, you call the cops," I said. "This guy looks to be operating purely vanilla, but he can still kill you just fine."

"I know, Harry."

"If you see him, do not approach him—and don't let your dad do it, either."

Molly rolled her eyes in exasperation. Then she muttered a quick word and vanished. Gone. She was standing within an arm's length of me, but I couldn't see her at all. "Let's see the bozo shoot this," said her disembodied voice.

"And while we're at it, let's hope he isn't using a heat-sensitive scope," I said drily.

She flickered back into sight, giving me an arch look. "The *point* is that I'm perfectly capable of keeping a lookout and yelling if there's trouble. I'll go with Dad to softball, and you'll be the second person I call if there's a whiff of peril."

I grunted. "Maybe I should go get Mouse. Let him stay with you, too."

"Maybe you should keep him close to the swords," Molly said quietly. "My dad's just a retired soldier. The swords are icons of power."

"The swords are bits of sharp metal. The men who hold them make them a threat."

"In case you hadn't noticed, my dad isn't one of those men anymore," Molly said. She tucked a trailing strand of golden hair behind one ear and frowned up at me worriedly. "Are you sure this isn't about you blaming yourself for what happened to my dad?"

"I don't blame myself," I said.

My apprentice arched an extremely skeptical eyebrow.

I looked away from her.

"You wanna talk to me about it?"

"No," I said. I suddenly felt very tired. "Not until I'm sure the swords are safe."

"If he knew where to send the pictures," Molly said, "then he knows where your house is."

"But he can't get inside. Even if he could get the doors or one of the windows to open, the wards would roast him."

"And your wards are perfect," Molly said. "There's no way anyone could get around them, ever. The way you told me those necromancers did a few years ago."

"They didn't go around," I said. "They went through. But I see your point. If I have to, I'll take one of the Ways to Warden's command center at Edinburgh and leave the swords in my locker."

Molly's eyes widened. "Wow. A locker?"

"Technically. I haven't used it. I've got the combination written down. Somewhere. On a napkin. I think."

"Does it hurt to be as suave as you, boss?"

"It's agonizing."

"Looks it." Her smile faded. "What are you going to do after you're sure the swords are safe?"

She hadn't thought it through. She didn't know what was going to happen in the next few minutes. So I gave her my best fake grin and said, "One step at a time, grasshopper. One step at a time."

I BEGAN POURING my will into my shield bracelet about half a mile from home. That kind of active magic wasn't good for the Beetle, but having a headless driver smash it into a building would be even worse. I fastened the buttons on my leather duster, too. The spells that reinforced the coat were fresh, and they'd once stood up to the power of a Kalashnikov assault rifle—but that was a world of difference from the power of a .50-caliber sniper round.

Buzz had missed his shot at the sword at Michael's house. It's really hard to tail someone without being noticed, unless you've got a team of several cars working together—and this had all the earmarks of a lone-gunman operation. Buzz hadn't been tailing me today, and unless he'd given up entirely—sure, right—that could only mean he was waiting for me somewhere. He'd had plenty of time to set up an ambush somewhere he knew I'd go.

Home.

The sword was my priority. I wasn't planning on suicide or anything, but at the end of the day, I was just one guy. The swords had been a thorn in the side of evildoers for two thousand years. In the long term, the world needed them a lot more than it needed one battered and somewhat shabby professional wizard.

As I came down the street toward my apartment, I stomped on the gas. Granted, in an old VW Beetle, that isn't nearly as dramatic as it sounds. My car didn't roar as much as it coughed more loudly, but I picked up speed and hit my driveway as hard as I could while keeping all the wheels on the ground. I skidded to a stop outside my front door as the engine rattled, pinged, and began pouring out black smoke, which would have been totally cool if I'd actually made it happen on purpose.

I flung myself out of the car, the sword in hand, and into the haze of smoke, my shield bracelet running at maximum power in a dome that covered me on all sides. I rushed toward the steps leading down to the front door of my basement apartment.

As my foot was heading down toward the first step, there was a flash of light and a sledgehammer hit me in the back. It spun me counterclockwise as it flung me down, and I went into a bad tumble down the seven steps to my front door. I hit my head, my shoulder screamed, and the taste of blood filled my mouth. My shield bracelet seared my wrist. Gravity stopped working, and I wasn't sure which way I was supposed to be falling.

"Get up, Harry," I told myself. "He's coming. He's coming for the sword. Get *up*."

I'd dropped my keys in the fall. I looked for them.

I saw blood all over the front of my shirt.

The keys lay on the concrete floor of the stairs. I picked them up and stared stupidly at them. It took me a minute to remember why I needed them, and then another minute to puzzle out which of the five keys on the ring went to my front door. My head was pounding and I felt sick; I couldn't get a breath.

I tried to reach up to unlock the door, but my left shoulder wouldn't hold my weight. I almost slammed my head against the concrete again.

I made it up to a knee. I shoved my key at the door.

He's coming. He's coming.

Blue sparks flew up, and a little shock lit up my arm with pain.

My wards. I'd forgotten about my wards.

I tried to focus my will again, but I couldn't get it to gel. I tried again, and again, and finally I was able to perform the routine little spell that disarmed them.

I shoved my key into the lock and turned it. Then I leaned against the door.

It didn't open.

My door is a heavy steel security door. I installed it myself, and I'm a terrible carpenter. It doesn't quite line up with the frame, and it takes a real effort to get it open and closed. I had grown used to the routine bump and thrust of my shoulders and hips that I needed to open it up—but like the spell that disarmed my wards, that simple task was, at the moment, beyond me.

Footsteps crunched in the gravel.

He's coming.

I couldn't get it open. I sort of flopped against it as hard as I could.

The door groaned and squealed as it swung open, pulled from the other side. Mouse, my huge, shaggy grey dog, dropped his front paws back to the ground, shouldered his way through the door, and seized my right arm by the biceps. His jaws were like a vise, though his teeth couldn't penetrate the leather. He dragged me indoors like a giant, groggy chew toy, and as I went across the threshold, I saw Buzz appear at the top of the stairs, a black shadow against the blue morning sky.

He raised a gun, a military sidearm.

I kicked the door with both legs, as hard as I could.

The gun barked. Real guns don't sound like the guns in the movies. The sound is flatter, more mechanical. I couldn't see the flash, because I'd moved the door into the way. Bullets pounded the steel like hailstones on a tin roof.

Mouse slammed his shoulder against the door and rammed it closed.

I fumbled at the wards, babbling in panicked haste, and managed to restore them just in time to hear a loud popping sound, a cry, and a curse from the other side of the door. Then I reached up and snapped the dead bolt closed for good measure.

Then I fell back onto the floor of my apartment and watched the ceiling spin for a while.

In two or three minutes, maybe, I was feeling a little better. My head and shoulder hurt like hell, but I could breathe. I tried my arms and legs; three of them worked. I sat up. That worked, too, though it made my left shoulder hurt like more hell, and it was hard to see straight through the various pains.

I knew several techniques for reducing and ignoring pain, some of them almost too effective—but I couldn't really seem to line any of them up and get them working. My head hurt too much.

I needed help.

I half crawled to my phone and dialed a number. I mumbled to the other end of the phone, and then lay back on the floor again and felt terrible. Buzz must have fallen back by now, knowing that the sound of the shots could attract attention. Now that the sword was behind the protection of my wards, there was no reason for him to loiter around outside my apartment—I hoped.

The next thing I knew, Mouse was pawing at the door, making anxious sounds. I dragged myself over to it, disarmed the wards, and unlocked it.

"Are these shell casings on the ground? Is this blood?" sputtered a little man in pale blue hospital scrubs and a black denim jacket. He had a shock of black hair like a startled haystack, and black wire-rimmed spectacles. "Holy Hannah, Harry, what happened to you?"

I closed the wards and the door behind him. "Hi, Butters. I fell down."

"We've got to get you to a hospital," he said, turning to reach for my phone.

I slapped my hand weakly down onto it, to keep him from picking it up. "Can't. No hospitals."

"Harry, you know I'm not a doctor."

"Yes, you are. I saw your business card." The effort of vocalizing that many syllables hurt.

"I'm a medical examiner. I cut up dead people and tell you things about them. I don't do live patients."

"Hang around," I said. "It's early yet." Still too many syllables.

"Oh, this is a load of crap," he muttered. Then he shook his head and said, "I need some more light."

"Matches," I mumbled. "Mantel." Better.

He found the matches and started lighting candles. "Next, I'll be getting out a big jar of leeches."

He found the first aid kit under my kitchen sink, boiled some water, and came over to check me out. I sort of checked out for a few minutes. When I came back, he was fumbling with a pair of scissors and my duster.

"Hey!" I protested. "Lay off the coat!"

"You've dislocated your shoulder," he informed me, frowning without stopping his work with the scissors. "You don't want to wriggle it around trying to take your shirt off."

"That's not what I—"

The pin that held the two halves of the scissors together popped as Butters exerted more pressure on their handles, and the two halves fell apart. He blinked at them in shock.

"Told you," I muttered.

"Okay," he said. "I guess we do this the hard way."

I won't bore you with the details. Ten minutes later, my coat was off, my shoulder was back in its socket, and Butters was pretending that my screams during the two failed attempts to put it back hadn't bothered him. I went away again, and when I came back, Butters was pressing a cold Coke into my hand.

"Here," he said. "Drink something. Stay awake."

I drank. Actually, I guzzled. Somewhere in the middle, he passed me several ibuprofen tablets and told me to take them. I did.

I blinked blearily at him as he held up my coat. He turned it around to show me the back.

There was a hole in the leather mantle. I flipped it up. Beneath the hole, several ounces of metal were flattened against the second layer of spell-toughened leather, about three inches below the collar and a hair to the right of my spine.

That was chilling. Even through my best defenses, that was how close I'd come to death.

If Buzz had shot me six inches lower, only a single layer of leather would have been between the round and my hide. A few inches higher, and it would have taken me in the neck, with absolutely no protection. And if he'd waited a quarter of a second longer, until my foot had descended to the first step leading down to my door, he would have sprayed my brains all over the siding of the boardinghouse.

"You broke your nose again," Butters said. "That's where some of the blood came from. There was a laceration on your scalp, too, which accounts for the rest. I stitched it up. You're holding your neck rigid. Probably whiplash from where the round hit you. There are some minor burns on your left wrist, and I'm just about certain you've got a concussion."

"But other than that," I muttered, "I feel great."

"Don't joke, Harry," Butters said. "You should be under observation."

"Already am," I said. "Look where it got me."

He grimaced. "Doctors are required to report gunshot wounds to the police."

"Good thing I don't have any gunshot wounds, eh? I just fell down some stairs."

Butters shook his head again and turned toward the phone. "Give me a reason not to do it, or I call Murphy right now."

I grunted. Then I said, "I'm protecting something important. Someone else wants it. If the police get involved, this thing would probably get impounded as evidence. That's an unacceptable outcome, and it could get a lot of people hurt."

"Something important," Butters said. "Something like a magic sword?"

I scowled at him. "How do you know that?"

He nodded at my hand. "Because you won't let go of it."

I looked down to find the burn-scarred fingers of my left hand clutching *Amoracchius*'s hilt in a white-knuckled grasp. "Oh," I said. "Yeah. Kind of a tip-off, isn't it?"

"Think you can let it go now?" Butters asked quietly.

"I'm trying," I said. "My hand's kind of locked up."

"Okay. Let's just go one finger at a time, then." Butters peeled my fingers off the sword, one at a time, until he had removed it from my grasp. My hand closed in on itself, tendons creaking, and I winced. It sort of hurt, but at the moment it was a really minor thing.

Butters set the sword aside and immediately took my left hand in his, massaging brusquely. "Murphy's going to be pissed if you don't call her."

"Murphy and I have disagreed before," I said.

Butters grimaced. "Okay. Can I help?"

"You are helping."

"Besides this," Butters said.

I looked at the little ME for a moment. Butters had been my unofficial doctor for a long time, never asking a thing in return. He'd waded into some serious trouble with me. Once, he'd saved my life. I trusted his discretion. I trusted him, generally.

So, as the blood started returning to my hand, I told him more or less everything about Buzz and the swords.

"So this guy, Buzz," Butters said. "He's just a guy."

"Let's don't forget," I said. "Despite all the nasties running around out there, it's just guys who dominate most of the planet."

"Yeah, but he's just a guy," Butters said. "How's that?"

I flexed my fingers, wincing a little. "It's good. Thanks."

He nodded and stood up. He went over to the kitchen and filled my dog's water bowl, then did the same for my cat, Mister. "My point is," he said, "that if this guy isn't a supermagical something, he had to find out about the swords like any other guy."

"Well," I said. "Yeah."

Butters looked at me over his spectacles. "So," he said, "who knew you had the swords?"

"Plenty knew I had Shiro's sword," I said. "But this guy tried to get to me through Michael. And the only ones who knew about *Amoracchius* were me, a couple of archangels, Michael, Sanya, and . . ."

Butters tilted his head, looking at me, waiting.

"And the Church," I growled.

———

ST. MARY OF the Angels is just about as big and impressive as churches get. In a city known for its architecture, St. Mary's more than holds its own. It takes up most of a city block. It's massive, stone, and as Gothic as black frosting on a birthday cake.

I'd watched my back all the way there and was sure no one was following me. I parked behind the church and marched up to the delivery door. Twenty seconds of pounding brought a tall, rather befuddled-looking old priest to the door.

"Yes?" he asked.

"I'm here to see Father Forthill," I said.

"Excuse me," he said.

"'S okay, Padre," I told him, clapping his shoulder and moving him aside less than gently. "I'll find him."

"Now, see here, young man—"

He might have said something else, but I didn't pay much attention. I walked past him, into the halls of the church, and headed for Forthill's room. I rapped twice on the door, opened it, and walked in on a priest in his underwear.

Father Forthill was a stocky man of medium height, with a fringe of white hair around his head, and his eyes were the color of robins' eggs. He wore boxers, a tank top, and black socks. A towel hung around his neck, and what hair he had left was wet and stuck to his head.

A lot of people would have reacted with outrage to my entrance. Forthill considered me gravely and said, "Ah. Hello, Harry."

I had come in with phasers set on snark, but even though I'm not particularly religious, I do have *some* sense of what is and isn't appropriate. Seeing a priest in his undies just isn't, especially when you've barged into his private chamber. "Uh," I said, deflating. "Oh."

Forthill shook his head, smiling. "Yes, priests bathe. We eat. We sleep. Occasionally, we even have to go to the bathroom."

"Yeah," I said. "Um. Yeah."

"I do rather need to get dressed," he said gently. "I'm saying Mass tonight."

"Mass?"

Forthill actually let out a short belly laugh. "Harry, you didn't think that I just sit around in this old barn awaiting my chance to make you sandwiches, bandage wounds, and offer advice?" He nodded to where a set of vestments was hung up on the wall. "On weeknights they let the junior varsity have the ball."

"We've got to talk," I said. "It's about the swords."

He nodded and gave me a quick smile. "Perhaps I'll put some pants on first?"

"Yeah," I said. "Sorry." I backed out of the room and shut the door.

The other priest showed up and gave me a gimlet eye a minute later, but Forthill arrived in time to rescue me, dressed in his usual black attire with a white collar. "It's all right, Paulo," he told the other priest. "I'll talk to him."

Father Paulo harrumphed and gave me another glare, but he turned and left.

"You look terrible," Forthill said. "What happened?"

I gave it to him unvarnished.

"Merciful God," he said when I'd finished. But it wasn't in an "Oh, no!" tone of voice. It was a slower, wearier inflection.

He knew what was going on.

"I can't protect the swords if I don't know what I'm dealing with," I said. "Talk to me, Anthony."

Forthill shook his head. "I can't."

"Don't give me that," I said with quiet heat. "I need to know."

"I'm sworn not to speak of it. To anyone. For any reason." He faced me, jaw outthrust. "I keep my promises."

"So you're just going to stand there," I snapped, "and do nothing."

"I didn't say that," Forthill replied. "I'll do what I can."

"Oh, sure," I said.

"I will," he said. "You have my word. You're going to have to trust me."

"That might come easier if you'd explain yourself."

His eyes narrowed. "Son, I'm not a fool. Don't tell me you've never been behind this particular eight ball before."

I looked for something appropriately sarcastic and edgy to say in response, but all I came up with was, "Touché."

He ran a hand over his mostly bald scalp, and I suddenly saw how much older Forthill looked than he had when I met him. His hair was even more sparse and brittle looking, his hands more weathered with time. "I'm sorry, Harry," he said, and he sounded sincere. "If I could . . . Is there anything else I could do for you?"

"You can hurry," I said quietly. "At the rate we're going, someone is going to get killed."

At the rate we'd been going, probably me.

I APPROACHED THE park with intense caution. It took me more than half an hour to be reasonably sure that Buzz wasn't there, somewhere, lurking with another .50-caliber salutation for me. Of course, he could have been watching from the window of one of the nearby buildings—but none of them were hotels or apartments, and none of the pictures taken in the park had been shot from elevation. Besides, if I avoided every place where a maniac with a high-powered rifle might possibly shoot me, I'd live the rest of my life hiding under my bed.

Still, there was no harm in exercising caution. Rather than walking across the open ground of the park to the softball field, I took the circuitous route around the outside of the park—and heard quiet little sobs coming from the shade beneath the bleachers opposite the ones where I'd sat with Michael.

Slowing my steps as I approached, I peered under the bleachers.

A girl in shorts, sneakers, and a powder blue team jersey was huddled up with her arms wrapped around her knees, crying quietly. She had stringy red hair and was skinny, even for someone her age. It took me a minute to recognize her as Alicia's teammate, the second basem—person.

"Hey, there," I said quietly, trying to keep my voice gentle. "You all right?"

The girl looked up, her eyes wide, and immediately began wiping at her eyes and nose. "Oh. Oh, yes. I'm fine. I'm just fine, sir."

"Right, right. Next you'll tell me you've got allergies," I said.

She looked up at me with a shaky little smile, huffed out a breath in the ghost of a laugh—and it transformed into another sob on her. Her face twisted up into an agonized grimace. She shuddered and wept harder, bowing her head.

I can be such a sucker. I ducked down under the bleachers and sat down beside her, a couple of feet away. The girl cried for a couple more minutes, until she began quieting down.

"I know you," she said a minute later, between sniffles. "You were talking to Coach Carpenter yesterday. A-Alicia said you were a friend of the family."

"I'd like to think so," I agreed. "I'm Harry."

"Kelly," she said.

I nodded. "Shouldn't you be practicing with the team, Kelly?"

She shrugged her skinny shoulders. "It doesn't help."

"Help?"

"I'm hopeless," she said. "Whatever it is I'm doing, I just screw it up."

"Well, that's not true," I said with assurance. "Nobody can be bad at *everything*. There's no such thing as a perfect screwup."

"I am," she said. "We've only lost two games all year, and both of them were because I screwed up. We go to the finals next week, and everyone's counting on me, but I'm just going to let them down."

Hell's bells, what a ridiculously tiny problem. But it was obvious that it was real to Kelly, and that it meant the world to her. She was just a kid. It probably looked like a much larger issue from where she was standing.

"Pressure," I said. "Yeah, I get that."

She peered at me. "Do you?"

"Sure," I said. "You feel like people's lives depend on you, and that if you do the wrong thing, they're going to be horribly hurt—and it will be your fault."

"Yes," she said, sniffling. "And I've been trying so hard, but I just can't."

"Be perfect?" I asked. "No, of course not. But what choice do you have?"

She looked at me uncertainly.

"Anything you do, you risk screwing up. You could do a bad job of crossing the street one day and get hit by a car."

"I probably could," she said darkly.

I held up my hand. "My point," I told her, "is that if you want to play it safe, you can stay at home and wrap yourself up in Bubble Wrap and never do anything."

"Maybe I should."

I snorted. "They still make you read Dickens in school? *Great Expectations*?"

"Yeah."

"You can stay at home and hide if you want—and wind up like Miss Havisham," I said. "Watching life through a window and obsessed with how things might have been."

"Dear God," she said. "You've just made Dickens relevant to my life."

"Weird, right?" I asked her, nodding.

Kelly let out a choking little laugh.

I pushed myself up and nodded to her. "I never saw you hiding over here, okay? I'm just gonna go do what I gotta do, and leave you to make the choice."

"Choice?"

"Sure. Do you want to put your cap back on and play? Or do you want to wind up an old maid wandering around your house in the rotting remains of a wedding dress and thirty yards of Bubble Wrap, plotting heartlessly against some kid named Pip?" I regarded her soberly. "There's really no middle ground."

"I'm pretty sure that's not right," she said.

"See there? I'm not much good at offering wise counsel, but that didn't stop me from trying." I winked at her and walked on, around behind the backstop to where Michael sat on the bleachers on the far side of the field.

Molly sat on a blanket underneath a tree maybe ten yards away, with earbuds trailing wires down into her shirt's front pocket, as if she were listening to a digital music player. It was an effort to blend into the background, I supposed, since she couldn't have been listening to one of those gizmos any more than I could have. She was wearing sunglasses, too, so I couldn't tell where her focus was, but I was sure she was being alert. She gave me the barest trace of a nod as I approached her father.

I sat down next to him and waited for it.

"Harry," Michael said, "you look awful."

"Yes, I do," I said. I told him about the attempted assassination and about my discussion with Forthill.

Michael frowned at the children practicing, his expression quietly disturbed. "The Church wouldn't do something like that, Harry. It isn't how they operate."

"People are people, Michael," I said. "People do things. They make mistakes."

"But it isn't the Church," he said. "If this person is part of the Church, he isn't acting with their blessing or under their instructions."

I shrugged. "Maybe. Maybe not. I don't think they were too happy with me when I was a couple of days late turning over the Shroud."

"But you did return it, safe and sound," Michael said.

"How many people know about the swords? How many knew that I had *Amoracchius*?"

He shook his head. "I'm not certain. Given the sorts of foes they contend with, the knowledgeable people within the Church are more than mildly secretive and security conscious."

I gestured around us. "Ballpark it for me."

He blew out a breath. "Honestly, I just don't know. I've personally met perhaps two hundred priests who understood our mission, but it wouldn't shock me if there were as many as six or seven hundred, worldwide. But among them, that kind of important information would be closely kept. Four or five, at most. Plus the Holy Father."

"I'm going to assume that il Papa didn't personally attempt to blow me away," I said gravely. "How do I find out about the others?"

"You might talk to Father For—"

"Been there, done that. He isn't a fountain of exposition."

Michael grimaced. "I see."

"So, other than him—"

He spread his hands. "I don't know, Harry. Forthill was my primary temporal contact."

I blinked. "He never talked to you about your support structure in the Church?"

"He was sworn to secrecy," Michael said. "I just had to trust him. Excuse me." He stood up and called to the softball team, "Thank you, ladies! Two laps of the park and we'll call it a day!"

The team began discarding gloves and such, and fell into a line to begin jogging around the exterior of the park, in no great hurry, talking and laughing as they went. I noticed that Kelly was among them and felt a little less like a complete incompetent.

"I'd really like to keep my brains on the inside of my skull," I told him when he sat down again. "And if one of the Church's top guys is leaking information or has sprung a gear, they need to know it."

"Yes."

I stared out at the now-empty softball diamond for a minute. Then I said, "I don't want to kill anybody. But Buzz is playing for keeps. I'm not going to pull any punches."

Michael frowned down at his hands. "Harry, you're talking about murder."

"What a shock," I said, "after taking one of those monster rounds in the back."

"There must be some way to end this without bloodsh—"

Over his shoulder, I saw Molly abruptly spring to her feet and whip off her sunglasses, staring across the park with a puzzled frown on her face. Then the girls from the team appeared from the direction in which Molly had been staring. The girls were running as fast as they could, screaming as they came.

"Coach!" screamed Kelly. "Coach! The man took her!"

"Easy, easy," Michael said, rising. He put his hands on Kelly's shoulders as Molly came hurrying over. "Easy. What are you talking about?"

"He came out of the van with one of those electric stunner things," Kelly babbled, through her panting. "He zapped her, and then he put her in the van and drove away."

Molly drew in a sudden breath and almost seemed to turn green.

Michael stared at the girl for a second, and then glanced at me. His eyes widened in horror. "Alicia!" he called, stepping past Kelly and looking wildly around the park. "Alicia!"

"He took her!" sobbed Kelly, her tears making her face blotchy. "He took her!"

"Kelly," I said, to get her attention. "What did he look like?"

She shook her head. "I don't—I can't . . . White, not really tall. His hair was cut really short. Like army haircuts."

Buzz.

He'd threatened Michael to get me to bring a sword out in the open, where it was vulnerable. Then he'd tried to kill me before I locked it away again. And when that failed, he tried something else.

"Molly," Michael said quietly. "Take the truck. Drive Sandra and Donna home. Call your mother on the way and tell her what's happened. Stay at the house."

"But—" Molly began.

Michael turned hard eyes to her and said, "Now."

"Yes, sir," Molly said instantly.

Michael tossed her the keys to the truck. Then he turned to a nearby equipment bag and smoothly withdrew an aluminum bat. He whipped it around in a flowing *rondello* motion, nodded as if satisfied, and turned to me. "Let's go. You're driving."

"Okay," I said. "Where?"

"St. Mary's," Michael said, his tone positively grim. "I'm going to talk to Forthill."

FORTHILL HAD JUST finished saying evening Mass when we showed up. Father Paulo greeted Michael like a long-lost son, and how was he doing, and of course we could wait for Forthill in his chambers. I suspected Paulo held deep reservations in regard to me. But that was okay. I wasn't feeling particularly trusting toward him, either.

We'd been waiting in Forthill's quarters for maybe five minutes when the old priest came in. He took one look at Michael and got pale.

"Talk to me about the order," Michael said quietly.

"My son," Forthill said. He shook his head. "You know that I—"

"He's taken Alicia, Tony."

Forthill's mouth dropped open. "What?"

"He's taken my daughter," Michael roared, his voice shaking the walls. "I don't care what oaths you've sworn. I don't care what the Church thinks needs to be kept secret. We have to find this man and find him now."

I blinked at Michael and found myself leaning a little away from him. The heat of his anger was palpable, a living thing that brought its own presence, its own gravity, into the room.

Forthill faced that anger like an old rock thrusting up stubbornly through a turbulent sea—worn and unmoving. "I will not break my oaths, Michael. Not even for you."

"I'm not asking you to do it for me," Michael said. "I'm asking you to do it for Alicia."

Forthill flinched. "Michael," he said quietly. "The order maintains security for a reason. Its enemies have sought to destroy it for two thousand years, and in that time the order has helped hundreds of thousands, even millions. You know that. A breach could put the entire order at risk—and that means more than my life, or yours."

"Or an innocent child's, apparently," I said. "I guess you're going to take that 'Suffer the little children to come unto Me' thing kind of literally, eh, Padre?"

Forthill looked from Michael to me, and then to the floor. He took a slow breath, and then smoothed his hands over his vestments. "It never gets any easier, does it? Trying to work out the right thing to do." He answered his own question. "No. I suppose it's often simpler to determine the proper path than it is to actually walk it."

Forthill rose and walked over to a section of the wood-paneled wall. He put his hands at the top-right and lower-left sections of the panel and, with a grunt, pushed it in. It slid aside, revealing a space the size of a closet, filled with file cabinets and a small bookshelf.

I traded a glance with Michael, who raised his eyebrows in surprise. He hadn't known about the hidey-hole.

Forthill opened a drawer and started thumbing through files. "The Ordo Malleus has existed, in one form or another, since the founding of the Church. Originally, we were tasked with the casting out of demons from the possessed, but as the Church grew, it became clear that we needed to be able to counter the threats from other enemies as well."

"Other enemies?" I asked.

"Various beings who were masquerading as gods," Forthill said. "Vampires and other supernatural predators. Wicked faeries who resented the Church's influence." He glanced at me. "Practitioners of witchcraft who turned their hand against the followers of Christ."

"Hell's bells," I muttered. "The Inquisition."

Forthill grimaced. "The Inquisition has become the primary reason Malleus maintains itself in secrecy—and why we very seldom engage in direct action ourselves. It's all too easy to let power go to your head when you're certain God is on your side. The Inquisition, in many ways, attempted to bring our struggle into the light—and because of the situation it helped create, more innocent men and women died than throughout centuries of the most savage, supernatural depredation.

"We support the Knights of the Cross and do whatever we can to counsel and protect God's children against supernatural threats—the way we protected the girl you brought to me the year Michael's youngest was born. Now the order recruits people singly, after years of personal observation, and maintains the highest levels of personal, ethical integrity humanly possible." He turned to us, with a file folder in his hands. "But as you pointed out earlier, Harry, we're only human."

I took the folder from him, opened it, and found Buzz's picture. I recognized the short haircut, and the severe lines of his chin and jaw. His eyes were new to me, though. They were as grey as stone, but less warm and fuzzy.

"'Father Roarke Douglas,'" I read. "'Age forty-three. Five eleven, one hundred eighty-five. Sniper for the Rangers, trained in demolitions, U.S. Army chaplain, parish priest in Guatemala, Indonesia, and Rwanda.'"

"Good Lord preserve us," Michael said.

"Yeah. A real holy warrior," I said. I eyed Forthill. "And this guy was brought in?"

"I've met Roarke on several occasions," Forthill said. "I was always impressed with his reserve and calm in the face of crisis. He repeatedly distinguished himself by acts of courage in protecting his parishioners in some of the most dangerous locations in the world." He shook his head. "But he . . . changed, in the last few years."

"Changed," Michael said. "How?"

"He became a strong advocate for . . . preemptive intervention."

"He wanted to hit back first, eh?" I asked.

"You wouldn't say that if you'd seen what life can be like in some of the places Father Douglas has lived," Forthill said. "It's not so simple."

"It never is," I said.

"He was, in particular, an admirer of Shiro's," Forthill continued. "When Shiro died, he was devastated. They had worked together several times."

"The way you worked with Michael," I said.

Forthill nodded. "Roarke was . . . not satisfied with the disposition of *Fidelacchius*. He made it known to the rest of Malleus, too. As time went by, he became increasingly frustrated that the sword was not being put to use."

I could see where this one was going. "And then I got hold of *Amoracchius*, too."

Forthill nodded. "He spent the last year trying to convince the senior members of Malleus that we had been deceived. That you were, in fact, an agent of an enemy power, who had taken the swords so they could not be used."

"And no one thought to mention the way those archangels gave orders that I was supposed to hold them?"

"They never appear to more than one or two people at a time—and you *are* a wizard, Harry," Forthill said. "Father Douglas hypothesized that you had created an illusion to serve your purpose, or else had tampered directly with our minds."

"And now he's on a crusade," I muttered.

Forthill nodded. "So it would seem."

I kept on reading the file. "He's versed in magic—well enough, at least, to be smart about how he deals with me. Contacts in various supernatural communities, like the Venatori Umbrorum, which probably explains that protective amulet." I shook my head. "And he thinks he's saving the world. The guy's a certifiable nightmare."

"Where is he?" Michael asked quietly.

"He could be anywhere," Forthill replied. "Malleus sets up caches of equipment, money, and so forth. He could have tapped into any one of them. I tried his cell phone. He's not returning my calls."

"He thinks you've been mind-scrambled by the enemy," I muttered. "What did you expect to accomplish?"

"I had hoped," Forthill said gently, "that I might ask him to be patient and have faith."

"I'm pretty sure this guy believes in faith through superior firepower." I closed the file and passed it back to Forthill. "He tried to kill me. He abducted Alicia. As far as I'm concerned, he's off the reservation."

Forthill's expression became distressed as he looked at me. He turned to Michael, beseeching.

Michael's face was bleak and unyielding, and quiet heat smoldered in his eyes. "The son of a bitch hurt my little girl."

I rocked a step backward at the profanity. So did Forthill. The room settled into an oppressive silence.

The old priest cleared his throat after a moment. He put the file back in the cabinet and closed the door. "I've told you what I know," he said. "I'm only sorry I can't do more."

"You can find her, can't you?" Michael asked me. "The way you found Molly?"

"Sure," I said. "But he's bound to be expecting that. Magic isn't a cure-all."

"But you can find her."

I shrugged. "He can't stop me from finding her, but he can damn well make sure that something happens to her if I do."

Michael frowned. "What do you mean?"

"Maybe he stashes her in a box that's being held fifty feet above the ground with an electromagnet, so that when I get close with an active spell up and running, it shorts out and she falls. The bastard is smart and creative."

Michael's knuckles popped as his hands closed into fists.

"Besides," I said, "we don't need to find him."

"No?"

"No," I said. "We've got the swords. He's got the girl." I turned to go. "He's going to find us."

FATHER DOUGLAS CALLED Michael's house later that night, and asked for me. I took the call in Michael's office.

"You know what I want," he said, without preamble.

"Obviously," I said. "What do you have in mind?"

"Bring the swords," he said. "Give them to me. If you do so without attempting any tricks or deceptions, I will release the girl to you unharmed. If you involve the police or attempt anything foolish, she will die."

"How do I know you haven't killed her already?"

The phone rustled, and then Alicia said, "H-Harry? I'm okay. H-he hasn't hurt me."

"Nor do I want to," Father Douglas said, taking the phone back. "Satisfied?"

"Can I ask you something?" I said. "Why are you doing this?"

"I am doing God's work."

"Okay, that doesn't sound too crazy or anything," I said. "If you're so tight with God, can you really expect me to believe that you'll be willing to murder a teenage girl?"

"The world needs the swords," he replied in a level, calm voice. "They are more important than any one person. And while I would never forgive myself, yes. I will kill her."

"I'm just trying to get you to see the fallacious logic you're using here," I said. "See, if I'm such a bad guy to have stolen the swords, then why would I give a damn whether or not you murder some kid?"

"You don't have to be evil to be ambitious—or wrong. You don't want to see the girl harmed. Give me the swords and she won't be."

There clearly wasn't going to be any profitable discussion of the situation here. Father Douglas was going to have his way, regardless of the impediments of trivial things like rationality.

"Where?" I asked.

He gave me an address. "The roof. You come to the east side of the building. You show me the swords. Then you come up and make the exchange. No staff, no rod. Just you."

"When?"

"One hour," he said, and hung up.

I put the phone down, looked at Michael, and said, "We don't have much time."

THE BUILDING IN question stood at the corner of Monroe and Michigan, overlooking Millennium Park. I had to park a couple of blocks away and walk in, with both swords stowed in a big gym bag. Father

Douglas hadn't specified where I was supposed to stand and show him the swords, but the streetlights adjacent to the building were all inexplicably dark except for one. I ambled over to the pool of light it cast down onto the sidewalk, opened the bag, and held out both swords.

It was hard to see past the light, but I thought I saw a gleam on the roof. Binoculars?

A few seconds later, a red light flashed twice from the same spot where I'd thought I had seen something.

This would be the place, then.

I'd brought my extremely illegal picklocks with me, but as it turned out, I didn't need to use them. Father Douglas had already circumvented the locks and, presumably, the security system. The front door was open, as was the door to the stairwell. From there, it was just one long, thigh-burning hike up to the roof.

I emerged into cold, strong wind. You get up twenty stories or so and you run into that a lot. It ripped at my duster, and set it to flapping like a flag.

I peered around the roof, at spinning heat pumps and AC units and various antennae, but saw no one.

The beam of a handheld floodlight hit me, and I whirled in place. The light was coming from the roof of the building next to mine. Father Douglas flipped it off, and after blinking a few times, I could see him clearly, standing in the wind in priestly black, his white collar almost luminous in the ambient light of the city. His grey eyes were shadowed, and he was maybe a day and a half past time to shave. At his feet on the rooftop lay a long plank, which he must have used to cross from this rooftop to the next.

Alicia, blindfolded and with a gag in her mouth, sat in a chair next to him, her wrists bound to its arms.

Father Douglas lifted a megaphone. "That's far enough," he said. I could hear him over the heavy wind. "That's detcord she's tied up with. Do you know what that is?"

"Yeah."

He held up his other hand. "This is the detonator. As long as it's sending a signal, she's fine. It's a dead-man switch. If I drop it or let it go, the signal stops and the cord goes off. If the receiver gets damaged and stops receiving the signal, the cord goes off. If you start using magic and destroy one of the devices, it goes off."

"That's way better than the electromagnet thing," I muttered to myself. I raised my voice and bellowed, "So how do you want to do this?"

"Throw them."

"Disarm the explosives first."

"No. The girl stays where she is. Once I'm gone, I'll send the code to disarm the device."

I considered the distance. It was a good fifteen-foot jump to get from one rooftop to the other—an easy throw.

"Douglas," I shouted, "think about this for a minute. The swords aren't just sharp and shiny. They're symbols. If you take one up for the wrong reasons, you could destroy it. Believe me, I know."

"The swords are meant for better things than to molder in a dingy basement," he replied. He held up the detonator. "Surrender them now."

I stared at him for a long second. Then I tossed the entire bag over. It landed at his feet with a clatter. He bent down to open it.

I steeled myself. This was about to get dicey. I hadn't counted on the dead-man switch or a fifteen-foot-long jump.

Father Douglas opened the bag. The smoke grenade Michael had rigged inside it in his workshop went off with a heavy thud. White smoke billowed back into his face. I took three quick steps and hurled myself into the air. For an awful portion of a second, twenty stories of open gravity yawned beneath me, and then I hit the edge of the other roof and collided with Father Douglas. We went down together.

I couldn't think about anything but the detonator, and I clamped down on that with my left hand, crushing his fingers beneath mine so that he couldn't release it. He jabbed his thumb at my right eye, but I ducked my head and he got nothing but bone. He slammed his head against my nose—*again* with the nose, Hell's bells that hurt—and drove a knee into my groin.

I let him, seizing his arm with both hands now, squeezing, trying to choke off the blood to his hand, to weaken it so I could take the detonator from him. His left fist slammed into my temple, my mouth, and my neck. I bent my head down and bit savagely at his wrist, eliciting a scream of pain from him. I slammed my weight against him, slipping some fingers into his grasp, and got one of them over the pressure trigger. Then I wrenched with my whole body, twisting my shoulders and hips for leverage, and ripped the detonator away from him.

He rolled away from me instantly and seized the bag; then he was up and running for a doorway leading down into the building.

I let him go and rushed over to Alicia. The dark-haired girl was trembling uncontrollably.

Detcord is basically a long rubber tube filled with explosive compound. It's a little thicker than a pencil, flexible, and generally set off by an electrical charge. Wrap detcord around a concrete column and set it off, and the explosion will cut through it like a piece of dry bamboo. Alicia was tied to the chair with it. If it went off, it would cut her to pieces.

The detonator was a simple setup—a black plastic box hooked to a twelve-volt battery, which was in turn connected to a wire leading to the detcord. A green light on the detonator glowed cheerily. It matched a cheery green light on the dead-man switch transmitter in my hand. If what Douglas had said was accurate and the light went out, things wouldn't be nearly so cheery.

If I let go of the switch, it would stop the signal to the detonator, which would then complete the circuit, send current to the detcord, and boom. In theory, I should be able to cut the wire leading from the battery and render it harmless—as long as Douglas hadn't rigged the device to detonate if that happened.

I didn't have much time. The electronics of the transmitter wouldn't last long around me, even though I hadn't used any magic around them. I had to get the girl out now.

I made the call based upon what I knew about Father Douglas. He seemed like he might have good intentions, despite all his shenanigans. So I gambled that he wouldn't want the girl to die by any means other than a conscious decision from someone—either him letting go of the trigger or me blowing the transmitter by using magic.

I took out my pocketknife, opened it with my teeth, and slashed at the heavy plastic tubing that held her tied down. I cut through the tube once, unwound it from first one arm, then the other, and she was free. She clawed away the blindfold and gag, her fingers still clumsy from being bound.

"Come on!" I said. I grabbed her arm and hauled her out of the chair and away from the explosives. She staggered, leaning against me, and I ran for the stairs.

As we got to the first landing, my ongoing presence apparently became too much for the transmitter. Something sparked and crackled inside the plastic case, the cheery green light went out, and there was a huge and horrible sound from above and behind us. I managed to get between Alicia and the stairwell wall as the pressure wave caught us and threw us into it. It slammed my already-abused head into the wall.

I staggered under the pain for a minute and forced my way through it, like a drowning man clawing for the surface.

"Come on," I croaked to Alicia. "Come on. We have to go."

She looked at me with dull, stunned eyes, so I just grabbed her hand and started down the stairs with her, stuffing the heavy transmitter into my duster pocket with the other hand. We had only a few minutes before the place would be swarming with police and firefighters. I didn't particularly feel like answering their questions about why my fingerprints were on an expensive transmitter and showed trace evidence of explosive residue.

Going down all those stairs was only slightly less taxing than going up had been, and my legs were going to be complaining at me for days. We got to the bottom and I led Alicia out into an alley, then out to Monroe. I looked wildly up and down the street. Michael's truck was there waiting right where it was supposed to be, out in front of the original building. I put my fingers to my lips and let out a shrill whistle.

Michael's truck pulled into the street and stopped in front of us. I hurried Alicia forward. The door swung open, and Molly leaned out, taking Alicia's hand and pulling her in. I went in right behind her, though it made things awfully cozy in the pickup's cab.

"He's loose with the swords," I said. "Did you do it?"

"Did it," Molly replied, and promptly handed me a dashboard compass with one of her own golden hairs stuck to it with clear tape. The needle pointed firmly to the east, instead of to the north. The grasshopper had set up a basic tracking spell, one of the handier tricks I know.

"He's probably moving on foot through the park," I told Michael. "Circle around to Lakeshore, get us in front of him."

"Are you all right, baby?" Michael asked.

Alicia fumbled for his hand and squeezed it tight. Then she leaned against Molly and started crying.

"Hurry," I told Michael. "He's got to know we've bugged the swords somehow. If he finds those hairs Molly tied onto the hilts, we're done."

"He won't get away," Michael said with perfect confidence, and slammed the accelerator down as we approached an intersection sporting a bright red light. Maybe it was divine intervention, or fate, or just good driving, but the truck shot through the intersection, missing two other cars by inches, and sailed on forward.

The needle on the compass pointed steadily toward the park as we went, but then abruptly began to traverse from one side to the other. I looked up ahead of me and saw a dark form sprinting across the road that separated the park from Lake Michigan.

"There!" I shouted, pointing. "There he is!"

Michael pulled over to the side of the road, and I hit the ground before the truck had stopped moving, sprinting after Father Douglas. He was in good shape, covering the ground in long, loping strides. Normally it wouldn't have been a contest to catch him. I run three or four days a week, to train for situations exactly like this one. Of course, when I practice, I'm not generally concussed, weary, and sporting a recently dislocated shoulder. Douglas was holding his lead as we sprinted down the beach, and I was tiring more rapidly than I should have.

So I cheated.

I reached into my pocket, drew out the heavy transmitter, and flung it at him as hard as I could. The black plastic device struck him on the back of the head, shattering, and sending several heavy batteries flying.

Father Douglas staggered and couldn't keep his balance at the pace he was moving. He went down in the sand. I rushed over to him and seized the bag with the swords, only to have him sweep one leg out in a martial arts move, then kick my legs out from beneath me. I went down, too.

Father Douglas ripped at the bag, but I clung grimly, while we fought and kicked at each other—until the bag tore open under the strain and spilled the swords onto the sand.

He seized the hilt of *Fidelacchius*, a katana-type sword that was built to look like a simple, heavy walking stick, until you drew the blade. I seized *Amoracchius*, scabbard and all, and barely brought the sheathed broadsword up in time to deflect a sweeping slash from Father Douglas.

He gained his knees and swung again, and I had all I could do to lift the sheathed sword and fend off the strike. Blow after blow rained down on me, and there was no time to call upon my power, no opportunity to so much as rise to my knees—

Until a size-fourteen work boot hit Father Douglas in the chest and threw him back.

Michael stood over me, an aluminum baseball bat in his right hand. He put out his other hand, and I slapped *Amoracchius* into it. He gripped it midblade, like some kind of giant crucifix, and, with his bat held in a guard position, limped toward Father Douglas. The priest stared at Michael with wide eyes. "Stay back," he said. "I don't want to hurt you."

"Who says you're able to?" Michael rumbled. "Put down the sword, and I'll let you go."

Douglas stared at him with those cold grey eyes. "I can't do that."

"Then I'll put you down and take the sword anyway. It's over, Roarke. You just don't realize it yet."

Father Douglas wasted no more time on talk, but came at Michael, the katana whirling.

Michael batted (no pun intended) the attack aside like a cat swatting down moths, the baseball bat spinning.

"Slow," he said. "Too slow to hit a half-blind cripple. You don't know the first thing about what it means to bear a sword."

Douglas snarled and came at him again. Michael defeated this attack, too, with contemptuous ease, and followed it by smacking Douglas across one cheek with the hilt of the sheathed sword.

"It means sacrifice," Michael said as Douglas reeled. "It means forgetting about yourself, and what you want. It means putting your faith in the Lord God Almighty." He swung a pair of blows, which Douglas defended against, barely—but the third, a straight thrust with the baseball bat's tip, drove home into his solar plexus. Douglas staggered to one knee.

"You *abandoned* your duty," Douglas gasped. "The world grows darker by the day. People cry out for our help—and you would have the swords sit with this creature of witchcraft and deceit?"

"You arrogant child," Michael snarled. "The Almighty Himself has made His will known. If you are a man of faith, then you must abide by it."

"You have been lied to," Douglas said. "How could God ignore His people when they need His protection so badly?"

"That is not for us to know!" Michael shouted. "Don't you *see*, you fool? We are only men. We see only in one place at one time. The Lord knows all that might be. Would you presume to say that you know better than our God what should be done with the swords?"

Douglas stared at Michael.

"Are you stupid enough to believe that He would want you to cast aside your beliefs to impose your will upon the world? Do you think

He wants you to murder decent men and abduct innocent *children*?"
The bat struck *Fidelacchius* from Douglas's hands, and Michael followed it with a pair of crushing blows, one to the shoulder and one to the knee. Douglas went down to the sand in a heap.

"Look at yourself," Michael said, his words hard and merciless. "Look at what you have done in God's name. Look at the bruises on my daughter's arms, at the blood on my friend's face, and then tell me which of us has been deceived."

Again, the bat swept down, and Douglas fell senseless to the sand.

Michael stood over the man for a moment, his entire body shaking, the bat still upraised.

"Michael," I said quietly.

"He hurt my little girl, Harry." His voice shook with barely repressed rage.

"He isn't going to hurt her now," I said.

"He hurt my little girl."

"Michael," I said, gently, "you can't. If this is how it has to be, I'll do it. But you can't, man."

His eyes shifted back toward me for just a second.

"Easy, easy," I told him. "We're done here. We're done."

He stared for another long, silent moment. Then he lowered the bat, very slowly, and bowed his head. He stood there for a minute, his chest heaving, and then dropped the bat. He settled down onto the sand with a wince.

I got up and collected *Fidelacchius*, returning it to its sheath.

"Thank you," Michael said quietly. He offered me *Amoracchius*'s hilt.

"Are you sure?" I asked.

He nodded, smiling wearily. "Yes."

I took the sword and looked at Douglas. "What do we do with him?"

Michael stared at him silently for a moment. In the background, we could hear emergency vehicles arriving to attend to the aftermath of the rooftop explosion. "We'll bring him with us," Michael said. "The Church will deal with its own."

———

I SAT IN the chapel balcony at St. Mary's, staring down at the church below me and brooding. Michael and Forthill had been seeing to Father Douglas, who wasn't going anywhere under his own locomotion for a while. They had him in a bed somewhere. It had hurt to watch Michael, moving in what was obviously great pain, hobble around the room helping to make Douglas feel better. I'd have been content to dump the asshole in an alley somewhere and leave him to his fate.

Which might, just possibly, be one reason I was never going to be a Knight.

I had also swiped Forthill's flask of Scotch from his room, and it was keeping me company in the balcony—two more reasons I was never going to be a Knight.

"Right at the end, there," I said to no one in particular, "those two started speaking a different language. I mean, I understood all the words, and I understood the passion behind them, but I don't get how they connect. You know?"

I sipped some more Scotch. "Come to think of it, there are a lot of things I don't get about this whole situation."

"And you want an explanation of some kind?" asked a man seated in the pew beside me.

I just about jumped out of my skin.

He was an older man. He had dark skin and silver-white hair, and he wore a workman's blue jumpsuit, like you often see on janitors. The name tag read JAKE.

"You," I breathed. "You're the archangel. You're Uriel."

He shrugged. The gesture carried acknowledgment, somehow.

"What are you doing here?" I asked—maybe a bit blearily. I was concussed and half the flask was gone.

"Perhaps I'm a hallucination brought on by head trauma and alcohol," he said.

"Oh," I said. I peered at him, and then offered him the flask. "Want a belt?"

"Very kind," he said, and took a swig from the flask. He passed it back to me. "I don't exactly make it a habit to do this, but if you've got questions, ask them."

"Okay," I said. "Why did you guys let Michael get so screwed up?"

"We didn't let him do anything," Jake replied calmly. "He chose to hazard himself in battle against the enemy. The enemy chose to shoot him, and where to point the gun and when to pull the trigger. He survived the experience."

"So in other words, God was doing nothing to help."

Jake smiled. "Wouldn't say that. But you got to understand, son. God isn't about making good things happen to you, or bad things happen to you. He's all about you making choices—exercising the gift of free will. God wants you to have good things and a good life, but He won't gift wrap them for you. You have to choose the actions that lead you to that life."

"Free will, huh?"

"Yes. For example, your free will on that island."

I eyed him and sipped more Scotch.

"You saw the Valkyrie staring at Michael. You thought he was in danger. So even though it was your turn, you sent him up to the helicopter in your place."

"No good deed goes unpunished," I said, with one too many *sh* sounds. "That's where he got hurt."

Jake shrugged. "But if you hadn't, you'd have died in that harness, and he'd have died on that island."

I scowled. "What?"

Jake waved a hand. "I won't bore you with details, but suffice to say that your choice in that moment changed everything."

"But you lost a Knight," I said. "A warrior."

Jake smiled. "Did we?"

"He can barely walk without that cane. Sure, he handled Douglas, but that's a far cry from dealing with a Denarian."

"Ah," Jake said, "you mean warrior in the literal sense."

"What other kind of warrior is there?" I asked.

"The important kind."

I frowned again.

"Harry," Jake said, sighing. "The conflict between light and darkness rages on so many levels that you literally could not understand it all. Not yet, anyway. Sometimes that battlefield is a literal one. Sometimes it's a great deal more nebulous and metaphorical."

"But Michael and I are literal guys," I said.

Jake actually laughed. "Yeah? Do you think we angled to have you brought into this situation because we needed you to beat someone up?"

"Well. Generally speaking. Yeah." I gestured with the flask. "Pretty much all we did was beat up this guy who had good intentions and who was desperate to do something to help."

Jake shook his head. "The real war happened when you weren't looking."

"Huh?"

"Courtney," Jake said. "The little girl who almost got hit by a car."

"What about her?" I asked.

"You saved her life," he said. "Moreover, you noted the bruise on her cheek—one she acquired from her abusive father. Your presence heightened her mother's response to the realization that her daughter was being abused. She moved out the next morning." He spread his hands. "In that moment, you saved the child's life, prevented her mother from alcohol addiction in response to the loss, and shattered a generational cycle of abuse more than three hundred years old."

"I . . . um."

"Chuck the electrician," Jake continued. "He was drunk because he'd been fighting with his wife. Two months from now, their four-year-old daughter is going to be diagnosed with cancer and require a marrow transplant. Her father is the only viable donor. You saved his life with what you did—and his daughter's life, too. And the struggle that family is going to face together is going to leave them stronger and happier than they've ever been."

I grunted. "That smells an awful lot like predestination to me. What if those people choose something different?"

"It's a complex issue," Jake admitted. "But think of the course of the future as, oh, flowing water. If you know the lay of the land, you can make a good guess where it's going. Now, someone can always come along and dig a ditch and change that flow of water—but honestly, you'd be shocked how seldom people truly choose to exercise their will within their lives."

I grunted. "What about second baseperson Kelly? I saved her life, too?"

"No. But you made a young woman feel better in a moment where she felt as though she didn't have anyone she could talk to. Just a few kind words. But it's going to make her think about the difference those words made. She's got a good chance of winding up as a counselor to her fellow man. The five minutes of kindness you showed her is going to help thousands of others." He spread his hands. "And that only takes into account the past day. Despair and pain were averted, loss and tragedy thwarted. Do you think you haven't struck a blow for the light, Warrior?"

"Um . . ."

"And last but not least, let's not forget Michael," he said. "He's a good man, but where his children are involved, he can be completely irrational. He was a hairbreadth from losing control when he stood over Douglas on the beach. Your words, your presence, your will helped him to choose mercy over vengeance."

I just stared at him for a moment. "But . . . I didn't actually mean to do any of that."

He smiled. "But you chose the actions that led to it. No one forced you to do it. And to those people, what you did saved them from danger as real as any creature of the night." He turned to look down at the church below and pursed his lips. "People have far more power than they realize, if they would only choose to use it. Michael might not be cutting demons with a sword anymore, Harry. But don't think for a second that he isn't still fighting the good fight. It's just harder for you to see the results from down here."

I swigged more Scotch, thinking about that.

"He's happier now," I said. "His family, too."

"Funny how making good choices leads to that."

"What about Father Douglas?" I asked. "What's going to happen?"

"For the most part," Jake said, "that will be up to him. Hopefully, he'll choose to accept his errors and change his life for the better."

I nodded slowly. Then I said, "Let's talk about my bill."

Jake's eyebrows shot up. "What?"

"My bill," I said, enunciating. "You dragged me into this mess. You can pay me, same as any other client. Where do I send the invoice?"

"You're . . . you're trying to bill the Lord God Almighty?" Jake said, as if he couldn't quite believe it.

"Hel—uh, heck no," I said. "I'm billing *you*."

"That isn't really how we work."

"It is if you want to work with me," I told him, thrusting out my jaw. "Cough up. Otherwise, maybe next time I'll just stand around whistling when you want me to help you out."

Jake's face broadened into a wide, merry grin, and laughter filled his voice. "No, you won't," he said, and vanished.

I scowled ferociously at the empty space where he'd been a moment before. "Cheapskate," I muttered.

But I was pretty sure he was right.

LAST CALL

—from *Strange Brew*, edited by P. N. Elrod

Takes place between *Small Favor*
and *Turn Coat*

Having already written a mead-themed short story, I wasn't quite sure what to do with this one. But hey, it was Pat Elrod asking me, and I've never been good at saying no, and I decided to tread upon what is very nearly holy ground, in the Dresden Files—the forces of darkness were going to violate Mac's beer.

Naturally, Harry gets to respond just as many readers would: Oh, snap!

This was a fairly lighthearted piece, for me, anyway, and I tried to carry the same sense of energy and pace through this story that you get from the really good "Monster of the Week" episodes of the *X-Files*. I'll have to make it up to Mac sometime. . . .

All I wanted was a quiet beer.

That isn't too much to ask, is it—one contemplative drink at the end of a hard day of professional wizarding? Maybe a steak sandwich to go with it? You wouldn't think so. But somebody (or maybe Somebody) disagreed with me.

McAnally's Pub is a quiet little hole in the wall, like a hundred others in Chicago, in the basement of a large office building. You have to go down a few stairs to get to the door. When you get inside, you're at eye level with the creaky old ceiling fans in the rest of the place, and you have to take a couple of more steps down from the entryway to get to the pub's floor. It's lit mostly by candles. The finish work is all hand-carved, richly polished wood, stained a deeper brown than most would use, and combined with the candles, it feels cozily cavelike.

I opened the door to the place and got hit in the face with something I'd *never* smelled in Mac's pub before—the odor of food being burned.

It should say something about Mac's cooking that my first instinct was to make sure the shield bracelet on my left arm was ready to go as I drew the blasting rod from inside my coat. I took careful steps forward into the pub, blasting rod held up and ready. The usual lighting was dimmed, and only a handful of candles still glimmered.

The regular crowd at Mac's, members of the supernatural community of Chicago, were strewn about like broken dolls. Half a dozen people lay on the floor, limbs sprawled oddly, as if they'd dropped unconscious in the middle of calisthenics. A pair of older guys who were always playing chess at a table in the corner lay slumped across the table. Pieces were spread everywhere around them, some of them broken, and the old chess clock they used had been smashed to bits. Three young women who had watched too many episodes of *Charmed*, and who always showed up at Mac's together, were unconscious in a pile in the corner, as if they'd been huddled there in terror before they collapsed—but they were spattered with droplets of what looked like blood.

I could see several of the fallen breathing, at least. I waited for a long moment, but nothing jumped at me from the darkness, and I felt no sudden desire to start breaking things and then take a nap.

"Mac?" I called quietly.

Someone grunted.

I hurried over to the bar and found Mac on the floor beside it. He'd been badly beaten. His lips were split and puffy. His nose had been broken. Both his hands were swollen and purple—defensive wounds, probably. The baseball bat he kept behind the bar was lying next to him, smeared with blood—probably his own.

"Stars and stones," I breathed. "Mac."

I knelt down next to him, examining him for injuries as best I could. I didn't have any formal medical training, but several years' service in the Wardens in a war with the vampires of the Red Court had shown me more than my fair share of injuries. I didn't like the look of one of the bruises on his head, and he'd broken several fingers, but I didn't think it was anything he wouldn't recover from.

"What happened?" I asked him.

"Went nuts," he slurred. One of his cut lips reopened, and fresh blood appeared. "Violent."

I winced. "No kidding." I grabbed a clean cloth from the stack on the shelf behind the bar and ran cold water over it. I tried to clean some of the mess off his face. "They're all down," I told him as I did. "Alive. It's your place. How do you want to play it?"

Even through as much pain as he was in, Mac took a moment to consider before answering. "Murphy," he said finally.

I'd figured. Calling in the authorities would mean a lot of questions and attention, but it also meant everyone would get medical treatment sooner. Mac tended to put the customer first. But if he'd wanted to keep it under the radar, I would have understood that, too.

"I'll make the call," I told him.

THE AUTHORITIES SWOOPED down on the place with vigor. It was early in the evening, and we were evidently the first customers for the night shift EMTs.

"Jesus," Sergeant Karrin Murphy said from the doorway, looking around the interior of Mac's place. "What a mess."

"Tell me about it," I said glumly. My stomach was rumbling, and I was thirsty besides, but it just didn't seem right to help myself to any of Mac's stuff while he was busy getting patched up by the ambulance guys.

Murphy blew out a breath. "Well, brawls in bars aren't exactly uncommon." She came down into the room, removed a flashlight from her jacket pocket, and shone it around. "But maybe you'll tell me what really happened."

"Mac said his customers went nuts. They started acting erratic and then became violent."

"What, all of them? At the same time?"

"That was the impression he gave me. He wasn't overly coherent."

Murphy frowned and slowly paced the room, sweeping the light back and forth methodically. "You get a look at the customers?"

"There wasn't anything actively affecting them when I got here," I said. "I'm sure of that. They were all unconscious. Minor wounds, looked like they were mostly self-inflicted. I think those girls were the ones to beat Mac."

Murphy winced. "You think he wouldn't defend himself against them?"

"He could have pulled a gun. Instead, he had his bat out. He was probably trying to stop someone from doing something stupid, and it went bad."

"You know what I'm thinking?" Murphy asked. "When something odd happens to everyone in a pub?"

She had stopped at the back corner. Among the remnants of broken chessmen and scattered chairs, the circle of illumination cast by her flashlight had come to rest on a pair of dark brown beer bottles.

"Ugly thought," I said. "Mac's beer, in the service of darkness."

She gave me a level look. Well. As level a look as you *can* give when you're a five-foot blonde with a perky nose, glaring at a gangly wizard most of seven feet tall. "I'm serious, Harry. Could it have been something in the beer? Drugs? A poison? Something from your end of things?"

I leaned on the bar and chewed that thought over for a moment. Oh, sure, technically it could have been any of those. A number of drugs could cause psychotic behavior, though admittedly it might be hard to get that reaction in everyone in the bar at more or less the same time. Poisons were just drugs that happened to kill you, or the reverse. And if those people had been poisoned, they might still be in a lot of danger.

And once you got to the magical side of things, any one of a dozen methods could have been used to get to the people through the beer they'd imbibed—but all of them would require someone with access to the beer to pull it off, and Mac made his own brew.

In fact, he bottled it himself.

"It wasn't necessarily the beer," I said.

"You think they all got the same steak sandwich? The same batch of curly fries?" She shook her head. "Come on, Dresden. The food here is good, but that isn't what gets them in the door."

"Mac wouldn't hurt anybody," I said quietly.

"Really?" Murph asked, her voice quiet and steady. "You're sure about that? How well do you really know the man?"

I glanced around the bar, slowly.

"What's his first name, Harry?"

"Dammit, Murph." I sighed. "You can't go around being suspicious of everyone all the time."

"Sure I can." She gave me a faint smile. "It's my job, Harry. I have to look at things dispassionately. It's nothing personal. You know that."

"Yeah," I muttered. "I know that. But I also know what it's like to be dispassionately suspected of something you didn't do. It sucks."

She held up her hands. "Then let's figure out what did happen. I'll go talk to the principals, see if anyone remembers anything. You take a look at the beer."

"Yeah," I said. "Okay."

AFTER BOTTLING IT, Mac transports his beer in wooden boxes like old apple crates, only more heavy-duty. They aren't magical or anything. They're just sturdy as hell, and they stack up neatly. I came through the door of my apartment with a box of samples and braced myself against the impact of Mister, my tomcat, who generally declares a suicide charge on my shins the minute I come through the door. Mister is huge and most of his mass is muscle. I rocked at the impact, and the bottles rattled, but I took it in stride. Mouse, my big shaggy dogosaurus, was lying full on his side by the fireplace, napping. He looked up and thumped his tail on the ground once, then went back to sleep.

No work ethic around here at all. But then, he hadn't been cheated out of his well-earned beer. I took the box straight down the stepladder to my lab, calling, "Hi, Molly," as I went down.

Molly, my apprentice, sat at her little desk, working on a pair of potions. She had maybe five square feet of space to work with in my cluttered lab, but she managed to keep the potions clean and neat, and still had room left over for her Latin textbook, her notebook, and a can of Pepsi, the heathen. Molly's hair was kryptonite green today, with silver tips, and she was wearing cutoff jeans and a tight blue T-shirt with a Superman logo on the front. She was a knockout.

"Hiya, Harry," she said absently.

"Outfit's a little cold for March, isn't it?"

"If it were, you'd be staring at my chest a lot harder," she said, smirking a little. She glanced up, and it bloomed into a full smile. "Hey, beer!"

"You're young and innocent," I said firmly, setting the box down on a shelf. "No beer for you."

"You're living in denial," she replied, and rose to pick up a bottle.

Of course she did. I'd told her not to. I watched her carefully.

The kid's my apprentice, but she's got a knack for the finer aspects of magic. She'd be in real trouble if she had to blast her way out of a situation, but when it comes to the cobweb-fine enchantments, she's a couple of lengths ahead of me and pulling away fast—and I figured this had to be subtle work.

She frowned almost the second she touched the bottle. "That's . . . odd." She gave me a questioning look, and I gestured at the box. She ran her fingertips over each bottle in turn. "There's energy there. What is it, Harry?"

I had a good idea of what the beer had done to its drinkers—but it just didn't make sense. I wasn't about to tell her that, though. It would be very anti-Obi-Wan of me. "You tell me," I said, smiling slightly.

She narrowed her eyes at me and turned back to her potions, muttering over them for a few moments, and then easing them down to a low simmer. She came back to the bottles and opened one, sniffing at it and frowning some more.

"No taste testing," I told her. "It isn't pretty."

"I wouldn't think so," she replied in the same tone she'd used while working on her Latin. "It's laced with . . . some kind of contagion focus, I think."

I nodded. She was talking about magical contagion, not the medical kind. A contagion focus was something that formed a link between a smaller amount of its mass after it had been separated from the main body. A practitioner could use it to send magic into the main body, and by extension into all the smaller foci, even if they weren't in the same physical place. It was sort of like planting a transmitter on someone's car so that you could send a missile at it later.

"Can you tell what kind of working it's been set up to support?" I asked her.

She frowned. She had a pretty frown. "Give me a minute."

"Ticktock," I said.

She waved a hand at me without looking up. I folded my arms and waited. I gave her tests like this one all the time—and there was always a time limit. In my experience, the solutions you need the most badly are always time-critical. I'm trying to train the grasshopper for the real world.

Here was one of her first real-world problems, but she didn't have to know that. So long as she thought it was just one more test, she'd tear into it without hesitation. I saw no reason to rattle her confidence.

She muttered to herself. She poured some of the beer out into the beaker and held it up to the light from a specially prepared candle. She scrawled power calculations on a notebook. And twenty minutes later, she said, "Hah. Tricky, but not tricky enough."

"Oh?" I said.

"No need to be coy, boss," she said. "The contagion looks like a simple compulsion meant to make the victim drink more, but it's really a psychic conduit."

I leaned forward. "Seriously?"

Molly stared blankly at me for a moment. Then she blinked and said, "You didn't *know*?"

"I found the compulsion, but it was masking anything else that had been laid on the beer." I picked up the half-empty bottle and shook my head. "I brought it here because you've got a better touch for this kind of thing than I do. It would have taken me hours to puzzle it out. Good work."

"But . . . you didn't *tell* me this was for real." She shook her head dazedly. "Harry, what if I hadn't found it? What if I'd been wrong?"

"Don't get ahead of yourself, grasshopper," I said, turning for the stairs. "You *still* might be wrong."

THEY'D TAKEN MAC to Stroger, and he looked like hell. I had to lie to the nurse to get in to talk to him, flashing my consultant's ID badge and making like I was working with the Chicago cops on the case.

"Mac," I said, coming to sit down on the chair next to his bed, "how are you feeling?"

He looked at me with the eye that wasn't swollen shut. "Yeah. They said you wouldn't accept any painkillers."

He moved his head in a slight nod.

I laid out what I'd found. "It was elegant work, Mac. More intricate than anything I've done."

His teeth made noise as they ground together. He understood what two complex, interwoven enchantments meant as well as I did—a serious player was involved.

"Find him," Mac growled, the words slurring a little.

"Any idea where I could start?" I asked him.

He was quiet for a moment, then shook his head. "Caine?"

I lifted my eyebrows. "That thug from Night of the Living Brews? He's been around?"

He grunted. "Last night. Closing." He closed his eyes. "Loudmouth."

I stood up and put a hand on his shoulder. "Rest. I'll chat him up."

Mac exhaled slowly, maybe unconscious before I'd gotten done speaking.

I found Murphy down the hall.

"Three of them are awake," she said. "None of them remember anything for several hours before they presumably went to the bar."

I grimaced. "I was afraid of that." I told her what I'd learned.

"A psychic conduit?" Murphy asked. "What's that?"

"It's like any electrical power line," I said. "Except it plugs into your mind—and whoever is on the other end gets to decide what goes in."

Murphy went a little pale. She'd been on the receiving end of a couple of different kinds of psychic assault, and it had left some marks. "So do what you do. Put the whammy on them, and let's track them down."

I grimaced and shook my head. "I don't dare," I told her. "All I've got to track with is the beer itself. If I try to use it in a spell, it'll open me up to the conduit. It'll be as if I drank the stuff."

Murphy folded her arms. "And if that happens, you won't remember anything you learn, anyway."

"Like I said," I told her, "it's high-quality work. But I've got a name."

"A perp?"

"I'm sure he's guilty of something. His name's Caine. He's a con. Big, dumb, violent, and thinks he's a brewer."

She arched an eyebrow. "You got a history with this guy?"

"Ran over him during a case maybe a year ago," I said. "It got ugly. More for him than me. He doesn't like Mac much."

"He's a wizard?"

"Hell's bells, no," I said.

"Then how does he figure in?"

"Let's ask him."

MURPHY MADE SHORT work of running down an address for Herbert Orson Caine, mugger, rapist, and extortionist—a cheap apartment building on the south end of Bucktown.

Murphy knocked at the door, but we didn't get an answer.

"It's a good thing he's a con," she said, reaching for her cell phone. "I can probably get a warrant without too much trouble."

"With what?" I asked her. "Suggestive evidence of the use of black magic?"

"Tampering with drinks at a bar doesn't require the use of magic,"

Murphy said. "He's a rapist, and he isn't part of the outfit, so he doesn't have an expensive lawyer to raise a stink."

"Howsabout we save the good people of Chicago time and money and just take a look around?"

"Breaking and entering."

"I won't break anything," I promised. "I'll do all the entering, too."

"No," she said.

"But—"

She looked up at me, her jaw set stubbornly. "No, Harry."

I sighed. "These guys aren't playing by the rules."

"We don't know he's involved yet. I'm not cutting corners for someone who might not even be connected."

I was partway into a snarky reply when Caine opened the door from the stairwell and entered the hallway. He spotted us and froze. Then he turned and started walking away.

"Caine!" Murphy called. "Chicago PD!"

He bolted.

Murph and I had both been expecting that, evidently. We both rushed him. He slammed the door open, but I'd been waiting for that, too. I sent out a burst of my will, drawing my right hand in toward my chest as I shouted, *"Forzare!"*

Invisible force slammed the door shut as Caine began to go through it. It hit him hard enough to bounce him all the way back across the hall, into the wall opposite.

Murphy had better acceleration than I did. She caught up to Caine in time for him to swing one paw at her in a looping punch.

I almost felt sorry for the slob.

Murphy ducked the punch, then came up with all of her weight and the muscle of her legs and body behind her response. She struck the tip of his chin with the heel of her hand, snapping his face straight up.

Caine was brawny, big, and tough. He came back from the blow with a dazed snarl and swatted at Murphy again. Murph caught his arm, tugged him a little one way, a little the other, and using his own arm as a fulcrum, sent him flipping forward and down hard onto the floor.

He landed hard enough to make the floorboards shake, and Murphy promptly shifted her grip, twisting one hand into a painful angle, holding his arm out straight, using her leg to pin it into position.

"That would be assault," Murphy said in a sweet voice. "And on a police officer in the course of an investigation, no less."

"Bitch," Caine said. "I'm gonna break your—"

We didn't get to find out what he was going to break, because Murphy shifted her body weight maybe a couple of inches, and he screamed instead.

"Whaddayou want?" Caine demanded. "Lemme go! I didn't do nothin'!"

"Sure you did," I said cheerfully. "You assaulted Sergeant Murphy, here. I saw it with my own eyes."

"You're a two-time loser, Caine," Murphy said. "This will make it number three. By the time you get out, the first thing you'll need to buy will be a new set of teeth."

Caine said a lot of impolite words.

"Wow," I said, coming to stand over him. "That sucks. If only there were some way he could be of help to the community. You know, prove how he isn't a waste of space some other person could be using."

"Screw you," Caine said. "I ain't helping you with nothing."

Murphy leaned into his arm a little again to shut him up. "What happened to the beer at McAnally's?" she asked in a polite tone.

Caine said even more impolite words.

"I'm pretty sure that wasn't it," Murphy said. "I'm pretty sure you can do better."

"Bite me, cop bitch," Caine muttered.

"Sergeant Bitch," Murphy said. "Have it your way, bonehead. Bet you've got all kinds of fans back at Stateville." But she was frowning when she said it. Thugs like Caine rolled over when they were facing hard time. They didn't risk losing the rest of their adult lives out of simple contrariness—unless they were terrified of the alternative.

Someone or, dare I say it, something had Caine scared.

Well, that table could seat more than one player.

The thug had a little blood coming from the corner of his mouth. He must have bitten his tongue when Murphy hit him.

I pulled a white handkerchief out of my pocket and, in a single swooping motion, stooped down and smeared some blood from Caine's mouth onto it.

"What the hell?" he said, or something close to it. "What are you doing?"

"Don't worry about it, Caine," I told him. "It isn't going to be a long-term problem for you."

I took the cloth and walked a few feet away. Then I hunkered down and used a piece of chalk from another pocket to draw a circle around me on the floor.

Caine struggled feebly against Murphy, but she put him down again. "Sit still," she snapped. "I'll pull your shoulder right out of its socket."

"Feel free," I told Murphy. "He isn't going to be around long enough to worry about it." I squinted up at Caine and said, "Beefy, little bit of a gut. Bet you eat a lot of greasy food, huh, Caine?"

"Wh-what?" he said. "What are you doing?"

"Heart attack should look pretty natural," I said. "Murph, get ready to back off once he starts thrashing." I closed the circle and let it sparkle a little as I did. It was a waste of energy—special effects like that almost always are—but it made an impression on Caine.

"Jesus Christ!" Caine said. "Wait!"

"Can't wait," I told him. "Gotta make this go before the blood dries out. Quit being such a baby, Caine. She gave you a chance." I raised my hand over the fresh blood on the cloth. "Let's see now—"

"I can't talk!" Caine yelped. "If I talk, she'll know!"

Murphy gave his arm a little twist. "Who?" she demanded.

"I can't! Jesus, I swear! Dresden, don't—it isn't my fault. They needed bloodstone, and I had the only stuff in town that was pure enough! I just wanted to wipe that smile off that bastard's face!"

I looked up at Caine with a gimlet eye, my teeth bared. "You ain't saying anything that makes me want you to keep on breathing."

"I *can't*," Caine wailed. "She'll *know!*"

I fixed my stare on Caine and raised my hand in a slow, heavily overdramatized gesture. "*Intimidatus dorkus maximus!*" I intoned, making my voice intentionally hollow and harsh, and stressing the long vowels.

"Decker!" Caine screamed. "Decker, he set up the deal!"

I lowered my hand and let my head rock back. "Decker," I said. "That twit."

Murphy watched me and didn't let go of Caine, though I could tell she didn't want to keep holding him.

I shook my head at Murphy and said, "Let him scamper, Murph."

She let him go, and Caine fled for the stairs on his hands and knees, sobbing. He staggered out, falling down the first flight, from the sound of it.

I wrinkled up my nose as the smell of urine hit me. "Ah. The aroma of truth."

Murphy rubbed her hands on her jeans as if trying to wipe off something greasy. "Jesus, Harry."

"What?" I said. "You didn't want to break into his place."

"I didn't want you to put a gun to his head, either." She shook her head. "You couldn't really have . . ."

"Killed him?" I asked. I broke the circle and rose. "Yeah. With him right here in sight, yeah. I probably could have."

She shivered. "Jesus Christ."

"I wouldn't," I said. I went to her and put a hand on her arm. "I wouldn't, Karrin. You know that."

She looked up at me, her expression impossible to read. "You put on a really good act, Harry. It would have fooled a lot of people. It looked . . ."

"Natural on me," I said. "Yeah."

She touched my hand briefly with hers. "So, I guess we got something?"

I shook off dark thoughts and nodded. "We've got a name."

———

BURT DECKER RAN what was arguably the sleaziest of the half-dozen establishments that catered to the magical crowd in Chicago. Left Hand Goods prided itself on providing props and ingredients to the black magic crowd.

Oh, that wasn't so sinister as it sounded. Most of the trendy, self-appointed Death Eater wannabes in Chicago—or any other city, for that matter—didn't have enough talent to strike two rocks together and make sparks, much less hurt anybody. The really dangerous black wizards don't shop at places like Left Hand Goods. You could get everything you needed for most black magic at the freaking grocery store.

But, all the same, plenty of losers with bad intentions thought Left Hand Goods had everything you needed to create your own evil empire—and Burt Decker was happy to make them pay for their illusions.

Me and Murphy stepped in, between the display of socially maladjusted fungi on our right, a tank of newts (PLUCK YOUR OWN *#%$ING EYES, the sign said) on the left, and stepped around the big shelf of quasi-legal drug paraphernalia in front of us.

Decker was a shriveled little toad of a man. He wasn't overweight, but his skin looked too loose from a plump youth combined with a lifetime of too many naps in tanning beds. He was immaculately groomed, and his hair was a gorgeous black streaked with a dignified silver that was like a Rolls hood ornament on a VW Rabbit. He had beady black eyes with nothing warm behind them, and when he saw me, he licked his lips nervously.

"Hiya, Burt," I said.

There were a few shoppers, none of whom looked terribly appealing. Murphy held up her badge so everyone could see it and said, "We have some questions."

She might as well have shouted, "Fire!" The store emptied.

Murphy swaggered past a rack of discount porn DVDs, her coat open just enough to reveal the shoulder holster she wore. She picked one up, gave it a look, and tossed it on the floor. "Christ, I hate scum vendors like this."

"Hey!" Burt said. "You break it, you bought it."

"Yeah, right," Murphy said.

I showed him my teeth as I walked up and leaned both my arms on the counter he stood behind. It crowded into his personal space. His cologne was thick enough to stop bullets.

"Burt," I said, "make this simple, okay? Tell me everything you know about Caine."

Decker's eyes went flat, and his entire body became perfectly still. It was reptilian. "Caine?"

I smiled wider. "Big guy, shaggy hair, kind of a slob, with piss running down his leg. He made a deal with a woman for some bloodstone, and you helped."

Murphy had paused at a display of what appeared to be small, smoky quartz geodes. The crystals were nearly black, with purple veins running through them, and they were priced a couple of hundred dollars too high.

"I don't talk about my customers," Decker said. "It isn't good for business."

I glanced at Murphy. "Burt. We know you're connected."

She stared at me for a second, and sighed. Then she knocked a geode off the shelf. It shattered on the floor.

Decker winced and started to protest, but the words died on his lips.

"You know what isn't good for business, Decker?" I asked. "Having a big guy in a grey cloak hang out in your little Bad Juju Mart. Your customers start thinking that the Council is paying attention, how much business do you think you'll get?"

Decker stared at me with toad eyes, nothing on his face.

"Oops," Murphy said, and knocked another geode to the floor.

"People are in the hospital, Burt," I said. "Mac's one of them—and he was beaten on ground held neutral by the Unseelie Accords."

Burt bared his teeth. It was a gesture of surprise.

"Yeah," I said. I drew my blasting rod out of my coat and slipped enough of my will into it to make the runes and sigils carved along its length glitter with faint orange light. The smell of wood smoke curled up from it. "You don't want the heat this is gonna bring down, Burt."

Murphy knocked another geode down and said, "I'm the good cop."

"All right," Burt said. "Jesus, will you lay off? I'll talk, but you ain't gonna like it."

"I don't handle disappointment well, Burt." I tapped the glowing ember tip of the blasting rod down on his countertop for emphasis. "I really don't."

Burt grimaced at the black spots it left on the countertop. "Skirt comes in asking for bloodstone. But all I got is this crap from South Asscrack. Says she wants the real deal, and she's a bitch about it. I tell her I sold the end of my last shipment to Caine."

"Woman pisses you off," Murphy said, "and you send her to do business with a convicted rapist."

Burt looked at her with toad eyes.

"How'd you know where to find Caine?" I asked.

"He's got a discount card here. Filled out an application."

I glanced from the porn to the drug gear. "Uh-huh. What's he doing with bloodstone?"

"Why should I give a crap?" Burt said. "It's just business."

"How'd she pay?"

"What do I look like, a fucking video camera?"

"You look like an accomplice to black magic, Burt," I said.

"Crap," Burt said, smiling slightly. "I haven't had my hands on anything. I haven't done anything. You can't prove anything."

Murphy stared hard at Decker. Then, quite deliberately, she walked out of the store.

I gave him my sunniest smile. "That's the upside of working with the grey cloaks now, Burt," I said. "I don't need proof. I just need an excuse."

Burt stared hard at me. Then he swallowed, toadlike.

———

"SHE PAID WITH a Visa," I told Murphy when I came out of the store. "Meditrina Bassarid."

Murphy frowned up at my troubled expression. "What's wrong?"

"You ever see me pay with a credit card?"

"No. I figured no credit company would have you."

"Come on, Murph," I said. "That's just un-American. I don't bother with the things, because that magnetic strip goes bad in a couple of hours around me."

She frowned. "Like everything electronic does. So?"

"So if Ms. Bassarid has Caine scared out of his mind on magic . . ." I said.

Murphy got it. "Why is she using a credit card?"

"Because she probably isn't human," I said. "Nonhumans can sling power all over the place and not screw up anything if they don't want to. It also explains why she got sent to Caine to get taught a lesson and wound up scaring him to death instead."

Murphy said an impolite word. "But if she's got a credit card, she's in the system."

"To some degree," I said. "How long for you to find something?"

She shrugged. "We'll see. You get a description?"

"Blue-black hair, green eyes, long legs, and great tits," I said.

She eyed me.

"Quoting," I said righteously.

I'm sure she was fighting off a smile. "What are you going to do?"

"Go back to Mac's," I said. "He loaned me his key."

Murphy looked sideways at me. "Did he know he was doing that?"

I put my hand to my chest as if wounded. "Murphy," I said. "He's a friend."

I LIT A bunch of candles with a mutter and a wave of my hand, and I stared around Mac's place. Out in the dining area, chaos reigned.

Chairs were overturned. Salt from a broken shaker had spread over the floor. None of the chairs were broken, but the framed sign that read ACCORDED NEUTRAL TERRITORY was smashed and lay on the ground near the door.

An interesting detail, that.

Behind the bar, where Mac kept his iceboxes and his wood-burning stove, everything was as tidy as a surgical theater, with the exception of the uncleaned stove and some dishes in the sink. Nothing looked like a clue.

I shook my head and went to the sink. I stared at the dishes. I turned and stared at the empty storage cabinets under the bar, where a couple of boxes of beer still waited. I opened the icebox and stared at the food, and my stomach rumbled. There were some cold cuts. I made a sandwich and stood there munching it, looking around the place and thinking.

I didn't think of anything productive.

I washed the dishes in the sink, scowling and thinking up a veritable thunderstorm. I didn't get much further than a light sprinkle, though, before a thought struck me.

There really wasn't very much beer under the bar.

I finished the dishes, pondering that. Had there been a ton earlier? No. I'd picked up the half-used box and taken it home. The other two boxes were where I'd left them. But Mac usually kept a legion of beer bottles down there.

So why only two now?

I walked down to the far end of the counter, a nagging thought dancing around the back of my mind, where I couldn't see it. Mac kept a small office in the back corner, consisting of a table for his desk, a wooden chair, and a couple of filing cabinets. His food service and liquor permits were on display on the wall above it.

I sat down at the desk and opened the filing cabinets. I started going through Mac's records and books. Intrusive as hell, I know, but I had to figure out what was going on before matters got worse.

And that was when it hit me—matters getting worse. I could see a mortal wizard, motivated by petty spite, greed, or some other mundane motivation, wrecking Mac's bar. People can be amazingly petty. But nonhumans, now—that was a different story.

The fact that this Bassarid chick had a credit card meant she was methodical. I mean, you can't just conjure one out of thin air. She'd taken the time to create an identity for herself. That kind of forethought indicated a scheme, a plan, a goal. Untidying a Chicago bar, neutral ground or not, was not by any means the kind of goal that things from the Nevernever set for themselves when they went undercover into mortal society.

Something bigger was going on, then. Mac's place must have been a side item for Bassarid.

Or maybe a stepping-stone.

Mac was no wizard, but he was savvy. It would take more than cheap tricks to get to his beer with him here, and I was betting he had worked out more than one way to realize it if someone had intruded on his place when he was gone. So, if someone wanted to get to the beer, they'd need a distraction.

Like maybe Caine.

Caine made a deal with Bassarid, evidently—I assumed he gave her the bloodstone in exchange for being a pain to Mac. So, she ruins Mac's day, gets the bloodstone in exchange, end of story—nice and neat.

Except that it didn't make a lot of sense. Bloodstone isn't exactly impossible to come by. Why would someone with serious magical juice do a favor for Caine to get some?

Because maybe Caine was a stooge, a distraction for anyone trying to follow Bassarid's trail. What if Bassarid had picked someone who had a history with Mac, so that I could chase after him while she . . . did whatever she planned to do with the rest of Mac's beer?

Wherever the hell that was.

It took me an hour and a half to find anything in Mac's files—the first thing was a book. A really old book, bound in undyed leather. It was a journal, apparently, and written in some kind of cipher.

Also interesting, but probably not germane.

The second thing I found was a receipt, for a whole hell of a lot of money, along with an itemized list of what had been sold—beer, representing all of Mac's various heavenly brews. Someone at Worldclass Limited had paid him an awful lot of money for his current stock.

I got on the phone and called Murphy.

"Who bought the evil beer?" Murphy asked.

"The beer isn't evil. It's a victim. And I don't recognize the name of the company. Worldclass Limited."

Keys clicked in the background as Murphy hit the Internet. "Caterers," Murphy said a moment later. "High end."

I thought of the havoc that might be about to ensue at some wedding or bar mitzvah and shuddered. "Hell's bells," I breathed. "We've got to find out where they went."

"Egad, Holmes," Murphy said in the same tone I would have said, "Duh."

"Yeah. Sorry. What did you get on Bassarid?"

"Next to nothing," Murphy said. "It'll take me a few more hours to get the information behind her credit card."

"No time," I said. "She isn't worried about the cops. Whoever she is, she planned this whole thing to keep her tracks covered from the likes of me."

"Aren't we full of ourselves?" Murphy grumped. "Call you right back."

She did.

"The caterers aren't available," she said. "They're working the private boxes at the Bulls game."

I RUSHED TO the United Center.

Murphy could have blown the whistle and called in the artillery, but she hadn't. Uniformed cops already at the arena would have been the first to intervene, and if they did, they were likely to cross Bassarid. Whatever she was, she would be more than they could handle.

She'd scamper or, worse, one of the cops could get killed. So Murphy and I both rushed to get there and find the bad guy before she could pull the trigger, so to speak, on the Chicago PD.

It was half an hour before the game, and the streets were packed. I parked in front of a hydrant and ran half a mile to the United Center, where thousands of people were packing themselves into the building for the game. I picked up a ticket from a scalper for a ridiculous amount of money on the way, emptying my pockets, and earned about a million glares from Bulls fans as I juked and ducked through the crowd to get through the entrances as quickly as I possibly could.

Once inside, I ran for the lowest level, the bottommost ring of concession stands and restrooms circling entrances to the arena—the most crowded level, currently—where the entrances to the most expensive ring of private boxes were. I started at the first box I came to, knocking on the locked doors. No one answered at the first several, and at the next, the door was opened by a blonde who, in an expensive business outfit showing a lot of décolletage, had clearly been expecting someone else.

"Who are you?" she stammered.

I flashed her my laminated consultant's ID, too quickly to be seen. "Department of Alcohol, Tobacco, and Firearms, ma'am," I said in my official's voice, which is like my voice only deeper and more pompous. I've heard it from all kinds of government types. "We've had a report of tainted beer. I need to check your bar, see if the bad batch is in there."

"Oh," she said, backing up, her body language immediately cooperative. I pegged her as somebody's receptionist, maybe. "Of course."

I padded into the room and went to the bar, rifling bottles and opening cabinets until I found eleven dark brown bottles with a simple cap with an *M* stamped into the metal—Mac's mark.

I turned to find the blonde holding out the half-empty bottle number twelve in a shaking hand. Her eyes were a little wide. "Um. Am I in trouble?"

I might be. I took the beer bottle from her, moving gingerly, and set it down with the others. "Have you been feeling, uh, sick or anything?" I asked as I edged toward the door, just in case she came at me with a baseball bat.

She shook her head, breathing more heavily. Her manicured fingernails trailed along the V-neck of her blouse. "I . . . I mean, you know." Her face flushed. "Just looking forward to . . . the game."

"Uh-huh," I said warily.

Her eyes suddenly became warmer and very direct. I don't know what it was exactly, but she was suddenly filled with that energy women have that has nothing to do with magic and everything to do with creating it. The temperature in the room felt as if it went up about ten degrees. "Maybe you should examine me, sir."

I suddenly had a very different idea of what Mac had been defending himself from with that baseball bat.

And it had turned ugly on him.

Hell's bells, I thought I knew what we were dealing with.

"Fantastic idea," I told her. "You stay right here and get comfortable. I'm going to grab something sweet. I'll be back in two shakes."

"All right," she cooed. Her suit jacket slid off her shoulders to the floor. "Don't be long."

I smiled at her in what I hoped was a suitably sultry fashion and backed out. Then I shut the door, checked its frame, and focused my will into the palm of my right hand. I directed my attention to one edge of the door and whispered, *"Forzare."*

Metal squealed as the door bent in its frame. With any luck, it would take a couple of guys with crowbars an hour or two to get it open again—and hopefully Bubbles would pitch over into a stupor before she did herself any harm.

It took me three more doors to find one of the staff of Worldclass Limited—a young man in dark slacks, a white shirt, and a black bow tie, who asked if he could help me.

I flashed the ID again. "We've received a report that a custom microbrew your company purchased for this event has been tainted. Chicago PD is on the way, but meanwhile I need your company to round up the bottles before anyone else gets poisoned drinking them."

The young man frowned. "Isn't it the Bureau?"

"Excuse me?"

"You said Department of Alcohol, Tobacco, and Firearms. It's a bureau."

Hell's bells, why did I get someone who could think *now*?

"Can I see that ID again?" he asked.

"Look, buddy," I said. "You've gotten a bad batch of beer. If you don't round it up, people are going to get sick. Okay? The cops are on the way, but if people start guzzling it now, it isn't going to do anybody any good."

He frowned at me.

"Better safe than sorry, right?" I asked him.

Evidently, his ability to think did not extend to areas beyond asking stupid questions of well-meaning wizards. "Look, uh, really you should take this up with my boss."

"Then get me to him," I said. "Now."

The caterer might have been uncertain, but he wasn't slow. We hurried through the growing crowds to one of the workrooms that his company was using as a staging area. A lot of people in white shirts were hurrying all over the place with carts and armloads of everything from crackers to cheese to bottles of wine—and a dozen of Mac's empty wooden boxes were stacked up to one side of the room.

My guide led me to a harried-looking woman in catering wear, who listened to him impatiently and cut him off halfway through. "I know, I know," she snapped. "Look, I'll tell you what I told Sergeant Murphy. A city health inspector is already here, and they're already checking things out, and I am *not* losing my contract with the arena over some pointless scare."

"You already talked to Murphy?" I said.

"Maybe five minutes ago. Sent her to the woman from the city, over at midcourt."

"Tall woman?" I asked, feeling my stomach drop. "Blue-black hair? Uh, sort of busty?"

"Know her, do you?" The head caterer shook her head. "Look, I'm busy."

"Yeah," I said. "Thanks."

I ran back into the corridor and sprinted for the boxes at midcourt, drawing out my blasting rod as I went and hoping I would be in time to do Murphy any good.

A FEW YEARS ago, I'd given Murphy a key to my apartment, in a sense. It was a small amulet that would let her past the magical wards that defend the place. I hadn't bothered to tell her the thing had a second purpose—I'd wanted her to have one of my personal possessions, something I could, if necessary, use to find her if I needed to. She would have been insulted at the very idea.

A quick stop into the men's room, a chalk circle on the floor, a muttered spell, and I was on her trail. I actually ran past the suite she was in before the spell let me know I had passed her, and I had to backtrack to the door. I debated blowing it off the hinges. There was something to be said for a shock-and-awe entrance.

Of course, most of those things couldn't be said for doing it in the middle of a crowded arena that was growing more crowded by the second. I'd probably shatter the windows at the front of the suite, and that could be dangerous for the people sitting in the stands beneath them. I tried the door, just for the hell of it and—

It opened.

Well, dammit. I much prefer making a dramatic entrance.

I came in and found a plush-looking room, complete with dark, thick carpeting, leather sofas, a buffet bar, a wet bar, and two women making out on a leather love seat.

They looked up as I shut the door behind me. Murphy's expression was, at best, vague, her eyes hazy, unfocused, the pupils dilated until you could hardly see any blue, and her lips were a little swollen with kissing. She saw me, and a slow and utterly sensuous smile spread over her mouth. "Harry. There you are."

The other woman gave me the same smile with a much more predatory edge. She had shoulder-length hair, so black, it was highlighted with dark, shining blue. Her green-gold eyes were bright and intense, her mouth full. She was dressed in a grey business skirt-suit, with the jacket off and her shirt mostly unbuttoned, if not quite indecent. She was, otherwise, as Burt Decker had described her—statuesque and beautiful.

"So," she said in a throaty, rich voice, "this is Harry Dresden."

"Yes," Murphy said, slurring the word drunkenly. "Harry. And his rod." She let out a giggle.

I mean, my God. She *giggled*.

"I like his looks," the brunette said. "Strong. Intelligent."

"Yeah," Murphy said. "I've wanted him for the longest time." She tittered. "Him and his rod."

I pointed said blasting rod at Meditrina Bassarid. "What have you done to her?"

"I?" the woman said. "Nothing."

Murphy's face flushed. "Yet."

The woman let out a smoky laugh, toying with Murphy's hair. "We're getting to that. I only shared the embrace of the god with her, Wizard."

"I was going to kick your ass for that," Murphy said. She looked around, and I noticed that a broken lamp lay on the floor, and the end table it had sat on had been knocked over, evidence of a struggle. "But I feel so *good* now. . . ." Smoldering blue eyes found me. "Harry. Come sit down with us."

"You should," the woman murmured. "We'll have a good time." She produced a bottle of Mac's ale from somewhere. "Come on. Have a drink with us."

All I'd wanted was a beer, for Pete's sake.

But this wasn't what I had in mind. It was just wrong. I told myself very firmly that it was wrong. Even if Karrin managed, somehow, to make her gun's shoulder rig look like lingerie.

Or maybe that was me.

"Meditrina was a Roman goddess of wine," I said instead. "And the bassarids were another name for the handmaidens of Dionysus." I nodded at the beer in her hand and said, "I thought maenads were wine snobs."

Her mouth spread in a wide, genuine-looking smile, and her teeth were very white. "Any spirit is the spirit of the god, mortal."

"That's what the psychic conduit links them to," I said. "To Dionysus. To the god of revels and ecstatic violence."

"Of course," the maenad said. "Mortals have forgotten the true power of the god. The time has come to begin reminding them."

"If you're going to muck with the drinks, why not start with the big beer dispensary in the arena? You'd get it to a lot more people that way."

She sneered at me. "Beer, brewed in cauldrons the size of houses by machines and then served cold. It has no soul. It isn't worthy of the name."

"Got it," I said. "You're a beer snob."

She smiled, her gorgeous green eyes on mine. "I needed something real. Something a craftsman took loving pride in creating."

This actually made sense, from a technical perspective. Magic is about a lot of things, and one of them is emotion. Once you begin to mass-manufacture anything, by the very nature of the process, you lose the sense of personal attachment you might have to something made by hand. For the maenad's purposes, it would have meant that the mass-produced beer had nothing she could sink her magical teeth into, no foundation upon which to lay her complex compulsion.

Mac's beer certainly qualified as being produced with pride—real, personal pride, I mean, not official corporate spokesperson pride.

"Why?" I asked her. "Why do this at all?"

"I am hardly alone in my actions, Wizard," she responded. "And it is who I am."

I frowned and tilted my head at her.

"Mortals have forgotten the gods," she said, hints of anger creeping into her tone. "They think the White God drove out the many gods. But they are here. We are here. I, too, was worshipped in my day, mortal man."

"Maybe you didn't know this," I said, "but most of us couldn't give a rat's ass. Raining down thunderbolts from on high isn't exclusive territory anymore."

She snarled, her eyes growing even brighter. "Indeed. We withdrew and gave the world into your keeping—and what has become of it? In two thousand years, you've poisoned and raped Mother Earth, who gave you life. You've cut down the forests, fouled the air, and darkened Apollo's chariot itself with the stench of your smithies."

"And touching off a riot at the Bulls game is going to make some kind of point?" I demanded.

She smiled, showing sharp canines. "My sisters have been doing football matches on the continent for years. We're expanding the franchise." She drank from the bottle, wrapping her lips around it and making sure I noticed. "Moderation. It's disgusting. We should have strangled Aristotle in his crib. Alcoholism—calling the god a *disease*!" She bared her teeth at me. "A lesson must be taught."

Murphy shivered, and then her expression turned ugly, her blue eyes focusing on me.

"Show your respect to the god, Wizard," the maenad spat. "Drink. Or I will introduce you to Pentheus and Orpheus."

Greek guys. Both of whom were torn to pieces by maenads and their mortal female companions in orgies of ecstatic violence.

Murphy was breathing heavily now, sweating, her cheeks flushed, her eyes burning with lust and rage. And she was staring right at me.

Hooboy.

"Make you a counteroffer," I said quietly. "Break off the enchantment on the beer and get out of my town, now, and I won't FedEx you back to the Aegean in a dozen pieces."

"If you will not honor the god in life," Meditrina said, "then you will honor him in *death*." She flung out a hand, and Murphy flew at me with a howl of primal fury.

I ran away.

Don't get me wrong. I've faced a lot of screaming, charging monsters in my day. Granted, not one of them was small and blond and pretty from making out with what might have been a literal goddess. All the same, my options were limited. Murphy obviously wasn't in her right mind. I had my blasting rod ready to go, but I didn't want to kill her. I didn't want to go hand to hand with her, either. Murphy was a dedicated martial artist, especially good at grappling, and if it came to a clinch, I wouldn't fare any better than Caine had.

I flung myself back out of the room and into the corridor beyond before Murphy could catch me and twist my arm into some kind of Escher portrait. I heard glass breaking somewhere behind me.

Murphy came out hard on my heels and I brought my shield bracelet up as I turned, trying to angle it so that it wouldn't hurt her. My shield flashed to blue-silver life as she closed on me, and she bounced off it as if it had been solid steel, stumbling to one side. Meditrina followed her, clutching a broken bottle, the whites of her eyes visible all the way around the bright green, an ecstatic and entirely creepy expression of joy lighting her face. She slashed at me, three quick, graceful motions, and I got out of the way of only one of them. Hot pain seared my chin and my right hand, and my blasting rod went flying off down the corridor, bouncing off people's legs.

I'm not an expert like Murphy, but I've taken some classes, too, and more important, I've been in a bunch of scrapes in my life. In the literal school of hard knocks, you learn the ropes fast, and the lessons go bone-deep. As I reeled from the blow, I turned my momentum into a spin and swept my leg through Meditrina's. Goddess or not, the maenad didn't weigh half what I did, and her legs went out from under her.

Murphy blindsided me with a kick that lit up my whole rib cage with pain, and she had seized an arm before I could fight through it. If it had been my right arm, I'm not sure what might have happened—

but she grabbed my left, and I activated my shield bracelet, sheathing it in sheer, kinetic power and forcing her hands away.

I don't care how many aikido lessons you've had—they don't train you for force fields.

I reached out with my will and screamed, *"Forzare!"* Then I seized a large plastic waste bin with my power. With a flick of my hand, I flung it at Murphy. It struck her hard and knocked her off me; I back-pedaled. Meditrina had regained her feet and was coming for me, bottle flickering.

She drove me back into the beer-stand counter across the hall, and I brought up my shield again just as her makeshift weapon came forward. Glass shattered against it, cutting her own hand—always a risk with a bottle. But the force of the blow was sufficient to carry through the shield and slam my back against the counter. I bounced off some guy trying to carry beer in plastic cups and went down soaked in brew.

Murphy jumped on me then, pinning my left arm down as Meditrina started raking at my face with her nails, both of them screaming like banshees.

I had to shut one eye when a sharp fingernail grazed it, but I saw my chance as Meditrina's hands—hot, horribly strong hands—closed over my throat.

I choked out a gasped, *"Forzare!"* and reached out my right hand, snapping a slender chain that held up one end of a sign suspended above the beer stand behind me.

A heavy wooden sign that read, in large cheerful letters, PLEASE DRINK RESPONSIBLY, swung down in a ponderous, scything arc and struck Meditrina on the side of the head, hitting her like a giant's fist. Her nails left scarlet lines on my throat as she was torn off me.

Murphy looked up, shocked, and I hauled with all my strength. I had to position her before she took up where Meditrina left off. I felt something wrench and give way as my thumb left its socket, and I howled in pain as the sign swung back, albeit with a lot less momentum now, and clouted Murphy on the noggin, too.

Then a bunch of people jumped on us, and the cops came running.

———

WHILE THEY WERE arresting me, I managed to convince the cops that there was something bad in Mac's beer. They got with the caterers and rounded up the whole batch, apparently before more than a handful of people could drink any. There was some wild behavior, but no one else got hurt.

None of which did me any good. After all, I was soaked in Budweiser and had assaulted two attractive women. I went to the drunk tank, which angered me mainly because I'd never gotten my freaking beer. And to add insult to injury, after paying exorbitant rates for a ticket, I hadn't gotten to see the game, either.

There's no freaking justice in this world.

Murphy turned up in the morning to let me out. She had a black eye and a sign-shaped bruise across one cheekbone.

"So let me get this straight," Murphy said. "After we went to Left Hand Goods, we followed the trail to the Bulls game. Then we confronted this maenad character, there was a struggle, and I got knocked out."

"Yep," I said.

There was really no point in telling it any other way. The nefarious hooch would have destroyed her memory of the evening. The truth would just bother her.

Hell, it bothered me—on more levels than I wanted to think about.

"Well, Bassarid vanished from the hospital," Murphy said. "So she's not around to press charges. And, given that you were working with me on an investigation, and because several people have reported side effects that sound a lot like they were drugged with Rohypnol or something—and because it was you who got the cops to pull the rest of the bottles—I managed to get the felony charges dropped. You're still being cited for drunk and disorderly."

"Yay," I said without enthusiasm.

"Could have been worse," Murphy said. She paused and studied me for a moment. "You look like hell."

"Thanks," I said.

She looked at me seriously. Then she smiled, stood up on her tip-toes, and kissed my cheek. "You're a good man, Harry. Come on. I'll give you a ride home."

I smiled all the way to her car.

LOVE HURTS

—from *Songs of Love and Death,*
edited by George R. R. Martin
and Gardner Dozois

Takes place between *Turn Coat*
and *Changes*

Gardner Dozois has a bunch of awards for his anthologies because he's *good* at them, and I leapt at his invitation to contribute to the anthology he was working on with George R. R. Martin, originally titled *Star-Crossed Lovers.* Despite my enthusiasm, finding a starting point for a Dresden story was sort of a puzzler for me, since Harry Dresden might be in the top three Star-Influence-Free lovers in the whole contemporary-fantasy genre. How was I going to bring him into a story with a theme like that?

Answer: Get him into the thick of things next to Murphy when seemingly random love spells are running amok through the city. After that, all I had to do was apply his usual streak of luck and cackle madly to myself while typing.

The title of the anthology changed to *Songs of Love and Death* after I had written the story, which is probably a good thing. Otherwise, I may have tried to find a way to fit a death-metal battle of the bands into the margins somewhere. No one deserves that.

Murphy gestured at the bodies and said, "Love hurts."

I ducked under the crime scene tape and entered the Wrigleyville apartment. The smell of blood and death was thick. It made gallows humor inevitable.

Murphy stood there looking at me. She wasn't offering explanations. That meant she wanted an unbiased opinion from CPD's Special Investigations consultant—who is me, Harry Dresden. As far as I know, I am the only wizard on the planet earning a significant portion of his income working for a law enforcement agency.

I stopped and looked around, taking inventory.

Two bodies, naked, male and female, still intertwined in the act. One little pistol, illegal in Chicago, lying upon the limp fingers of the woman. Two gunshot wounds to the temples, one each. There were two overlapping fan-shaped splatters of blood, and more had soaked into the carpet. The bodies stank like hell. Some very unromantic things had happened to them after death.

I walked a little farther into the room and looked around. Somewhere in the apartment, an old vinyl was playing Queen. Freddie wondered who wanted to live forever. As I listened, the song ended and began again a few seconds later, popping and scratching nostalgically.

The walls were covered in photographs.

I don't mean there were a lot of pictures on the wall, like at Great-grandma's house. I mean covered in photographs. Entirely. Completely papered.

I glanced up. So was the ceiling.

I took a moment to walk slowly around, looking at pictures. All of them, every single one of them, featured the two dead people together, posed somewhere and looking deliriously happy. I walked and peered. Plenty of the pictures were near-duplicates in most details, except that the subjects wore different sets of clothing—generally cutesy matching T-shirts. Most of the sites were tourist spots within Chicago.

It was as if the couple had gone on the same vacation tour every day, over and over again, collecting the same general batch of pictures each time.

"Matching T-shirts," I said. "Creepy."

Murphy's smile was unpleasant. She was a tiny, compactly muscular woman with blond hair and a button nose. I'd say she was so cute, I just wanted to put her in my pocket, but if I tried to do it, she'd break my arm. Murph knows martial arts.

She waited and said nothing.

"Another suicide pact. That's the third one this month." I gestured at the pictures. "Though the others weren't quite so cuckoo for Cocoa Puffs. Or, ah, in medias res." I shrugged and gestured at the obsessive photographs. "This is just crazy."

Murphy lifted one pale eyebrow ever so slightly. "Remind me— how much do we pay you to give us advice, Sherlock?"

I grimaced. "Yeah, yeah. I know." I was quiet for a while and then said, "What were their names?"

"Greg and Cindy Bardalacki," Murphy said.

"Seemingly unconnected dead people, but they share similar patterns of death. Now we're upgrading to irrational and obsessive behavior as a precursor. . . ." I frowned. I checked several of the pictures and went over to eye the bodies. "Oh," I said. "Oh, hell's bells."

Murphy arched an eyebrow.

"No wedding rings anywhere," I said. "No wedding pictures. And . . ." I finally found a framed family picture, which looked to have been there for a while, among all the snapshots. Greg and Cindy were both in it, along with an older couple and a younger man.

"Jesus, Murph," I said. "They weren't a married couple. They were brother and sister."

Murphy eyed the intertwined bodies. There were no signs of struggle. Clothes, champagne flutes, and an empty bubbly bottle lay scattered. "Married, no," she said. "Couple, yes." She was unruffled. She'd already worked that out for herself.

"Ick," I said. "But that explains it."

"Explains what?"

"These two. They were together—and they went insane doing it. This has the earmarks of someone tampering with their minds."

Murphy squinted at me. "Why?"

I spread my hands. "Let's say Greg and Cindy bump into Bad Guy X. Bad Guy X gets into their heads and makes them fall wildly in love and lust with each other. There's nothing they can do about the feelings—which seem perfectly natural—but on some level they're aware that what they're doing is not what they want, and dementedly wrong besides. Their compromised conscious minds clash with their subconscious"—I gestured at the pictures—"and it escalates until they can't handle it anymore, and bang." I shot Murphy with my thumb and forefinger.

"If you're right, they aren't the deceased," Murphy said. "They're the victims. Big difference. Which is it?"

"Wish I could say," I said. "But the only evidence that could prove it one way or another is leaking out onto the floor. If we get a survivor, maybe I could take a peek and see, but barring that, we're stuck with legwork."

Murphy sighed and looked down. "Two suicide pacts could—technically—be a coincidence. Three of them, no way it's natural. This feels more like something's MO. Could it be another one of those Skavis vampires?"

"They gun for loners," I said, shaking my head. "These deaths don't fit their profile."

"So you're telling me we need to turn up a common denominator to link the victims? Gosh, I wish I could have thought of that on my own."

I winced. "Yeah." I glanced over at a couple of other SI detectives in the room, taking pictures of the bodies and documenting the walls and so on. Forensics wasn't on-site. They don't like to waste their time on the suicides of the emotionally disturbed, regardless of how bizarre they might be. That was crap work, and as such had been dutifully passed to SI.

I lowered my voice. "If someone is playing mind games, the Council might know something. I'll try to pick up the trail on that end. You start from here. Hopefully, I'll earn my pay and we'll meet in the middle."

"Right." Murph stared at the bodies, and her eyes were haunted. She knew what it was like to be the victim of mental manipulation. I didn't reach out to support her. She hated showing vulnerability, and I didn't want to point out to her that I'd noticed.

Freddie reached a crescendo that told us love must die.

Murphy sighed and called, "For the love of God, someone turn off that damn record."

"I'M SORRY, HARRY," Captain Luccio said. "We don't exactly have orbital satellites for detecting black magic."

I waited a second to be sure she was finished. The presence of so much magical talent on the far end of the call meant that at times the lag could stretch out between Chicago and Edinburgh, the headquarters of the White Council of Wizards. Anastasia Luccio, captain of the Wardens, my ex-girlfriend, had been readily forthcoming with the information the Council had on any shenanigans going on in Chicago— which was exactly nothing.

"Too bad we don't, eh?" I asked. "Unofficially—is there anyone who might know anything?"

"The Gatekeeper, perhaps. He has a gift for sensing problem areas.

But no one has seen him for weeks, which is hardly unusual. And frankly, Warden Dresden, you're supposed to be the one giving *us* this kind of information." Her voice was half teasing, half deadly serious. "What do you think is happening?"

"Three couples, apparently lovey-dovey as hell, have committed dual suicide in the past two weeks," I told her. "The last two were brother and sister. There were some seriously irrational components to their behavior."

"You suspect mental tampering," she said. Her voice was hard.

Luccio had been a victim, too.

I found myself smiling somewhat bitterly at no one. She had been, among other things, mindboinked into going out with me. Which was apparently the only way anyone would date me, lately. "It seems a reasonable suspicion. I'll let you know what I turn up."

"Use caution," she said. "Don't enter any suspect situation without backup on hand. There's too much chance that you could be compromised."

"Compromised?" I asked. "Of the two people having this conversation, which one of them exposed the last guy rearranging people's heads?"

"Touché," Luccio said. "But he got away with it because we were overconfident. So use caution, anyway."

"Planning on it," I said.

There was a moment of awkward silence, and then Anastasia said, "How have you been, Harry?"

"Keeping busy," I said. She had already apologized to me, sort of, for abruptly walking out of my personal life. She'd never intended to be there in the first place. There had been a real emotional tsunami around the events of last year, and I wasn't the one who had gotten the most hurt by them. "You?"

"Keeping busy." She was quiet for a moment and then said, "I know it's over. But I'm glad for the time we had together. It made me happy. Sometimes I—"

Miss feeling that, I thought, completing the sentence. My throat felt tight. "Nothing wrong with happy."

"No, there isn't. When it's real." Her voice softened. "Be careful, Harry. Please."

"I will," I said.

I STARTED COMBING the supernatural world for answers and got almost nothing. The Little Folk, who could usually be relied on to provide some kind of information, had nothing for me. Their memory for detail was very short, and the deaths had happened too long ago to get me anything but conflicting gibberish from them.

I made several mental nighttime sweeps through the city using the scale model of Chicago in my basement, and got nothing but a headache for my trouble.

I called around the Paranet, the organization of folk with only modest magical gifts, the kind who often found themselves being preyed upon by more powerful supernatural beings. They worked together now, sharing information, communicating successful techniques, and generally overcoming their lack of raw magical muscle with mutually supportive teamwork. They didn't have anything for me, either.

I hit McAnally's, a hub of the supernatural social scene, and asked a lot of questions. No one had any answers. Then I started contacting the people I knew in the scene, starting with the ones I thought most likely to provide information. I worked my way methodically down the list, crossing out names, until I got to *Ask random people on the street*.

There are days when I don't feel like much of a wizard. Or an investigator. Or a wizard investigator.

Ordinary PIs have a lot of days like that, where they look and look and look for information and find nothing. I get fewer of those days than most, on account of the whole wizard thing giving me a lot more options—but sometimes I come up goose eggs, anyway.

I just hate doing it when lives may be in danger.

———

FOUR DAYS LATER, all I knew was that nobody knew about any black magic happening in Chicago, and the only traces of it I *did* find were the minuscule amounts of residue left from black magic wrought by those without enough power to be a threat (Warden Ramirez had coined the phrase "dim magic" to describe that kind of petty, essentially harmless malice). There were also the usual traces of dim magic performed subconsciously from a bed of dark emotions, probably by someone who might not even know they had a gift.

In other words, goose eggs.

Fortunately, Murphy got the job done.

Sometimes hard work is way better than magic.

MURPHY'S SATURN HAD gotten a little blown up a couple of years back, sort of my fault, and what with her demotion and all, it would be a while before she'd be able to afford something besides her old Harley. For some reason, she didn't want to take the motorcycle, so that left my car, the ever trusty (almost always) *Blue Beetle*, an old-school VW Bug that had seen me through one nasty scrape after another. More than once, it had been pounded badly, but always it had risen to do battle once more—if by battle one means driving somewhere at a sedate speed, without much acceleration and only middling gas mileage.

Don't start. It's paid for.

I stopped outside Murphy's little white house, with its little pink rose garden, and rolled down the window on the passenger side. "Make like the Dukes of Hazzard," I said. "Door's stuck."

Murphy gave me a narrow look. Then she tried the door. It opened easily. She slid into the passenger seat with a smug smile, closed the door, and didn't say anything.

"Police work has made you cynical," I said.

"If you want to ogle my butt, you'll just have to work for it like everyone else, Harry."

I snorted and put the car in gear. "Where we going?"

"Nowhere until you buckle up," she said, putting her own seat belt on.

"It's my car," I said.

"It's the law. You want to get cited? 'Cause I can do that."

I debated whether or not it was worth it while she gave me her cop look—and produced a ballpoint pen.

I buckled up.

Murphy beamed at me. "Springfield. Head for I-55."

I grunted. "Kind of out of your jurisdiction."

"If we were investigating something," Murphy said. "We're not. We're going to the fair."

I eyed her sidelong. "On a date?"

"Sure, if someone asks," she said offhandedly. Then she froze for a second, and added, "It's a reasonable cover story."

"Right," I said. Her cheeks looked a little pink. Neither of us said anything for a little while.

I merged onto the highway, always fun in a car originally designed to rocket down the Autobahn at a blistering one hundred kilometers an hour, and asked Murphy, "Springfield?"

"State Fair," she said. "That was the common denominator."

I frowned, going over the dates in my head. "State Fair only runs, what? Ten days?"

Murphy nodded. "They shut down tonight."

"But the first couple died twelve days ago."

"They were both volunteer staff for the fair, and they were down there on the grounds setting up." Murphy lifted a foot to rest her heel on the edge of the passenger seat, frowning out the window. "I found Skee-Ball tickets and one of those chintzy stuffed animals in the second couple's apartment. And the Bardalackis got pulled over for speeding on I-55, five minutes out of Springfield and bound for Chicago."

"So *maybe* they went to the fair," I said. "Or maybe they were just taking a road trip or something."

Murphy shrugged. "Possibly. But if I assume that it's a coincidence, it doesn't get me anywhere—and we've got nothing. If I assume there's a connection, we've got a possible answer."

I beamed at her. "I thought you didn't like reading Parker."

She eyed me. "That doesn't mean his logic isn't sound."

"Oh. Right."

She exhaled heavily. "It's the best I've got. I just hope that if I get you into the general area, you can pick up on whatever is going on."

"Yeah," I said, thinking of walls papered in photographs. "Me, too."

THE SMELLS ARE what I enjoy the most about places like the State Fair. You get combinations of smells at such events like none found anywhere else. Popcorn, roast nuts, and fast food predominate, and you can get anything you want to clog your arteries or burn out your stomach lining. Chili dogs, funnel cakes, fried bread, majorly greasy pizza, candy apples, ye gods. Evil food smells amazing—which is either proof that there is a Satan or some equivalent out there, or that the Almighty doesn't actually want everyone to eat organic tofu all the time. I can't decide.

Other smells are a cross section, depending on where you're standing. Disinfectant and filth walking by the Porta-Potties, exhaust and burned oil and sun-baked asphalt and gravel in the parking lots, sunlight on warm bodies, suntan lotion, cigarette smoke and beer near some of the attendees, the pungent, honest smell of livestock near the animal shows, stock contests, or pony rides—all of it charging right up your nose. I like indulging my sense of smell.

Smell is the hardest sense to lie to.

Murphy and I started in midmorning and began walking around the fair in a methodical search pattern. It took us all day. The State Fair is not a rinky-dink event.

"Dammit," she said. "We've been here all day. You sure you haven't sniffed out anything?"

"Nothing like what we're looking for," I said. "I was afraid of this."

"Of what?"

"A lot of times, magic like this—complex, long-lasting, subtle, dark—doesn't thrive well in sunlight." I glanced at the lengthening shadows. "Give it another half hour and we'll try again."

Murphy frowned at me. "I thought you always said magic isn't about good and evil."

"Neither is sunshine."

Murphy exhaled, her displeasure plain. "You might have mentioned it to me before."

"No way to know until we tried," I said. "Think of it this way: Maybe we're just looking in the exact wrong place."

She sighed and squinted around at the nearby food trailers and concession stands. "Ugh. Think there's anything here that won't make me split my jeans at the seams?"

I beamed. "Probably not. How about dogs and a funnel cake?"

"Bastard," Murphy growled. Then, "Okay."

HALFWAY THROUGH MY second hot dog, I realized we were being followed.

I kept myself from reacting, took another bite, and said, "Maybe this is the place after all."

Murphy had found a place selling turkey drumsticks. She had cut the meat from the bone and onto a paper plate, and she was eating it with a plastic fork. She didn't stop chewing or look up. "Whatcha got?"

"Guy in a maroon tee and tan BDU pants, about twenty feet away off your right shoulder. I've seen him at least two other times today."

"Doesn't necessarily mean he's following us."

"He's been busy doing nothing in particular all three times."

Murphy nodded. "Five eight or so, long hair? Little soul tuft under his mouth?"

"Yeah."

"He was sitting on a bench when I came out of the Porta-Potty," Murphy said. "Also doing nothing." She shrugged and went back to eating.

"How do you want to play it?"

"We're here with a zillion people, Harry." She deepened her voice and blocked out any hint of a nasal tone. "You want I should whack him until he talks?"

I grunted and finished my hot dog. "Doesn't necessarily mean anything. Maybe he's got a crush on you."

Murphy snorted. "Maybe he's got a crush on *you*."

I covered a respectable belch with my hand and reached for my funnel cake. "Who could blame him." I took a bite and nodded. "All right. We'll see what happens, then."

Murphy nodded and sipped at her Diet Coke. "Will says you and Anastasia broke up a while back."

"Will talks too much," I said darkly.

She glanced a little bit away. "He's your friend. He worries about you."

I studied her averted face for a moment and then nodded. "Well," I said, "tell Will he doesn't need to worry. It sucked. It sucks less now. I'll be fine. Fish in the sea, never meant to be, et cetera." I paused over another bite of funnel cake and asked, "How's Kincaid?"

"The way he always is," Murphy said.

"You get to be a few centuries old, you get a little set in your ways."

She shook her head. "It's his type. He'd be that way if he were twenty. He walks his own road and doesn't let anyone make him do differently. Like . . ."

She stopped before she could say who Kincaid was like. She ate her turkey leg.

A shiver passed over the fair, a tactile sensation to my wizard's senses. Sundown. Twilight would go on for a while yet, but the light left in the sky would no longer hold the creatures of the night at bay.

Murphy glanced up at me, sensing the change in my level of tension. She finished off her drink while I stuffed the last of the funnel cake into my mouth, and we stood up together.

THE WESTERN SKY was still a little bit orange when I finally sensed magic at work.

We were near the carnival, a section of the fair full of garishly lit rides, heavily slanted games of chance, and chintzy attractions of every kind. It was full of screaming, excited little kids, parents with frayed patience, and fashion-enslaved teenagers. Music tinkled and brayed tinny tunes. Lights flashed and danced. Barkers bleated out cajolement, encouragement, and condolences in almost-equal measures.

We drifted through the merry chaos, our maroon-shirted tail following along ten to twenty yards behind. I walked with my eyes half closed, giving no more heed to my vision than a bloodhound on a trail. Murphy stayed beside me, her expression calm, her blue eyes alert for physical danger.

Then I felt it—a quiver in the air, no more noticeable than the fading hum from a gently plucked guitar string. I noted its direction and walked several more paces before checking again, in an attempt to triangulate the source of the disturbance. I got a rough fix on it in under a minute and realized I had stopped and was staring.

"Harry?" Murphy asked. "What is it?"

"Something down there," I said, nodding to the midway. "It's faint. But it's something."

Murph inhaled sharply. "This must be the place. There goes our tail."

We didn't have to communicate the decision to each other. If the tail belonged to whoever was behind this, we couldn't let him get away to give the culprit forewarning—and odds were excellent that the sudden rabbit impersonation by the man in maroon would result in his leading us somewhere interesting.

We turned and gave pursuit.

A footrace on open ground is one thing. Running through a crowded carnival is something else entirely. You can't sprint, unless you want to wind up falling down a lot and attracting a lot of attention. You have to hurry along, hopping between clusters of people, never really getting the chance to pour on the gas. The danger in a chase like this isn't that the quarry will outrun you, but that you'll lose him in the crowd.

I had a huge advantage. I'm freakishly tall. I could see over everyone and spot Mr. Maroon bobbing and weaving his way through the crowd. I took the lead and Murphy followed.

I got within a couple of long steps of Maroon, but was interdicted by a gaggle of seniors in Shriners caps. He caught a break at the same time, a stretch of open ground beyond the Shriners, and by the time I got through, I saw Maroon handing tickets to a carnie. He hopped up onto a platform, got into a little roller coaster–style car, and vanished into an attraction.

"Dammit!" Murphy said, panting. "What now?"

Behind the attraction, advertised as the Tunnel of Terror, there was an empty space, the interior of a circle of several similar rides and games. There wouldn't be anyone to hide behind in there. "You take the back. I'll watch the front. Whoever spots him gives a shout."

"Got it." Murphy hurried off around the Tunnel of Terror. She frowned at a little plastic barrier with an AUTHORIZED PERSONNEL ONLY notice on it, then calmly ignored it and went on over.

"Anarchist," I muttered, and settled down to wait for Maroon to figure out he'd been treed.

He didn't appear.

The dingy little roller coaster car came wheezing slowly out of the opposite side of the platform, empty. The carnie, an old fellow with a scruffy white beard, didn't notice—he was dozing in his chair.

Murphy returned a few seconds later. "There are two doors on the back," she reported, "both of them chained and locked from the outside. He didn't come out that way."

I inhaled and nodded at the empty car. "Not here, either. Look, we can't just stand around. Maybe he's running through a tunnel or something. We've got to know if he's inside."

"I'll go flush him out," she said. "You pick him up when he shows."

"No way," I said. "We stay with our wing"—I glanced at Murphy—"person. The power I sensed came from somewhere nearby. If we split up, we're about a million times more vulnerable to mental manipulation. And if this guy is more than he appears, neither of us wants to take him solo."

She grimaced, nodded, and we started toward the Tunnel of Terror together.

The old carnie woke up as we came up the ramp, let out a wheezing cough, and pointed to a sign that required us to give him three tickets each for the ride. I hadn't bought any, and the ticket counter was more than far enough away for Maroon to scamper if we stopped to follow the rules.

"Sir," Murphy said, "a man we're looking for just went into your attraction, but he didn't come out again. We need to go in and look for him."

He blinked gummy eyes at Murphy and said, "Three tickets."

"You don't understand," she said. "A fugitive may be hiding inside the Tunnel of Terror. We need to check and see if he's there."

The carnie snorted. "Three tickets, missy. Though it ain't the nicest room you two could rent."

Murphy's jaw muscles flexed.

I stepped forward. "Hey, man," I said. "Harry Dresden, PI. If you wouldn't mind, all we need to do is get inside for five minutes."

He eyed me. "PI, huh?"

I produced my license and showed it to him. He eyed it and then me. "You don't look like no private investigator I ever saw. Where's your hat?"

"In the shop," I said. "Transmission gave out." I winked at him and held up a folded twenty between my first and second fingers. "Five minutes?"

He yawned. "Naw. Can't let nobody run around loose in there." He reached out and took the twenty. "Then again, what you and your lady friend mutually consent to do once you're inside ain't my affair." He rose, pulled a lever, and gestured at the car. "Mount up," he leered. "And keep your, ah, extremities inside the car at all times."

We got in, and I was nearly scalded by the steam coming out of Murphy's ears. "You just had to play along with that one."

"We needed to get inside," I said. "Just doing my job, Sergeant."

She snorted.

"Hey, Murph, look," I said, holding up a strap of old, worn leather. "Seat belts."

She gave me a look that could have scoured steel. Then, with a stubborn set of her jaw, secured the flimsy thing. Her expression dared me to object.

I grinned and relaxed. It isn't easy to really get Murph's goat and get away with it.

On the other side of the platform, the carnie pulled another lever, and a moment later the little cart started rolling forward at the blazing speed of one, maybe even two miles an hour. A dark curtain parted ahead of us, and we rolled into the Tunnel of Terror.

Murphy promptly drew her gun—it was dark, but I heard the scratch of its barrel on plastic as she drew it from its holder. She snapped a small LED flashlight into its holder beneath the gun barrel and flicked it on. We were in a cramped little tunnel, every surface painted black, and there was absolutely nowhere for Maroon to be hiding.

I shook out the charm bracelet on my left wrist, preparing defensive energies in case they were needed. Murph and I had been working together long enough to know our roles. If trouble came, I would defend us. Murphy and her Sig would reply.

A door opened at the end of the little hallway, and we rolled forward into an open set dressed to look like a rustic farmhouse, with a lot of subtle details meant to be scary—severed fingers at the base of the chicken-chopping stump, just below the bloody ax, glowing eyes appearing in an upstairs window of the farmhouse, that kind of thing. There was no sign of Maroon and precious little place for him to hide.

"Better get that seat belt off," I told her. "We want to be able to move fast if it comes to that."

"Yeah," she said, and reached down, just as something huge and terrifying dropped onto the car from the shadows above us, screaming.

Adrenaline hit my system like a runaway bus, and I looked up to see a decidedly demonic scarecrow hanging a few feet above our heads, bouncing on its wires, and playing a recording of cackling, mad laughter.

"Jesus Christ," Murphy breathed, lowering her gun. She was a little white around the eyes.

We looked at each other and both burst into high, nervous laughs.

"Tunnel of Terror," Murphy said. "We are *so* cool."

"Total badasses," I said, grinning.

The car continued its slow grind forward, and Murphy unfastened the seat belt. We moved into the next area, meant to be a zombie-infested hospital. It had a zombie mannequin, which burst out of a closet near the track, and plenty of gore. We got out of the car and scouted a couple of spots where he might have been but wasn't. Then we hopped into the car again before it could leave the set.

So it went, on through a ghoulish graveyard, a troglodyte-teaming cavern, and a literal Old West ghost town. We came up with nothing, but we moved well as a team, better than I could remember doing with anyone before. Everything felt as smooth and natural as if we'd been moving together our whole lives. We did it in total silence, too, divining what each other would do through pure instinct.

Even great teams lose a game here or there, though. We came up with diddly and emerged from the Tunnel of Terror with neither Maroon nor any idea where he'd gone.

"Hell's bells," I muttered. "This week has been an investigative suckfest for me."

Murphy tittered again. "You said *suck*."

I grinned at her and looked around. "Well," I said, "we don't know where Maroon went. If they hadn't made us already, they have now."

"Can you pick up on the signal-whatsit again?"

"Energy signature," I said. "Maybe. It's pretty vague, though. I'm not sure how much more precise I can get."

"Let's find out," she said.

I nodded. "Right, then." We started around the suspect circle of attractions, moving slowly and trying to blend into the crowds. When a couple of rowdy kids went by, one chasing the other, I put an arm around her shoulders and drew her into the shelter of my body so she wouldn't get bowled over.

She exhaled slowly and did not step away from me.

My heart started beating faster.

"Harry," she said quietly.

"Yeah?"

"You and me . . . Why haven't we ever . . ." She looked up at me. "Why not?"

"The usual, I guess," I said quietly. "Trouble. Duty. Other people involved."

She shook her head. "Why not?" she repeated, her eyes direct. "All these years have gone by. And something could have happened, but it never did. Why not?"

I licked my lips. "Just like that? We just decide to be together?"

Her eyelids lowered. "Why not?"

My heart did the drum solo from "Wipeout."

Why not?

I bent my head down to her mouth and kissed her, very gently.

She turned into the kiss, pressing her body against mine. It was a little bit awkward. I was most of two feet taller than she was. We made up for grace with enthusiasm, her arms twining around my neck as she kissed me, hungry and deep.

"Whoa," I said, drawing back a moment later. "Work. Right?"

She looked at me for a moment, her cheeks pink, her lips a little swollen from the kiss, and said, "Right." She closed her eyes and nodded. "Right. Work first."

"Then dinner?" I asked.

"Dinner. My place. We can order in."

My belly trembled in sudden excitement at that proposition. "Right." I looked around. "So let's find this thing and get it over with."

We started moving again. A circuit around the attractions got me no closer to the source of the energy I'd sensed earlier.

"Dammit," I said, frustrated, when we'd completed the pattern.

"Hey," Murphy said. "Don't beat yourself up about it, Harry." Her hand slipped into mine, our fingers intertwining. "I've been a cop a long time. You don't always get the bad guy. And if you go around blaming yourself for it, you wind up crawling into a bottle or eating your own gun."

"Thank you," I said quietly. "But . . ."

"Heh," Murphy said. "You said *but*."

We both grinned like fools. I looked down at our entwined hands. "I like this."

"So do I," Murphy said. "Why didn't we do this a long time ago?"

"Beats me."

"Are we just that stupid?" she asked. "I mean, people, in general. Are we really so blind that we miss what's right there in front of us?"

"As a species, we're essentially insane," I said. "So, yeah, probably." I lifted our hands and kissed her fingertips. "I'm not missing it now, though."

Her smile lit up several thousand square feet of the midway. "Good."

The echo of a thought rattled around in my head: *Insane . . .*

"Oh," I said. "Oh, hell's bells."

She frowned at me. "What?"

"Murph . . . I think we got whammied."

She blinked at me. "What? No, we didn't."

"I think we did."

"I didn't see anything or feel anything. I mean, *nothing*, Harry. I've felt magic like that before."

"*Look* at us," I said, waving our joined hands.

"We've been friends a long time, Harry," she said. "And we've had a couple of near misses before. This time we just didn't screw it up. That's all that's happening here."

"What about Kincaid?" I asked her.

She mulled over that one for a second. Then she said, "I doubt he'll even notice I'm gone." She frowned at me. "Harry, I haven't been this happy in . . . I never thought I could feel this way again. About anyone."

My heart continued to go pitty-pat. "I know exactly what you mean," I said. "I feel the same way."

Her smile warmed even more. "Then what's the problem? Isn't that what love is supposed to be like? Effortless?"

I had to think about that one for a second. And then I said, carefully and slowly, "Murph, think about it."

"What do you mean?"

"You know how good this is?" I asked.

"Yeah."

"How right it feels?"

She nodded. "Yeah."

"How easy it was?"

She nodded energetically, her eyes bright.

I leaned down toward her for emphasis. "It just isn't fucked-up enough to really be you and me."

Her smile faltered.

"My God," she said, her eyes widening. "We got whammied."

WE RETURNED TO the Tunnel of Terror.

"I don't get it," she said. "I don't . . . I didn't feel anything happen. I don't feel any different now. I thought being aware of this kind of thing made it go away."

"No," I said. "But it helps sometimes."

"Do you still . . . ?"

I squeezed her hand once more before letting go. "Yeah," I said. "I still feel it."

"Is it . . . Is it going to go away?"

I didn't answer her. I didn't know. Or maybe I didn't want to know.

The old carnie saw us coming, and his face flickered with apprehension as soon as he looked at us. He stood up and looked from the control board for the ride to the entranceway to the interior.

"Yeah," I muttered. "Sneaky bastard. You just try it."

He flicked one of the switches and shambled toward the tunnel's entrance.

I made a quick effort of will, raised a hand, and swept it in a horizontal arc, snarling, "*Forzare!*" Unseen force knocked his legs out from beneath him and tossed him into an involuntary pratfall.

Murphy and I hurried up onto the platform before he could get to his feet and run. We needn't have bothered. The carnie was apparently a genuine old guy, not some supernatural being in disguise. He lay on the platform moaning in pain. I felt kind of bad for beating up a senior citizen.

But hey. On the other hand, he did swindle me out of twenty bucks.

Murphy stood over him, her blue eyes cold, and said, "Where's the bolt-hole?"

The carnie blinked at her. "Wha?"

"The trapdoor," she snapped. "The secret cabinet. Where is he?"

I frowned and walked toward the entranceway.

"Please," the carnie said. "I don't know what you're talking about!"

"The hell you don't," Murphy said. She leaned down and grabbed the man by the shirt with both hands and leaned closer, a snarl lifting her lip. The carnie blanched.

Murph could be pretty badass for such a tiny thing. I loved that about her.

"I can't," the carnie said. "I can't. I get paid not to see anything. She'll kill me. She'll kill me."

I parted the heavy curtain leading into the entry tunnel and spotted it at once—a circular hole in the floor about two feet across, the top end of a ladder just visible. A round lid lay rotated to one side, painted as flat black as the rest of the hall. "Here," I said to Murph.

"That's why we didn't spot anything. By the time you had your light on, it was already behind us."

Murphy scowled down at the carnie and said, "Give me twenty bucks."

The man licked his lips. Then he fished my folded twenty out of his shirt pocket and passed it to Murphy.

She nodded and flashed her badge. "Get out of here before I realize I witnessed you taking a bribe and endangering lives by letting customers use the attraction in an unsafe manner."

The carnie bolted.

Murphy handed me the twenty. I pocketed it, and we climbed down the ladder.

WE REACHED THE bottom and went silent again. Murphy's body language isn't exactly subtle—it can't be, when you're her size and working law enforcement. But she could move as quietly as smoke when she needed to. I'm gangly. It was more of an effort for me.

The ladder took us down to what looked like the interior of a buried railroad car. There were electrical conduits running along the walls. Light came from a doorway at the far end of the car. I moved forward first, shield bracelet at the ready, and Murphy walked a pace behind me and to my right, her Sig held ready.

The doorway at the end of the railroad car led us into a large workroom, teeming with computers, file cabinets, microscopes, and at least one deluxe chemistry set.

Maroon sat at one of the computers, his profile in view. "Dammit, Stu," he snarled. "I told you that you can't keep coming down here to use the john. You'll just have to walk to one of the—" He glanced up at us and froze in midsentence, his eyes wide and locked on Murphy's leveled gun.

"Stu took the rest of the night off," I said amiably. "Where's your boss?"

A door opened at the far end of the workroom and a young woman

of medium height appeared. She wore glasses and a lab coat, and neither of them did anything to make her look less than gorgeous. She
looked at us and then at Maroon and said, in a precise, British accent,
"You idiot."

"Yeah," I said. "Good help is hard to find."

The woman in the lab coat looked at me with dark, intense eyes,
and I sensed what felt like a phantom pressure against my temples, as
if wriggling tadpoles were slithering along the surface of my skin. It
was a straightforward attempt at mental invasion, but I'd been practicing my defenses for a while now, and I wasn't falling for something
that obvious. I pushed the invasive thoughts away with an effort of will
and said, "Don't meet her eyes, Murph. She's a vampire. Red Court."

"Got it," she said, her gun never moving from Maroon.

The vampire looked at us both for a moment. Then she said, "You
need no introduction, Mr. Dresden. I am Baroness LeBlanc. And our
nations are not, at the moment, in a state of war."

"I've always been a little fuzzy on legal niceties," I said. I had several devices with me that I could use to defend myself. I was ready to
use any of them. A vampire in close quarters is nothing to laugh at.
LeBlanc could tear off three or four of my limbs in the time it takes
to draw and fire a gun. I watched her closely, ready to act at the slight-
est semblance of an attack. "We both know the war is going to start
up again eventually."

"You are out of anything reasonably like your territory," she said,
"and you are trespassing upon mine. I would be well within my rights
under the Accords to kill you and bury your torso and limbs in individual graves."

"That's the problem with this ride," I complained to Murphy.
"There's nothing that's actually *scary* in the Tunnel of Terror."

"You did get your money back," she pointed out.

"Ah, true." I smiled faintly at LeBlanc. "Look, Baroness. You know
who I am. You're doing something to people's minds, and I want it
stopped."

"If you do not leave," she said, "I will consider it an act of war."

"Hooray," I said in a Ben Stein monotone, spinning one forefinger in the air like a New Year's noisemaker. "I've already kicked off one war with the Red Court, and I will cheerfully do it again if that is what is necessary to protect people from you."

"That's irrational," LeBlanc said. "Completely irrational."

"Tell her, Murph."

"He's completely irrational," Murphy said, her tone wry.

LeBlanc regarded me impassively for a moment. Then she smiled faintly and said, "Perhaps a physical confrontation is an inappropriate solution."

I frowned. "Really?"

She shrugged. "Not all of the Red Court are battle-hungry blood addicts, Dresden. My work here has no malevolent designs. Quite the opposite, in fact."

I tilted my head. "That's funny. All the corpses piled up say differently."

"The process *does* have its side effects," she admitted. "But the lessons garnered from them serve only to improve my work and make it safer and more effective. Honestly, you should be supporting me, Dresden, not trying to shut me down."

"Supporting you?" I smiled a little. "Just what is it you think you're doing that's so darned wonderful?"

"I am creating love."

I barked out a laugh.

LeBlanc's face remained steady, serious.

"You think that *this*, this warping people into feeling something they don't want to feel is *love*?"

"What is love," LeBlanc said, "if not a series of electrochemical signals in the brain? Signals that can be duplicated, like any other sensation."

"Love is more than that," I said.

"Do you love this woman?"

"Yeah," I said. "But that isn't anything new."

LeBlanc showed her teeth. "But your current feelings of longing and desire are new, are they not? New and entirely indistinguishable from your genuine emotions? Wouldn't you say, Sergeant Murphy?"

Murphy swallowed but didn't look at the vampire. LeBlanc's uncomplicated mental attack might be simple for a wizard to defeat, but any normal human being would probably be gone before they realized their minds were under attack. Instead of answering, she asked a question of her own. "Why?"

"Why what?"

"Why do this? Why experiment with making people fall in love?"

LeBlanc arched an eyebrow. "Isn't it obvious?"

I sucked in a short breath, realizing what was happening. "The White Court," I said.

The Whites were a different breed of vampire from the Reds, feeding on the life essence of their victims, generally through seduction. Genuine love and genuine tokens of love were their kryptonite, their holy water. The love of another human being in an intimate relationship sort of rubbed off on you, making the very touch of your skin an anathema to the White Court.

LeBlanc smiled at me. "Granted, there are some aberrant effects from time to time. But so far, that's been a very small percentage of the test pool. And the survivors are, as you yourself have experienced, perfectly happy. They have a love that most of your kind seldom find and even more infrequently keep. There are no victims here, Wizard."

"Oh," I said. "Right. Except for the victims."

LeBlanc exhaled. "Mortals are like mayflies, Wizard. They live a brief time, and then they are gone. And those who have died because of my work at least died after days or weeks of perfect bliss. There are many who ended a much longer life with less. What I'm doing here has the potential to protect mortalkind from the White Court forever."

"It isn't genuine love if it's forced upon someone," Murphy said, her tone harsh.

"No," LeBlanc said. "But I believe the real thing will very easily grow from such a foundation of companionship and happiness."

"Gosh, you're noble," I said.

LeBlanc's eyes sparkled with something ugly.

"You're doing this to get rid of competition," I said. "And, hell, maybe to try to increase the world's population. Make more food."

The vampire regarded me levelly. "There are multiple motivations behind the work," she said. "Many of my Court agreed to the logic you cite when they would never have supported the idea of strengthening and defending mortals."

"Ohhhhh," I said, drawing the word out. "You're the vampire with a heart of gold. Florence Nightingale with fangs. I guess that makes it okay, then."

LeBlanc stared at me. Then her eyes flicked to Murphy and back. She smiled thinly. "There is a special cage reserved for you at the Red Court, Dresden. Its bars are lined with blades and spikes, so that if you fall asleep, they will cut and gouge you awake."

"Shut up," Murphy said.

LeBlanc continued in a calmly amused tone. "The bottom is a closed bowl nearly a foot deep, so that you will stand in your own waste. And there are three spears with needle-sized tips waiting in a rack beneath the cage, so that any who pass you can pause and take a few moments to participate in your punishment."

"Shut *up*," Murphy growled.

"Eventually," LeBlanc purred, "your guts will be torn out and left in a pile at your feet. And when you are dead, your skin will be flayed from your body, tanned, and made into upholstery for one of the chairs in the Red Temple."

"Shut up!" snarled Murphy, and her voice was savage. Her gun whipped over to cover LeBlanc. "Shut your mouth, bitch!"

I realized the danger an instant too late. It was exactly the reaction LeBlanc had intended to provoke. "Murph! No!"

Once Murphy's Sig was pointing elsewhere, Maroon produced a gun from beneath his desk and raised it. He was pulling the trigger even before he could level it for a shot, blazing away as fast as he could move his finger. He wasn't quite fifteen feet away from Murphy, but the first five shots missed her as I spun and brought the invisible power of my shield bracelet down between the two of them. Bullets hit the shield with flashes of light and sent little concentric blue rings rippling through the air from the point of impact.

Murphy, meanwhile, had opened up on LeBlanc. Murph fired almost as quickly as Maroon, but she had the training and discipline necessary for combat. Her bullets smacked into the vampire's torso, tearing through pale flesh and drawing gouts of red-black blood. LeBlanc staggered to one side—she wouldn't be dead, but the shots had probably rung her bell for a second or two.

I lowered the shield as Maroon's gun clicked on empty, lifted my right fist, and triggered the braided energy ring on my index finger with a short, uplifting motion. The ring saved back a little energy every time I moved my arm, storing it so that I could unleash it at need. Unseen force flew out from the ring, plucked Maroon out of his chair, and slammed him into the ceiling. He dropped back down, hit his back on the edge of the desk, and fell into a senseless sprawl on the floor. The gun flew from his fingers.

"I'm out!" Murphy screamed.

I whirled back to find LeBlanc pushing herself off the wall, regaining her balance. She gave Murphy a look of flat hatred, and her eyes flushed pure black, iris and sclera alike. She opened her mouth in an inhuman scream, and then the vampire hiding beneath LeBlanc's seemingly human form exploded outward like a racehorse emerging from its gate, leaving shreds of pale, bloodless skin in its wake.

It was a hideous thing—black and flabby and slimy looking, with a flaccid belly, a batlike face, and long, spindly limbs. LeBlanc's eyes bulged hideously as she flew toward me.

I brought my shield up in time to intercept her, and she rebounded from it, to fall back to the section of floor already stained with her blood.

"Down!" Murphy shouted.

I dropped down onto my heels and lowered the shield.

LeBlanc rose up again, even as I heard Murphy take a deep breath, exhale halfway, and hold it. Her gun barked once.

The vampire lost about a fifth of her head as the bullet tore into her skull. She staggered back against the wall, limbs thrashing, but she still wasn't dead. She began to claw her way to her feet again.

Murphy squeezed off six more shots, methodically. None of them missed. LeBlanc fell to the floor. Murphy took a step closer, aimed, and put another ten or twelve rounds into the fallen vampire's head. By the time she was done, the vampire's skull looked like a smashed gourd.

A few seconds later, LeBlanc stopped moving.

Murphy reloaded again and kept the gun trained on the corpse.

"Nice shootin', Tex," I said. I checked out Maroon. He was still breathing.

"So," Murphy said, "problem solved?"

"Not really," I said. "LeBlanc was no practitioner. She can't be the one who was working the whammy."

Murphy frowned and eyed Maroon for a second.

I went over to the downed man and touched my fingers lightly to his brow. There was no telltale energy signature of a practitioner. "Nope."

"Who, then?"

I shook my head. "This is delicate, difficult magic. There might not be three people on the entire White Council who could pull it off. So . . . it's most likely a focus artifact of some kind."

"A what?"

"An item that has a routine built into it," I said. "You pour energy in one end, and you get results on the other."

Murphy scrunched up her nose. "Like those wolf belts the FBI had?"

"Yeah, just like that." I blinked and snapped my fingers. "*Just* like that!"

I hurried out of the little complex and up the ladder. I went to the tunnel car and took the old leather seat belt out of it. I turned it over and found the back inscribed with nearly invisible sigils and signs.

Now that I was looking for it, I could feel the tingle of energy moving within it. "Hah," I said. "Got it."

Murphy frowned back at the entry to the Tunnel of Terror. "What do we do about Billy the Kid?"

"Not much we can do," I said. "You want to try to explain what happened here to the Springfield cops?"

She shook her head.

"Me, either," I said. "The kid was LeBlanc's thrall. I doubt he's a danger to anyone without a vampire to push him into it." Besides, the Reds would probably kill him on general principles, anyway, once they found out about LeBlanc's death.

We were silent for a moment, then stepped in close to each other and hugged gently. Murphy shivered.

"You okay?" I asked quietly.

She leaned her head against my chest. "How do we help all the people she screwed with?"

"Burn the belt," I said, and stroked her hair with one hand. "That should purify everyone it's linked to."

"Everyone," she said slowly.

I blinked twice. "Yeah."

"So once you do it . . . we'll see what a bad idea this is. And remember that we both have very good reasons to not get together."

"Yeah."

"And . . . we won't be feeling *this* anymore. This . . . happy. This complete."

"No. We won't."

Her voice cracked. "Dammit."

I hugged her tight. "Yeah."

"I want to tell you to wait awhile," she said. "I want us to be all noble and virtuous for keeping it intact. I want to tell you that if we destroy the belt, we'll be destroying the happiness of God knows how many people."

"Junkies are happy when they're high," I said quietly, "but they don't need to be happy. They need to be free."

I put the belt back into the car, turned my right hand palm up, and murmured a word. A sphere of white-hot fire gathered over my fingers. I flicked a hand, and the sphere arched gently down into the car and began charring the belt to ashes. I felt sick.

I didn't watch. I turned to Karrin and kissed her again, hot and urgent, and she returned the kiss frantically. It was as though we thought we might keep something from escaping our mouths if they were sealed together in a kiss.

I felt it when it went away.

We both stiffened slightly. We both remembered that we had decided the two of us couldn't work out. We both remembered that Murphy was already involved with someone else and that it wasn't in her nature to stray.

She stepped back from me, her arms folded across her stomach.

"Ready?" I asked her quietly.

She nodded, and we started walking. Neither of us said anything until we reached the *Blue Beetle*.

"You know what, Harry?" she said quietly from the other side of the car.

"I know," I told her. "Like you said, love hurts."

We got into the Beetle and headed back to Chicago.

AFTERMATH

—original novella

Takes place an hour or two after
the end of *Changes*

To quote a great man: 'Nuff said.

can't believe he's dead.

Harry Dresden, Professional Wizard. It sounds like a bad joke. Like most people, at first I figured it was just his schtick, his approach to marketing himself as a unique commodity in private investigation, a job market that isn't ever exactly teeming with business.

Well, that's not entirely true. I knew better. I'd seen something that the rules of the normal world just couldn't explain, and he was right in the middle of it. But I did what everyone does when they run into the supernatural: I told myself that it was dark, and that I didn't really know what I had seen. No one else had witnessed anything to support me. They would call me crazy if I tried to tell anyone about it. By the time a week had passed, I had half convinced myself that I hallucinated the whole thing. A year later, I was almost certain it had been some kind of trick, an illusion pulled off by a smarmy but savvy con.

But he was for real.

Believe me, I know. Several years and several hundred nightmares later, I know.

He was the real thing.

God. I was already thinking about him in the past tense.

"Sergeant Murphy," said one of the lab guys. Dresden was almost one of our own, in Special Investigations. We'd pulled every string we had to get a forensics team on the site. "Excuse me, Sergeant Murphy."

I turned to face the forensic tech. He was cute, in a not-quite-grown, puppyish kind of way. The ID clipped to his lapel said his name was Jarvis. He looked nervous.

"I'm Murphy," I said.

"Um, right." He swallowed and looked around. "I don't know how to tell you this, but . . . my boss said I shouldn't be talking to you. He said you were on suspension."

I looked at him calmly. He wasn't more than average height, but that put his head about eight and a half inches over mine. He still had that whippet thinness that some twentysomethings hang on to for a while after their teenage years. I smiled at him and tried to put him at ease. "I get it," I said. "I won't tell anyone if you won't."

He licked his lips nervously.

"Jarvis," I said, "please." I gestured at the bloodstain on the exterior of the cabin of a dumpy little secondhand boat, the lettering on which proclaimed it the *Water Beetle*. "He is my friend."

I didn't say *was*—not out loud. You don't ever do that until you've found the remains. It's professional.

Jarvis exhaled and looked around. I thought he looked as if he might throw up.

"The blood spatter suggests that whoever was struck there took a hit somewhere in his upper torso. It's impossible to be sure, but"—he swallowed—"it was a heavy spray. Maybe an arterial hit."

"Or maybe not," I said.

He was too young to notice the way I was grasping at straws. "Or maybe not," he agreed. "There's not enough blood on the site to call it a murder, but we think most of it . . . We didn't find the round. It went through the victim, and both walls of the, uh, boat there. It's probably in the lake."

I grunted. It's something I picked up over a fifteen-year career in law enforcement. Men have managed to create a complex and utterly impenetrable secret language consisting of monosyllabic sounds and partial words—and they are apparently too thick to realize it exists. Maybe they really are from Mars. I'd been able to learn a few Martian phrases over time, and one of the useful ones was the grunt that meant *I acknowledge that I've heard what you said; please continue.*

"Smears on the deck and the guardrail suggest that the victim went over the side and into the water," Jarvis continued, his tone subdued. "There's a dive team on the way, but . . ."

I used the Martian phrase for *You needn't continue; I know what you're talking about.* It sounded a lot like the first grunt to anyone without a Y chromosome, but I really did get it.

Lake Michigan is jealous and protective of her dead. The water's depth and the year-round cold temperatures that go with it mean that corpses don't tend to produce many gasses as they decompose. As a result, they often don't bob to the surface, like you see in all those cop shows on cable. They just lie on the bottom. No one knows how many poor souls' earthly remains rest in the quiet cold of Michigan's depths.

"It hasn't been long," I said. "Even if he fell off the back, into the open water, he can't have gone far."

"Yes, ma'am," Jarvis said. "Um. If you'll excuse me."

I nodded at him and shoved my hands into the pockets of my coat. Night was coming on, but it wouldn't make a lot of difference—the lake wasn't exactly crystal clear on the best days. The divers would have to use flashlights, day or night, even though we weren't more than fifty yards from shore, on the docks of the marina the *Water Beetle* called home. That would limit the area of water they could search at any given moment. The cold would impose limits on their dive time. Sonar might or might not be useful. This close to Chicago, the lake floor was cluttered with all kinds of things. They'd have to get lucky to get a good radar hit and find him.

If he was in there, he'd been there for several hours, and the wind had been rising the whole time, stirring the surface of the lake. Harry's corpse would have had plenty of time to fall to the bottom and begin to drift.

The dive team probably wasn't going to find him. They'd try, but . . .

Dammit.

I stared hard at the lengthening shadows and tried to make my tears evaporate through sheer will.

"I'm . . . very sorry, Sergeant," Jarvis said.

I replied with the Martian for *Thank you for your concern, but at the moment I need some space.* That one's easy. I just stared forward without saying anything, and after a moment, Jarvis nodded and toddled off to continue working.

A while later, Stallings was standing next to me, wearing his badge prominently out on his coat. After I'd been busted back to sergeant, Stallings had replaced me as the head of Special Investigations, Chicago's unofficial monster squad. We dealt with the weird stuff no one would accept, and then lied about what we'd been doing so that everything fit neatly into a report.

Stallings was a big, rawboned man, comfortably solid with age, his hair thinning on top. He had a mustache like Magnum's. I'd been his boss for nearly seven years. We got along well with each other. He never treated me like his most junior subordinate—more like an adviser who had been made available to the new commander.

The forensics boys were sealing the doors of the little boat with crime scene tape, having taken enough samples and photographs to choke a rhinoceros, before anyone spoke.

"Hey," he said.

"Hey."

He exhaled through his nose and said, "Hospital checks have come up with zip."

I grimaced. They would. When Harry got hurt, the hospital was the last place he wanted to be. He felt too vulnerable there—and he worried that the way a wizard's presence disrupted technology could hurt or kill someone on life support, or do harm to some innocent bystander.

But there was so much blood on the boat. If he was that badly hurt, he couldn't have gone anywhere on his own power. And down here, anyone who had found him would have called emergency services.

And the blood trail led to the lake.

I shook my head several times. I didn't want to believe it, but you can't make fact into fiction, no matter how much denial you've got to draw upon.

Stallings sighed again. Then he said, "You're on suspension, Murphy. And this is a crime scene."

"Not until we know a crime's been committed," I said. "We don't absolutely know anyone's been hurt or killed. Right now, it's just a mess."

"God dammit," he said, his voice weary. "You're a civilian now, Karrin. Get away from the fucking scene. Before someone gets word to Rudolph about this and Infernal Affairs comes down here to toss your ass in jail."

"On any other day, I would think you were talking sense," I said.

"I don't care what you think," he said. "I care what you do. And what you're going to do is turn around, walk over to your car, get in it, go home, and get a good night's sleep. You look like a hundred miles of bad road. Through Hell."

See, most women would have been a little put out by a remark like that. Especially if they were wearing slacks that flattered their hips and butt, with a darling red silk blouse and a matching silver necklace and two bracelets, studded with tiny sapphires, which they'd inherited from their grandmother. And more makeup than they usually wore in a week. And new perfume. And great shoes.

By any measure, that kind of remark was insulting. When you were dressed for a date, it was more so.

But Stallings wasn't trying to piss me off. The insult was Martian, too, for something along the lines of *I have so much regard for you that I went out of my way to create this insult so that we can have the fun of a mildly adversarial conversation. See how much I care?*

"John," I replied, using his first name, "you are a sphincter douche." Translation: *I love you, too.*

He gave me a quiet smile and nodded.

Men.

He was right. There was nothing I could do here.

I turned my back on the last place I'd seen Harry Dresden and walked back to my car.

IT HAD BEEN a long day, starting most of two days before, including a gunfight at the FBI building—which the news was still going insane about, especially after the office building bombing a couple of days before that—and a pitched battle at an ancient Mayan temple that ended in the utter destruction of the vampires of the Red Court.

And after that, things had gotten really dangerous.

I'd shown up to that ratty old boat where Harry was crashing, dressed in the outfit Stallings had insulted. Harry and I were supposed to go grab a few drinks and . . . and see what happened.

Instead, I'd found nothing but his blood.

I didn't think I would sleep, but two days plus of physical and psychological stress made it inevitable. Nightmares came to haunt me, but they didn't make much of an impression. I'd seen worse in the real world. I did cry, though. I remember that—waking up in the middle of the night from bad dreams that were old hat by now, sobbing my eyes out in pure reaction to the events of the past two days.

It happens. You feel overwhelmed, you cry, you feel better, and you go back to sleep.

If you don't get it, don't ask. It doesn't really translate into Martian.

I WOKE UP to a firm knock at my front door. I got out of bed, my Sig in my hand, and flicked a quick glance out the window at the backyard. It was empty, and there was no one at the door that led into my kitchen. Only after I had checked my six o'clock did I go to the front door, glancing quickly out the window in the hall as I went.

I recognized the stout young man standing on the porch, and I relaxed somewhat. Since I slept in an oversized T-shirt, I grabbed a pair of sweats and hopped into them, then went to see the werewolf standing at my door.

Will Borden didn't look like a werewolf. He was about five five, five six, and built like an armored car, all flat, heavy muscle. He wore glasses, his brown hair was cut short and neat, and you would never have guessed, from looking at him, that he and his friends had been responsible for a forty percent drop in crime in a six-block radius around the University of Chicago—and that didn't even take into account the supernatural predators that had been driven away and that now avoided the neighborhood. Strictly speaking, I probably should have arrested him as a known vigilante.

Of course, strictly speaking, I wasn't a cop anymore. I wouldn't be arresting anybody. Ever again.

That thought hit my stomach like a lead wrecking ball, and no amount of bravado or discipline could keep it from hurting. So I turned away from it.

I answered the door, and said, "Hello, Will."

"Sergeant Murphy," he said, nodding at me. "Got a minute?"

"It's early," I said, not bothering to correct his form of address.

"I need your help," he said.

I took a deep breath through my nose.

It wasn't as though I had to go to work. It wasn't as though I had a hot date waiting for me.

Part of me longed to slam the door in Will's face and go back to bed. I'd always thought that kind of selfish reaction had been a fairly small portion of my character. Today, it felt huge.

The house was silent and empty behind me.

"Okay," I said. "Come in."

I SEATED HIM at the kitchen table and went back to my room to put on clothes that looked a little less pajama-like. When I came back out, Will had gotten the coffeepot going, and brew was already a finger deep in the little glass pitcher.

I popped some bread in the toaster and watched it carefully to make sure it didn't burn. My toaster was an old one, but even so I didn't need to be watching it. It just gave me something to do until the coffee was done.

I took the finished toast and coffee to the table, a bit for each of us, and set out a jar of strawberry preserves. Will accepted the food readily and, naturally, wolfed it down. We did all of that in silence.

"Okay," I said, settling back in my chair and studying him. "What help?"

"Georgia's gone," he said simply.

I kept myself from wincing. Georgia was Will's wife. They'd been together since they were barely out of high school. They'd learned to be werewolves together, apparently. I liked them both. "Tell me."

"Work had me out of town," he said. "Omaha. Georgia is getting ready to defend her dissertation. She stayed home. We both watched the news—about Dresden's office building and the terrorists at the FBI. We were worried but . . . I got a call from her late last night. She was . . ." His face became pale. "She was almost incoherent. Terrified. She wasn't making any sense. Then the call cut off abruptly." His voice shook. "She was screaming. I tried to call the cops, but . . ."

I nodded. "But if it was something bad enough to make her scream, there wouldn't be much the cops could do to help. And between the bombing and the attack, they were all overworked, anyway. They'll get to it as soon as they can."

"Yeah," Will said. "So I left a message with Dresden's service and came back to Chicago. The apartment door was broken, maybe kicked in. The place was a wreck." He swallowed. "She was gone. And I couldn't pick up a trail. I went to Harry's place, but . . . There was still smoke coming up from what was left. Then I came here."

I nodded slowly. Then I asked, "Why?"

He blinked and looked at me as if I'd broken out into a musical number. "Seriously?"

"Yeah."

"He always told us that if we ever needed him but couldn't find him, we were supposed to go to you. That you were the person in this city who could help us better than anyone else."

I stared at him for a minute. Then I said, "Yeah. I can just see him saying that." I shook my head. "And never bothering to mention it to me."

I'll give Will credit—he was obviously terrified, but he managed to try a joke. "He probably thought you were formidable enough without the confidence boost from something like that."

"Like I need his approval to be confident," I muttered. I studied Will for a moment. I knew him well enough to know there was something off in his behavior. He was too quiet. Will wasn't the sort of man to sit at a table fiddling with his napkin when his wife was missing and quite possibly in danger. He was terrified, frightened to such a degree that it was nearly paralytic. I recognized the look.

I'd seen it in the mirror often enough.

"What aren't you telling me, Will?" I asked quietly.

He closed his eyes and shivered as a tear tracked down each cheek.

"Georgia's pregnant," he whispered. "Seven months."

I nodded. Then I pushed the rest of my coffee away and got up. "Let me get my coat."

"It's supposed to be nice today," Will said.

"With the coat, I can carry more guns," I said.

"Oh," he said. "Right."

WILL'S APARTMENT WAS a wreck. The lock had been smashed, though the door was still in one piece. The furniture was askew. A few things were broken. Paperback books had been knocked off a shelf. A laptop computer lay on its side, a blue screen of death glaring from its monitor. A mug of cocoa had been spilled and lay in a drying puddle on the hardwood floor.

I looked back and forth for a moment, frowning. The spill lay near the laptop, and both were to the right side of a comfortable-looking recliner, which had been bowled over backward. There was a therapeutic contoured pillow lying a few feet beyond that.

"So," I said, "maybe it went like this. The attacker kicks in the door. There's a partial impression of a shoe's tread on it. Georgia's sitting in her chair, there, working on her computer." I frowned some more. "She drink a lot of cocoa?"

"No," Will said. "Only when she's really upset. She jokes about it being self-medication."

So she'd been upset already, even before the attack. She was sitting in the chair with her laptop and her cocoa and . . . I walked over to the fallen chair and found a simple household wireless phone lying behind it.

"Something besides the prospect of an attack had upset her," I said. "She took the time to make a cup of cocoa, and you don't do that when there's a maniac at the door. She made herself a comfort drink and huddled up in her chair to call you. Do you have any idea what could have upset her like that?"

Will shook his head. "Normally, no. But she's been on a hormone crazy train the past few months. She's overreacted to a lot of things."

I nodded and stood there, just trying to absorb it all, to get an image of how things might have fit together. I pictured Georgia, a long, lean, willowy woman, curled up in the recliner, her face blotchy, her eyes red, almost curling up around her baby and the sound of her husband's voice.

Someone broke the door in with a single kick and rushed her. Georgia was a fighter, accustomed to combat, even if it was mostly when she was in the form of another creature. She used the first defense she could bring to bear—her legs. As her attacker rushed her, she kicked out with both legs, trying to shove him away. But he had too much momentum, and instead Georgia's kick had flung her chair over backward.

A pregnant woman nowhere near as lithe or graceful as she usually was, she turned and tried to get away.

"There's no blood," I said.

The attacker had dragged her out by main force. Either he'd beaten her with his fists and feet—easy, on a pregnant woman, who would instinctively curl her body around her unborn child, so that blows landed mostly on the back, ribs, and buttocks—or else he'd choked her unconscious. Either way, he'd subdued her without, apparently, drawing blood.

Then they left.

I shook my head.

"What do you think?" Will asked.

"I think you don't want to know."

"No, I don't," he said. "But I need to."

I nodded. I repeated my theory and its supporting evidence. It made Will go pale and silent.

"How was her hand-to-hand?" I asked him.

"Fair. She used to teach women's self-defense seminars on campus. I don't think she's ever had to use it in earnest. . . ." His voice trailed off as he stared at the fallen chair.

"What did you find out that I couldn't?" I asked. "I mean, with the whole werewolf thing."

He shook his head. "The human brain isn't wired for serious scent-processing," he said. "Not like a wolf's, anyway. Shifting . . . sort of turns up the volume in your nose, but it's really hard to sort things out. I can follow a trail if I'm on it soon enough, but when a bunch of scents get mixed together, it's a crap shoot. In here there's new paint, spilled cocoa, the last day or two of meals. . . ." He shrugged.

"Magic never seems to make things any easier," I said.

Will snorted faintly. "Dresden keeps saying the same thing."

I felt an odd pain in my chest. I ignored it. I walked over to the apartment's little kitchen and studied it for a minute. Then I said, "So she's a cocoa junkie."

"Well, she's functional."

"She drink instant?"

"Are you kidding?" The pitch and cadence of his voice changed a little, becoming slightly higher and more clearly inflected, in what was probably an unconscious imitation of his wife. "It's the Spam of cocoas."

I got a pen out of my pocket and used it to lift a second cup, this one with a bit of lipstick smeared on the rim. The bottom of the cup was sticky with the residue of real cocoa, the kind you make from milk and chocolate. Some of it was still liquid enough to stir as the cup shifted. I showed it to him.

"Georgia doesn't wear makeup," he half whispered.

"I know," I said. "And the cocoa in this cup has been sitting out for about the same length of time as the cocoa in the other cup. So the next question we need to answer: Who was drinking cocoa with Georgia when the door broke in?"

Will shook his head. "Either it's the attacker's scent or it's someone we know. Someone who is over a lot."

I nodded. "Redhead, right? The one who likes wearing the tight shirts."

"Andi," Will said. "And Marcy. She moved back to town after Kirby's funeral. Their scents are here, too."

"Marcy?"

"Little mousey girl. Brown hair. She and Andi had kind of a thing in school."

"Liberal werewolves," I said. "Two words rarely seen adjacent to each other."

"Lots of people experiment in college," Will said. "You probably did."

"Yeah," I said. "I tried getting into watching European football. It didn't work out."

"Neither did Marcy and Andi."

"Bad blood there?"

"Not that I know of. They were still roommates after they split."

"But Marcy left town."

Will nodded. "She wanted into the animation business. She pulled a job at Skywalker. Seriously cool stuff."

"So cool that she left it to come back here?"

Will shrugged a shoulder. "She said it was more important for her to be here to help us. And she lived in a cardboard box or something, socked most of her money into the bank. Says the interest is enough to get by on for now."

I decided to remain skeptical on that story. "You happen to remember if either of them wears this color lipstick?"

He shook his head. "Sorry. Not really the kind of thing I notice."

If I remembered right, most guys who looked at Andi wouldn't be entirely certain whether or not she *had* lips afterward. But she'd probably have back problems at some point. "Okay," I said. "Maybe the cops will be here soon, and maybe not. Either way, I don't think we should wait around for them."

Will nodded. "What are we going to do?"

"This isn't exactly high-dollar soundproof housing. Someone in this building must have heard or seen something."

"Maybe," Will said, though he didn't sound confident.

I turned to leave the apartment and tried not to notice the little crib and changing table that had already been set up just beyond the open door of the apartment's second bedroom. "We won't know until we ask. Come on."

CANVASSING A BUILDING isn't particularly fun work. It's awkward, boring, repetitive, and frustrating. Most of the people you talk to don't want to be talking to you and want out of the conversation as quickly as possible—or else they're just *delighted* to be talking to you, and want to keep talking to you even though they don't know a damn thing. You have to ask the same questions over and over again, get the same answers over and over again, and generally look like you're an idiot without a single clue.

And you pretty much are, or you wouldn't be canvassing the building in the first place. You grow a thick skin fast for that kind of thing when you do police work.

"This is getting us nowhere," Will said after the umpteenth door, his frustration and worry finally boiling over to the point that it was beginning to outweigh his terror for his wife and child. He turned to face me, his stance unconsciously confrontational, his shoulders squared, his chest thrust out, his hands clenched into fists. "We need to do something else."

Ah, masculine assertiveness—I've got nothing against it, as long as it helps get the job done instead of making it harder. "Yeah?" I asked him. "You think we'd be better off walking down the street calling her name, Will?"

"N-no, but—"

"But what?" I asked him, keeping my tone reasonable while facing him with an equal amount of ready-to-kick-your-ass Martian body language. *You do not intimidate me.* "You came to me for help. I'm giving it to you. Either you work with me or you tell me you want to go it alone. Right now."

He backed off, unclenching his hands and looking away. I relaxed as well. Will hadn't meant to deliver a threat to me, as such, but he was a hell of a lot bigger and stronger than I was. Stronger isn't everything, but simple mass and power mean a lot in a fight, and Will had the ferocity and killer instinct to make them count even more heavily than most. He'd never considered—hell, probably never *noticed*—the full depth of the statement he was making with his stance and clenched fists.

It's another in a long list of things that Martians hardly ever think about: Almost any woman knows that almost any man is stronger than she is. Oh, men know they're stronger, but they seldom actually stop to think through the implications of that simple reality—implications that are both unnerving and virtually omnipresent, if you aren't a Martian. You think about life differently when you know that half the people you see have the physical power to do things to you, regardless of whether you intend to allow it—and even implied threats of physical violence have to be taken seriously.

Will hadn't intended to frighten me. He just wanted to find his wife.

"I know it's frustrating," I told him, "but it's the best way to find out something we didn't know before."

"We've been through the whole building," he snapped. "The most we've got is a neighbor a couple of floors up who heard a thump."

"Which tells us there wasn't much of a fight," I said, "or they'd have probably heard it. Fights are loud, Will, even when only one person is fighting. A building like this, everyone knows it when the neighbor beats his wife."

"Somebody should have heard her scream."

"Maybe it wasn't as loud as you thought. It was right in your ear. And it upset you. If it ended quickly enough, it might not even have woken anyone up."

I looked out the hallway window, toward more of the same sort of apartment building across the parking lot. Will wasn't going to be terribly helpful in his current state. "I'm going to check across the lot, see if anyone happened to see or hear anything last night. I want you to call Andi and Marcy. Get them over here if you can reach them. After that, go over your phone's caller ID, Georgia's cell phone's caller ID, her e-mail. See if anyone odd has been in contact with her."

"Okay," he said, frowning—but nodding.

"Control your emotions, Will. Stay calm," I told him. "Calm's the best way to think, and thinking's the best way to find Georgia and help her."

He inhaled deeply, still nodding. "Look, Sergeant. . . . One of the guys in that building . . . Maybe you shouldn't go over there by yourself."

I smiled sweetly at him.

He lifted his empty hands as if I'd pointed a gun. "Right. Sorry."

THREE BUILDINGS HAD apartments in them that faced out on the common parking lot in general, and had a view of the Bordens' apartment in particular. I stood in the parking lot, looking up at the windows for a moment, and then started with the building on the left.

Most of an hour later, I hadn't learned anything else, and I figured out my main problem: I wasn't Harry Dresden.

Dresden would have looked around with a vague expression on his face and wandered around, bumping into things and barely comporting himself with professional caution, even at a crime scene. He'd ask a few questions that wouldn't make much sense on the surface, make a few remarks he thought were witty, and glibly insult anyone who appeared to be a repressive authority figure. Then he'd do something that didn't make any goddamn sense, and produce results out of thin air, like a magician pulling a rabbit out of his hat.

If Harry were here, he could have taken some hairs out of Georgia's hairbrush, done something stupid-looking with them, and followed her across the town or the state or, for all I knew, to the other side of the universe. He could have told me more about what had happened at Georgia's than I could have known, maybe even identified the perp, in general or specifically. And, if things got hot when we went after the bad guy, he would have been there, throwing fire and lightning around as if they were his own personal toys, created especially and exclusively for him to play with.

Watching Dresden operate was usually one of two things: mildly amusing or positively terrifying. On a scene, his whole personal manner always made me think of autistic kids. He never met anyone's eyes for more than a flickering second. He moved with the sort of exaggerated caution of someone who was several sizes larger than normal, keeping his hands and arms in close to his body. He spoke a little bit softly, as if apologizing for the resonant baritone of his voice.

But when something caught his attention, he changed. His dark, intelligent eyes would glitter, and his gaze became something so intense that it could start a fire. During the situations that changed from investigation to desperate struggle, his whole being shifted in the same way. His stance widened, becoming more aggressive and confident, and his voice rose up to become a ringing trumpet that could have been clearly heard from opposite ends of a football stadium.

Quirky nerd, gone. Terrifying icon, present.

Not many "vanillas," as he called nominally normal humans, had seen Dresden standing his ground in the fullness of his power. If we had, more of us would have taken him seriously—but I had decided that for his sake, if nothing else, it was a good thing that his full capabilities went unrecognized. Dresden's power would have scared the hell out of most people, just like it had scared me.

It wasn't the kind of fear that makes you scream and run. That's fairly mild, as fear goes. That's Scooby Doo fear. No. Seeing Dresden in action filled you with the fear that you had just become a casualty of evolution—that you were watching something far larger and infinitely more dangerous than yourself, and that your only chance of survival was to kill it, immediately, before you were crushed beneath a power greater than you would ever know.

I had come to terms with it. Not everyone would.

In fact . . . it might be for that very reason that someone had put the hit on him. A bullet that strikes from long range and goes cleanly through a human body, and then through the hull of a boat, twice, leaving a series of neat holes, is almost certainly a *very* high-powered rifle round. A professional rifleman shooting from a good way out was one of the things Dresden had acknowledged had a real chance of taking him out cleanly. He might be a wizard, a wielder of tremendous power and knowledge (as if they're any different), but he wasn't immortal.

Quick, tough, tricky as hell, sure. But not untouchable.

Not in any number of senses. I should know, having touched him— even if I hadn't touched him anywhere near soon or often enough. . . .

And now I never would.

Dammit.

I pushed thoughts of the man out of my head before I started crying again. It's hard enough to pull off an air of authority when you're five feet tall, without also having red, watery eyes and a running nose.

Dresden was gone. His cheesy jokes and his corny sense of humor were gone. His ability to know the unknowable, to fight the unfightable, and to find the unfindable was gone.

The rest of us were just going to have to carry on as best we could without him.

———

I KNOCKED ON doors and talked to a lot of people, most of them college-age kids attending school in town. I got a whole lot of nothing about Georgia, though I did get tips on some drug sales that had gone down in the parking lot. I'd pass them on to the right people on the force, where they would become more scenery for the endless march of the war on drugs and wouldn't amount to anything. The tips did prove the point I'd made to Will, though: Neighbors see things. Maybe I just hadn't talked to the right neighbor yet.

When I hit building three, I felt the change in climate as I went through the door. It was more run-down than the other apartments. Some fresh graffiti marked an interior wall. More of the doors had double dead bolts on them. The carpet was old and stained. The pane of a window had been broken out and replaced with a piece of wood. The whole place screamed that unpleasant sorts were lurking about, making the building's super reluctant to maintain the halls and foyer, maybe forcing him to continue dealing with problems and damage over and over again.

I couldn't hear any music.

That's unusual in buildings like that one, mostly inhabited by students. Kids love their music, however mind-numbing or ear-rending it might be, and you can almost always hear at least a beat thumping somewhere nearby.

Not here, though.

I kept my eyes open, tried to grow a new pair for the back of my head, and started knocking on doors.

"NO," LIED A small, fragile-looking woman who said her name was Maria, a resident of the third floor. She hadn't opened the door more than the security chain allowed. "I didn't hear or see anything."

I tried to make my smile reassuring. "Ma'am, the way this usually works is that I ask you a question, and *then* you tell me a lie. If you give me a dishonest answer before I have the chance to ask the question, it offends my sense of propriety."

Her head shook in quick, jerky spasms as her eyes widened. "N-no. I'm not lying. I don't know anything."

Maria tried to shut the door. I got my boot into it first. "You're lying," I said, gently. "You're scared. I get that. I've gotten the same treatment from almost everyone in the building."

She looked away from me, as if seeking an escape route. "I'll c-call the police."

"I am the police," I said. Which was technically true. They hadn't fired me yet.

"Oh, God," she said. She shook her head more and more, desperation in the gesture, "I don't want to be . . . I can't be seen talking to you. Go *away*."

I lifted my eyebrows. "Ma'am, please. If you're in trouble . . ."

I wasn't sure she'd even heard me. I'd seen women like her often enough to know the look. She was terrified of something, probably a husband or boyfriend or a string of husbands and boyfriends, and maybe a father before that. She was living scared, and she'd been doing it for a long time. Fear had ground away at her, and the only way she'd been able to survive was by capitulating.

Maria was damaged goods. She shook her head, sobbing, and just started pushing at the door. I was about to pull my foot out and go away. You can't force someone to accept your help.

"Is there some kind of problem here?" asked a booze-roughened voice.

I turned to face a wooly mammoth of a man. He was well over six feet tall and probably weighed three of me, though more of it was mass than muscle. He wore a white undershirt that showed off his belly, and a button-down shirt with the name RAY embroidered on one breast.

He looked at me and at the apartment door and scowled. "Mary, you got some kind of problem?"

Maria had gone still, like a rabbit that suspects a predator is nearby. "No, Ray," she whispered. "It's nothing."

"Sure as hell don't sound like nothing," Ray said. He folded his arms. "I'm trying to get the city out here to fix the lights on the street and the fuse box, and you're making enough noise to fuck up my conversation all the way down the hall."

"I'm sorry, Ray," Maria whispered.

Something flickered behind Ray's eyes, an ugly little light. "Jesus, I give you all that extra time to pay off on the rent, and you treat me like this?"

Maria sounded as though someone were strangling her. "It was an accident. It won't happen again."

"We'll talk," he said.

Maria flinched as if the words had smeared her with grime.

My hand clenched into a fist.

Well, dammit.

I'd seen Ray's type before, too—bullies who never managed to outgrow the playground; people who liked having power over others and who controlled them through fear. He was big, and he thought that made him more powerful than everyone else. The worm probably had a record, probably had done some time, probably for something fairly gutless. For guys like Ray, sometimes prison only convinces them what dangerous badasses they are, serving as a confirmation and validation of their status as predators.

Ray looked from Maria to me, with that same ugly light in his eyes. "You're the super?" I asked.

He grunted in Martian. *Fuck off and die.*

It's an expressive language, Martian.

"What's it to you?" he asked.

"I'm the curious sort," I said.

"Fuck off and die," Ray said, in English, this time. "Get out." He looked past me to Maria. "Close that goddamn door."

"I—I've been trying," Maria said. My foot and my heavy black work boot were both still between the door and its frame.

Flat rage hit Ray's eyes, and it was aimed at Maria. That made up my mind for me. Ray was obviously an abuser and one who took out his frustrations wherever he damn well pleased instead of upon their source. He was going to be unhappy with me, and when he realized he couldn't take it out on me, Maria would be the recipient of his rage. It more or less obliged me to protect her.

And I wasn't going to enjoy doing it even one little bit, either. Honest.

"Get your foot out of the door before I tear it off," Ray growled.

"Suppose I don't," I said.

"Last chance," Ray said, his eyes narrowing to slits. He was breathing faster, now, and I could see sweat beading on his brow. "Get out of here. Now."

"Or what?" I asked, mildly. "You gonna hit me, Ray?"

Self-control was not one of Ray's strong suits. He spat out the word "Bitch," spraying spittle with it as he did. He moved toward me, all three-hundred-and-change pounds of him, his hands balled into fists the size of cantaloupes.

There was something Ray didn't know about me: I know martial arts.

I'm not a truly advanced student, but I've practiced every day since I was seventeen. I started with Aikido, then Wing Chun, then Jujitsu. I've studied Kali, Savate, Krav Maga, Tae Kwan Do, Judo, boxing, and Shaolin Kung Fu. It sounds impressive laid out like that, but it really isn't. Once you get two or three arts down, the next dozen or so come pretty quick. Since they are all addressing the same problem, and because human bodies are human bodies, regardless of which continent you're on, they share characteristic motions and timing.

Ray swept a fist at me in a looping punch a kiddie-league fighter could have avoided, so I took my foot out of Maria's door and ducked it. He kept coming forward in a fleshy avalanche, while I went under his arm and took a pair of steps to one side on a diagonal angle. He tried to grab me as I slipped loose, but he wound up losing his balance badly in doing it. I gave him a helpful push with the first two knuckles of my left fist, right in the kidney.

Ray smashed into the drywall and left dents. I thought about how long it had taken him to build up speed, and I took several steps back. He turned, screaming a vicious oath, and came at me, gathering sluggish momentum like an overloaded tractor trailer. I had to back up another pair of steps to give him enough space to move into a wobbling run.

He didn't bother with a punch this time. He simply grabbed at me with his huge arms. I timed it carefully, and dropped to the floor at the last instant, sweeping my leg out in an almost-gentle kick that did nothing except prevent his right foot from proceeding forward and to the floor in proper rhythm with his left.

The bigger they are, the harder they fall. Ray fell pretty hard.

He staggered up to his hands and knees and swiped a paw at me in another grab.

Jesus Christ. Basic self-defense instructors would kill to have a video of this. He was coming at me with every stupid-aggressive move he possibly could, as if working his way through a list.

There were a lot of things I could have done with the gift he'd made me of his hand, but in real conflict, I don't get fancy. I go with simple, fast, and reliable. I let him grab my wrist, then broke his grip, wrapped him into a wrist lock, and applied pressure.

That kind of hold has very little to do with muscle or mass. That one is all about exploiting the machinery of the human body. It wouldn't have mattered if Ray was in shape. He could have looked like Schwarzenegger as Conan, and he would have been just as helpless. Human joints are all built to more or less the same specifications, out of similar materials, no matter how much muscle or lard is on top of them. They're vulnerable, if you know how to use them against your opponent.

I did.

Three hundred plus pounds of body odor, stupid and mean, slammed down onto the worn, dirty carpeting in the hallway, as if dropped from a crane.

While he lay there, stunned, I twisted his wrist straight up and behind him, keeping his arm locked straight with my other hand. From there, I could literally take his arm out of his shoulder socket with about as much effort as it would take to push a grocery cart. And I could make him hurt—a lot, if need be—in order to discourage him from trying any more stupid moves.

Being Ray, he tried stupid again, screaming and thrashing against the lock. I sighed and kept control, and he and his face relived his crushing impact with the carpet. We repeated that several times, until the lesson began to drill its way through to Ray—he wasn't going anywhere. It would hurt if he tried.

"So I've been talking to people in several buildings," I said in a calm, conversational tone. Ray was puffing like an engine. "I was wondering if you could tell me if you saw anything odd or unusual last night? Probably between two and three in the morning?"

"You're breaking my fucking arm!" Ray growled—or tried to. It had been watered down with whine.

"No, no, no," I said. "If I broke your arm, you'd hear a snapping sound. It sounds a lot like a tree branch breaking, actually, though a little more muffled. What you have to worry about is me dislocating your arm at the shoulder and elbow. That's worse, overall. Just as painful and it takes a hell of a lot more effort to recover."

"Jesus," Ray said.

"Are you telling me that Jesus was visiting between two and three last night? I'm dubious, Ray."

"I didn't see nothing!" he said a few panting seconds later. "All right? Jesus Christ, I didn't see nothing!"

"Aha," I said. "You sound like an honest man." I used my bracing arm to reach for my coat pocket, then tossed my badge down onto the floor in front of him.

He stared at it for a long second, and then his face went white.

"Here's what happens," I said very quietly. "You're going to resign from your job. You'll write a very nice letter to your boss, and then you get out of this building. You're gone by noon tomorrow."

"You can't do that," he said.

"I can do whatever I want," I said. "Which of us do you think the judge will believe, Ray?"

That isn't how I approached law enforcement. It isn't how any good cop does, either. But the criminals are always willing, even eager, to believe the absolute worst about cops. I think it makes them feel better if they can convince themselves that the police are just like them, only with badges and a paycheck.

"You're going, one way or another. You don't play ball, I send the city inspector in here to verify all the code violations on this building. Fire extinguishers are missing. The smoke detectors are years old, and most of the ones that aren't missing entirely are just hanging from their wires. You've got mold and fungus issues all over the place. Lights are out. There's trash piling up outside." I yawned. "On top of that, there are drug deals going down in your parking lot, Ray. I figure you're in on that."

"No," he said. "No, I'm not!"

"Sure you are. It fits you, doesn't it? And here you are assaulting an officer." I shook my head sadly. "So when the building fails inspection, maybe even makes it into the paper, you'll be fired anyway. And on top of that, I'll finger you in the drug deals. I'll press charges for assault. How many strikes do you already have on you, big guy? Can you handle two more?"

"You're bluffing," he said.

"Maybe," I admitted. "On the other hand . . . maybe I just give John Marcone a call and tell him how you're helping some of his street-level guys run some deals behind his back."

Invoking the name of Marcone to a Chicago criminal is as significant as invoking the name of a saint to a devout Catholic. He's the biggest fish in the pond, the head of organized crime in Chicago—and damn good at it. His people fear him, and even cops take him very, very seriously. One day he'd slip up and CPD, the FBI, or maybe the IRS would nail him. Until then, he was the deadliest predator in the jungle.

Ray shuddered.

"Look up, Ray," I said quietly.

He did, and he saw what I had seen a moment before.

Doors were open all up and down the hallway. People stood in them, men and women, children, parents, the elderly. They all stood there silently and watched a little blond woman handling big mean Ray as if he were an unruly child.

Their eyes were very hard. And there wasn't any fear in them now.

"Look at them, Ray," I said.

He did. He shuddered again. Then his body stopped straining, and he sagged down.

"I'll go," he said.

"Fucking right you will." I shoved on his arm, and he screamed with pain—but I hadn't dislocated it. I only did it to give myself a moment to pick up my badge and step out of grab range, just in case he was too dumb to quit.

He wasn't. He simply lay there like a beached shark.

"I'll be checking back here, Ray. Regularly. If I think you've harmed any of these people, stolen or broken their property—hell, if I hear that you gave them a dirty *look*, I am going to find you and shove a bundle of rusty rebar up your ass. I promise."

I took out one of my business cards, now obsolete, I supposed, and wrote down a phone number. I took the card to Maria and held it out for her. "If you have any trouble, you call this number on the back. You ask for Lieutenant Stallings. Tell him Murphy gave you the number."

Maria bit her lip. Then she looked at Ray and back to me.

She took the card with a hurried, nervous little motion and scampered back, closing her apartment door. Several locks clicked shut.

I didn't say anything else. I walked out of the building. I was halfway across the lot, heading back to Will's place, when I heard quick footsteps coming behind me. I turned with one hand close to my Sig, but relaxed when I recognized Maria.

She stopped in front of me and said, "I s-saw something."

I nodded and waited.

"There were some odd sounds, late last night. Like . . . like thumps.

And a little while later, a car rolled in. It pulled up to the building across the lot, and a man got out and left it running, like he wasn't worried about it being stolen."

"Did you recognize him?" I asked.

Maria shook her head. "But he was big. Almost as big as Ray, but he . . . You know, he moved better. He was in shape. And he was wearing an expensive suit."

"What else can you tell me about him?" I asked.

Maria shrugged. "Not . . . not anything, really. I saw him come out again, right away. Then he got into the car and drove away. I didn't see any plates or anything. I'm sorry."

"Nothing to be sorry about," I said quietly. "Thank you."

She nodded and turned to scurry back toward her building. Then she stopped and looked back at me. "I don't know if it matters," she said, "but the man had one of those army haircuts."

I stiffened a little. "Do you remember what color hair?"

"Red," she said. "Like, bright orange-red." She swallowed. "If it matters."

It mattered—but I didn't want to scare her, so I nodded and smiled, then said, "Thank you, Maria. Seriously."

She tried to smile back and did pretty well. Then she looked around her, as if uncomfortable standing in so much open space, and hurried back to her building.

A big guy in a suit with a bright red crew cut—it was almost word for word the short description in the notes of the file that CPD kept for a man named Hendricks.

Hendricks was a former college football player. He weighed upward of three hundred pounds, none of it excess. He had been under suspicion for several mysterious disappearances, mostly of criminal figures who seemed to have earned his boss's displeasure. And his boss had, presumably, sent him to Will and Georgia's building late last night.

But why?

To get an answer, I was going to have to talk to Hendricks's boss.

I had to go see "Gentleman" John Marcone.

———

THE POLICE KNOW where Marcone can be reached. Finding him doesn't do diddly to let us nail him. The fact that he has his fingers in so many pies means that not only do we have to work against Marcone and his shadowy empire, but we have our own superiors and politicians breathing down our necks as well. Oh, they never say anything directly, like, "Stop arresting Marcone's most profitable pimps." Instead, we get a long speech about racial and socioeconomic profiling. We get screams from political action committees. We get vicious editorial pieces in the newspapers and on TV.

We mostly stay quiet and keep plugging away at our jobs. Experience has taught us that hardly anyone ever cares what we think or have to say. They demand answers, but they don't want to listen.

I'm not saying that cops are a bunch of white knights. I'm just saying that the politicians can spin things all sorts of ways if it means that they're guaranteed stacks of cash for their campaign chests—or that Marcone's blackmailers won't expose some dark secret from their pasts.

I still had friends in the CPD. I called one who worked in the Organized Crime Division and asked him where I could find Marcone.

"Aw, Murph," Malone said. He sounded weary. "This ain't the time."

"Since when have you been big on punctuality?" I asked. "I need this. It's about Dresden."

Malone grunted. Dresden had saved his uncle from some kind of possession or (and I still have trouble with the concept when I say it), an evil enchantment. The elder Malone had been suffering to a degree I had never seen elsewhere. Cops and medics and so on couldn't do a thing for the man. Dresden had walked in, shooed everyone else out of the room, and five minutes later Malone was sane again, if worse for wear. It had made an impression on Malone's nephew.

"Okay," he said. "Give me a couple minutes. They got everyone with a star running around the city looking for bin Laden or Bigfoot or whoever else might have blown up that building. I ain't slept in two days. And the FBI is coming down like a freaking cloud of angry mama birds, after what happened at their office." He cleared his throat. "Um. I heard you might have been around there."

I grunted. Neutrally.

"Weird stuff, huh?"

I sighed. Internal Affairs or the FBI might still have my phone tapped, and I was reluctant to say much.

On the other hand, what were they going to do? Take my career away?

"Serious weirdness. The same flavor as the kind that hit the old Velvet Room." That was where Dresden had fought a whole bunch of vampires and wound up burning down the entire house.

Malone whistled. "Was it as bad as that guy down in the SI holding tank?"

The kid meant the loup-garou. We were stupid enough to lock Harley MacFinn in a normal cell. He transformed into this hideous Ice Age–looking thing. It was half the size of an old Buick and it could only loosely be called a wolf. Brave men had died that night, fighting with weapons that were utterly useless against the loup-garou. Carmichael, my old partner, had died there, all but throwing himself into the thing's jaws to buy me a few seconds.

I feel nauseated when I think about it.

"I don't know, really. Things happened too fast. I rounded up some people, went down a stairway and out. SWAT went in, but by the time they did, there was nothing left but staff hiding in closets and under desks, and a lot of bodies."

"Jesus," he said.

"Malone, I need this," I pressed firmly.

"Call you back in a minute," he said.

I put my phone back into my coat pocket and looked at Will. We were both standing on the sidewalk in front of his apartment.

"This is crazy," Will said quietly. "Vampires hitting a government building? Blowing up buildings in a major city? They don't *do* that."

"If they followed all the rules, they wouldn't be bad guys," I said.

"It's just . . ." He swallowed. "I really wish Harry was around. He'd have a take on it."

"That makes two of us."

Will shook his head. "I've been too crazy to even ask. . . . Where is he?"

I glanced at him and away, keeping my face still.

The color drained out of Will's cheeks. "No. He's not. . . . It doesn't work like that."

"We don't know where he is," I said. "He was staying out on that ratty boat he uses until he could find somewhere else to sleep. We found blood. Bullet holes. Blood trail leading into the lake."

Will shook his head. "But . . . if he was hurt, he wouldn't go to a hospital. He'd call Waldo Butters." He took his cell phone from his pocket. "He's in my contacts. We can call—"

"I know about Butters, Will," I interrupted gently. "I called him first thing after I saw the blood. He hasn't heard from Harry."

"Oh my . . . Oh my God," Will said, his voice a whisper.

I felt like I'd just double-tapped Santa Claus.

"Maybe he isn't dead," I said. "Maybe it was somebody else with the same blood type who got shot. Or maybe Dresden pulled one of his tricks and just vanished, whoosh, off to . . . a wizard hospital somewhere."

"Yeah," Will said, nodding. "Yeah, maybe. I mean, he can do all kinds of things, right?"

"All kinds of things," I said.

Including dying. But I didn't say that.

DETECTIVE MALONE WAS good to his word, and five minutes later we were heading for a building on the north edge of Bucktown, another renovation project Gentleman Johnnie's mostly legitimate business interests had secured. He had purchased, refurbished, updated, and preserved more than a dozen buildings in the city over the past several years. He'd been feted and decorated and honored at various society functions, as a man who was preserving the native beauty of Chicago architecture, saving it from being destroyed and forgotten, et cetera.

If you didn't consider the drugs, gambling, prostitution, extortion, and other shadow franchises he ruled, I guess he was a real citizen hero.

Contractors were hard at work on the building as we came in, and a security guard in a white shirt and black pants walked over to us with a frown as I entered the building. Will was at my back. I hoped that if things went nutty, I wouldn't have to drag him with me when I shot my way out.

I felt myself smile at that image, mostly because of its fantasy content. If blood was spilled in Marcone's headquarters, I wouldn't live long enough to drag anybody out.

"No trespassers," the guard said firmly. "This is a construction site. Dangerous. You'll have to leave."

I eyed the man and said, "I'm here to see John Marcone."

The guard eyed me. Then he got on his little radio and spoke into it. A moment later, a voice squawked an answer. "Mr. Marcone is not available."

"Yes, he is," I said. "Go tell him Karrin Murphy is here to see him."

"I'm afraid not," he said. "You'll have to leave."

He had a gun, a 9mm Glock, I noted.

I took out the little leather wallet with my police ID in it, and said, "If you make me open this, it gets official. There will be official questions, official paperwork, and lots of men in uniform trespassing all over your site." I held the wallet out as if presenting a crucifix to a vampire, fingers poised as if to open it. "Do you want to be the one who gives your boss that kind of headache?"

His eyes moved from me to Will. He looked quickly away. Then he took a few steps back toward the interior of the building and had a low, rather emphatic conversation with his radio.

I folded my arms and tapped one foot impatiently.

"Would you really do that?" Will asked me.

"Can't," I said. "I'm getting fired. But they don't know that."

Will made a choking sound.

The guard came back and said, "Through that door. Two floors down. Then take your first left, and you'll see it." He coughed. "You'll have to leave any weapons with me."

I snorted and said, "Like hell." Then I brushed past him, nudging him slightly aside with my shoulder as though spoiling for a fight. Martian for *It is inappropriate for you to screw with me in any way.*

He got the message. He didn't try to stop us.

Will's quiet chuckle followed me down the stairs.

MARCONE'S OFFICE WAS located in what appeared to be a dining hall. The room was huge and tiled, and several contractors—most of them brawnier and more heavily tattooed than the average laborer—sat at long tables, eating. Caterers kept several serving tables of food stocked with the same attention and care that I would have expected in a high-society gala. It was brightly lit, and a raised stage at one end of the room, which would presumably host a full orchestral band if one were present, had instead been loaded with computers and office furniture.

The portrait of a busy executive, Marcone sat at an enormous old desk, holding a phone to his ear with one shoulder, his business shirt rolled up to his elbows.

Everything about him screamed "successful patriarch." His suit jacket, hung over the back of his chair, was worth more than some small nations. His loosened tie, a simple silver number rather than a bright "power" tie, bespoke confidence and strength that needed no such sartorial declaration. His hands were broad and looked strong. There were scars on his knuckles. His short, conservatively cut hair was dark, except for just enough silver at his temples to announce a man in his physical and mental prime. He was well built and obviously kept himself in shape, and his features were regular and appealing. He was by no means beautiful, but his face projected strength and competence.

He looked like a man others would willingly follow.

Two other people stood on the stage, slightly behind him, testimony to his ability to lead. The first was a woman, a blond amazon more than six feet tall in a grey business suit. She had the legs that had been cruelly denied me at birth, the bitch. Her name was Gard, and Dresden had believed she was an actual, literal Valkyrie.

The other was Hendricks. He wasn't truly ugly, but he reminded me of a gargoyle, anyway, a slab-muscled being with a misshapen appearance and beady eyes, ready to leap into action on behalf of the man he watched over. His eyes tracked me as I approached. Gard's blue eyes focused on me for a moment, then skipped past me to Will. She narrowed her eyes and murmured something toward Marcone.

Chicago's resident lord of the underworld gave no indication that he'd heard her, and I caught the last few lines of a conversation as I approached.

"You'll just have to do it yourself." He paused, listening. Then he said, "I don't have the proper resources for such a thing—and even if I did, I wouldn't waste them by sending them there blind and unprepared. You'll have to use your own people." He paused again and then said, "Neither of us will ever be scratching each other's back, mutually or otherwise. I will not send my people into danger without more information. Should you change your mind, you may feel free to contact me. Good day."

He hung up the phone and then turned toward me. He had eyes the color of several-days-old grass clippings. They were opaque, reptilian. He made a steeple of his fingertips and said, "Ms. Murphy."

"News travels fast," I said.

"To me. Yes." His mouth turned up in a heartless smile. "Which are you here for? Work or revenge?"

"Why would I want revenge on such a pillar of the community?"

"Dresden," he said simply. "I assume you're here because you think me responsible."

"What if I am?" I asked.

"Then I would advise you to leave. You wouldn't live long enough to take your gun from your coat."

"And besides," I said, "you didn't do it. Right? And you have a perfectly rational reason to explain why you didn't even want him dead."

He shrugged, a motion he managed to infuse with elegance. "No more than any other day, at any rate," he said. "I had no need to assassinate Dresden. He'd been working diligently to get himself killed for several years—as I pointed out to him a few days ago."

I kept my heart on lockdown. The cocky bastard's tone made me want to scream and tear out his eyes. I wouldn't give him the satisfaction of knowing he'd rattled me. "I'm here for another reason."

"Oh?" he asked politely.

Too politely. He knew. He'd known why I was coming since before I came through the door. I stopped and played the past several hours back in my imagination, before I spotted where I'd contacted his net.

"Maria," I said. "She was one of yours."

Hendricks eyed Gard.

She rolled her eyes and withdrew a twenty-dollar bill from her jacket pocket. She passed it to the big man.

Hendricks pocketed it with a small, complacent smile.

Marcone took no evident note of the interaction. "Yes. The superintendent you met had been providing the means for some of my competitors to operate. Maria was observing his business partners, so that we could track them back to their source and encourage them to operate elsewhere."

I stared at him, hard. "She just let Ray treat her like that?"

"And was well paid to do it," Marcone replied. "Admittedly, she was looking forward to closing the contract."

Maria hadn't been a broken little mouse. Hell, she was one of Marcone's troubleshooters. It was a widely used euphemism for hitters in Marcone's outfit. Everyone knew it was the troubleshooter's job to identify trouble within the organization—and shoot it.

"And you're just standing there, sharing all this with me?" I asked.

His expression turned bland. "It isn't as though I'm confessing to a police officer, is it, Ms. Murphy?"

I clenched my teeth. I swear. Scratch out his goddamn eyes. "That was why Maria came running out after me—she took enough time to call in, report, and ask you for instructions."

Marcone nodded his head, very slightly.

"And she was also why Hendricks showed up," I continued. "Maria saw or heard something and reported in."

Marcone spread his hands. "You apprehend the situation."

I clenched a fist again to let out some of the anger his deliberate choice of words had inspired.

"Why?" Will demanded suddenly, stepping forward to stand beside me. I noted that both Will and I were under average height. We stood staring up at Marcone on the raised stage. It was hard not to feel like an extra in the cast of *Oliver—Please, sir, may I have some more?*

"Why?" he repeated. "Why did you send your man to my apartment?"

Marcone tilted his head slightly to regard Will. "What are you willing to pay for such information, young man?"

Will's upper lip lifted away from his teeth. "How about I don't tear you and your goons into hamburger?"

Marcone regarded Will for maybe three seconds, his face blank. Then he made a single, swift motion. I barely saw the gleam of metal as the small knife flickered across the space between them, and buried itself two inches deep in Will's right biceps. Will let out a cry and staggered.

My own hands went toward my coat, but Gard had lifted a shotgun from behind a cabinet, and leveled it on me as my fingers touched the handle of my Sig. Hendricks had produced a heavy-caliber pistol from his suit, though he hadn't aimed at anyone. I stopped, then moved my fingers slowly from my gun.

Will ripped the knife out of his arm, then turned to Marcone, his teeth bared.

"Don't confuse yourself with Dresden, Mr. Borden," Marcone said, his voice level and cold. His eyes were something frightening, pitiless. "You don't have the power to threaten me. The instant you begin to change, Ms. Gard here will fire on Ms. Murphy—and then upon you." His voice dropped to a barely audible murmur. "The next time you offer me a threat, I will kill you."

Will's breaths came in pained gasps, each exhalation tinged with a growl. But he didn't answer. The room had become completely quiet. The men who were eating lunch had stopped moving, as if frozen in place. No one looked directly at the confrontation, but all of them were watching from the corners of their eyes. A lot of hands were out of sight.

"He means it, Will," I said quietly. "This won't help her."

Marcone left it like that for a moment, staring at Will, before he settled back into his chair again, his eyes becoming hooded and calm once more. "Have you given thought to your next career move, Ms. Murphy? I'm always looking for competent help. When I find it, I pay a premium for it."

I wondered where he'd heard about my suspension, but I supposed it wasn't important. He had more access to the CPD than most cops. I asked him, calmly, "Does the job involve beating you unconscious and throwing you into a cell forever?"

"No," Marcone said, "although it offers an excellent dental plan. And combined with your pension check, it would make you a moderately wealthy woman."

"Not interested," I said. "I will never work for you."

"Never is a very long time, Ms. Murphy." Marcone blinked slowly and then sighed. "Clearly, the atmosphere has become unproductive," he said. "Ms. Gard, please escort them both from the premises. Give them the information they want."

"Yes, sir," Gard said. She lowered the shotgun slowly. Then she returned it to its place behind the desk, picked up a file folder from it, and walked out to Will and me. I stooped and picked up the dropped, bloodstained knife before she could reach it. Then I wiped it clean on a pocket handkerchief, taking the blood from it, before offering the handle to Ms. Gard. I was more or less ignorant about magic, but I knew that Gard knew more about it than I, and that blood could be used in spells or incantations or whatever, to the great detriment of the bleeder. By wiping the blood from the blade, I'd prevented them from having an easy way to get to Will.

Gard smiled at me very slightly and nodded her head in what looked like approval. She took the knife, slipped it into a pocket, and then said, "This way, please."

We followed her back out of the room. Will walked with his left hand pressed to his right biceps, his expression furious. There was blood, but not much of it. His shirt was soaking it up, and he'd clamped his hand hard over the wound. The knife hadn't hit any major blood vessels, or he'd have been on the floor by now. We'd clean it up once we were out of here.

"You may know," Ms. Gard said, as we walked, "that Mr. Marcone's business interests are varied. Some of them have fierce competitors."

"Drugs," I said. "Extortion. Prostitution. Those are the money-makers. There's always competition for territory."

Gard continued as if she hadn't heard me. "Competition has increased rather dramatically of late, and it has consisted of increasingly competent personnel. We've also had a number of issues with involuntary employee dereliction."

Will let out a snort. "Does she mean what I think she means?"

"Hitters," I said quietly. "Marcone's been losing people." I frowned. "But there hasn't been any particular increase in the number of homicides."

"They haven't been killed," Gard said, frowning. "They've vanished. Quickly. Quietly. Sometimes with minimal signs of a struggle."

Will inhaled sharply. "Georgia."

Gard passed me the folder. I opened it and found a simple printout of a Web browser document. "'Craigslist,'" I read, for Will's benefit. "'Talent search, Chicago. Standard compensation for new talent. Contact for delivery dates.' And there's an e-mail address."

"I know some of the business Dresden was involved in yesterday," she said quietly. "In the past twenty-four hours, announcements like this have appeared in London, Chicago, New York, Los Angeles, Paris, Rome, Berlin. . . ."

"I get the point," I said. "Something big is happening."

"Exactly," Gard said. She glanced at Will and said, "Someone is rounding up those mortals possessed of modest supernatural gifts."

"Talent search," I said.

"Yes," Gard said. "I don't know who or what is behind it. We haven't been able to get close. Whoever they are, they're quite well-informed, and they know our personnel."

"Why was Hendricks at my apartment?" Will asked.

"Maria saw someone force your wife and another young woman out of the building and into a car. We know about your gifts, obviously. Marcone sent Hendricks to case the scene to look for any evidence of our opponent's identity. He found nothing." She shook her head. "From here on, I have only conjecture," Gard said. "I'll give it to you if you want it."

"You don't need to," I told her. "Someone started picking on the little guys in town within a few hours of Dresden's shooting. He never would have stood for something like that. So whoever is responsible for these disappearances might well be behind the shooting, too."

"Excellent," Gard said, nodding in approval. "We don't really specialize in finding people." She glanced down at me. "But you do."

"I am not doing this for Marcone," I snarled.

We reached the building's entrance, and Ms. Gard looked at me thoughtfully. "A word of advice: Be cautious what official channels you use for assistance. We aren't the only ones who have compromised the local authorities."

"Yes," I said. "I know how it works."

Gard frowned at me and then nodded her head a little more deeply than was usual. "Of course. My apologies."

I frowned at her, trying to figure out what she meant. There wasn't any trace of sarcasm or irony in her words or her body language. Damn. I wasn't used to confronting non-Martians. "Nothing to apologize for," I said, after a hesitation. "I didn't sleep well last night."

She studied me for a moment. "I can't tell if what I'm seeing in you is courage or despair. I'd ask, but I'm almost sure you wouldn't know the answer."

"Excuse me?"

Gard nodded. "Exactly." She sighed. "I'm sorry. About Dresden. He was a brave man."

I suddenly felt furious that she had spoken of Harry in the past tense. It wasn't anything I hadn't done in my thoughts—but I hadn't spoken the words aloud, either. "They haven't found a body," I told her, and I heard a fierceness in my voice I had not intended. "Don't write him off just yet."

The Valkyrie gave me a smile that bared her canine teeth. "Good hunting," she bade us, and then went back inside the building.

I turned to Will and said, "Let's take care of your arm."

"It's fine," Will said.

"Don't play tough guy with me," I said. "Let me see."

Will sighed. Then he took his hand away from the wound. There was a slit in his shirtsleeve, where the knife had gone in. It was too high up on his arm to make rolling the sleeve up practical, so I tore it a little wider and examined the wound.

It wasn't bleeding. There was an angry, swollen purple line over the puncture mark. It wasn't a scab, either. It was just . . . healing, albeit into a damn ugly scar.

I whistled softly. "How?"

"We've been experimenting," Will said quietly. "Closing an injury isn't really much different from shifting back into human form. My arm still hurts like hell, but I can stop bleeding—probably. If it isn't too bad. We're not sure about the limits. Leaves a hell of a mark, though." His stomach gurgled. "And the energy for it has to come from somewhere. I'm starving."

"Neat trick."

"I thought so." Will kept pace beside me as we headed back to the car. "What do we do next?"

"Food," I said. "Then we contact the bad guys."

He frowned. "Won't that just, you know . . . warn them that we're on to them?"

"No," I said. "They'll want to meet me."

"Why?"

I looked up at him. "Because I'm going to be selling them some new talent."

WE WENT TO my place.

There wasn't much point in setting the dogs on the owner of the e-mail address. It would prove to be anonymous, and given what I had for hard evidence, even if I could get someone to pay attention to me, by the time it went through channels and peeled away all the red tape and got a judge somewhere to move, I was sure the address would be old news, and anyone connected to it would long since have departed.

I might have gotten some help from a friend at the Bureau, except that in the wake of the Red Court attack on their headquarters building, they would be going crazy looking for the "terrorists" responsible. They, too, were long since departed. Dresden had seen to that.

The TV news was all about the bombing, the attack, while everyone speculated about who had done what and used the occasion to put forward their own social and political agendas.

People suck. But they're the only ones around who can keep the lights on.

I turned Will loose on my fridge and then sent him out to make a few discreet inquiries of the local supernatural scene. I heard his car door close when he returned, about the time the daylight was turning golden orange. It looked like it would be another cold night.

There was the sound of a second car door closing.

Will knocked at the front door, and I answered it with my gun held low and against my leg. There proved to be a girl with him. She was a little taller than I, which still put her below average, and I had pencils bigger around than she was. Her glasses were oversized, her hair thin, straight, and the same brown of a house mouse's fur. Still, there was something in the way she held herself that put up the hairs on the back of my neck. The young woman might be a lightweight, but so were rats—and you didn't want to trap one of them in a corner if you could avoid it. She contained a measure of danger that demanded respect.

Her eyes flickered to my face and then down to my gun hand in the same first half second of recognition. She stopped slightly behind Will, her body language wary.

"Murphy," Will said, nodding—but he didn't try to come in or make any other movement that might force me to react. "Uh, maybe you remember Marcy? We were all at Marcone's place, stuck down in that muddy pit? Drugged?"

"Good times?" the young woman asked hopefully.

"My partner died the day before, when the loup-garou gutted him. Not so much," I said. I looked at Will. "You trust her?"

"Sure," Will said without a second's hesitation.

Maybe I'm getting cynical as I age. I stared at Marcy hard for a second before I said, "I don't."

No one said anything for a minute. Then Will said, "I'm vouching for her."

"You're emotionally involved, Will," I said. "It's compromising your judgment. Marcone could have put a bullet through your head instead of tossing that little knife at you. If Dresden was standing here telling you to be suspicious, what would you do?"

Will's expression darkened. But I saw him get ahold of himself and take a deep breath. "I don't know," he said finally. "I don't know. I've known Marcy for years."

"You knew her years ago," I corrected him with gentle emphasis.

Marcy rubbed one foot against the other calf, and stood looking down, her eyes on her feet. It looked like a habitual stance, social camouflage. "She's right, Will," she said in a quiet voice.

Will frowned at her. "How?"

"She should be suspicious of me, given the circumstances. I've been back in town for what? Two weeks? And something like this happens? I'd be worried, too." She looked up at me, her expression uncertain. "I want to help, Sergeant Murphy," she said. "What do we do?"

I stared at them both, thinking. Dammit, this was another one of those Dresden things. He could have pinched his nose for a second, then swept his gaze over them and reported whether or not they were who they said they were. Supernatural creatures are big on shapeshifting. They use it to get in close to their prey. In an attack like that, a mortal has the next-best thing to zero probability of escaping.

I knew. It had been done to me. The sense of chagrin and helplessness is terrible.

"To start with," I said, "let me see if you can come in."

Marcy frowned at me. "What do you mean?"

"I mean that if you're a shapeshifter or something, you might not have an easy time coming over the threshold."

"Christ, Sergeant," Will began. "Of course she's a shapeshifter. So am I."

I glowered at them both. "If she's who she says she is, she won't have a problem," I said.

Will sighed and looked at Marcy. "Sorry."

"No, it's fine," the young woman said. "It's smart to be careful."

Marcy held her hands out to her sides, in plain sight, and stepped into the house. "Good enough?"

Houses are surrounded by a barrier of energy. Dresden always called it the threshold. It's all murky magic stuff to me, but the general guideline is that anything that's too hideously supernatural can't come in without being invited. A threshold will stop spirits, ghosts, some vampires (but not others), and will generally ward away things that intend to eat your face.

Not everything. Not hardly. But a lot of things.

"No," I said, and put my gun away. "But it's a start." I nodded to a chair in the living room. "Sit down."

She did, and she sat looking down at her hands, which were folded in her lap.

Will followed Marcy in and gave me a look that meant, in Martian, *What the hell do you think you're doing?*

I ignored him.

"Marcy," I said, "why didn't you respond to Will when he tried to contact you earlier?"

"I tried," she said. "I called back as soon as I got the message, but I didn't have Will's cell number. Only Georgia's."

"Why not?" I asked.

"Um," she said, "I just got back into town. And Georgia doesn't need any stress. And he's married. I mean, you don't just go asking for a husband's phone number. You know?"

Which was reasonable, put that way. I nodded, neither approving nor disapproving.

"I left messages on the answering machine at the apartment," Marcy said. "It was all I could do."

"And I checked the messages after I'd run your errands," Will said. "I called her back and had her come over. She swept for scents, and then we came here."

"Will," I said, firmly, "please let me handle this?"

He clenched his jaw and subsided, leaning against a wall.

I turned back to where Marcy sat and continued towering over her, a posture of parental-style authority. "Tell me about your relationship to Georgia."

"We're friends," Marcy said. "Close friends, really. I think of her as a close friend, I mean. She was very kind to me when Andi broke it off with me. And we were friends for years before that."

I nodded. "Did Will explain what was going on?"

She nodded. "Georgia and Andi have been taken."

"How do you know it was Andi with Georgia?"

"Because I was there," Marcy said. "I mean, not last night, but the night before last. Will was out of town and we had a girls' night."

"Girls' night?"

"We hung out and made fondue and watched movies and lied about how we all looked better now than when we first met. Well, except that Andi actually does." She shook her head. "Um, anyway, we stayed up late talking, and Andi slept in the guest bed and I slept on the couch." She glanced up at my eyes for the first time. "That was when we had the nightmares."

"Nightmares?"

She shuddered. "I . . . I don't want to think about it. But all three of us had an almost identical nightmare. It was the worst for Georgia. She was . . ." She looked at Will. "It was as if she hadn't quite woken up out of the dream. She kept jerking and twitching." She gave me a weak smile. "Took two cups of cocoa to snap her out of it."

I kept my face neutral and gave her nothing. "Go on."

"Me and Andi talked about it and decided that one of us should stay with her. We were going to trade off, like, until Will came home."

"The first night was Andi, I take it?"

Marcy nodded, biting her lip. "Yes."

"Sounds reasonable," I said. Reasonable, logical—and impossible to verify.

And the kid was shaking.

Jesus Christ, Karrin, said a gentler voice inside me. *What are you doing? She's scared to death.*

I tried to make my tone a little warmer. "What do you know about their abduction, specifically, Marcy? Can you tell me anything at all that might point toward the identity of the kidnappers?"

She shook her head. "I can't think of anything that I picked up beforehand. But I'm certain it was Andi and Georgia who were taken."

"How can you be sure?" I asked.

Will cleared his throat and spoke quietly. "Marcy's got a nose. She's better with scents than any of the rest of us."

I eyed Marcy. "Could you pick up their trail?"

"They were taken downstairs and loaded into the back of a

car," Marcy said promptly. "An older model, burning too much oil. But I couldn't follow them after that. I think I'll be able to recognize the scent of their captors, though, if I run into it."

I nodded. She'd gotten a ton more out of the scene than Will had. Such a talent could be damn useful.

All the same, I wasn't sure. She sounded sincere to me, and I'm pretty good at knowing when someone isn't. But there's always a better liar out there. I just wasn't sure.

But . . . you have to trust someone, sometime. Even when it seems risky, when lives are on the line.

Maybe even especially then.

"Okay," I said calmly, and took a seat in another chair. "Will," I asked, "what did you find out?"

"There are half a dozen other folks who have gone missing in the past day and a half," Will said. "At least, that's how many Bock and McAnally know about. Word about the kidnappings is out on the Paranet, and has been spreading since yesterday morning. People are moving places in groups of three and four, at least. McAnally's is packed. The community knows something is up. They're scared."

Marcy nodded. "It isn't just Chicago. It's happening all over the country. Group leaders are keeping everyone informed, asking after their people, reporting them missing to the local cops, for whatever good that might do. . . ." Her voice trailed off into a little squeak as she looked at me. "Um. Sorry."

I ignored her. Martian for *This is easier for all of us if we just pretend I didn't hear it*. "Will, did you turn up anything we can use?"

He shook his head. "No one has seen or heard anything at any of the disappearances. But there are rumors that someone found a gang of Red Court vampires torn apart in a basement across town. Maybe that has something to do with what's going on."

"It doesn't," I said, firmly. "Not directly, at least. Dresden killed the Red Court."

Will blinked. "You mean . . . those vampires in the basement?"

"I mean the Red Court," I said. "All of them."

Will let out a quiet whistle. "Uh. Wow. That's pretty big magic, I guess."

"Yeah," I said.

Marcy's face was twisted up in a frown of concentration. "Was . . . was this the night before last, by any chance?"

I glanced aside at her and nodded once.

"If there was a really big surge of magic . . . maybe that explains the dreams," she said. "It wasn't just the three of us. The night before last, a lot of people—Paranet people, I mean—had nightmares, too. Some of them were bad enough that people haven't slept since. A couple of folks wound up in the hospital." She blinked at Will. "That's what happened with you, Will."

"What do you mean?" Will said.

"When Georgia called you. She'd had the nightmare twice, during the day, when she tried to sleep. She must have had it again and tried to call you."

"There's no point in speculation for now." I looked at Will. "In short, more people missing, bad dreams, everyone is gathering in defensive herds. That about it?"

"More or less," Will said. "What did you get?"

"I sent an e-mail to the address Marcone gave us. Told them I had a talent in need of placement. I got a public phone location. I'm supposed to be there to answer a call at nine tonight."

Will frowned. "So they can get a look at you first, right?"

"Probably."

"You shouldn't look like you," Marcy blurted. Her face colored slightly. "I mean, like, you're the supernatural cop in Chicago. Everyone knows that. And it makes sense that anyone planning something here wouldn't have much trouble finding out who might actually get in their way."

"Unfortunately," I said, "I don't have a different look."

Will looked at Marcy, frowning, and then said, "Ah. Makeover."

"We have a little time," Marcy said, nodding.

"Hey," I said.

"She's right, Ms. Murphy," Will said. "You've been seen with Dresden a lot. And, no offense, but not many people look like you do."

"Meaning?" I asked him. I smiled.

Will's eyes might have checked the distance between himself and the door. "Meaning you're outside the norm for adult height and weight," he said. "Exceptionally so. We should do what we can to make it harder to identify you."

Will had a point, I supposed. Annoying as it might be, his logic was sound. And I was almost certainly a little sensitive where my height was concerned. I sighed. "All right. But if I hear montage music starting to play, I'm cutting it short."

Will, seeming to relax, nodded. "Cool."

Marcy nodded with him. "So what about Will and me? I mean, what do the two of us do?"

I looked at the pair of young werewolves and pursed my lips. "How do you feel about duct tape?"

WHEN I ANSWERED the pay phone outside a small grocery store on Belmont, I felt like an idiot. In the windows of a darkened shop across the street, I could see my reflection.

Halloween had come early this year. I wore boots not unlike Herman Munster's, with elevator soles about three inches thick, making me look taller. My hair was dyed matte black and was slicked down to my skull. There was so much product in it, I was fairly sure it would deflect bullets. I wore some black dance tights Marcy had donated to the cause, a black T-shirt, and a black leather jacket in a youth size.

My face was the worst part of the disguise. I was all but smothered beneath the makeup. Dark tones of silver that faded to black made a mess of my eyes, altering their shape by means of suggestion, through clever application of liner. In the evening light, I might have looked Asian. My lips were darkened, too, a shade of wine red that somehow managed to complement the eye shadow. The lipstick changed the shape of my mouth slightly and made my lips look fuller.

I glowered at the reflection. This costume had exactly one thing going for it: I didn't look a thing like me.

The phone rang and I picked it up, jerking it off the base unit as if impatient. I glared around me, my eyes tracking across every spot I thought could contain an observer, and said, "Yeah?"

"The merchandise," murmured a soft, sibilant voice with an odd accent. "Describe."

There was something intrinsically unsettling about the voice. The hairs on the back of my neck stood up. "One male and one female, mid- to late-twenties. Shapeshifters."

There was a rustle of static over the line, unless the speaker could make an extremely odd hissing sound. All things considered, I gave it even odds.

"Ten thousand," said the voice.

I could have played it a couple of different ways. The kinds of people who get into this sort of deal come in about three general types: greedy, low-life sons of bitches; cold professionals engaged in a business transaction; and desperate amateurs who are in over their heads. I'd already decided to try to come across as the first on the list.

"Forty thousand," I shot back instantly. "Each."

There was a furious sound on the other end of the phone. It wasn't a human sound, either.

"I could pluck out your eyes and cut your tongue into slivers," hissed the voice. Something about it scared the hell out of me, touching on some instinctual level that Ray, in all his repulsive mass, had not. I felt myself shudder, despite my effort not to do so.

"Whatever," I said, trying to sound bored. "Even if you could do it, it gets you nothing. But hey, no skin off my ass either way."

There was a long silence on the other end of my phone. I thought I felt some kind of pressure building behind my eyelids. I told myself it was my imagination.

"Yo, anyone there?" I complained. "Listen. Are you up for doing some business, or did I just waste my time?"

After another pause, the voice hissed something in a bubbling, serpentine tongue. The phone rustled, as if changing hands, and a very deep male voice said, "Twenty thousand. Each."

"I'm not selling the female for less than thirty."

"Fifty total, then," rumbled the new voice. It sounded entirely human.

"Cash," I demanded.

"Done."

I kept tracking the street with my eyes, looking for their spotter, but saw no one. "How do you handle delivery?"

"There's a warehouse."

"Fat chance. I pull in there, you'll just pop me and make the body disappear along with the freaks."

"What do you suggest?" rumbled the voice.

"Buttercup Park. Thirty minutes. One carrier. Carrier hands me half the cash. Then carrier verifies the merchandise in the back of my truck. Carrier hands me the rest of the money. I hand him the keys to the vehicle carrying the merchandise. We all walk away happy."

The deep-voiced man thought about it for a moment and then grunted. Translation: *Agreed.* "How will you identify me?"

I snorted and said, "Park isn't huge, tough guy. And it ain't my first rodeo."

I hung up on him, then went back to my motorcycle and left, heading for Buttercup Park. A lighted sign hanging outside a bank told me it was a quarter after nine. The metro traffic grid was dying down for the night. I got there in a little more than fifteen minutes, parked my Harley in a garage, and made my way to where Georgia's high-dollar SUV was waiting in the same structure. I went around to the back and opened the hatch. Will was just finishing wrapping Marcy in what appeared to be several layers of duct tape, covering her in a swath from her hips to her deltoids, trapping her arms against her sides. She was wearing a simple sundress with, I assumed, nothing underneath. I guess when you change into a wolf, you don't take your ensemble with you—being trapped in undies made for a different *species* could prove awkward in a fight.

Will looked up and gave me a quick nod of greeting. "All set?"

"So far. You're sure you won't have a problem getting out?" I asked.

Will snorted. "Claws, fangs. It'll sting a bit, when it tears out the hair. Nothing serious."

"Spoken like someone who's never had his legs waxed," Marcy said in a nervous, forcedly jovial tone. She might have looked like a skinny little thing, but the muscles showing on her legs were lean and ropy.

Will tore off the end of the duct tape and passed the roll to me. He sat down on the open floor in the back of the SUV, the seats of which had been folded away to make room for the "prisoners." He stripped out of his shirt, leaving only a pair of loose sweats. I started wrapping him.

"Tighten your muscles," I said. "When I'm done, relax them. It should leave you enough room to maintain blood flow."

"Right," Will said. "Houdini." He contracted the muscles in his upper body and the duct tape creaked. Damn, the kid was built. Given that I was more or less leaning against his naked back to reach around him with the roll of tape, it was impossible not to notice.

Dresden hadn't been muscled as heavily as Will. Harry'd had a runner's build, all lean, tight, dense muscle that . . .

I clenched my jaw and kept wrapping tape.

"One more time," I said. "I meet the contact, then bring him here." I held up the SUV's remote control fob. "I'll disarm the security system so you know we're coming. If you hear me say the word *red*, it means things aren't going well. Get loose and help me jump the contact. We'll question him, find out where the other specials are being kept. Otherwise, sit tight, and make like you got hit with tranquilizer darts. I'll shadow you back to their HQ."

"What then?" Marcy asked.

"We'll have to play that by ear," I said. "If there aren't many of them, we'll hit them and get your people out. If they've got a lot of muscle, I'll make a call. If I can get a large force here, they'll run rather than fight."

"Can you be sure of that?" Will asked.

"Dresden said that to the supernatural world, bringing in mortal authorities was equated with nuclear exchanges. No one wants to be the one to trigger a new Inquisition of some kind. So any group with a sense of reason will cut their losses rather than tangle with the cops."

"The way they didn't tangle with FBI headquarters?" Will asked.

I had sort of hoped no one would notice that flaw in my reasoning. "That was an act of war. This is some kind of profit-gaining scheme."

"Come on, Karrin," Will said. "You've got to know better than that."

"This is a professional operation," I said. "Whoever is behind it is depending on distraction and speed to enable them to get away with it. They'll already have their escape plan ready to go. If a bunch of cars and lights come at them, I think their first instinct will be to run rather than fight."

"Yeah," Marcy said, nodding. "That makes sense. You've always said supernatural predators don't want a fight if they can avoid one, Will."

"Lone predators don't," Will said, "but this is an organization. And you might have noticed how a lot of supernatural types are a couple of french fries short of a Happy Meal. And I'm talking about more than here, tonight. More than Georgia and Andi. More than just Chicago."

I frowned at him. "What do you mean?"

He leaned forward, his eyes intent. "I mean that if Dresden just blew up the Red Court . . . that means the status quo is *gone*. There's a power vacuum, and every spook out there is going to try to fill it. The rules have *changed*. We don't know *how* these people are going to react."

A sobering silence fell over us.

I hadn't followed the line of reasoning, like Will had. Or rather, I hadn't followed it far enough. I'd only been thinking of Dresden's cataclysm in terms of its effect on my city, upon people who were part of my life.

But he was right. Dear God, he was right. The sudden demise of the Red Court, with consequences that would reach around the whole world, would make the fall of the Soviet Union look like a minor organizational crisis.

"So, what?" I asked. "We back out?"

"Are you kidding?" Will said. "They took my wife. We go get her and anyone else they've taken."

"Right," Marcy said firmly, from where she lay on the bed of the vehicle.

I felt a smile bare my teeth. "And if they fight?"

Will's face hardened. "Then we kick their fucking ass."

"Ass," said Marcy, nodding.

I finished wrapping Will in the duct tape. He exhaled slowly and relaxed. He took a few experimental breaths and then nodded. "Okay. Good."

"Lie down, both of you. I'll be back with the buyer."

"Be careful," Will said. "If you aren't back in twenty minutes, I'll come looking."

"If I'm not back in twenty minutes, there won't be much point in finding me," I said.

Then I shut them into the SUV and headed for the park.

BUTTERCUP PARK WASN'T exactly overwhelming. There were grass, playground equipment, and a tree or two on an island bordered by four city streets. That was pretty much it. It was the sort of place my low-life persona would choose. It was out in the open, and there was not much to break up the line of sight. It was a good location for criminals with mutual trust issues to meet up. Each could be sure the other was alone. Each could be reasonably sure the other wouldn't start shooting, right out there in front of God and everybody.

The park, as it should have been, was empty. The surrounding streetlights left little hidden on the green grass, but the playground equipment cast long, asymmetric shadows.

A man sat on one of the swings. He was huge—the biggest individual I'd ever seen. He was heavy with muscle, though it was an athlete's balanced build—made for action, not for display. His hips strained the heavy flexible plastic seat of the swing to the horizontal. He must have been better than seven feet tall.

He was quietly sitting there, completely still, watching and waiting. His head was shaved and his skin was dark. He wore a simple outfit—black chinos and a thin turtleneck sweater. If the October chill was bothering him, it didn't show. I stomped over toward him in my Munster boots. When I was about thirty feet away, he turned his head toward me. His gaze was startling. His eyes were blue-white, as on some northern sled dogs, and looked nearly luminous in the half shadows.

He lifted his eyebrows as I came closer, then rose and bowed politely from the waist. I realized that he wasn't seven feet tall. He was more like seven foot four or five.

"Good evening," he said. His basso rumble was unmistakable. This was the person I had spoken to earlier.

I stopped in front of him and put a hand on my hip, eyeing him as if I wasn't much impressed. "As long as you brought the money, it will be," I drawled.

He reached into a cavernous pocket in his pants and drew out a brick wrapped in plastic. He tossed it to me. "Half."

I caught it and tore open the plastic with my teeth. Then I started counting the money, all of it in nonsequential Ben Franklins.

A trace of impatience entered my contact's voice. "It's all there."

"Talking to me is just going to make me lose count and start over," I said. "What am I supposed to call you?"

"Nothing," he said. "No one. I am nothing to you."

"Nothing it is," I replied. The bills were bound in groups of fifty. I counted one out and compared its thickness to that of the others, then flipped through just to be sure Nothing wasn't trying to short me by throwing some twenties into the middle of the stack. Then I stuck the money in my jacket pocket and said, "We're in business."

Nothing inclined his head a bit. "The merchandise?"

"Come with me," I said, injecting my voice with breezy confidence.

I turned to stomp back toward the garage parking lot, and Nothing paced along beside me.

Already, this wasn't going well. This guy was huge. I was good, but training and practice can get you only so far. The old saying is that a good big man will beat a good little man. Which is sexist as all get-out, but no less true. Levels of skill being equal, whoever has the size and weight advantage damn near always wins. Nothing probably outweighed all three of us together, and I already had a sense, from the way he held himself and moved, that he was a person accustomed to violence. He was good.

I could shoot him (probably), but I didn't need a dead trafficker on my hands. I needed one who could talk—which meant I was going to have to let Will and Marcy be taken.

"How long you fellas setting up shop?" I asked him as we walked. "Might be able to come up with another one, if the price is right."

Nothing looked at me for a moment before speaking. "If you cannot do it by dawn, do not bother."

"Maybe. We'll see how this plays out."

Nothing shrugged and kept on walking. I caught sight of our reflection in a passing window—Biker Barbie and Bigfoot. I tried to keep out of his reach as we walked, but there was only so much sidewalk, and Nothing's arms looked long enough to slap me from the middle of the street.

As we walked, I noticed the smell. The man just smelled *wrong*. I wasn't sure what it was—something . . . musty, vaguely like the scent of stagnant water and rotting fish. It hung in the air around him.

"You aren't really human, are you," I noted as we walked into the parking garage—and away from any potential witnesses.

"Not anymore," he replied.

As he spoke, the collar of the turtleneck . . . stirred. It rippled, as if something had moved beneath it.

"Well, I am," I said. "Completely worthless for whatever you're doing collecting specials. So don't be thinking you can get three for the price of two."

Nothing looked down at me with those unsettling eyes. "You are pathetic."

I put a little extra swagger into my step. "Careful what you say there, big guy. You'll turn me on."

Nothing made a small, quiet sound of disgust and shook his head. It was hard not to smile as I watched him pigeonhole me into "scum, treacherous, decadent."

"It's right up here."

"Before we approach the vehicle," he said, "you should know that if you have associates waiting in ambuscade, I will break their necks—and yours."

I lifted my hands. "Jesus. Show a little trust, will you? We're all capitalists here." I pointed the fob at the SUV and disarmed the alarm with a little electronic chirp. The lights flashed once. I tossed him the keys. "That one. I'll stay back here if you like."

"Acceptable," he said, and strode to the SUV. Watching him bend down to look in was like a scene from *Jurassic Park*. He opened the rear hatch and then lifted his hands to his neck for a moment. He tugged the turtleneck down a little.

The skin of Nothing's neck was deformed with narrow flaps of skin, somehow, and it took me a few seconds to realize what I was looking at.

Gills.

The man had *gills*. And he was breathing through them. They opened and closed in a rhythm not far removed from a dog's sniffing.

"Werewolves," he said. "Valuable."

"They make good pets?" I asked.

He reached in and seized Will, lifting him with one hand. The young man remained limp, his eyes closed.

"Their blood has unique properties. What did you use to subdue them?"

"Roofies. The way my dating life has been going, I keep some on hand."

He made a dissatisfied sound and tugged his collar up again. "The drug might lower their value."

"I hope not," I said. "This has been such a nice conversation. I'd hate for it to end in a gunshot."

Nothing turned his head slightly and gave me a very cold little smile.

I felt threatened enough to produce my gun without even consciously thinking about it. I held it in two hands, pointed at the ground near his feet. We stayed that way, facing off for several seconds. Then he shrugged a shoulder. He produced another brick of bills and threw it to me, along with the truck keys. Then he gathered up Marcy and tossed her over one shoulder, and Will over the other.

He turned to the entrance of the garage and made several sharp, popping clicks as he went, producing with an odd quiver of his chest and throat a sound that was somehow familiar. They must have been a signal. A moment later, a van with rental-agency plates pulled up to the curb and stopped.

A man dressed identically to Nothing rolled open the side door. Nothing put the two werewolves inside, then followed them, somehow compressing his bulk enough to get into the van. The driver pulled back into traffic a second later. The entire pickup had taken less than ten seconds.

I got back onto my motorcycle and rolled out of the garage with my lights off before their van had gotten to the end of the block. Then, settling in to follow them from several car lengths back, I tried to make like a hole in the air.

Nothing and his driver headed for the docks, which was hardly unanticipated. Chicago supports an enormous amount of shipping traffic that travels through the Great Lakes, and offloads cargo to be transferred to railroads or trucking companies for shipment throughout the United States. Such ships remain one of the best means for moving illegal goods without being discovered.

There are plenty of storage buildings down by the docks, and Nothing went to one of the seedier, more run-down warehouses on the waterfront. I noted the location and went on by without stopping. Then I circled around, killed the engine with the bike still in motion, and came coasting back over the cracked old asphalt, the whisper of my tires lost in the susurrus of city sounds and water lapping the lakeshore.

There wasn't much to see. The warehouse had a single set of standard doors, and several large steel doors that would roll up to allow crates and shipping containers to be brought inside. They were all closed. A single guard, a man in a watch cap and a squall coat, wandered aimlessly around outside the building, smoking cigarettes and looking bored.

I got rid of the damn clunky Munster boots and pulled on the black slippers I always wore on the practice mat. I pulled weapons and gear out of the bike's saddlebags, attached the items to the tactical harness under my coat, and slipped closer. I stayed where it was dark, using the shadows to hide my approach. Then I found a particularly deep patch of darkness and waited.

It took a seemingly endless five minutes for the guard to get close enough for me to shoot him with a Taser.

Darts leapt out and plunged into his chest, trailing shining wires, and I pulled the trigger while he jerked and twitched and fell to the ground. I wasn't sure if this guy was human or not, but I wasn't taking chances. I kept the juice on him until I was sure he was down for the count. When I let up, he just lay there on his side, curled up halfway into a fetal position, quivering and twitching while drool rolled out of his mouth.

Actually, he sort of reminded me of my second husband in the morning.

I jerked the darts out of him and shoved the Taser and the trailing wire into my jacket pocket. It would take too much time to reset it for use, and I had a bad feeling that the electronic device wouldn't do me much good inside the warehouse. I could have slapped some heavy restraining ties on him—but I would be happier if anyone who found the downed man had no idea what had happened to him.

So much for the easy part.

My P-90 hung easily from the tac harness, its stock high, its barrel hanging down the line of my body. I took a moment to screw a suppressor onto the end of the gun and lifted it to firing position against my shoulder. The little Belgian assault weapon was illegal for a civilian to own within city limits; the suppressor, too. If I got caught with them, I'd be in trouble. If I got caught *using* them, I'd do time. Both of those consequences were subordinate to the fact that if I didn't go in armed for bear, I might not live to congratulate myself on my sterling citizenship.

Well, there's no such thing as a perfect solution, is there.

I moved quietly back to the entry door, silenced weapon tight against my shoulder. I duckwalked, my steps quick and small and rolling, to keep my upper body level as it moved. I'd put a red dot sight on the P-90, and it floated in my vision as a translucent crosshair of red light. The sight made the weapon, to some degree, point and click. The idea was for the bullets to go wherever the crosshairs were centered. I had it sighted for short work. Even though I'd seen more action than practically any cop in the country—thanks to Dresden—I could count on one hand the number of times I'd used a weapon in earnest against a target more than seven or eight yards away.

Standing next to the entry door, I tested the knob. It turned freely. So, the folks inside had been relying on their guard to keep intruders out.

I thought of the first hissing voice I'd spoken to on the phone and shivered. They wouldn't be relying on purely physical defenses. But I knew something about those, too. Harry's defenses had been deadly dangerous—but to create them, apparently you had to use the energy of a threshold, which only grew up around an actual home. This old warehouse was a place of business and didn't have a threshold. So, if a spell had been put up to guard the door, it would have to be fairly weak.

Of course, *weak* was a relative term in Dresden's vocabulary. It might hit me only hard enough to break bones, instead of disintegrating me completely—if there was a spell there at all.

I hated this magic crap.

Screw it. I couldn't just stand here all night.

I turned the doorknob slowly, keeping my body as far to one side as possible. Then I pushed in gently, and the door swung open by an inch or three. When nothing exploded or burst into wails of alarm, I eased up next to it and peeked into the building.

It was like looking into another world.

Green and blue light crawled and slithered up the walls and over the warehouse's interior, eerie and subtly unsettling, each color moving in waves of differing widths and speeds. The strange scent of water and fish was strong inside. There were *things* on the wall—*growths* was all I could call them. Ugly patches of some kind of lumpy, rough substance I didn't recognize were clumped all around the walls and ceiling of the warehouse in roughly circular patches about six feet across.

Cages were scattered all around the floor—a bunch of five-foot cubes made of heavy steel grid. People were locked up in several of them, the doors held shut by heavy chains. Most of them just sat, staring at nothing, or lay upon their sides doing the same thing, completely motionless. That wasn't normal. Even someone who was drugged but conscious would show a little more animation than that. This meant magic was involved, some kind of invasive mental stuff, and a little voice in my head started screaming.

I've been subjected to that kind of invasion, more than once.

It's bad.

My legs felt weak. My hands shook. The rippling colors of light on the walls became something sinister, disorienting, the beginnings of another attack on my mind. Jesus Christ, I wanted to turn around and scurry away, as swiftly and as meekly as possible. In fact, I tried to. My legs quivered as if preparing to move, but the motion drew my gaze across another row of cages, and I saw Georgia.

She was naked, kneeling, her hands wrapped gently around her swelling stomach, cradling her unborn child. Her head was bowed in a posture of meekness, and her sleek shoulders and neck were relaxed.

But I saw her eyes, open and staring at the bottom of the cage, and I saw the defiance flickering in them.

Whatever held the others held Georgia as well—but she evidently had not been subdued as readily as they had. She was still fighting them.

Something deep inside me, something hard and fierce and furious, locked my legs into place. I stared at Georgia, and I knew I couldn't run. I remembered that Will and Marcy were in there, waiting for me to announce that the moment was right to change form and fight. I remembered that nearly all of those people in the cages were young, even younger than the werewolves—including the youngest of all, in Georgia's cage.

I remembered blood splattered on the weathered cabin of a boat—and that there was no one but me coming to help those kids.

The fear changed form on me. It disguised itself as reason. *Don't go in*, it told me. *Know your limits. Send for help.*

But the only serious help I could get would be SI—and they would be putting their own careers, as well as their lives, on the line if they came to my aid. I could send for the regular police, drop in an anonymous call, but in this part of town it might take half an hour for them to show up. Even when they did arrive, they'd be lambs to the slaughter. Most of the force had no idea what really went on in the city's darkest shadows.

You could go get the Sword, said my fear. *You know where it is. You know how strong it makes you.*

Not many people could honestly say they'd wielded a magic sword against the forces of darkness, but I'm one of them. *Fidelacchius*, the Sword of Faith, lay waiting for the hand of someone worthy to wield it against the powers of darkness. In the final battle with the Red Court, that hand had been mine. In the darkest moment of that fight, when all seemed lost, it had been my hand upon *Fidelacchius* that had tipped the balance, enabling Dresden to prevail. And I had felt a Power greater than I supporting me, guiding my movements, and, for a single, swift moment, entering into me and making use of my lips and tongue to pronounce sentence upon the murderous creatures surrounding us.

I could go for the Sword. Odds were it would be of some help.

But I knew that if I did, I would have taken the easy path. I would have turned away from a source of terror for the most excellent, rational of reasons. And the next time I faced the same kind of fear, it would be a little easier to turn away, a little easier to find good reasons not to act.

The Sword was a source of incredible power—but it was nothing but cool, motionless steel without the hand that could grip it, the muscles that would move it, the eyes and the mind that would guide it. Without them, the Sword was nothing.

I stopped and stared down at my shaking hand. Without my hand, my mind, my will, the Sword was nothing. And if that was true, then it must also be true that my hand was what mattered. That it had been my hand, my will that had made the difference.

And my hand was right here. In fact, I had two of them.

My breathing steadied and slowed. Sword or no Sword, I had sworn to serve and protect the people of this city. And if I turned away from that oath now, if I gave in to my fear, even for the most seductively logical of reasons, then I had no right to take up the Sword of Faith in any case.

My hands stopped shaking and my breathing slowed and steadied, bringing the terror under control. I whispered a quick, almost entirely mental prayer to St. Jude, the patron of lost causes and policemen. It sounded something like, "OhGodohGodohGod. *Help*."

I nudged the door open a few more inches, then slid into the warehouse, moving with as much speed and silence as I possessed, my gun at the level and ready.

I MOVED DOWN the length of the warehouse, mostly hidden behind a shelving unit more than twenty feet high. It was stacked with pallets, loading gear, storage bins, and the occasional barrel or box of unknown provenance. The shifting, constantly wavering light made an excellent cover for motion, and I timed my steps to move in rhythm with the dancing illumination.

The hairs on the back of my neck stood up, and it felt like every inch of my skin was covered in gooseflesh. I'd been in the presence of dangerous magic often enough to know the feeling of dark power in motion. It had been like this at Chichen Itza, and in the waters off the island of Demonreach, and in the Raith Deeps, and at Arctis Tor, and in the nest of Black Court vampires, and at . . .

You get the point. This wasn't my first rodeo.

The most important thing would be to take out Nothing's presumptive boss, and fast—preferably before anyone knew I was here at all. The warehouse reeked of magic, and if a mortal goes into a fair fight against a wizard, the mortal loses. Period. They have power that is literally almost unimaginable, and if the bad guy got a chance to defend himself, the only uncertainty remaining would be how much creativity he put into killing me.

At the end of the shelving unit, there was a rolling ladder, one made to run all the way up and down the shelves and provide easy access. The warehouse was darker up near the ceiling than at floor level. I didn't even slow down. I went up the ladder to the top of the shelving unit and froze in place, getting a good, clear look at the enemy for the first time.

There were half a dozen of them including Nothing, and they all shopped at the same store. Their outfits were conspicuous due to their uniformity, though some instinct made me think that they had been intended as disguises—that individuality, as a concept, wasn't of any particular concern to Nothing and his crew. Nothing was, by far, the largest of the men, though none of them looked like featherweights.

They were loading cages into a railroad cargo container, a fairly common sight on large ships, some of which could carry hundreds of the metal boxes. The cages had been sized to stack exactly into the railroad car, two across and three high, with no consideration whatsoever for the human cargo. There were no blankets, no pads—nothing but metal cages and vulnerable skin.

I spotted Andi's cage, not far from Georgia's. The redheaded girl had evidently lacked some critical capacity to resist whatever had been done to her. She lay on her back, staring blankly up at the roof of her cage. The werewolf girl was a bombshell. Even lying in completely passive relaxation, her curves beckoned the eye—but the hollow despair of her expression was haunting.

Nothing was standing over Will and Marcy, who lay limp and motionless on the floor at his feet. A couple of turtlenecks were hauling an empty cage toward them. "How long will it take?" he was asking a third man.

"Without knowing the exact drug, several hours," the man replied. His voice was plainly human, and sounded nothing like whoever it was I'd spoken to on the phone. "Perhaps more."

Nothing frowned. "Can you make a determination of their viability by dawn?"

"If I am able to isolate the substance that incapacitated them before then," he said. "I have no means of determining how many attempts will be required. It will take as long as it takes."

"He will not be pleased," Nothing said.

The man bowed his head. "My life for the master. I will do all in my power to serve him. Should he be disappointed in me, it is meet for him to take my life."

Nothing nodded. "Be about it."

The man turned and walked quickly away, holding two small vials of rich red blood in his hand—samples from Will and Marcy, I assumed.

By then, the empty cage had arrived. Nothing picked up Marcy and lifted her toward the waiting cage. I bit down on a curse. If I let him imprison her, a full third of my team would be neutralized, as helpless as the prisoners who had already been taken. But if I started the music early, I risked throwing away my sucker punch. Nothing's master might show up at any time.

On the other hand, Nothing seemed to be large and in charge. Perhaps the hissing person I'd spoken to on the phone had left matters in Nothing's shovellike hands. Or perhaps I'd read the situation incorrectly. What if one of the other turtlenecks had been the first speaker, and Nothing was really the boss?

I made up my mind and settled the P-90's crosshair onto Nothing's head, a little below the tip of his nose. The weapon was set for automatic fire, and while I could control the weapon fairly well, especially when it was loaded with subsonic rounds, the recoil would tend to carry the weapon's muzzle higher after the first shot.

Against anything human, more than one round to the head would be overkill: When the merely mortal goes up against the supernatural, there's no such *thing* as overkill.

I snuggled the gun in close and tight, took a deep breath in, let it halfway out, held it, and began to slowly squeeze the weapon's trigger.

The instant before the trigger would have broken, there was a shimmering in the air and a man stepped out of it, appearing as if from nowhere.

I backed off the tension on my finger, feeling my heart surge with unspent adrenaline.

The man was of medium height, with sallow skin and greasy, straight black hair that hung past his shoulders. His lips were very thick and his mouth very wide, almost to the point of deformity. His large eyes were dark and watery and bulging, his nose sunken, as small as any I had ever seen. He was soaking wet and naked, his limbs scrawny and long, his hands very, very wide. Except for the hair, I couldn't help but compare him to a frog—a sullen, vicious frog.

The man let out a sound somewhat like a muffled belch, then vomited water onto the floor. Flaps of skin at his neck flared in and out, spewing smaller sprays of water several times, until he drew in a breath through his mouth, evidently filling his lungs with air.

All of the turtlenecks turned to face the creature and fell to their knees, including Nothing, who calmly set Marcy aside and went into a full kowtow, his palms flat on the floor, his forehead pressed down onto his knuckles.

"Sssssso," he hissed, "did the insssolent creature deliver our prizesss?"

I recognized the voice from the telephone.

"Yes, my lord," rumbled Nothing. "As promised and in plenty of time to move."

"Did you sssstrike the bitch down?"

Nothing rocked back and then bowed again, somehow giving the impression that he was doing it more deeply. "She was clever enough to build safeguards into the meeting. I could not do so without attracting attention."

Frogface hissed. "I will sssettle with the mortal another time," he said. "Sssuch insssolence cannot be countenanced."

"No, my lord."

"Bring the new acquisitionsss. I will bind them."

"They have been given drugs, my lord. The binding could damage them."

Without looking particularly excited about it, Frogface kicked Nothing in the armpit. The blow was a more powerful one than Frogface's frame would suggest he was capable of giving. It flung Nothing from his hands and knees and onto his side by main force.

"Bring them."

"I obey," wheezed Nothing. He rose unsteadily and went to pick up Will. He dropped the young werewolf onto the floor beside Marcy.

"Sssuch disgussssting thingsss, mortalsss," Frogface murmured. His eyes lifted to Georgia in her cage. "She hasss not yet capitulated."

"No, my lord," Nothing muttered.

"Interesssting," Frogface said, and a leer spread over his broad mouth. "When we arrive, transport her to my chambers. We will sssee what is left of her ssstrength when the ssspawn is taken from her womb."

Jesus, men can be assholes. Even when they're barely human. Frog-face was officially elected.

Georgia shuddered. She lifted her head, very slowly, as if it had been held down with vast weights—and the glare she turned on Frog-face was nothing less than murderous.

Frogface chuckled at the expression and turned to face Will and Marcy. He dipped his fingers into a pouch that hung around his neck, almost invisible against his leathery skin, and withdrew what looked like a small seashell from it. He leered at the motionless Marcy and said, "Firssst, the female."

He closed his eyes and made a low sound in his throat, then began chanting words that bubbled and gobbled out from between his rubbery lips.

Now I've got you, I thought to myself, and sighted the gun on Frog-face's rubbery lips. I didn't have Dresden's knowledge of magic, but I knew any wizard was vulnerable when they began working forces, the way Frogface was doing. The concentration needed was intense. If I'd understood Dresden correctly, it would mean that Frogface would have to be focusing his entire attention on his spell—leaving nothing remaining for defending his sallow hide.

The air began to shimmer around Frogface's hands, and fine, slithering tendrils emerged from the brightly colored shell and began to drift down toward Marcy, a cloud of tendrils as fine as a cobweb.

Certain now of my target, I breathed, held it, and squeezed the trigger.

Say what you like about the Belgians. They can make some fine weaponry.

The silenced P-90 barely whispered when the burst of automatic fire erupted from the end of the suppressor. There was no flash, no thunder—just a soft, wheezing sound and the *click* of the gun's action cycling. Thanks to the subsonic ammunition, the discharge itself actually made less noise than the rounds striking Frogface's skull.

There were several wet, loud cracking sounds, and every one of the rounds I'd fired struck home. One round would have been messy enough. When half a dozen of them hit, Frogface's head quite literally exploded, shattered to pulp and shards of bone by the bullets' impact, and two-thirds of his skull, from the upper lip on up, simply vanished into green-blooded spray.

There was a flash of angry red light from the seashell. Frogface let out a high-pitched, tinny scream, and the near-headless body began to topple, thrashing wildly.

The turtlenecks all came to their feet, looking around in wide-eyed confusion. My weapon had given them absolutely no clue as to where the attack had come from. I sighted in on Nothing, but from my angle, any rounds that went through him would threaten Will and a caged prisoner, beyond him.

I shifted targets, settling the red crosshairs on another turtleneck standing just past Will. I squeezed off another whispering burst of a half-dozen or so rounds, and the creature's neck exploded into a cloud of scarlet gore the consistency of mucus. It went limp, settling to the floor like a deflating balloon.

Nothing's pale-eyed gaze snapped over toward me, and I saw his gaze track the fall of brass bullet casings from where they bounced off the floor back up to my position on the shelves.

He let out an enraged sound, pulled a short tube from his pocket, and pointed it at me. I moved, sliding back down the ladder to the floor, hardly moving more slowly than if I'd fallen. There was a high-pitched whistle, and something that looked like a small, spiny sea urchin flew past me, just over my head, close enough for the wind of its passage to stir dark-dyed hairs. It slammed into the wall behind me and remained there, quivering, as its spines punched through the metal siding and stuck. Drops of yellow-green liquid fell from the tips of some of the spines, and began smoking and eating small holes in the concrete floor.

Yikes.

Throaty popping, clicking sounds from several sources filled the air, an exchange of what could only be language. I ran for the far end of the shelving unit as the dark forms of the turtlenecks started moving toward me. I caught glimpses of them between the boxes and containers stacked on the lowest shelf, running with the lithe, floating agility of professional athletes.

I ran past a clump of the growth on the wall, a little lower than most, and as I approached, it suddenly fluoresced with bioluminescent color. On sheer instinct, I threw myself flat to the concrete floor and slid past on my belly as the lumpy growths began hissing, and jets of mist, the same color as the fluid covering the urchin spines, began to spray forth at random. The smell was hideous, and I scrambled back to my feet and kept running down the aisle, staying as far from the wall as I could.

If I'd been half a step slower, I would have died. There was a great crash, and Nothing smashed through the lowest level of the shelving unit, thrusting aside a steel drum and a wooden crate the size of a coffin as if they'd been made of Styrofoam. His fingers missed grabbing onto me by inches.

A second turtleneck beat me to the end of the shelf. I opened up with the P-90, praying that a ricochet wouldn't kill one of the prisoners, but my target moved with the speed of a striking serpent, bounding forward to plant a foot against the steel wall of the warehouse, six feet off the ground. Using only a single leg, he kicked off into a backflip that carried him back past the end of the shelf and out of my line of fire.

The damn thing hadn't been moving fast enough to dodge bullets—but he'd been moving fast enough to dodge *me*, and I was the one doing the aiming. A round might have clipped one of his legs, but that was all, and Nothing was pounding up behind me, gaining despite his mass. I felt like a squirrel being pursued by a German shepherd; if he caught me, it would end about the same way.

So I played squirrel, and instead of running in the open, I turned ninety degrees to my right and dove between two stacks of pallets on the lowest shelf. I took a little skin off an arm in hurling myself between them and emerged onto the open warehouse floor. I heard Nothing's shoes squealing on the floor as he applied the brakes behind me.

A turtleneck was coming straight at me, on a direct line from the cages not yet loaded into the railroad car. I brought the P-90 up and dropped to one knee. The turtleneck rushed forward, his pale blue eyes wide and staring. He held an inward-curving knife in one hand and carried it low and close to his leg. He knew how to use it.

I put the scarlet crosshairs on his sternum and squeezed the trigger. The instant before the shots would have sputtered out of the gun, the turtleneck leapt straight up, flipping once in the air as he went over me.

After seeing the incredible quickness of the other not-quite-humans, I'd been waiting for the dodge. As soon as his feet left the floor, I spun to my left, opening fire the instant the end of the barrel was clear of the prisoners. Bullets hissed through the air like a great scythe—and in the edge of my vision, I saw the turtleneck I'd wounded seconds before. He'd come charging toward me while I'd aimed at his buddy, and the sudden turn took him by surprise. There was no aiming involved—it was a brute-force approach. I emptied the rest of the clip at him and prayed I could leave him no safe space in which to dodge.

St. Jude gets a lot of business, but sometimes he comes through. The hissing, puffing little gun spat out a line of deadly projectiles and intersected the turtleneck's path, tearing a row of five or six holes across his upper body. The turtleneck screamed and went down.

But the one who'd leapt over me dropped back down, adjusting swiftly to the situation, and then whipped the hooked knife across my belly.

Almost anyone else in town would have been killed. The knife struck with enormous power, and its blade was sharp. Standard Kevlar-style body armor wouldn't have done a damn thing to stop it. I'd stopped wearing the standard stuff, thanks to one too many exciting outings with Dresden. I wore a double-thickness vest now—and sandwiched between the layers of antiballistic fabric was a corselet of tightly linked titanium rings, manufactured for me by one of Dresden's friends, the wife of a retired Fist of God.

The knife sliced right through the Kevlar. It split a ring or three, but then the tip caught in the titanium. Instead of spilling my intestines upon the ground, the superhumanly powerful blow wound up dragging me along and flung me across the concrete floor. I went down into a roll and spread out the force of the fall, coming back up to my feet, already having released the empty magazine from the P-90. I was reaching for the fresh one when another turtleneck abruptly closed in on me from behind and slipped a slim, iron-hard arm around my neck.

I barely got a hand inside the loop of his arm before he could lock the choke on me, and I twisted like an eel to get out. His strength was far superior to mine, but then, whose wasn't? Even in grappling, strength isn't absolutely everything. The turtleneck might have been faster than I, but I had the advantage of experience. My timing was good enough to let me sense the opening, the lack of pressure in the weakest part of his hold, and I managed to writhe out of his grip—only to have a forearm smash down across my shoulders, driving me to the floor.

As I went down, I saw that the turtleneck with the knife was only a few steps away. I'd never escape a pair of them.

I didn't have time to get another magazine into the P-90, so I rolled with it and smashed the heavy polymer stock of the weapon into the nearest turtleneck's kneecap.

He screamed and seized me by the neck of the leather jacket, shaking me like a doll.

At which point Will and Marcy gave Nothing's companions an object lesson as to why werewolves instill terror in mortal hearts and minds.

There was a flash of dark fur, a snarl, a horrible, tearing sound, and the turtleneck screamed. He started listing to one side, and I realized that one of the werewolves had just severed the hamstring of the turtleneck's unwounded leg. We both went down. I twisted out of the leather jacket, though I had to drop the P-90 and let it hang from my harness to do it, and rolled free of the turtleneck. An instant later, a second, slightly lighter brown form, teeth gleaming, darted past the fallen turtleneck and ripped out what would have been the jugular vein on a human being.

Apparently, it was close enough for government work. The turtleneck thrashed in dying agony as mucuslike red blood bubbled from the gaping wound.

And suddenly there were two beasts from the nightmares of mankind standing on either side of me, facing the enemy. They were wolves, one large and dark, the other slightly smaller and lighter, but both heavily laden with muscle and thick fur, and their golden eyes burned with awareness—and fury.

Faced with a pair of murderous werewolves, the knife-wielding turtleneck slid to a sudden, uncertain halt.

In the sudden silence that followed, the sound of me slapping a fresh magazine into the P-90 and racking the first round into the chamber was a sharp trio of clicks. *Pop. Click-clack.*

See, Nothing? I thought. *I can make ominous noises, too.*

I brought the weapon back up and snarled, "Lose the knife."

The turtleneck hesitated for half a second, eyes darting left and right, then released it. The steel chimed as the knife hit the floor.

I kept the weapon on him, the trigger half pulled. Yeah, it wasn't the safe, smart way to operate, but frankly I wouldn't lose any sleep if I accidentally shot this guy. He was just too damn fast to give up any advantage at all.

"There were five of them," I said to the wolves. "How many did you handle, including the one that was on me?"

The more lightly colored wolf let out two precise, low barks.

"I got two," I said. "That leaves this one and the big guy."

A complex sequence of clicks and pops drifted through the air, and the lights went out, plunging the warehouse into perfect darkness.

Instinctively, my finger tightened on the trigger, and I sent a burst of rounds out almost before the lights were gone. But I was literally shooting blind against a foe who had supernatural reflexes and had also known, thanks to those damn clicks, what was about to happen. I heard the rounds hammer through the far wall.

The wolves snarled and started forward—the warehouse wasn't a light-tight darkroom, and a wolf's eyes actually see better in near darkness than in full light. The gloom was no obstacle to them. But I seized handfuls of fur and hissed, "Wait."

Their momentum dragged me several inches forward before they slowed down, but I said, "The growths on the wall spray out acid, at least seven or eight feet. Don't get suckered in close to one. The big guy has something like a gun. Go."

The wolves bounded out from beneath my hands, leaving me alone in the darkness.

Clicks and pops continued to bounce around the empty space of the warehouse, impossible for me to localize. They were an ongoing thing, every couple of seconds, and I couldn't shake the idea that they were coming closer and closer to me.

Even as I crouched there, defenseless and hating it, my hands were scrabbling at the pouch on my tac vest. If there was too much magic running amok, flashlights might not be reliable. Magic screws up technology when there's too much of both of them around, and you don't take chances with something as important as being effectively struck blind. I'd prepared the tac vest with this kind of situation in mind.

I opened the pouch and pulled out a flare, popping the pull cord, which struck it to life as I did. Red light glared into the darkness, and I lifted the flare over my head and out of my own vision in my left hand. I held the P-90 in my right. The small weapon could be fired in one hand, no problem, and while it wouldn't be as accurate, I could still send bursts downrange almost as well as I could two-handed.

The pops and clicks continued, everywhere and nowhere. I had no idea where Will and Marcy were, and Nothing and the other turtle-neck had an awful lot of shadow to hide in. I realized I was essentially sitting in the middle of an open floor under a spotlight, a perfect target for Nothing and his weird little urchin-gun, and I retreated toward the caged prisoners.

"Georgia," I said, crouching down beside her. I studied the door of the cage, and found that the thing wasn't even locked. It had a ring for a padlock on it, but the door's mechanism was simply cycled closed. I spun it open and pulled open the cage door. "Georgia. Can you move?"

She lifted her head and stared at me grimly. Then she turned her body and leaned forward, moving as though underwater, and slowly began to crawl out of the cage. I hurried to Andi's cage and opened that door as well—but the girl did not so much as blink or stir a finger when I urged her to get out. So much for reinforcements. I felt useless. I couldn't go out there into the dark to join Will and Marcy in the hunt. I'd be worse than useless, stumbling around out there. They'd be forced to take their attention from their attack in order to protect me.

"Murphy," Georgia said. "M-Murphy."

I hurried to her side. "I'm here. Are you hurt?"

She shook her head. "N-n-no . . . L-listen." She lifted her head to meet my eyes, her neck wobbling like a paraplegic's. *"Listen."*

Clicks. Pops. Once, a hackle-raising snarl. The whishing sound of an urchin flying through the air, and the sharp *pong* of its hitting a metal exterior wall.

"The guards," Georgia said. "Sonar."

I stared at her for a second, and then clued in to what she was talking about. The clicks and pops had sounded familiar because I *had* heard them before, or something very close to them—from dolphins, at the Shedd Aquarium. Dolphins sent out sharp pulses of sound and used them to navigate, and to find prey in the dark.

I dropped the flare on the ground well away from Georgia and began unscrewing the suppressor on the P-90. "Will! Marcy!" I shouted, unable to keep the snarl out of my voice. "They're about to go blind!"

Then I pointed the weapon up and off at an angle that I thought would send the rounds into the nearby lake, flicked the selector to single fire, and began methodically triggering rounds. The second clip had been loaded with standard, rather than subsonic, ammo, and without the suppressor to dampen the explosion of the propellant, the supersonic rounds roared out, painfully loud. The flash at the muzzle lit the entire warehouse in strobes of white light. I didn't fire them in rhythm or any particular pattern. I had no idea how actual sonar worked in biological organisms, but I'd taken several nephews as a pack to see the *Daredevil* movie, and rhythmic sounds seemed to create a more ordered picture than random bursts of noise.

As I worked my way through the fifty-round magazine, I could all but hear Dresden's mockery, his voice edged with adrenaline, the words coming through a manic grin, as I'd heard several times before. *Murph, when you're reaching out to movie concepts that involved millions of dollars in special effects for your tactical battle plan, I think you can pretty safely take that as an indicator that you are badly out of your depth.*

But as the last round left the gun, I heard one of the turtlenecks screaming in pain—a horrible cry that ended abruptly. And then the warehouse fell silent again—only to be invaded by another steady series of rhythmic clicks.

And this time they were definitely getting closer.

I unclipped the P-90 and set it aside. I had only the two clips for the weapon. But my Sig came into my hand with the smooth familiarity of long practice, and I moved, away from Georgia and the other prisoners, around behind the empty cages that had been meant for Will and Marcy. I nearly screamed when I kicked a dead body and found the other turtleneck lying in a pool of viscous blood—apparently the other bad guy Will and Marcy had seen to.

Some instinct warned me I was in danger, and I dropped flat. Another sea urchin projectile streaked over me; a second struck a bar in the empty cage and slammed into its floor, acid chewing at the steel. Then there was a third whispering projectile that rushed away from me.

A wolf began to scream in agony—horrible, horrible high-pitched screams.

Nothing had just pulled the same trick I had—shooting at me and enticing one of his other enemies into the open as he did, then spinning to fire at an unexpected moment. Will or Marcy had just paid a horrible price for their aggression.

I came to my knees with a cry of fury and flung my flare. It went high into the air, spinning, spreading red light wide and thin around the inside of the warehouse. I saw a massive black form ahead of me, turning, the tube of his projectile weapon swinging back toward me.

The Sig was faster.

I had already slid into a Weaver stance, and I slammed out a trio of shots, swift, steady, and practiced, all aimed at the upper torso, to avoid any chance of hitting one of the wolves. I know at least one of the shots scored a hit on Nothing. The flare landed, still blazing. I saw the black outline of his silhouette twist in agony, then heard a quavering grunt escape him. He moved away from the flare and out of my vision. An instant later, I saw a wolf leap across the scarlet pool of light, and I started squeezing out more rounds from the Sig. I staggered them just as I had the shots from the P-90, hoping to blind Nothing as the wolf attacked.

The magazine emptied in a few seconds, though I hadn't meant to fire that many shots. The excitement of the fight was making it hard to stay level. I ejected the empty mag, slapped in a fresh one, and pulled a second flare from my tac vest, bringing it to hissing life as I started forward, my gun extended.

I could hear Nothing fighting with a wolf. His voice emanated from his huge chest, a basso growl of rage every bit as angry and animalistic as the snarls of the wolf fighting him. I used the sound as my guide and rushed forward. The other wolf kept on screaming in agony, its shrieks slowly changing and becoming more and more eerily human.

The scarlet light of the flare fell across Nothing and the wolf-version of Will just as Nothing flung the wolf to the concrete floor with bone-jarring force. Will let out a shriek of pain, and bones popped and crackled—but he retained enough awareness to roll out of the way as Nothing sent one huge foot stomping down at his skull.

I started putting rounds into Nothing's chest from maybe fifteen feet away.

I was shooting one-handed and was hyped up on adrenaline. It wasn't an ideal state for marksmanship. But I wasn't trying for points on a target—this was instinct shooting, the kind of accuracy that comes only with endless hours of practice, with thousands and thousands of rounds sent downrange. It takes a lot of work to make that happen.

I'd worked.

I was using a 9mm weapon. The rounds were on the small side for real combat—and Nothing was on the other end of the combat universe from small. He turned toward me, and I saw he no longer had the projectile tube—or two of the fingers on the hand that had been holding it. One of the wolves had tried for his throat and evidently had torn open the fine cloth of the sweater's neck, because I could see his gills flaring as he charged me.

Shots struck home in his torso. I was aiming for the heart, which few people realize is fairly low in the chest, a couple of inches below the left nipple. I hit him with every shot, six, seven, eight. . . .

It takes an attacker about two seconds to close a gap of thirty feet and get within range for a strike with a knife or fist. Nothing was about five feet closer than that. Eight shots, all of them hits, was damn solid combat shooting.

It just wasn't enough.

Nothing plowed into me like a runaway truck, sending me sprawling. We both hit the concrete. Pushing against him, I barely managed to keep his weight from coming down on my chest so that it came down somewhere around my hips instead. He seized my right hand and squeezed.

Pain. Tendons tearing. Bones cracking. He shook his arm once, and my Sig went tumbling away.

I didn't hesitate. I just doubled up, leaning toward him, and rammed the blazing end of the flare into the open flap of his gills.

He screamed, louder than a human being could have, and both

hands flew to his throat to clutch at the flare. I got a leg free and kicked him in the chin, hard, driving down with all the power of my leg behind a crushing heel. I heard something crack, and he screamed, flinching. I freed my other leg and scrambled away from him, clutching awkwardly at my right ankle with my left hand.

Nothing tore the flare out, his pale eyes nearly luminous with rage, and came after me, roaring.

I had never been more frightened in my life. I couldn't get to the damn holdout gun before he reached me, so I did the only thing I could. I ran, blind, into the dark, and he came after me like a rabid locomotive.

I knew I didn't have much room left. I knew that I would hit a wall in a few seconds, and that then he'd have me. I could only pray that the shots I'd put in him were more serious than his reaction to them indicated—that he was already bleeding massively, and that the extra few seconds would be enough time to let him die.

But somewhere inside, I knew better.

I was playing out of my league, and I had known that from the beginning.

Beautiful light suddenly fluoresced in front of me—the acid growths on the walls. I slammed to a stop in front of the weird clumps of material and saw little tendrils and orifices on the growths tracking and orienting on me.

I turned to face Nothing.

He came in, insanely huge, insanely strong, and roaring in a terrible fury.

But terrible fury alone doesn't win fights. In fact, it can be a deadly weakness. In the second it took him to reach me, I touched the center of calm in myself, earned with endless hours of practice and discipline. I judged the distance and the timing. It felt as if I had forever to work out what I would need to do.

And then I did to Nothing exactly what I'd done to Ray.

As he closed, I ducked under his huge hands, spinning to sweep my right leg across his right foot, just as it was about to hit the floor. Preternaturally strong though he may have been, gravity pulled him just as hard as it had Ray, and his joints operated in exactly the same fashion. His right foot was driven to tangle with his left, and he went smashing forward into the wall.

Into the growth.

Into the spurting cloud of acidic spray that erupted from it, aiming at me.

I rolled away to one side, frantically, but I needn't have worried. Nothing's vast bulk shielded me from the acid spray. I turned over and backed away awkwardly on my butt and my left hand, staring at Nothing in sheer fascination.

He didn't scream. I think he was trying. The acid must have torn his throat apart, first thing. He sort of recoiled, staggering, and fell to his knees. I could see his profile dimly in the distant light of the flare and the glow of the acid fungus. It . . . just dissolved; seeing it was like watching time-lapse photography of a statue being worn away by wind and rain. Fluids pooled around his knees. He took several agonized breaths—and then there were sucking sounds, as the acid ate into his chest wall. And then there were no sounds at all.

He tried to get up, twice. Then he settled down onto his side as if going to sleep.

The acid kept chewing at him, even after he was dead.

The stench hit me, and I retched horribly.

I backed farther away and sat for a second with my knees up against my chest, my good arm wrapped around them, and sobbed. I hurt so much.

I hurt so much.

And my arm throbbed dully.

"Dammit, Dresden," I said into the silence in a choked voice. "Dammit. Here I am doing your job. Dammit, dammit, dammit."

I got to my feet a moment later. I recovered the second flare. I found my gun. I went to do what I could for Will and Marcy, who would both live.

After that, I went around the warehouse and methodically put another half-dozen rounds into the head of each and every fallen turtle-neck. And I used a can of paint thinner I found in a corner to set their master on fire, just to be sure.

There's no such thing as overkill.

I STOOD IN the open loading door with Will, facing into a wind that blew from the east, over the lake, cool and sweet. There was nothing between us and the water but forty feet of paved loading area. It was quiet. There had been no reaction to the events in the building.

Behind us, lying in quiet rows on the concrete floors, were the prisoners, each of them freed from their respective cages. Even though his left shoulder had been badly dislocated, Will had done most of the heavy lifting, dragging the cages out of the railroad car so I could open them and, with Marcy's and Georgia's help, drag the prisoners out.

Marcy came up to stand beside us, wearing her sundress once more. Her right shoulder looked hideous. The urchin projectile had struck her, and two tines had sunk in deeply. Acid had gone into the muscle and dribbled down from the other tines to slither over her skin, burning as it went. The tines had been barbed, but the acid had liquefied the skin immediately around the barbs, and I had been forced to pry the projectile out with a knife. Marcy had stopped the bleeding, the same way Will had, but her arm was somewhat misshapen, and the scar tissue was truly impressive in its hideousness.

That didn't seem to overly worry the young woman, whom I would never again be able to compare to a mouse in any fashion. But she looked exhausted.

"She's sleeping," Marcy reported quietly to Will.

"Good," Will said. His voice sounded flat, detached. He was hurting a lot. He looked at me, eyes dull, and said, "Think this will work?"

"Sunrise," I said quietly, nodding, and glanced back at the rows of motionless prisoners. "It has a kind of energy, a force of positive re-newal in it. It should wipe away the spells holding them."

"How do you know?" Will asked.

"Dresden," I said.

Marcy tilted her head suddenly and said, "Someone's coming."

I stood by the door, ready to pull it down, as a car, a silver Beemer, came around the corner of the warehouse into the paved loading lot. It stopped maybe thirty feet away, and Ms. Gard got out of it. She looked at me for a moment, then came around to the front of the car and stood there, waiting. The eastern wind blew her long blond hair toward us, like a gently rolling banner.

"Wait here," I said quietly.

"You sure?" Will asked.

"Yeah."

He nodded. "Okay."

I stepped out, went down a short set of concrete stairs to the level of the lot, and walked over to face Gard.

She looked at me expressionlessly for a moment, and then at the prisoners. She shook her head slowly and said, "You did it."

I didn't say anything.

"That's fomor magic," she said quietly. "One of their lesser sorcerers and his retainers."

"Why?" I asked her. "Why are they doing this?"

Gard shook her head and shrugged. "I don't know. But there are teams like it operating all over the world right now."

"Not in Chicago," I said quietly.

"Not in Chicago," she agreed. And her mouth stretched into a slow, genuine grin. She bowed to me from the waist, a gesture of antiquated, stately grace, and said, "There are few mortals with courage enough to face the fomor and their minions. Fewer still with skill enough to face them and win." Her eyes grew serious, and she lost the smile. "Hail, Warrior."

Dresden would have known how to respond to that kind of anachronistic gibberish. I nodded back to her and said, "Thank you."

"My employer owes you a debt, it seems."

"Didn't do it for him."

"But your actions are significant regardless," she said. "This is the second time the fomor have attempted to move on Chicago—and failed." She was quiet for a moment and then said, "If you told him you wanted your job back, he could make it happen. Without further obligation."

I stood very still for a long, silent minute.

Then I sighed, very tired, and said, "Even if I was sure he wouldn't try to use it as leverage down the line . . . If Marcone got it for me, I wouldn't want it. I'll make my own way."

Gard nodded, her eyes steady, and she looked back at the warehouse again. "There's another position you might consider. Monoc Securities is always hiring. My boss is always pleased to find those with the proper"—she pursed her lips—"frame of mind. Considering your experience and skill set, I think you could do very well as one of our security consultants."

"And work for guys like Marcone?" I asked.

"You should bear in mind that this is the second such incursion of the fomor," Gard said in a level voice. "And there have been a half-dozen others nosing at the city in the last eight months alone. All of them have been turned away, courtesy of Marcone."

"He's swell," I said.

"He keeps his word," Gard replied, "which puts him a step above most of your own superiors, in my opinion. Like him or not, he has defended this city. It's no minor thing."

"Every predator defends its territory," I said. "Pass."

Her eyes glittered with amusement, and she shook her head. "Vadderung would definitely find you interesting. You've even got the hair for it. Don't be surprised if you get a call sometime."

"It's a free country," I said. "Is there anything else?"

Gard turned to look at the rapidly lightening eastern horizon, and looked from there to the prisoners. "You seem to have things fairly well contained."

I nodded.

"Don't worry too much about the scene," Gard said. "Hardly any-one ever noses around places like this."

But that wasn't what she meant. Gard was telling me that the evidence—the bodies, the rounds, the weapons, all of it—was going to disappear. Marcone's people were very, very good at making evidence vanish. In this particular case, I wasn't sure I minded. It would protect Will and Marcy, both of whom had left blood there, and it would also cover me.

And Gard hadn't made me ask for it.

She held up her hand, palm up—another one of those gestures, their meanings forgotten by everyone except for long-term wackjobs like Dresden. I returned it. She nodded in approval, got into her car, and left.

Will came up to stand at my side, watching her go. Then both of us turned to watch the sun beginning to rise over the lake.

"He's really gone," Will said quietly. "Dresden, I mean."

I frowned and stared at the waters that had, by every rational indication, swallowed Dresden's lifeblood. I didn't answer him.

"Was she telling the truth, you think? That Marcone's the one standing in the gap now?"

"Probably," I said, "to some degree. But she was wrong."

"Wrong how?"

"Dresden's not gone," I said. I touched a hand lightly to my brow. "He's here." I touched Will's bare chest, on the left side. "Here. With-out him, without what he's done over the years, you and I would never have been able to pull this off."

"No," he agreed. "Probably not. Definitely not."

"There are a lot of people he's taught. Trained. Defended. And he's been an example. No single one of us can ever be what he was. But together, maybe we can."

"The Justice League of Chicago?" Will asked, smiling slightly.

"Dibs on Batman," I said.

His smile turned into a real grin for a minute. Then sobered. "You really think we can do it?"

I nodded firmly. "We'll cover his beat."

"That will be a neat trick, if you can do it," Will said.

"If *we* can do it," I corrected him. "I'll need a deputy, Will. Someone I trust. You."

He was quiet for a moment. Then he nodded. "I'm in. But you're talking about some very, ah, disparate personalities. How long can you keep it up?"

My answer surprised even me. "Until Dresden gets back."

Will frowned. "You really think that's possible?"

I shook my head. "It doesn't seem to be. But . . . There's this voice inside me that keeps pointing out that we haven't seen a body. Until I have . . ."

The sun rose over the horizon, burning gently through the morning haze over the lake, and golden light washed over us, warm and strong. We turned to watch the prisoners, and as the light touched them, they began to shudder. Then they began to stir. The first to rise was Georgia.

Will sucked in a long, slow breath, his eyes shining.

"Until I have," I said quietly, "I can't believe he's dead."

We walked back to the warehouse together, to see to the business of getting the prisoners safely home.